Praise for *The Ghosts' High Noon*:

"Mr. Carr has brought a meticulous learning to the task, a good eye, and all the tricks of the trade."
—Alfred Kazin, *Books*

"Mr. Carr argues the case with great ingenuity."
—*Manchester Guardian*

"For connoisseurs."—*Saturday Review of Literature*

John Dickson Carr
THE GHOSTS' HIGH NOON

Carroll & Graf Publishers, Inc.
New York

Copyright © 1969 by John Dickson Carr

Published by arrangement with Clarice M. Carr

First Carroll & Graf edition 1990

Carroll & Graf Publishers, Inc.
260 Fifth Avenue
New York, N.Y. 10001

ISBN: 0-88184-673-2

Manufactured in the United States of America

To Edna Seaman, with gratitude

CONTENTS

PART ONE: *Blindfold Quest*   9

PART TWO: *Quest of Phantoms*   83

PART THREE: *Lover's Quest*   155

PART FOUR: *Quest of a Murderer*   225

Notes for the Curious   299

PART ONE:

BLINDFOLD QUEST

1

THE TRAIN LEFT Washington at 10:45 P.M. Starting at Manhattan, it was the New York-Atlanta-New Orleans Limited, number 37, the most luxurious train on a southerly run. When it pulled out of Union Station at Washington, that Monday night in October of the year 1912, Jim Blake had just swung aboard.

And this chronicle must begin with the reason for his journey.

Half-past nine of the same morning—Monday, October 14th—had found Jim Blake finishing breakfast in his bachelor apartment on the south side of Gramercy Park in New York, with stout Mrs. McCool standing by to tidy up afterwards. A little over middle height, lean, and not ill-looking in a strongly Anglo-Saxon way, Jim at thirty-five might be accounted a very fortunate man. He had just poured another cup of coffee and lighted his first cigarette when the telephone rang.

The call came from Colonel Harvey at Harper's. Ebullient Colonel George Harvey, president of the stately old publishing house in Franklin Square, was also the very active editor of *Harper's Weekly*, with his name spread across its cover every Saturday. And George Harvey had many talents. He charmed authors; he hypnotized the press; he had steered the firm through a bad financial crisis at the turn of the century. But nowadays not everybody trusted his judgment; he had been spending so heavily on publicity that the directors were alarmed.

Colonel Harvey's voice, impressive if a trifle strident, rang heartily over the wire. Today he had chosen to be avuncular.

"Morning, Jim, boy! Didn't get you out of bed, did I?"

"No, not at all. If there's something on your mind, Colonel Harvey . . ."

"There is, my lad. Despite your new-found prosperity and freedom from ancient shackles, are you still game to take on a special assignment for the *Weekly*?"

"With pleasure, if it interests me. What's the assignment?"

"A supplementary question," said Colonel Harvey. "How well do you know New Orleans?"

"Hardly at all."

The telephone refused to believe this.

"Oh, come on! You were at college in the South, and yet you're not familiar with New Orleans?"

"It's just one of those things. Richmond and Charleston I know well, and Atlanta pretty well. Years ago, as an undergraduate, I was in New Orleans once to visit a classmate named Leo Shepley, and had a high old time in my unregenerate days. But that's about all. Having been abroad for so long . . ."

"Jim, a good newspaperman can land on his feet anywhere. This story that needs your particular touch: I'm betting you'll jump at it."

"You haven't told me what it is."

"And I don't think I will, on the phone."

"Is it as secret as all that?"

"It's not secret at all. Can you manage to come down here and see me this morning?"

"Yes, of course. In about an hour?"

"Good! I haven't looked up trains yet, but you may have to move fast. Better pack a bag ahead of time, just in case."

"Expect me by ten-thirty or even earlier, Colonel Har-

vey. The bag shall be packed and waiting. 'Bye, Colonel."
Jim hung up the receiver and turned. "Mrs. McCool . . ."

"Your bag's a'ready packed, sor," announced Mrs.
McCool, emerging from the bedroom with a small suitcase
in her hand. "I knew ye'd be nayding ut as soon as I
heard 'twas Colonel Harvey. Colonel Harvey!" Her voice
grew lyrical. "A grand name, wid bugles in ut! And whin
would the gintleman 'a' been a colonel, now? In the Spanish War, maybe, like Colonel Roosevelt?"

"Well, no. He was once appointed military aide to a
former governor of New Jersey. In the sense you mean,
he's no more a real colonel than the first Cornelius
Vanderbilt was a real commodore. But he came by the title
honestly, as such things go; he still uses it."

"Good luck to him, sor, and to you too! Dhen it's off to
New Orleans you'll be?"

"Yes, very probably. Thanks for packing the bag, Mrs.
McCool."

"No thanks nayded; it's me pleasure. But New Orleans,
now!" Mrs. McCool brooded darkly. "Yon's a place o' sin
and wickedness, I've heard tell."

"It's a civilized city, Mrs. McCool. And a broadminded
one, too."

"Broadminded, is it? If ye mane booze and women,
which is what ye do mane, say so plain and shame the
divil! Not that I'd call ye loose or immoral, worse dhan
what most men are: though in London, be all accounts,
you were more took wid a couple o' freezin' Englishwomen
dhan befits a Yankee gintleman o' Scotch descent."

His partiality to Albion's daughters Jim could not deny.
But for verbal accuracy he was something of a purist.

"Scots descent, Mrs. McCool," he corrected rather
sharply. "Scotch comes out of a bottle."

"Sure 'tis enough o'*dhat* ye've had, I'll be bound, though
you're no soak ayther!" Again her tone changed. "Oh,
bedad, who am I to criticize me betters? Now galong
widja to Colonel Harvey, and to New Orleans too if it

must be! 'Tis damn few Englishwomen will be tempting you dhere, glory be!''

Taking his hat, the suitcase, and a morning paper at whose headlines he had scarcely glanced, Jim tramped downstairs and out into a winelike autumn day, brisk but not at all chilly, with tattered trees inside the railings of the square. He crossed the street to his bank, the Gramercy Park branch of the Atlas Title & Trust Co., and drew out more than enough cash to see him through.

Then, pondering. . . .

On his return to America a year ago, with *The Count of Monte Carlo* piling up royalties, he had bought a fifty-horsepower Peerless and learned to drive it. Now he wished he had waited. The 1912 Cadillac featured an automatic electric starting-device (no more need to wrench at a crank, if this worked), and electric lamps instead of cumbersome acetylene gas.

Still, the Peerless was a first-rate car. For an instant Jim toyed with the notion of driving it to Franklin Square this morning, though only for an instant.

New York had changed during his absence abroad; but then, as you so constantly heard, this city was always changing. The new Pennsylvania Station had been open for two years. The stone lions of a new Public Library haughtily faced Fifth Avenue. They had almost finished the new Goliath of the Woolworth Building, soaring sixty floors above Broadway between Barclay Street and Park Place.

But the problem of tangled traffic, a horse-drawn parade now complicated by far-from-silent automobiles, changed only for the worse. Much though he enjoyed motoring, Jim Blake seldom drove in town except when on his way out of it or returning. Since most cars still had the steering-wheel on the right-hand side, it was no easy matter to judge oncoming traffic in a crowded street.

At least motor-cabs had become plentiful. Crossing Gramercy Park again, Jim hailed one outside the club next door to his own address. As the cab chugged west to

Fourth Avenue, then south past Union Square for the long run down Broadway, he settled back and unfolded his morning paper.

"This job for the *Weekly!* . . ." he said to himself.

Harper's Weekly, subtitled 'A Journal of Civilization,' had been a potent political force ever since the cartoons of the late Thomas Nast did so much to break Boss Tweed in the eighteen-seventies. Whatever assignment Colonel Harvey had in mind, Jim fervently hoped it had no concern with politics.

And yet you couldn't escape politics wherever you turned. As election day drew nearer, every newspaper shook to the uproar of a three-cornered fight for the Presidency of the United States in which the Republican incumbent, William Howard Taft, was challenged both by Governor Wilson for the Democrats and by rambunctious Theodore Roosevelt for the Progressive or Bull Moose party he had created when the Republican bosses refused to nominate him at Chicago. Mr. Wilson said Roosevelt was a megalomaniac, Mr. Roosevelt said Wilson looked and talked like an apothecary's clerk, and both of them made remarks anything but flattering to Mr. Taft.

They were still at it; today Colonel Roosevelt would make a speech in Milwaukee. But even T.R., that perennial headline-grabber and God's gift to cartoonists, had been almost pushed off page one. War exploded in the Balkans, with Bulgaria, Serbia, Greece, and Montenegro united to march against Turkey. A European conflagration must at all costs be averted.

Here in New York, over the week-end, there had been a conference of Democratic bigwigs at the Hotel Astor. The liner *Mauretania* would sail this afternoon for Southampton and Cherbourg, bearing . . .

Oh, never mind!

At shortly past ten o'clock Jim's cab set him down at the House of Harper. Plagued by disastrous fires since the firm's founding almost a century ago, the brothers Harper of the middle eighteen-fifties had determined on an edifice which should be as nearly as possible fireproof. And they had succeeded. There it stood, outwardly little changed but for smoke-grime, rearing five storeys of brick and stone and iron in the shadow of the Brooklyn Bridge.

Telling the cab-driver to wait, Jim strode through the main entrance, under Benjamin Franklin's statue over the doorway, and up a massive staircase, twelve feet wide, to what they still called the first or counting-room floor.

It always seemed darkish here, despite boasted tall windows. On the right, at the telephone switchboard, sat amiable Miss Polly Wrench, with her starched shirtwaist and her high-piled hair, to clock junior employees in and out.

"*Good morning,* Mr. Blake! How are you?"

"Never better, Polly. How's yourself?"

"A little sad, I'm afraid; no real reason." Then Polly grew slightly kittenish. "And who is it this morning, o most valued author? Mr. Alden, or . . . no, sorry! It must be Colonel Harvey, isn't it?"

"Being on the switchboard, Polly, you know it is. May I leave this suitcase while I go on upstairs?"

"Yes, of course you may! Just put it down there. I'll look after it."

Even the inside of the old premises, Jim reflected, could have changed little beyond certain necessary concessions to the present. Electric light, yes. Telephones, yes. Modern printing machinery, for the secondary building across the courtyard behind this one, obviously yes. But no elevator; never an elevator! That would have been too easy.

On each floor above the street, in good repair still, a covered bridge led to the round brick tower in the courtyard. Inside that tower rose the famous spiral staircase, of wrought iron to last forever, which had known the tread of so many writers and artists. And Colonel Harvey was only one flight up. Jim Blake, in excellent physical condition, took the stairs at a run.

Venerable old Henry M. Alden, editor of *Harper's Monthly Magazine,* had his office on the same floor as

Colonel Harvey. But whereas Mr. Alden's lair was little more than a dusty, paper-crammed cubicle with one window, the president and general editor occupied quarters of spaciousness and luxury near splendor.

Above shoulder-high bookcases or panels of carved mahogany, above walls smooth with some material that glistened like gold-tinted burlap, a frieze of paintings by Harper artists ran all the way round the office. Against one wall hung a large framed photograph of J. P. Morgan, who had been more than generous with loans when they were needed.

George Brinton McClellan Harvey, that self-made man from Vermont, sat behind his flat-topped desk with a cigar upthrust in one corner of his mouth and his right hand pressing flat the open pages of a railway guide. Large shell-rimmed spectacles, no less than his eternal cigar and rather flamboyant clothes, made him a figure easy to identify. Though the dark hair might be sprinkled with gray, his vitality had abated not one ounce. With the courtliest of gestures he motioned Jim to a chair.

"In case I misunderstood you," he began in a tone less courtly, "or misjudged the effect a little success so often has, let's get one thing quite straight." The next words were fired at his visitor. "You're *not* too proud to cover ordinary news as you used to do?"

"No, naturally I'm not too proud! Why should I be?"

Colonel Harvey took the cigar out of his mouth and drew himself up.

"It's well to remember," he announced, "that *I* began as a newspaperman, too. I've come a fairly long way, it may be stated without immodesty, since I won my first job on a small-town sheet at three dollars a week. But that's not the point. Let's consider someone else."

Here Colonel Harvey cleared his throat.

"Mr. James Blake," he continued, addressing the photograph of J. P. Morgan as though Jim were not there at all. "Scion of a good old family much respected in Westchester County since their forebears trekked north from Virginia at the beginning of the eighteenth century.

Because one of those Virginia forebears helped to found the College of William and Mary in 1693, it's a family tradition that the eldest son in each generation shall attend our second oldest institution of learning. The present James Blake, an only child, graduated class of 1900. Being an admirer of Richard Harding Davis, who first popularized the newspaperman as a romantic figure . . ."

"Mr. Davis himself was something of a romantic figure," Jim pointed out. "He still is, though he must be almost fifty."

"Dick's the same age as I am," rapped Colonel Harvey. "*He* was managing editor of the *Weekly* from '90 to '94, and neither of us is quite ready for the boneyard just yet. But we'll return to James Blake. Being an admirer of Dick Davis, and having family influence behind him, he landed a job as cub reporter on the New York *Banner*.

"Let's be fair to the fellow. He had a knack of writing vivid news stories, and the nose or the luck to find news on his own, though with a regrettable taste for crime reporting when left to his own choice. And he did pretty well. In '04 he was made the *Banner*'s London correspondent, a post he filled for the next seven years.

"In 1911 he wrote a novel, *The Count of Monte Carlo*, allegedly based on real-life intrigue and spying—crime again, please notice!—under the surface of European diplomacy. To everybody's surprise, including my own, *The Count of Monte Carlo* became a runaway best seller on both sides of the Atlantic. Today Jim Blake plies his trade only as 'our special correspondent.' He can afford to be choosy."

"Forgive me, Colonel, but who's being choosy? You said you had a job for me, and here I am."

"Then listen carefully, Jim. In the second congressional district of Louisiana . . ."

"So we're back to politics, are we? It's a *political* assignment you've got in mind?"

"Yes, of course it is. At a time like this, what else did

you expect? Have you been following 'Comment' in the
Weekly?''

"I have, Colonel. And it's good, rousing stuff. But the
Weekly has concentrated on taking potshots at Teddy Roosevelt. Even apart from all the cartoons inside, at least four
times this year he's been caricatured on the cover as
something between a circus clown and Benedict Arnold.
The editorial notes usually end in a kind of refrain: 'Down
with the demagogue! Smash the third term! Save the re-
public!' You seem to have Teddy Roosevelt on the brain.''

"He's got *himself* on the brain, hasn't he? *'Vox populi,
vox mei'*: that's Teddy.''

"And you've stopped booming Governor Wilson; it's
been many a long month since you last cheered for Governor Wilson. Nothing's gone wrong between you two, has
it? There's a rumor . . .''

"It's more than a rumor; it's ancient history.'' Colonel
Harvey inhaled smoke deeply. "I asked Brother Wilson
straight out whether he thought my support was hurting
him. He said he believed it was. In the popular mind, it
would seem, the House of Harper is associated with
the House of Morgan. That's all right for New York
or the East generally, he claimed, but it's rank poison
to the chawbacons west of the Mississippi.

"They say I got mad and went sour on Brother Wilson,
which is a lie. I was a little hurt, that's all. When practically single-handed I made that man governor of New
Jersey, I've got a *right* to feel a little hurt. He might have
been more tactful with his friends.

"But make no mistake, my lad. I'm still supporting T.
Woodrow, though I don't make so much noise about it;
I'm with him all the way to November 5th. He'll win; he
deserves to win; and, anyway, this year the Democrats
could win with anybody except Brother Bryan. Now are
you ready to listen to my proposition?''

"I'm all attention.''

Colonel Harvey crushed out his cigar in an ashtray. He

rose up, bustled across the office, then bustled back to his chair and stared hard at his guest through the big spectacles.

"The first two congressional districts of Louisiana," he said, "are both in New Orleans, adjoining parishes on each side of Canal Street. The Democratic candidate for the House of Representatives from the second district is a young lawyer, about the same age as you, called . . . By the way, Jim, what's your middle name? Or have you got one?"

"Yes. It's Buchanan, a family name. But I've never used it in a by-line. Why do you ask?"

"Because this man running for Congress is also a James Blake. There's never likely to be any confusion between you: he's James *C*. Blake, C. for Claiborne, a good old name, too; his friends call him Clay. He's a colorful character and a good speaker, they tell me; everybody seems to like him. Jim, I want a personality story on Clay Blake."

Jim made a last stand against that hypnotic eye.

"But why, of all things, a political assignment for *me*? Both Wilson and Roosevelt claim to be progressives. I'm a conservative, even a reactionary, insofar as I'm anything at all; I distrust progressives and hate reformers. In the name of sanity, Colonel, why a political assignment for *me*?"

"First," said Colonel Harvey, "because the personality piece is what you do best. The one you wrote for me eighteen months ago, about that actress What's-her-name, was a real daisy. Every reader felt he'd actually met the woman and knew what she was like. Second, because this isn't merely politics; it's human interest. And that's not all. When you first walked in here I spoke about ordinary news, which this isn't. There may be a big story in it."

"How so?"

"Don't worry about the 'progressive' angle; Clay Blake, like most Southerners, is as conservative as you are. Candidates for Congress, as a general rule, are a dime a dozen; nobody cares. This one's different. He can't help being elected, because he's unopposed; no Republican has had a

Chinaman's chance there since they kicked out the last carpetbagger in 1877. So apparently he can't help being elected. But the underground wire has it that some enemy is out to ruin him.''

"Who's trying to ruin him? And how?''

"That's what my spies can't tell me. I'm hoping you can find out. At least there's something damned funny going on in the Crescent City. Surely that interests an under-the-surface merchant like you?''

Jim stood up and extended his hand.

"You're bloody well right it interests me, Colonel! I'm sorry if I backed away too soon.''

"Then you'll take it on?''

"With pleasure. I don't know New Orleans, but I know somebody who can give me a line on conditions there.''

Colonel Harvey, after gripping Jim's hand, snatched another cigar out of his pocket and used it like an orchestra leader's baton.

"Let's understand each other. I want copy, tentatively, for this Saturday's issue. If there's any prospect of a real story, perhaps even a chance to beat the wire services, just conceivably I might give you another week to make good. But I'd prefer *something* for this Saturday. And you know our deadline, late Thursday, so there'll be no time to mail your story. Either telegraph it from New Orleans, or phone through to rewrite as you used to do in your salad days. Got that?''

"Got it. Any further instructions?''

"There's the matter of your train. No need to rush off this morning, I find. Your best bet,'' and Colonel Harvey tapped the railway guide, "is the New York–Atlanta–New Orleans Limited, very much travel de luxe, leaving Penn Station 4:48 P.M. You'll be off today, Monday, and arrive Terminal Station, New Orleans, early Wednesday morning. How's that?''

"It won't do, I'm afraid.''

"Won't do?'' yelped Colonel Harvey. "What do you mean, it won't do?''

"I said, didn't I, that there's someone who can supply the information I must have?"

"You mean the friend and classmate I've heard you mention once or twice in the past? What's his name: Leo Somebody?"

"No, not Leo Shepley. Leo's a rake and a *bon viveur,* though anybody who takes him for a fool will get a healthy shock. He used to come to New York for periodic hell-raising when I was with the *Banner,* but I haven't seen the old so-and-so in about eight years."

"Well, then?"

"The man I mean is Charley Emerson, formerly of New Orleans. He made history on the *Sentinel,* the best police reporter in the country and *the* authority on his home beat."

"The *Sentinel,* eh?" Colonel Harvey began fishing in his pockets. "That's old Alec Laird's pride and joy, if I'm not mistaken. Alec must be in his dotage by this time, but I hear he's picked a good successor. And the name of George Harvey, Jim, is open-sesame at the *Sentinel.* If you need any help, just present this card to the managing editor."

"I'll have the card, if I may; but I can get what I need from Charley Emerson, thanks. Not long ago he received a legacy from some well-heeled relative: no fortune, but enough for a comfortable retirement. He lives in Washington now, quote, 'to observe the inanities of the political scene.' If I'm to waylay Charley right away, it means a local train to Washington; there's one at noon. So I can't possibly take the train you—" Jim stopped suddenly. "Here, hold on!"

"What's the matter with you, boy?"

"If this crack Limited is Atlanta–New Orleans, it must stop at Washington."

"It does stop at Washington; there's a lieover of twenty minutes or so. Great God in the bushes! You *can* take the *de luxe* after all, boarding at Washington tonight!"

"That's the general idea."

"Then everything's in order, Jim; the rest is up to you. Your usual fee, plus a walloping bonus if you come up with something good. And expenses, of course."

"Speaking of that, Colonel, will expenses run to a lower berth both ways?"

"My dear fellow," Colonel Harvey said with a touch of grandeur, "you'll be representing *Harper's Weekly*. Take a drawing-room and occupy it in solitary state. No, wait! A train from here at noon should get you to Gastown not much later than six o'clock. And you know Dice Reynolds, our man in Washington?"

"Yes."

"Right! I'll phone Dice to make the New Orleans reservation and meet you at Union Station with the tickets. That's about all, except . . . in case I want to get in touch with you, at what hotel will you be staying in New Orleans?"

"It had better be the St. Charles; that's the only one I know."

Jim stood up and took his hat from the desk. Colonel Harvey bustled after him as he made for the door.

"One last word, my lad. Forget this obsession of yours about crime and the police. Take it from a man who was once managing editor of old Joe Pulitzer's *World:* mysterious happenings in real life aren't at all like mysterious happenings in a story by Conan Doyle or Arthur B. Reeve. Or in *The Count of Monte Carlo* either. Where you're going, there'll be no beautiful and enigmatic English girl to distract you from business. And you'll meet no spy of the German Emperor, who turns out to be something else at the end of the book. It's a straight job of reporting; keep it that way. Now goodbye, good hunting, and don't let me down!"

Jim descended the spiral staircase, his footsteps ringing on iron and echoing back in the old tower. He had plenty of time for a noon train; it was not yet eleven. He had begun to enjoy this. And he felt unwontedly exuberant without knowing why.

Colonel Harvey was right, of course. He must not look for sensationalism round some corner or indeed round any corner: not at staid Harper's, not on a Southern Railway train to New Orleans, not even in New Orleans itself. If he had put more truth into *The Count of Monte Carlo* than anybody would believe, it was because some people on this earth really did lead lives of adventure and intrigue, walking with danger as though with a mistress.

But not Jim Blake; never Jim Blake!

And yet, if he faced sober truth, would he have wanted a life like that? Could he have endured a life like that? Franz von Graz didn't enjoy it; Franz was the original haunted man. In the novel, of course, Franz's identity had been so disguised that he could be called a fictitious character. But what had happened, eventually, to that Austrian in the service of Imperial Germany? Was he jailed or dead, either through some slip of his own or because, as Franz feared, the Wilhelmstrasse had decided he knew too much?

Jim reached the counting-room floor: darkish, as always, with its pervasive aroma of damp and old Bibles. There sat Polly Wrench behind the switchboard. Jim retrieved his suitcase, thanked Polly, and started down the very broad staircase to the entrance lobby.

He had the best of all possible worlds. He would become involved in no sensationalism, and wanted none. He was a detached observer, a reporter: no more. Nothing personal could . . .

Then it happened.

Vaguely he had heard light footfalls rap across the counting-room floor and descend the staircase at his back. He glanced over his right shoulder just as the girl behind him, four or five steps up, caught her heel on a tread and pitched headforemost.

Jim's suitcase bumped down the steps and skittered across tile in the lobby. He did not see the suitcase after dropping it; his arms were too full of femininity. Jim had to brace himself as he caught her, or they both would have gone rolling like the suitcase.

He staggered but kept his balance, his left arm underneath her waist, taking the weight against arm and shoulder. Though not heavy, she was very supple. He became conscious of white silk blouse, of tailored blue-serge skirt and jacket, of heavy dark-gold hair under the small straw hat. A gold-mesh handbag swung by its chain from her right wrist.

In that undignified position, head down and tilted so far forward that Jim could not see her face, she spoke in a soft, slurred, breathless voice.

"Oh, this is awful!" And she shivered all over. "I can't think how . . . Put me down, won't you? *Please* put me down!"

He carried her to the foot of the stairs, slid his hands up under her arms, and set her down to face him.

"I say, I *am* sorry!" she cried. "I'm not even wearing one of those dreadful hobble skirts, so I can't think how I came to be so clumsy. It was good of you to catch me, but I do apologize. I am *so* frightfully sorry!"

And she looked up into his eyes.

Jim felt a trifle light-headed.

"Madam," he began oratorically, "you may regret the circumstances of our first encounter. Permit me to say I welcome them almost as much as I welcome you. You're British, aren't you?"

2

HER AGE he estimated in the middle twenties; as he afterwards learned, she was twenty-seven. "Beautiful" would have been too strong a word. But she was very pretty, with those healthy, fresh-complexioned good looks which seem to radiate innocence or even naïveté. Wide blue-green eyes contemplated him within a fringe of dark lashes. And yet nobody could have called this girl naïve. Despite her embarrassment and pouring contrition, the pink mouth showed a sense of humor struggling through. Her admirable bodily proportions seemed emphasized rather than concealed by the severe tailored costume.

For something else had occurred as they looked at each other.

The shock and tug of mutual attraction was a palpable force in that dusky entrance hall; it could almost be breathed. That she felt this as well as he did Jim could not doubt; the intense blue-green eyes communicated it before they retreated from him.

"British?" she said, trying to conquer confusion. "That's fairly obvious, I expect. Yes, I'm British. And you're Mr. Blake, aren't you?"

"How do you know that?"

"I've seen your photograph somewhere. You—you wrote that very entertaining book. And *you* used to live in England, didn't you? May I ask how long you've been back in the States?"

"Just a year: as of October, '11. Now, since you know *my* name . . . ?"

"Yes; how ungrateful of me! Mine is Matthews, Gillian Matthews. I'm usually called Jill."

"Then may I ask, Miss Jill Matthews, what you're doing on these sinister premises? Are you a writer or an artist?"

"Goodness, no! Nothing so fetching or glamourous! You, as a famous author . . ."

"I'm not a famous author; I'm a working newspaperman in quest of a story. But there's a cab waiting outside. May I offer you a lift uptown?"

"No, really!" Jill Matthews cried. "That won't do! That's dreadful!"

"Forgive me, but what's so dreadful about offering you a lift? It's not considered an insult even in London."

"Mr. Blake, you don't understand! That wasn't what I meant at all!"

"Much as I hate upsetting you, surely this alarm is out of all proportion to the actual suggestion? Since fate quite literally threw us together, we seem destined to become better acquainted. Is that idea so distasteful to you?"

"Really, Mr. Blake, you persist in misunderstanding!"

"How so?"

"It's not distasteful in the least. I shouldn't *mind* becoming better acquainted, as you choose to put it. But we can't become better acquainted; we *couldn't*, even if that were our dearest wish. I'm leaving New York today; I'm going home!"

By the *Mauretania*, no doubt. Jim's elbow brushed the newspaper he had thrust into his pocket; profanity wrote a fine legible script across his brain.

Is it ever thus? You meet the one girl for whom you could really go overboard: dark-gold hair, Circe in pink-and-white flesh, every potentiality to make a man dream; and she gets away from you before you can do one damned thing about it. On the other hand, today and tomorrow are not forever.

"As a matter of fact," he said, "I must catch a noon train for Washington on the first lap of my story assignment. But you, I gather, won't be leaving until afternoon. Are you staying with friends? Or at a hotel?"

"I'm at the McAlpin Hotel. Only . . . !"

"The McAlpin's not far from Pennsylvania Station; I can drop you at the hotel. At least there'll be time to exchange views, and find we have similar views on most created things. Then, when we meet again . . ."

"Oh, silly, how *can* we meet again?"

"Easily; I'm a man of leisure, as a general rule. And don't think I'm eccentric; here are some plain facts. This present assignment will take only a few days. Once I've learned the truth about somebody's plot to ruin an honest man, I'm strongly tempted to follow you wherever you are. You're quite a charmer, Jill; you would draw an anchorite from his cave and disturb the meditations of Marcus Aurelius himself. I *will* follow you, my sugar-candy witch, and catch up with you at last if I have to put Scotland Yard on your track."

"I—I almost wish you would. You're worse than eccentric; you're raving mad! And . . . and isn't that the woman from the switchboard, signalling to you up there?"

Jill had pointed. He swung round.

Polly Wrench was in fact standing at the head of the stairs, her arm raised.

"Mr. Blake!" called Polly.

At the look on her face as she peered past him, at the sudden scurry of footsteps here in the lobby, Jim whirled back again. The great doors to the street stood wide open, showing a throng of passers-by on the sidewalk beyond. Jill Matthews had gone.

"Mr. Blake!" shouted Polly. "Colonel Harvey wants to know—"

"So do I," Jim yelled back, and bolted into the street.

He couldn't see Jill: not for the moment, at least. Across the square stood three hackney carriages, two open and one closed, as well as a single motor-cab. Jim's own cab still waited, turned now to face the other direction. But its driver had disappeared, too.

Jill must have run hard. He saw her sitting in one of the open carriages over the way. He saw this just as its coachman's whip went up, and the carriage rolled out and was lost to sight in a press of other vehicles surging uptown.

Jim charged into the square, but had to turn back or be run down. Three seconds later the absent cab-driver emerged from a saloon, wiping his mouth with the back of his hand.

You couldn't shout instructions to follow a carriage no longer in view; you couldn't even tell by which of several routes she might be going. Jim went indoors for his suitcase, said, "Penn Station!" and then fumed all the way there.

Colonel Harvey had declared there was something damned funny going on in New Orleans. There was something equally damned funny about the behavior of Miss Jill Matthews. She didn't object to being called by her first name; she didn't object (on the contrary) to some muffled, frantic semi-lovemaking in the lobby at Harper's. But she wouldn't share a cab with him between Franklin Square and the McAlpin Hotel. Even the prospect she had characterized as "dreadful," and it explained nothing merely to say she was leaving for home.

Jim's first impulse, to call at the McAlpin en route, would have proved impracticable even if he had been sure she was really there. When he thought there would be time for both hotel and station, he had reckoned without midday traffic in New York.

Three times they were held up by stoppages, usually involving a brewer's dray or two. At Madison Square, bearing west along Twenty-third Street, the cab developed engine trouble and had to be coaxed back to life. When at length he reached the great new railway temple on Seventh Avenue, Jim had just time to buy the two necessary tickets and swing aboard before his train pulled out.

Blue-green eyes, seductive mouth: no! For the present, anyway, he must forget the infernal girl and concentrate on business. Settling back in a green-upholstered chair of the parlor car, with periodic excursions to the washroom-smoker for a cigarette, he added up the meagre store of facts he now had. Unless Charley Emerson could add greatly to them . . . !

It seemed a long haul to Washington. Dusk had gathered, towards the end of it, when the porter came along with a whisk-broom and brushed the cinders off the window-sill on to the right knee of Jim's trousers. It was almost time for a tip.

In the great hall at Union Station, another marble temple built after the plan of a Roman bath, he encountered Dice Reynolds of the *Weekly*. Dice, disgruntled to waspishness at not getting the New Orleans story for himself, handed him about a yard of ticket and the little green slip of the drawing-room reservation. His train would go at a quarter to eleven.

After leaving his bag at the checkroom, and telephoning to make sure he would find Charley Emerson at home, he emerged from the station into a high, cool emptiness spangled with pale lights. After the din of New York, Washington always seemed lethargic and slow-moving, little more than a sleepy Southern town.

Charley Emerson lived in the Congressional Apartments, at the corner of East Capitol Street diagonally across from the Congressional Library, where Charley in retirement indulged his twin hobbies of old books and toy trains. A cab took Jim there in short order, through streets of genteel boarding houses on the edge of near-slums.

Dusk was deepening, though a red gash still lay along the sky. The burnished dome of the Congressional Library had a gold gleam against night as Jim entered the smallish red-brick apartment-house, whose front windows faced south between the Library and East Capitol Park.

Charley Emerson, a wiry little terrier of a man with scruffy patches of gray-black hair and the scar of an old burn above his left ear, admitted him to a comfortable apartment on the second floor. In the living-room, lighted by a table lamp with a shade of mosaic glass in half a dozen colors, one wall seemed to be composed entirely of books. Against the opposite wall stood a long trestle-table, bearing the maze of tracks, signals, bridges, tunnels, and stations for a sleek little train powered by two dry-cell batteries attached to a transformer.

According to the occasion Charley could be either shatteringly frank or smooth with the noncommittal suavity of a trained diplomat. Tonight, it seemed, he had decided to be frank.

"All right!" he exclaimed, sighting along an extended forefinger. "You weren't very informative on the phone, but you've whetted my curiosity. Tell me what you want to know and I'll tell you what you'll have to know, as far as I'm sure I know it myself. First, though, do you mind an early dinner?"

"On the contrary, I've been looking forward to one. I had so rushed a morning that there was no time for lunch, and I'm ravenous."

"In the basement of this place there's a bar and grill to which I'll invite you presently. It's quite respectable; you could take your Aunt Nelly there. And the steaks aren't half bad. Now sit down and fire away."

Jim sat down and told his story, omitting only the episode of Jill Matthews.

Charley bent over the trestle-table, his hand on the switch of the transformer. The little train jerked forward suddenly, then whirred and clicked at a steady pace as Charley adjusted the speed. Lighting a Wheeling stogy (two for a nickel), he dropped into an easy chair beside the table and puffed in silence until Jim had finished.

"When people ask me about New Orleans," Charley remarked, "what seems to interest them most is the famous legalized red-light district known as Storyville: no less than thirty-eight blocks of the Vieux Carré around North Basin Street, containing everything from palatial houses where evening dress is obligatory to a twenty-five-cent crib in an alley. And it works, you know! Allowing brothels to operate, always provided they're run on the level and don't disturb the peace, is the one sane political move which . . ."

"I'm not concerned with Storyville, Charley. What's the inside information on Clay Blake?"

"Well . . ."

"Let's have it, please. If somebody's out to get him . . ."

Charley, face twisted up and an intent look in his eye, meditatively tapped ashes on the carpet.

"Clay's all right, Jim. He's as able a lawyer as we've got and a damn good fellow, though a little too intellectual for my taste. You're intelligent, Jim; you're not intellectual, thank God. Clay *is* intellectual. Now don't get the wrong idea! He's no Christer or holier-than-thou, as you'll understand very soon.

"He defeated Happy Chadwick for nomination in the Democratic primary, when most people thought Happy would have a walkover. Clay's just popular, that's all. The men like him; the women love him. The women may not be able to vote, but the hand that rocks the cradle still has a hell of a pull. And he's had the backing of two good friends. One of these friends is a man about town called Leo Shepley . . ."

Jim stared at him.

"Haven't I ever mentioned it, Charley? I know Leo Shepley very well, or I used to know him well in days gone by. But I shouldn't have taken him for a political type."

"He's not a political type. Still! Leo was the great college football star twelve or fifteen years ago, as I hardly have to remind you. Odd as it may seem, that still counts. He's got no very good reputation in polite circles, and he tears around in that red Mercer Raceabout until they wonder why he hasn't broken his fool neck. But they'll find excuses for him whatever he does. Clay's other friend . . . are you following me?"

"Intently."

"Clay's other friend is Alec Laird, now high khan of my old paper, the *Sentinel*."

"Just a minute, Charley! Colonel Harvey mentioned Alec Laird, but said he was so old that . . ."

"Easy, Jim! Your good colonel meant Alec senior, who founded the *Sentinel* and still owns it. I mean Alec's son, always called young Alec though he must be at least forty. Oh, these newspaper empires! Remember the two Gordon Bennetts, father and son, successive proprietors of the New York *Herald*?"

"Well?"

"Gordon Bennett the elder, dead these forty years, minded his shop and paid strict attention to the till. Whereas Gordon Bennett the younger was (and still is, to some limited extent) a real hellion." Charley writhed as though in torture. "Sweet, suffering *Jesus!*"

"What's the matter with you?"

"As far as the Lairds are concerned, that situation is exactly reversed. In his younger days, by all accounts, Alec the elder showed distinct tendencies towards skittishness. That doesn't go for Alec junior, who's as responsible a citizen as you'd want to pass the collection plate in church. Don't get *him* wrong either. Some say he's too fond of power; I worked for him and never noticed it. He may be a sobersides and an unredeemed puritan, but you can depend on Alec when you need somebody in your corner.

"Another branch of the Laird family—Peter Laird, young Alec's cousin, and the elderly dowager they call Madam Ironface—may be said to have a bearing on the present position of Clay Blake. It's Clay Blake we're concerned with, isn't it? James Claiborne Blake: no relation to you, as I'd already ascertained for myself, but candidate for Congress and virtually certain to be elected. It's time I mentioned what may well be the most important point about Clay at this moment. It's time I mentioned the woman."

"What woman?"

"The woman in his life," said Charley. "Does the name Yvonne Brissard mean anything to you?"

"Nothing at all."

Charley dropped the stogy into a china cuspidor and sat forward.

"Originally Yvonne was a New Orleans girl, born of good bourgeois Creole stock. When she was six or seven years old—some time ago; she's past thirty now—her parents took her abroad, to a dull provincial city in France. But Yvonne herself didn't stay dull or provincial. She grew up into a smashing beauty: dark hair, melting eyes, all the other appurtenances, too. When she was eighteen she cut loose from her family and went to Paris. To say she rang the bell there would be putting it mildly. In her chosen profession . . ."

"As a prostitute?"

"We don't call it that, Jim."

"Then what do we call it?"

"Hell's fire, man, do I need to stress the difference between the prostitute and the courtesan?"

"There's difference in degree, of course."

"That's putting it mildly, too. Your prostitute is nothing at all. Your courtesan, particularly in the moneyed circles of Europe, achieves eminence and a kind of left-handed respectability. Her furs, her diamonds, her bank account provide armor against clubs or poisoned darts. Almost every woman secretly envies her as she rolls past in her own carriage or car. She is above this world. In Paris, in Vienna, even in London . . .

"Jim, our Yvonne has had a really spectacular career. Her conquests have included a French cabinet minister, a British industrialist, even some sprig of minor royalty from the Balkans. And she kept 'em all dizzy. Her secret, it's claimed, is that she combines complete wantonness with an outwardly modest and well-mannered air that adds zest to the business.

"Now hear the next-to-latest development. In spring of

this year—furs, diamonds, bank account and all—Yvonne Brissard returned from Europe for an extended stay in the city where she was born.''

"To conquer New Orleans, too?"

"Oh, no. She wasn't 'received,' as the saying is, and didn't expect to be received. On the other hand, she did rent one of those fine mansions beside Bayou St. John, a district picturesque, rather mysterious, and still unspoiled even in this year 1912. How she persuaded the owner of that particular house to accept her as a tenant is something of a mystery in itself. But that's not the point. The point is that she met Clay Blake. Whereupon these two, the Creole siren and the Anglo-Saxon lawyer of excellent family but no particular wealth, fell for each other like a ton of bricks. Their affair, though discreetly conducted, has been sizzling with bright flames ever since.''

Jim sat up straight.

"Look here, Charley! Are you suggesting, is anybody suggesting, that Yvonne Brissard is part of the alleged plot against my namesake? That somebody may be using the woman to ruin him?"

"To ruin him? *In New Orleans?* Jim, are you bughouse?"

"I'm only asking . . ."

The rattle of the toy train endlessly circling had become almost a hypnosis. It stopped suddenly, leaving a void, as Charley stood up and touched the switch of the transformer.

"Food!" he proclaimed in a ringing voice. "You say you're starving; I know I am. That's enough for a first instalment; not one more word until we've put ourselves outside some grub! Come along downstairs.''

"But you haven't explained . . ."

"Nor will I, at the moment." Charley adjusted his cuffs. "Not one more word, I say, until the inner man can relax, too. Now stir your stumps and come along!''

What Charley had called the basement at the Congressional Apartments was in fact a semi-basement only a few feet, below the level of the street. Cramped and raftered, it had a faint alcoholic dampness to match its gloom. Entering from the back, they found the bar parallel to the left-hand wall and, on their right, wooden booths enclosing tables, each table with a dim little pink-shaded lamp. Towards the front, beyond the glass door at the end of this cavern, five or six stone steps led up to street level. An autumn wind swirled dead leaves outside.

They were the only customers in the place. Ensconced in a booth opposite Charley, and facing forward, Jim had the fidgets. If his host's apartment had been comfortable and commonplace, for some reason the atmosphere here seemed alien, furtive, even a trifle sinister.

Several times, as their meal progressed, he found his glance straying towards the front door. More than once he thought he saw a shadow stir on the glass, as of some other customer descending. It was only an impression from the corner of the eye, probably hallucinatory; the door never opened.

But he had small cause for complaint. Having ordered steaks done rare, they got steaks done rare. Jim drank beer; Charley drank Bourbon and water. Finally they sat back, replete, Charley lighting a stogy and Jim a cigarette, as the dispirited waiter brought coffee. Both pondered for some time. It was Charley who broke the silence.

"Jim, what are you thinking?"

" 'Lo, she that was the world's delight . . .' "

"I wish you wouldn't quote Swinburne so early in the evening. The world's delight, eh? Yvonne Brissard?"

"As a matter of fact, my thought bore no reference to Yvonne Brissard. All the same! If your interdict on questions is now lifted . . ."

"It's lifted, Jim. Anything goes."

"You keep in fairly close touch with your native city, I know. Have *you* heard the report of Clay Blake as potential victim of some dirty work?"

"I've heard the report, yes. However, since no dirty work has been attempted . . ."

"You won't even entertain the possibility that his affair with Yvonne Brissard may be used against him?"

"I deny the allegation and spurn the allegator." Charley puffed out his cheeks as though blowing away a feather. "Used against him in New Orleans, for Pete's sake?"

"His constituents aren't exactly cheering for it, are they?"

"Well, they're not horror-struck either. It just doesn't matter, that's all. Provided he behaves with reasonable discretion in public, which is what he's been doing, his constituents don't care how often he goes to bed with a favored wench. Would you care for proof?"

"We're not taking the case to court, Charley. At the same time . . ."

"If any evilly disposed people had wanted to use Yvonne against him, they'd have done it when he was running against Happy Chadwick in the primary. The affair was well under way at that time: everybody knew it, everybody talked about it. And there wasn't a ripple. As I think I told you, he beat Happy Chadwick hands down."

"Who's Happy Chadwick?"

"Happy Chadwick (Raymond P. Chadwick to you) is another lawyer, a middle-aged-to-elderly family man who keeps smiling whatever happens. He's got a lot of influence at Baton Rouge and in other places, too. But here's more irony, as with the two Lairds of the *Sentinel*. Clay Blake, our young intellectual, is all for conservatism and the status quo. It's mature Happy Chadwick who's the roaring progressive, afire to bust capitalists and let women vote. Also, as far as anybody knows, Happy's an honest man, too."

Jim groped for common sense.

"Let's sum up, shall we?" he suggested. "As an experienced observer, then, you've come to the conclusion there's nothing in it? That this whole tale about somebody's plot is nothing but a canard and a mare's-nest?"

"No, Jim, no! I don't say that at all!"

Charley Emerson had become desperately serious. His left eyelid was twitching, and shaky fingers all but upset his coffee-cup.

"Now listen, Jim. Colonel Harvey seems to have intimated you may be sitting on dynamite. It may be only a damp firecracker. Or it may be dynamite and worse than dynamite; it may be this murderous new stuff called TNT.

"Listen carefully, I say! Just in case there's a big story behind everything, who'd be interested in preventing you from getting it? Interested enough, for instance, to follow you from New York?"

"Follow me from . . . Holy cats, Charley, who's crazy now? Who'd follow me from New York? And why do you say that anyway?"

"Because, just outside the front door of this place . . ."

"Damnit, how do you know what's outside? You can't even see the door; you're sitting with your back to it."

"Yes; but I can see a fair sideways reflection in the mirror behind the bar. There's somebody hanging around outside. He's been there for some time; he ducks back every time you look in that direction.

"I'm a patient man, James; I can put up with practically anything. But I don't like my friends being spied on in my own bailiwick. And I want to know . . ."

Charley's stogy dropped on the table. Bouncing to his feet like an india-rubber cat, he spun round, charged at the door, and flung it open.

3

SILENCE.

Silence, that is, except for a scurry of dead leaves and the thump of Charley's footfalls as he bounced up the steps to the pavement.

Jim, rising to follow after he had balanced the burning stogy on the edge of an ashtray, got no farther than the open door. There he met Charley descending again.

The rising wind kept leaves a-dance. One of Washington's small and unsteady streetcars, whose lights would flicker off and then on again whenever the car rounded a curve, jolted past on its way to Lincoln Park. Charley closed the glass door.

"Anything wrong, Mr. Emerson?" asked the dispirited waiter. "It kinda looked as if—"

"No, Mike; not a thing wrong! I'm getting fanciful in my old age, that's all."

The waiter faded away; the bartender appeared sound asleep. Charley lowered his voice as he and Jim sat down again.

"There *was* somebody, though," he confided with great intensity. "It's true I'm getting old and my legs aren't what they were, or I'd have chased him as I once chased Emile the Slasher from upper Esplanade Avenue to a grog-shop by the French Market. Never mind! This jasper's been spying on you, Jim, though he can't have got much of an earful through that door."

"Easy, Charley! Probably it was only a loafer wondering if he could cadge something from the free-lunch counter. Even granted the moonstruck notion of spying, need it necessarily have been spying on me? It could just as well be spying on you."

"A retired old hack like C. Emerson? Not on your tintype, Jamie! He was interested in you; he had his eye on you, and took good care you didn't get a real look at him."

"Well, if *you* got a look at him, let's have a description of the fellow."

"I didn't get a real look at him either, and you know it! He was only a sideways reflection, a kind of shadow against the street-light out there. But I don't like this; I don't like it a little bit. Jim, do you carry a gun?"

"Good God, no! What would I be doing with a gun?"

"It might not be such a bad idea, considering the company you may be keeping in the next few days."

"Charley, what brought about this sudden conclusion that *anybody's* spying?"

"Instinct. I trust my instinct, which never fails. The present situation, fishy enough to start with, gets fishier and fishier as it goes along."

"Shades of Dion Boucicault! If you must turn the whole business to melodrama, all right; I like melodrama. And yet you haven't fully committed yourself on the most vexed question of all. Is there, or isn't there, some conspiracy against Clay Blake?"

"I think there is. I thought so even before you got here tonight. That's what whetted my curiosity."

"But you said . . . !"

"All I said was that, if evilly disposed people have it in for our esteemed Clay, they can't use Yvonne Brissard against him. They've got to have a hell of a lot more and a hell of a lot worse. I can't say what it is or who's behind it. And yet . . .

"Now get this. Less than ten days ago I was in New Orleans. I talked to the boys at the *Sentinel*; I dropped in at

City Hall; I kept my ears open all over the place. And I came to certain conclusions.''

Charley pushed aside his coffee-cup and picked up the stogy, setting both elbows on the table.

"Never mind proof; forget proof. Any newspaperman worth his salt doesn't make a whole string of deductions like Sherlock Holmes. He can *smell* something impending, as plain as the smell of sour beer in an Irishtown saloon. And you know it as well as I do.

"All right! In New Orleans, wherever I went, the one topic of conversation seemed to be Clay Blake and his fair Creole. Had the notorious Yvonne found true love at last, or was it only another interval *pour passer le temps?* What about Clay himself? Might he go the whole hog and ask her to marry him? If he did, ladies and gentlemen, what would be your verdict then?

"No, Jim; there's no proof of anything, unless you can supply it before somebody stops you. Let's you and I just look at the situation objectively, and see what *we* feel.

"Clay Blake and the two Lairds, father and son, all live in the Garden District, the best residential area in town. Along the shore of Bayou St. John, which in one sense may be considered outside town . . .''

"Charley, what's the topography got to do with this?''

"Hearken and perpend. I told you, remember, that another branch of the Laird family must figure in any account of Clay Blake?''

"Yes, Young Alec's cousin, Peter Laird, and a dowager you called Madam Ironface.''

"Don't call her that *to* her face, for the love of God, unless you want even more trouble than you're in already. I will now explain a seeming irrelevance.

"Old Alec Laird had a younger brother, Sam, since deceased. In one of the mansions beside Bayou St. John . . .''

"Is Bayou St. John near the Garden District?''

"No; it's very far from the Garden District in another direction, towards Lake Pontchartrain. *Will* you shut up and listen?''

"Sorry; go ahead."

"In one of the mansions beside Bayou St. John," Charley continued, "lived for many years the aristocratic Creole family of de Jarnac. The last male head of the family, Guy de Jarnac, died without spouse or issue in 1907. A picturesque figure, old Guy, who has left several legends. He was mad on automobiles, for one thing; behind the Villa de Jarnac he built a miniature racetrack which is kept in some kind of order to this day.

"Now roistering Guy de Jarnac had a younger sister, Mathilde, who idolized him. In the early eighteen-eighties, Mathilde de Jarnac married Sam Laird, old Alec's brother. As a wedding present to Sam and his bride, old Alec bought 'em another fine house near Bayou St. John, but on the opposite side of the road from the Villa de Jarnac, and a little closer to town.

"Sam and Mathilde Laird had one son, Peter, who's just under thirty now. Though it's said Mathilde de Jarnac Laird was gay and attractive in her youth, she's developed into a very formidable old dame. Nobody can remember when she came to be christened Madam Ironface, or by whom. It must have been one of the Lairds, who are so *damned* Anglo-Saxon they won't even Gallicize 'madam' by sticking an *e* on the end of it.

"Anyway! You can get some idea of Madam Ironface from the way she's brought up her only child.

"She's been a very indulgent mother, after her fashion. She's given Pete Laird everything he's wanted except the thing he's really wanted, and let him do anything at his will except whatever has *been* his will. 'The boy mustn't get hurt, the boy mustn't get hurt!' Even today, for the same reason, she won't let him drive a car of his own. Oh, no! He must have a chauffeur, the sort that used to be called a chauffeur-engineer and was preferably French, to take him everywhere. Raoul, his personal chauffeur, has been with the family for some time. At the beginning of this year she bought Pete a brand-new Cadillac, with the self-starting device a child could operate. Raoul still does the driving.

"In short, she's almost mothered Pete to death.

"Not that Pete Laird is or ever has been a mama's boy; far from it! He'd have won his letter at football if the old lady had allowed him to play football. He's got an eye for the women. He's not bookish, as the other male Lairds have been bookish and as Clay Blake is, too. Pete's hero is your friend Leo Shepley, the great football star of 1900. Any comment, Jim?"

Jim reflected.

"It's of interest as human nature," he said, "though hardly a very unusual family situation. And I don't see what any of it has to do with Clay Blake."

"You will in a moment, *mon vieux*. Guy de Jarnac, as already stated, died in 1907. Mathilde de Jarnac Laird, his sole surviving relative, inherited everything, including the Villa de Jarnac. She still occupied her own house over the road, Sam Laird having kicked the bucket a couple of years before Guy; but in honor of her brother she cherished the Villa de Jarnac with particular passion. Nobody must live in it, at least while *she* lived. It should stand forever empty, swept and garnished, a shrine to his memory."

Charley spread out his hands.

"End of March, this year! Spring in the air and in the blood. Yvonne Brissard arrived in New Orleans and put up at that connoisseurs' paradise, the Grunewald Hotel.

"Yvonne didn't stay long at the hotel. She let it be known she wanted a place of her own. Though not 'received,' again as already stated, she called on Mathilde Laird. And by some means (I can't tell you how), this more than considerable trollop persuaded Madam Ironface to rent her the Villa de Jarnac."

"Yvonne is still there, is she?"

"She's there in all her glory. And with Clay Blake as much on the premises as though he'd rented 'em himself."

"Are you acquainted with Mathilde Laird, Charley?"

"I've never met her socially, meaning she'd never have

condescended to meet *me*. But we have our spies everywhere. Ask anything you like.''

''What's *her* opinion of our candidate for Congress?''

''She's very fond of Clay. Another of her prime favorites, believe it or not, is the hell-roaring Leo Shepley. The pressures are piling up, aren't they? Can't you sense thunder in the air?''

''What particular thunder, for instance? There are inconsistencies, yes. But a little thought should provide an explanation for everything.''

''It'll explain everything, will it?'' Charley exploded. ''Will it explain how old Madam Ironface, a worse puritan moralist than Alec Laird, made up her mind to encourage flaming passion practically where she could see the blaze? Will it explain a persistent rumor that the Villa de Jarnac is haunted? Will it explain why Clay Blake and Peter Laird almost came to blows in public, and had to be dragged apart by main force?''

''*What?*''

''I'm telling you. I'm also telling you,'' said Charley, abruptly dragging out his watch, ''we're much later than I'd thought; it's getting on towards nine o'clock. Come on back up to my hangout, and I'll underline a few points before you have to catch your train. Mike, Mike, where the hell is that *bill?*''

''This is on me, Charley. *You* be quiet for a change.''

Five minutes later, they were again in the living-room of the ex-reporter's apartment. The toy train circled its track; Charley fumed and paced the floor, smoking incessantly.

''There's that big house amid the live-oaks,'' he said, ''with the covered way that still leads to the racetrack. These tales about a haunting aren't too impressive. I can't see the ghost of Guy de Jarnac roaring around the track in a spectral motor-car, or lurking in the hall to pinch some housemaid's behind. But the place is lonely and ghostly enough, and there's sufficient emotion among our cast of characters to blow any given roof off.''

"What about the near-fight between Clay Blake and Peter Laird?"

"It happened one night towards the middle of April, in the famous 'Cave' at the Grunewald Hotel. Clay was there . . ."

"In attendance on Mademoiselle Brissard?"

"He's never seen with her in public, didn't I say? On this occasion, apart from Pete Laird himself, not one of the other principals was present.

"Nobody knows what caused the trouble. To all appearances they were just having a sociable drink. But their voices went lower and lower as the atmosphere grew more heated, until Clay said, 'Why, you presumptuous—' Pete had just started to go for him, leading with a left, when all of a sudden Raoul, Pete's personal chauffeur, appeared out of nowhere and grabbed him. Then some strangers intervened for everybody's good."

"New Orleans, Charley, has at least the reputation for something else. It didn't get anywhere near a duel challenge, did it?"

"It didn't; it couldn't have. The last encounter under the Duelling Oaks, City Park, took place in 1889. Somebody sent a *challenge* as recently as four years ago, but the challenge wasn't accepted. No, Jim. The duello's as dead as Bernard de Marigny; the War between the States has been over for nearly fifty years. Whatever started the row between Clay and young Pete . . ."

"Could young Pete have his eye on Yvonne Brissard, too?"

"He could, I suppose, as anybody could. But it's never been suggested; and, anyway, his mother would have cut him off with a throw to first base. Anyone else you're interested in?"

"I could bear to hear a little something on everybody. For instance, what can you tell me about an influential politician named Raymond P. Chadwick, other than the fact that both he and Clay Blake are lawyers?"

"They've got a different approach, for one thing. Clay handles a lot of criminal cases and seems to like addressing juries. Happy Chadwick's the kind of lawyer who calls a backroom conference and settles out of court. He won't actually cheat anybody, but he'll get both your collar-buttons unless you're very careful. You see . . ."

For over an hour Charley continued to smoke and pace the floor, freely discussing all the persons he had mentioned but adding little more to Jim's knowledge. At length he stopped himself, stopped the toy train, and consulted his watch.

"I can't speak for you, my lad. Myself, I'm one of the people who like to be at stations well before train time."

"So am I. What about transportation?"

"There aren't many cabs in this area at night. Never mind. A friend of mine does part-time work in that way of business; Walt's usually on tap when I need him. Just a moment!"

Charley disappeared into the little hallway, and could be heard speaking in a conspiratorial voice to the telephone.

"That was Walt Winkelhorst," he explained, rubbing his hands together as he returned. "Be here in less than five minutes, Walt says. Now, Jim, since you enjoy playing detective . . ."

"I think I *might* have enjoyed playing detective, if I'd ever had the chance to do it."

"Well, you've got the chance now. See what you can discover about a conspiracy. First see Clay Blake himself, without letting on you think there's dirty work. You can reach him at his office or at home (he's in the phone book), and he'll make no difficulty about meeting you. If you need help or advice, go to the *Sentinel*."

"That's what Colonel Harvey said. He gave me a card to the managing editor."

"The managing editor is Bart Perkins, who'll do. So will Harry Furnival on the city desk. The man you give the card to is Alec Laird; you'll find him in the owner's office on the top floor. In the meantime . . ."

Charley darted to one of the two windows overlooking

East Capitol Street, and peered down with a hand shading his eyes.

"I don't *see* anybody lurking there," he reported after a pause. "Whoever's been spying on you . . ."

"Will you get it through your head, Charley, that there's no such person?"

"If that's what you think, rash adventurer, it won't be many hours before you learn your mistake. Get set for a shock when the thing blows up in your face. In the meantime, I say, just keep your eyes peeled and look a leedle oudt. That's not asking too much, is it?"

"No, but : . ."

"Walt Winkelhorst will be here any minute; he's only just up the road. You won't travel in style or grandeur, but he'll get you there. Don't let him soak you more than fifty cents, and . . . there!" Charley started. "You hear, Jim? That's the noise of the car now . . . it's pulling up . . . and there's Walt honking his horn. Goodbye, remember what I've counselled, and give my regards to the gang!"

The night had gone very still when Jim left the Congressional Apartments; not a breath of wind now stirred.

The car, a battered Stoddard Dayton tourer of several years back, faced west behind the soft glow of acetylene lamps. Walt Winkelhorst himself, youngish and fat and surly, had switched off its engine. Since this model had no windshield, Mr. Winkelhorst wore cap and goggles, though he lacked the long dust-coat motorists still needed in open country.

This model had no doors either: only apertures. Jim climbed into the back. Crank in hand, the driver descended from his perch, set the engine thumping, and mounted to his perch again. Away they went, bearing to the right, through a darkness only spangled with street-lights.

It was much the same course as that by which Jim had been driven from the station: genteel boarding houses on the edge of near-slums. But you breathed a good deal of dust in this car; you couldn't see too clearly either. Streets all but deserted, hardly another vehicle moving in either direction.

Except . . .

Jim sat back, not sure whether to be amused or irritated by Charley Emerson's fit of nerves. Reading ominous meanings into the behavior of some casual tramp! Spies, prowlers, God knew what! Whereas, of course . . .

They were within sight of Union Station, a pale shimmer beyond the immense sweep of its approach, when the driver spoke.

"Lookit!" he said suddenly. "If you're the famous Mr. Jim Blake . . . ?"

"My name is Blake. I'm not the famous anybody."

"Well, Charley Emerson said you was. All right; don't make no difference! Whoever you are, ain't nobody got it in fer you, have they?"

"Why do you ask that?"

"I can't be dead sure; some people just don't like to pass. But I think somebody's a-follerin' us. Look at them headlamps back there!"

Jim had already seen the car in their wake, only a black shape beyond the twin beams of its lamps. The glowing circles hung there, about thirty feet away; they neither grew nor diminished. Jim touched the driver's arm.

"Try speeding up a little and then slowing down," he suggested. "See if the fellow behind us does the same."

"I just *done* that, a little ways back. He done it, too. And don't tell me to shake him off, neither! That there's a new Thomas Flyer, and she's a beaut!"

"I won't tell you to shake him off. But there's something else you might do."

"What is it?"

"The station arcade seems clear of cars or carriages. He may not follow us there, or at least follow so closely, in which case he's an innocent motorist and it's only accident. Here's what you do if he's not so innocent. Try a burst of speed now. As we go in under the arcade, just before you swing left to let me off at the entrance, jam on your brake and pull up.''

"That might not be so bright, might it? What if he smacks into me?"

"He won't smack into you. If he does and there's any damage, you may hold me responsible." Jim leaned forward and pushed a ten-dollar bill into the breast pocket of his companion's coat. "There's some slight earnest that I mean what I say. After all, tramps don't ride in a Thomas Flyer."

"Howzzat?"

"Never mind. Will you do it?"

"Oh, I'll do it! I'm just crazy enough to do it, I reckon. But what you up to, Mr. Blake? What you tryin' to *prove?"*

"I want to know what this is all about," Jim said. "The only way to learn is to stand and face it."

A small wrath burned deep inside him. He had scoffed at Charley's suggestion of carrying a gun; he still scoffed at it. If Charley Emerson at sixty had not hesitated to charge unarmed against the enemy, he himself wouldn't be backward either.

Walt had instantly put on speed. The old Stoddard Dayton bucketed across the approach to the station, past scattered vehicles and over a pattern of streetcar tracks, under lights moon-wan. The Thomas leaped in pursuit, a reflected gleam on its high windshield.

Up loomed the station's white façade and arches. Jim rose to his feet and braced himself by gripping the top of the front seat. They swept in under the arcade; he just kept his balance as the car clanked, shivered, and stopped dead. Jim jumped out and down on the left-hand side, wheeling to face an oncoming pursuer.

The Thomas did not run him down; it did not even pursue further. Without slackening speed it swerved widely, made a full turn, and roared away in the direction of distant Pennsylvania Avenue. He had only a brief glimpse of the five-seater's two occupants: its hunched-over driver and another man in the back. Then he looked for the D.C. number-plate. The car had no number-plate.

Heat had crawled up under Jim's collar; he could feel the beating of his own heart. But a certain satisfaction warmed him, too. You stood to meet the enemy, and the enemy turned tail.

He looked at Walt Winkelhorst, who had again climbed down to use the crank.

"Well, we're here in good time, anyway. What do I owe you?"

"Ain't no charge, sir. This one's on the house."

"But . . . !"

"Charley Emerson said I'd try to overcharge you, didn't he? Well! Maybe I would 'a' done that, as a general thing; I'm ornery enough fer to do it. But you think I'm a goddam Yankee?" Walt demanded with sudden passion. "You think I got no conscience *at* all? Stickin' out of my pocket's the ten-case note you gimme 'thout no strings to it. You're a real sport, Mr. Blake, so this one's on the house."

Now glowing with satisfaction, Jim thanked him and went on into the station.

A handful of people straggled through the hall's marble vastness. There was not so much time as he had thought: the clock hands stood at 10:35.

He bought cigarettes at a counter devoted mainly to magazines and candy; the morning papers had not yet appeared. He redeemed his suitcase at the checkroom and handed it to one of the hovering redcaps. Though the bag was neither heavy nor inconvenient, he wanted the services of a guide.

"Atlanta–New Orleans Limited," he said, consulting separate tickets. "Drawing-room B, car sixteen. Do you know which gate?"

"Ah knows it, suh. Train been in mebbe fifteen minutes. Follow me."

After clear lights on marble in the main hall, the stone area beyond held grittiness and gloom. It was gloomier and grittier still in platform aisles between the Martian shapes of trains.

The shape of his own train, with steam up, rose massive and somber at Jim's left hand, emitting chinks of yellow light only at occasional window-corners or into the vestibules between each car. His redcap guide led him for some distance beside it before pointing to the numbered card in an end window.

"Put that bag in the drawing-room, please," Jim instructed, "and see me on your way back. Since I can't miss the train now, I'm in no hurry."

And he wasn't in a hurry, either.

The redcap swung up the iron steps to the vestibule, vanished into car sixteen, returned within twenty seconds, was rewarded, and hastened away.

Jim remained on the platform at the foot of the iron steps. One or two last-minute passengers still scrambled for the train. But most would be aboard already, berths made up, settling in for the night.

Well, now, what had been the meaning of the Thomas Flyer and its ultimate failure to pursue? With the excitement over and his pulses no longer hammering, what *might* an intelligent man make of it?

He couldn't take the business seriously now; or could he? If Charley had been right after all . . .

What sort of face had he expected to see as the Thomas bore down? He had not recognized either of its two occupants. On the other hand, he had been afforded so short a look, in uncertain light, that he might not have recognized either even if he had known both. It did smack of conspiracy, in a way; but why, in sanity's name, a conspiracy against Jim Blake?

All this was nonsense! Why think about faces anyway? There was only one face he wanted to see. At this time tonight the owner of that face would be somewhere out in the Atlantic, a passenger on the Cunarder *Mauretania*. And he had a job to do; he must concentrate on business.

Vaguely he became aware of someone standing near the

edge of the vestibule above, where a little light spilled out through the glass panel in the door of car sixteen. He himself couldn't stay here any longer; he had better find his drawing-room. Official activity boiled along the platform; a lantern swung and winked towards the head of the train. They would be under way at any moment, though he had heard no cry of *"Bo-o-ard!"*

What he did hear was a different noise altogether.

As though the engineer were playing games, a convulsive kind of shudder jolted through the whole line of cars. Metal whacked metal as couplings bumped together. The person standing above, flung off balance by the heave of the train, reeled and fell.

For the second time that day Jim's arms were full of femininity. But on this occasion she pitched backwards, face up. He stepped aside and caught her with both hands, left arm under her back and right arm under the fold of both knees.

"Enjoying yourself, Jill?" he asked affably. "Either the fates have determined it, or else *you're* the one who's following me."

4

SHE HAD CHANGED her tailored costume for a dress of some soft brownish material under a light, fleecy tan coat. The brim of her large hat brushed his cheek; the face of which he had dreamed was only a few inches from his own.

"Not *again?*" Jill Matthews gasped, utterly demoralized. "Dear, gracious heaven, not *you* I must thank for . . ."

"I fear so, though no thanks are needed. Permit me, madam, to anticipate your next words. 'Put me down, put me down!' All in good time, Jill. In a very few seconds they'll be closing up that vestibule. With your permission, then, I will just carry you back up the steps."

"The—the steps are awfully steep, though! And the first one's high off the ground."

"Not so very high, Jill. Observe beside me a thing like an overgrown wooden footstool with a slot in it, used for the convenience of passengers. *Facilis ascensus Averni,* as the poet didn't say. I hook the box closer with my foot: so. I stand up on it: so. Still carrying your delectable person, I mount the steps: so.

"But we won't stay here in the vestibule, Jill. There behind us is the porter, waiting to shut outer doors and seal 'em up. Which car are you in?"

"S-sixteen. *But . . . !*"

"So am I. With my right hand I turn the knob of the

door. We push through, we turn a little to the left, and . . . here in this aisle I set you down.''

The narrow aisle stretched between a short row of windows on the left and, on the right, a wall painted to resemble rosewood and pierced by the green-curtained doorway of the men's smoker and washroom. Since they were at the rear of the car, the continuation of that same wall would be the inner wall of drawing-room B.

''You're not going to New Orleans, too?'' the soft voice cried at him. ''Don't tell me *you're* going to New Orleans?''

''But I do tell you that. Here we both are, your own destination now evident.''

''Well,'' and she moved her shoulders, ''it's a free country, as they keep saying here. But really and truly, Jim, you needn't have deceived me like that. You said you were going to Washington!''

Smoothly gliding, almost stealthily and without a jerk, the train began to move. Jim studied his companion.

''I said I was going to Washington as the first stop on my trip. If deceit's to be our theme, young lady, what about your story to me? You said . . . no, stop! You didn't actually say you were sailing for England. You said you were going home.''

''And so I am! New Orleans *is* home: at least, it's been home for nearly seven months and the only home I have. I—I work there.''

''What do you work at, Jill?''

''Oh, please!'' she protested. ''Not everything at once, I beg! Do give me a chance to get my breath!''

She was already breathing quickly. She had retreated a step, the blue-green eyes full of some emotion very like fear. Despite Jill's slenderness, you could not help noting the well-defined shape of her hips. Then she seemed to wake up from a dream.

''No, now, really! Let's not fuss about unimportant things, shall we? We're here, as you say, and we ought to make the best of it. I got on at New York, of course; I'm in lower seven. Where are you?''

"An open-handed philanthropist named Colonel Harvey —he gives dinners to four hundred guests at Sherry's, as he did for William Dean Howells's seventy-fifth birthday in March—provided both berths of a drawing-room. If you'll accept a well-intentioned offer, I shall be very glad to swap the drawing-room for lower seven."

"No, Jim. Thanks loads, but I'd *rather* not. Besides, I've already . . ."

"You've already what? Had the offer of a swap from somebody else? Or what kind of offer?"

"No offer at all; I do wish you wouldn't keep misunderstanding! It's Drawing-room B, isn't it?"

"Yes. How do you know that?"

"I sat in there from New York to Washington, except when I was having dinner in the restaurant-car, and nobody turned me out or so much as said a word. That's why I'm at this end of the coach," Jill gestured slightly towards the green-curtained doorway, "rather than at the other end near the ladies'. Which reminds me: speaking of people who book whole drawing-rooms for themselves, there's a great friend of yours in A, also at that end."

"Oh? Who's the friend?"

"Leo Shepley. Quite sober, too."

"*You* know Leo, do you?"

"He's a friend of some friends of mine in New Orleans, that's all." Jill lifted candid eyes. "I know he'd love to see you, Jim! He talked a lot tonight about his old pal; he liked *The Count of Monte Carlo* almost as much as I did. And he's awfully intelligent, though you'd never guess it at first glance. Why not go and have a word with him now?"

"That's just what I'll do. There's nothing I'd like better, bar one thought that's been in my mind since eleven o'clock this morning. Lead the way, will you?"

Jill went ahead, walking on tiptoe.

The dim-lighted little alley opened into a dark aisle between tiers of upper and lower berths masked by heavy green curtains closely drawn. The scent of those curtains, faintly stuffy but not unpleasant, pervaded the whole car. There was a faint yellow glow from another little alley past drawing-room A.

The train had gathered speed, swaying and clicking. Jim opened the door of his own drawing-room for a quick glance inside. The ceiling light shone on polished wood edged with gilt. Both berths had been made up; his suitcase stood on the green-covered couch parallel to the berths. Jim closed the door and followed Jill.

Outside drawing-room A they encountered the conductor, who did conjuring tricks with Jim's yard of ticket before moving on. Jill had removed her large hat; she gestured with it towards the drawing-room door and lowered her voice.

"There you are; just knock. *He's* not asleep."

"Aren't you coming with me?"

"Not for a moment, if you don't mind. I want to freshen up a bit in the—the other place. Just knock, I say. I've warned him not to . . . oh, never mind!"

She stopped suddenly. And sudden jealousy bared poison fangs; Jim couldn't help it.

"Warned him not to . . . *what*, for the love of Mike? Jill, were you with Leo in New York?"

"In New York *with* him? Good gracious, no! I didn't even know he was *in* New York until we found ourselves on the same train and had dinner together. Until this evening I never so much as heard he was acquainted with you. Really, my dear man, I wish you wouldn't be so dashed peremptory!"

"And I wish *you* wouldn't be so dashed mysterious."

"I'm not trying to be mysterious, really and truly I'm not! You'll hear all about me presently. If I don't unburden myself and tell you every detail in the first ten minutes, it's not because there's anything dark or awful in my life. I hope you believe that much, Jim, because . . . because . . ."

"Yes?"

"Because I do so want you to believe it!" Once more

Jill looked up at him, almost with a prayer in her eyes. "Now you *will* excuse me for a few minutes, won't you?"

Then she was gone.

Jim meditated, cleared his throat, and knocked.

"Yes?" boomed a voice. "Whoever the hell you are, come on in!"

Leo Shepley, fully dressed, stood gaping at his visitor in the space between a made-up lower berth and the green-covered couch. Powerful, heavy of shoulders, outwardly he seemed to have changed little over the years, except that his face had acquired a reddish tinge and the bald patch showed through thinning light-brown hair.

That Leo was genuinely dumbfounded Jim couldn't doubt. And the reunion could be called a success. They shook hands with real pleasure and walloped each other on the back.

"Leo, you old bastard, how are you?"

"Jim, you unregenerate son-of-a-bitch, have you visited any good whorehouses recently?"

"Though I apologize for the oversight, I haven't even patronized one since you took me to Josie Somebody's in '98. You may remember . . ."

"Yeah, sure. You always did prefer amateur talent, didn't you? That's good judgment, Jim. As one of our more notorious madams is said to have remarked, 'These country club girls are ruining my business!' "

Many memories returned. In bygone days Leo's passion for wine, women, and football had been equalled only by his passion for practical jokes, which were never malicious but which so fretted his conscience that he lived in a bad dream until he had called off the joke or put matters right with its victim.

" 'Then here's a hand, my trusty fier, and gie's a hand o' thine,' " he roared now. "It *is* you, Jim? It really is you? I can hardly believe it!"

"Neither could Jill Matthews, when she bumped into me on the platform here a few minutes ago."

"Ah, our Jill! Yes, of course. She said she'd met you at

Harper's this morning, but seemed to think you were bound for Washington on an important story.''

"I'm bound for New Orleans, Leo. The story may or may not be important. I think you cán help me with it, if you will.''

"You betcha, Jim; any damn thing in the world!'' Then Leo blinked at him. "But how the holy hell do you come to be chasing a newspaper story? I heard you'd quit your job when you struck pay-dirt with *The Count of Monte Carlo*.''

"I did. This is a special assignment for *Harper's Weekly*. Did Jill tell you what *she* was doing at Harper's, by the way?''

"No. Just said she had business there. Part of her job, probably.''

"You don't happen to know what her job is, I suppose?''

"You're damn shouting I know what it is. Who'd think, now, that a gal with such obvious qualifications for you-know-what could be an efficient private secretary?''

"Jill's somebody's private secretary?''

"Yes. She works for old Ed Hollister, a big-money boy and financial manipulator who moves in such secretive ways that nobody can learn anything about him or even where to find him. Don't tell her I told you that, though, until she tells you herself. The secretary, in my estimation, has picked up too much of her boss's secretiveness. She's an elusive little devil, as you may have noticed.''

"Yes, I've noticed.''

"Smitten with the pretty Limey, are you?''

"More than smitten, Leo. I've fallen hard.''

"She's fallen for *you,* if anybody should ask old Uncle Leo, though I wouldn't embarrass Jill by intimating it to her. This afternoon, as soon as we were under way from New York, she sat down by herself in an empty drawing-room, and wouldn't say boo to anybody until I dragged her out for dinner. She had something on her mind then, again if anybody should ask me.''

Evidently Leo himself had something on his mind. Always garrulous, he was now hurling out words as though for a kind of barrier or screen.

"For quite a while, it seems, she's been much taken with that book you wrote. At dinner she told me she'd met the man who wrote it: a very romantic scene, as she described it, like Beatrix descending the stairs in *Henry Esmond*. When I said the rat who wrote the thing was an old friend of mine, she first went a funny color and backed away from the subject, then started asking questions about you, and finally retreated back to the drawing-room again."

"It happens to have been my drawing-room, Leo, though she didn't know it at the time. As soon as I see her again, I'm going to insist on her taking over that drawing-room and occupying it to the end of the line, while I doss down in the berth she reserved for herself. She hasn't agreed to it so far . . ."

"Maybe she won't agree at all. She could have had my quarters here, if she'd wanted 'em, with no favor asked in exchange. But would she do that little thing? Oh, no: wouldn't hear of it! Jill's a peculiar gal in some ways, even for a Britisher."

"As soon as I see her again, I said." Jim had begun to fret. "Look here, Leo, where do you suppose she's got to? She said she'd be joining us in a few minutes, which was more than a few minutes ago. Unless she turns up in the next few minutes, I'm going out to find her!"

Leo drew himself up.

"You're not going to do one goddamn thing, my friend, until we've had at least a drink or two to celebrate this reunion! It does call for a celebration, doesn't it?"

"No doubt about that much."

"The club car's closed for the night. I *could* grease some palms and get it opened again, but that hardly seems necessary even for so memorable an event. I've got a bottle of Bourbon with me, so we don't need anything except glasses and ice and soda. Just press that bell between the windows, will you?"

As Jim rang for the porter, a light knock at the door

heralded the entrance of Jill, who had now discarded coat as well as hat. She stood there sleek-limbed in the brownish dress, with the ceiling light shining on dark-gold hair and fair complexion, her hands clasped. Though the look of strain had not gone from her eyes, she seemed more at ease.

"Now, then, angel-face," Leo addressed her grandly, "what about it? Wouldn't *you* care for a small drink in honor of this great occasion?"

"I'd like one very much, thanks, provided we don't make a night of it and see the dawn up. Also, Leo, considering that people hereabouts are trying to sleep, it's not really necessary to *yell*."

"Who's yelling?" Leo shouted. "And there's no question of turning this into a brawl or anything like it. As I told you at dinner, I'm a reformed character nowadays."

"You're a reformed character?" Jim stared at him. "Since when?"

"Since about the middle of summer, that's when! Thinks I to myself, 'You're thirty-five years old, son; it's time you at least *started* to grow up.' And it works, Jim. God strike me dead, it really works!"

This flight of eloquence was interrupted by the porter, a stout, smiling, elderly character whom Leo addressed as Uncle Mose. Promising to bring what was required, the porter withdrew. Leo rummaged in a valise under the couch and produced a quart bottle of Old Kentucky.

"Now get this!" he continued impressively, holding the bottle aloft like the Statue of Liberty's torch. "I'm a responsible citizen now, as anybody at home can tell you. I take an interest in good government. I'm not cockeyed drunk every night. Any nice girl is safe from me, and I haven't even visited a—never mind; it's been too hot for that anyway! In New York, on this last occasion, my most extreme dissipation was to see a couple of shows: Billie Burke in *The Mind-the-Paint Girl* and John Barrymore in *The Affairs of Anatol*. Jill my wench, our friend Jim is on his way to New Orleans after an important story for *Har-*

per's Weekly. Don't you think we ought to hear about the assignment?''

"Anything you like," agreed Jill, who had sat down on the couch. "Speaking of shows, though, I'd much rather hear about *The Count of Monte Carlo*.''

''What do you mean, speaking of shows?'' demanded Leo. "What have shows got to do with Jim's book?''

"Those characters!" Jill seemed to be dreaming. "Count Dimitri, the Russian nobleman with the villa at Monaco, who's supposed to be working for Germany in the Kaiser's secret service, but turns out to be a British agent at the end! And the heroine, Marcia Allison!'' She appealed to Jim. "Is it true they're doing it as a play in London?''

"Yes; it's been in the works since the first of the year. A friend of mine at the Savage Club adapted it for the stage, and Sir George Alexander will put it on at the St. James's as soon as they've finished casting, with Alexander himself playing Count Dimitri. They wanted to get Constance Lambert for Marcia Allison, but in February she went off to Italy and it's got to be somebody else.''

"Did you ever meet Constance Lambert, Jim?''

"Yes, more than once. I did a personality story on her for *Harper's Weekly*.''

"Speaking of *Harper's Weekly*—'' Leo began.

''There's just one more question,'' pleaded Jill, ''I'd dearly love to ask, if I may. I read somewhere that at least some of the characters in that book were or are real people. Is that true, too?''

"Yes, but . . .''

"But what?''

Again the porter interrupted, this time bearing a tray with three glasses, a siphon of soda-water, and a bowl of cracked ice.

The train-wheels had acquired steady rhythm; a long blast of the whistle was torn behind them. While Jim sat down beside Jill, Leo carried Bourbon and mixers into the drawing-room's little lavatory, returning in short order with three drinks on the tray, to which he had added an ashtray from the dining-car.

"First stop Lynchburg, Virginia," he proclaimed, handing out glasses, putting the tray on the couch at Jim's left hand, and sitting down on the made-up berth opposite. "But that's at past three in the morning; we'll be sound asleep long before then.

"Now listen, Jim!" he went on, as they all ceremoniously touched glasses and drank. "It's a damn good yarn you wrote and nobody's more pleased than I am you rang the bell so hard. But we're not supposed to take it seriously, are we?"

"Take what seriously?"

"All this secret-service business! Cloak and dagger stuff: all the big nations spying on each other, possibly to end in a major European war?"

"Don't you read the papers, Leo? There's war in the Balkans already."

"There's always war in the Balkans. That means nothing by itself. I can't visualize Ruritania or Graustark as a real trouble-spot, though it just may happen sooner or later if the Prussian warlords decide on *der Tag*.

"No, Jim; we've gotten away from the point! What's this story you're after? Whom does it concern, for instance?"

"It concerns a partial namesake of mine, one James Claiborne Blake of New Orleans. Unlike some persons I could mention," and Jim carefully kept his eye away from Jill, "I'm going to be absolutely frank and tell you everything. I've got to tell you everything, Leo, if I ask you to back me up! Well, then . . ."

Neither of the other two commented. But he could almost feel the pressure of silence as he recounted the events of that day, from Colonel Harvey's office to the session with Charley Emerson, not excluding the lurker in the shadows outside.

"And that's *all?*" cried Jill, exhaling what might have been a breath of relief. "That's *absolutely* all?"

"That's all, but it's enough. I can't tell you who trailed

me from the Congressional Apartments to Union Station, if in fact there was somebody trailing me and I didn't imagine it. The one person who won't fit in anywhere is your obedient servant.

"Still, there they all are: Clay Blake, Yvonne Brissard, the various Lairds, and a politician named Raymond P. Chadwick. It seems generally agreed, Leo, that your friend Clay's affair with the notorious Yvonne won't do him any harm at all . . ."

"No, of course it won't do him any harm!"

"But you may have heard something yourself, especially since you've decided to become a good citizen. Is there a conspiracy, or isn't there? Who's behind it? And, if they're not using Yvonne Brissard, who or what are they using?"

Jim and Jill smoked cigarettes, the ashtray on the floor between couch and berth. Leo, after lighting a diminutive cigar, had let it go out. At some point in Jim's narrative he had sat up straight, his face heavy and lowering. The blinds were drawn on both windows behind him. Leo craned round, raising one blind to stare out at the dark countryside sweeping past under a yellow harvest moon. Abruptly he swung back, with that same heavy, lowering look, and surged to his feet like a boxer answering the bell.

"I wonder if it could be? Jesus Christ Almighty," he roared, "I wonder if it *could* be?"

"You wonder if what could be?"

"Clay wouldn't be mixed up with Flossie Yates. I don't think he's ever met Flossie Yates, though he must have heard her name. That's not important, is it? If you ask me, Jim, Clay's a much less decisive character than he seems to be. And I know, because deep down inside me I'm not very decisive myself. Merely being innocent wouldn't matter if they decided to . . ."

"Leo, will you kindly explain what you're talking about?"

"I'm talking about a game, Jim, that's been tried once or twice before. Somebody may be trying it now. It's almost foolproof; it never fails. And it's just about the wickedest game you ever heard of!''

Quick, sharp, and peremptory, there was a knock at the door.

Tension had grown in that drawing-room as the long story unfolded. Leo jumped at the sound of the knock. But he did not falter. He set down his glass on the floor and dropped the miniature cigar into the ashtray. Then, as though facing death or doom, he stalked to the door and threw it open.

There was nobody outside. The dark aisle between the tiers of berths stretched away empty to the faint glow from the little passage at the far end, by which they could see the white coat and glistening white eyeballs of the porter standing there.

Leo plunged along the aisle, checking a shout. He remembered to keep his voice down as he accosted the porter. The car swayed slightly; the wheels clicked; Jim in the doorway could hear only a muttered rumble of question and answer. Then Leo raced back.

"I've known Uncle Mose for years! He swears nobody ran in that direction, or ducked into one of the berths either. Whoever knocked at the door must have gone—"

Leo stabbed a finger in the other direction, at the companion dimly lighted alley past drawing-room A. It was Jim who took up the chase, striding along the alley almost at a run, past a green-curtained doorway of aspect far more sedate than that to the men's washroom. At the glass-panelled door to the double vestibule between this car and car fifteen ahead, for the second time that night he encountered the train's conductor, who was making cryptic markings in a little black book.

"Excuse me, Conductor: did you see somebody come this way about a minute and a half ago?"

The conductor, a man of immense dignity, squared his shoulders.

"I saw nobody, my good sir. There was nobody to see."

"He knocked at that drawing-room door and then made himself scarce in a hurry. If you're on your way through the train . . ."

"I am not on my way through the train. I have been through the train twice."

"But you keep on the move, don't you? You might have missed him."

The conductor drew out a large gold watch.

"I did not miss him, sir. It is now 11:59. I have been in this same position since approximately 11:54. When I tell you nobody passed this way until you did, you may take it as strict and absolute truth."

The train rounded a curve at such speed that Jim seized at the railing past the little windows on his right. Glancing back over his shoulder, he saw Leo Shepley at the other end of the alley. Jill herself hovered just behind Jim. She nodded towards the green-curtained doorway, and her voice was not steady when she spoke.

"There's nobody in the ladies' either," she said. "There's nobody *anywhere*. Merciful powers, are we on a haunted train?"

5

WHEN AFTERWARDS Jim thought back to the events of the ensuing thirty-two hours, between a few minutes before midnight on Monday and arrival in New Orleans at a few minutes before eight on Wednesday morning, he recalled them only as fragmentary scenes whose true meaning he never saw until step by step he saw everything.

Monday night's ructions had not ceased when the clock hands stood vertical. A bitter argument with Leo, which lasted until nearly one in the morning, was succeeded by a last argument with Jill. When Leo turned them out of drawing-room A, saying that as a reformed character he was damn well going to get *some* sleep, Jim led her gently to drawing-room B.

At that drugged and drowsy hour, with a dead world moving past outside, he thought he sensed in her a mood of wavering, even pliancy, which her eyes seemed to confirm. But Jill remained adamant.

"For the last time," she said, "I most certainly will *not* steal this drawing-room and turn you out of it!"

"You're not stealing anything. And you'll be much more comfortable here."

"What about you?"

"That's not the point."

"It is the point! Really, Jim! The very idea!"

"What's the matter, Jill? You sound as though I were trying to insult you."

"I know you're not trying to insult me, and I'm grateful. But you *will* do the most ridiculous things!"

"What's so ridiculous about it?"

"When that mysterious man in Washington followed you from your friend's flat to the railway station, you told your driver to pull up short and deliberately jumped down in front of the other car. You might have been *killed!*"

"I ran no risk whatever of being killed. The other car was a good fifty or sixty feet away. And even in this country, Jill, we're not so fond of violence that somebody who's following you will wallop into you with a ton of car just to prove you haven't eluded him."

"Now you're cross with me; please don't be cross with me! There's a reason, you know," she gave him a glance from under lowered eyelids, "why I c-can't and mustn't deprive you of your compartment. I mustn't even stay here any longer. You *could* hit me over the head with something, I daresay. But even you can't be fond enough of violence for that. Let's not argue any further, Jim. Good night."

The door closed after her. And that had been that.

Despite his forebodings of wakeful hours, he was so tired that he slept heavily. It was almost nine o'clock on a warmish, murky Tuesday morning, and the train had pulled in to stop at Salisbury, North Carolina, when the porter's insistent tapping roused him at last.

Jim shaved and dressed in haste. The body of the sleeping-car had resumed a normal daylight appearance, lines of green-upholstered seats facing each other down its length. Jill was nowhere in sight.

He pushed through to the dining-car, meeting a number of other passengers returning from it. Almost everybody had breakfasted. By herself at a table in the near-deserted dining-car, Jill sat with bacon and eggs before her and a newspaper on the adjacent chair.

Jill wore another severe tailored costume without looking at all severe in it. But she did not seem to be eating much. She started involuntarily as he loomed up beside the

table and sat down facing her across it. Her first words
took him aback.

"Not fond of violence, did you say?"

"I was only trying to say good morning, Jill. How are
you?"

"I'm p-perfectly fit, thanks. But you might look at this
newspaper." She took it up. "A boy on the platform was
selling them when we stopped at Salisbury twenty minutes
ago. I didn't really *want* the wretched paper; I only went
out for a breath of fresh air. Then I saw the headlines. One
of your presidential candidates, Mr. Roosevelt . . ."

Colonel Theodore Roosevelt, it seemed, had been on his
way to make a speech in Milwaukee when some lunatic
fired a bullet into his chest. The redoubtable Teddy, dis-
daining this, had insisted on making the scheduled speech
before he would allow any doctor to attend him.

"He's not badly hurt, fortunately," Jill continued, as
her companion glanced through the story. "They've taken
him to a hospital in Chicago, and he'll be campaigning
again in a day or two. I said I was perfectly fit, and I am.
However, what with everything else that's been happening, I'm afraid I'm a little . . . a little . . ."

"Of course you are, Jill; that business last night must
have given you a very bad time. I'm sorry if I was
inconsiderate."

"You weren't a bit inconsiderate; just the opposite! *I'm*
the one who was so stubborn that . . . that . . ."

"Well, well, well!" boomed another voice. Leo Shepley,
freshly groomed if reddish of jowl, drew out a chair and
sat down beside Jill.

"Yes, I've heard about Teddy Roosevelt's mishap; it's
all over the train. You may not agree with everything
Teddy says, but you've got to admire the old boy's guts.
Gently, brothers and sisters! Not another word, either of
you," Leo went on, though nobody had said a word,
"until Jim and I have had at least a bite to eat."

While the train sped through a countryside not yet deeply
tinged with autumnal colors, each newcomer wrote his

order on the pad beside each plate. When ham and eggs had been consumed and coffee poured, Jim offered Jill a cigarette, which she refused.

"Not in public, please, if you don't mind."

Leo backed her up with powerful gallantry.

"Your lightest wish, dear lady, shall be our command. *I'll* have a coffin nail, though. Next, Jim, about last night . . ."

"Lord, Leo, are we back on that same old round of argument?"

"We never did leave it, did we? Now listen you pestilential Yankee . . ."

"Suppose you do the listening, for once in your life!"

"Well?"

"Someone with a sense of humor knocked at the drawing-room door and then lit out. Let's face it, Leo. Unless you do believe in ghosts, which I gather isn't likely, then one person or the other has done some very tall lying. That story of the porter, for instance . . ."

"I tell you, Jim, I've known Uncle Mose for years! Clay Blake can vouch for him, too!"

"It's not a question of vouching for anyone; it's a question of fact. If the porter really stood for some minutes where he said he stood —'jes' lazin', lak'—then he had a clear view of the drawing-room door. How was it he didn't see the person who knocked?"

"But he did see the person who knocked. Dammit, Jim, we had him on the carpet afterwards and you heard him tell it yourself! The light was very bad, remember. What he saw was only a kind of shadow, like a man in a dark suit with back turned. The joker knocked sharply and then ducked into the alley leading past the women's whatnot to the car ahead. All Uncle Mose kept insisting, over and over, was that nobody ran *in his direction*. And of course the joker didn't; he ran the other way."

"Whereas the conductor, a responsible railroad official if any responsible official exists, will swear on a stack of Bibles nobody went that way either. Which of them is more likely to have been telling the truth?"

"What if both of 'em were telling the truth?"

"Leo, how could both have been telling the truth?"

"How could the unknown watcher have been trailing you in Washington? But somebody did. We've just got to find explanations for both problems, that's all!"

"I've already said I can't swear I was being trailed. However! For argument's sake, and just for the moment, let's assume it's a fact. With some concentration or even star-gazing, I might just conceivably find an explanation for that particular problem, because it's merely puzzling. But the problem of the vanishing joker isn't just puzzling or difficult to solve; unless somebody's lying, it's a flat physical impossibility.

"And so, Leo, we come to the crux of last night's argument. You keep saying we've got to find explanations for this or that. All right. Why the hell won't *you* explain?"

"Come again, old son?"

A gray cloud of tobacco-smoke had drifted above the table. Jim glanced at Jill, whose face was turned partly away. Then he looked Leo in the eyes.

"At risk of tedium, I had better repeat that my whole mission on this job is to find certain answers. Is there in fact a plot against Clay Blake? And, if so, how is the dirty work to be managed? If I knew the answer to that one, I should be more than halfway home. You do follow me, don't you?"

"Yes, of course. But . . . !"

"Last night, just before the appearance or non-appearance of the joker, you were visited with a great inspiration. Amid wild and whirling words, including mention of one Flossie Yates, you more than intimated you had the information I need. When the tumult about the joker had died down a little, and we were back in the drawing-room again, I asked you to explain. You froze; you drew yourself up; you stood on your dignity and refused to say one more word. What made you do that, Leo?"

"It was because I couldn't tell you then. And I can't tell you now!"

"Why not?"

"This is a delicate business, Jim; it's a *damn* delicate business."

"We're all aware of that. At the same time . . ."

"Clay's a great friend of mine, too, you know. Before I've made the most discreet and cautious inquiries at home, I mustn't open my big mouth at all. I can't even tell an old friend like you, or a model of discretion like Jill. I may have said too much already.

"Let's suppose I *am* right. And Clay's entirely innocent, as I'm sure he is. If I go talking or hinting too much to *anybody*, anybody at all, I myself may start the very accusation Clay's enemies want to start. It wouldn't get into the papers, of course. But just the rumor or report, more and more magnified as it spread, could play merry hell with any man. If you two knew, and either of you dropped an indiscreet word without meaning to . . ."

"May *I* ask a question?" interposed Jill.

"That depends on the question, little one. Let's hear it."

Jill's color had come up. Distressed, uncertain, she glanced sideways at Leo before lowering her eyes.

"I was just thinking," she said. "This accusation, whatever it is, must be an accusation of something perfectly dreadful!"

"A line of inquiry," Jim pointed out, "which can be carried still further. It's something abnormal or unnatural, is it? The slightest suggestion of homosexuality, for instance . . ."

Leo smote his fist on the table, so that glasses and china rang.

"What kind of friends do you think I have, for God's sake? No, Jim, I won't hear that for a minute! It's nothing at all abnormal or unnatural, at least in the way you mean."

"Then there's nothing left, surely, they can charge my namesake with. When he's safe in the arms of his high-priced siren, the guidfolk of your city seem to regard it with indulgence if not actual approval. Barring the abnormal or the unnatural, what could a man possibly do that would blow his career sky-high?"

"May I ask my question now?" murmured Jill.

"Look, little one, you've already . . ."

"Pardon me, Leo, but I haven't! I remarked that it must be an accusation of something dreadful, and Jim suggested what he did suggest. Since we seem to have decided on plain speaking, a rare thing nowadays except in theatrical circles or perhaps newspaper offices, I must confess something of that sort occurred to me, too. And plain speaking may be best after all. But I didn't ask my question, so I'll ask it now. Who's Flossie Yates? Is she what she sounds like?"

Leo leaned back and hooked his thumbs in the armholes of his vest.

"Well, now, me dear, that's part of the secret. You've discovered for yourself, I think, that old Uncle Leo can keep a secret when he promises he will. Who's Flossie Yates, the lady asks, and is she what she sounds like? Be more explicit, little one: what *does* she sound like?"

"Not like a prostitute, really, or at least not like one who's practising now. More like what they'd call in England an old . . . an old . . . !"

"I would spare your delicate ears, Jill. But you're the advocate of plain speaking. Are you by any chance trying to ask me whether Flossie's the madam of a brothel?"

"*Yes!*"

"In one sense the answer's yes; in another sense the answer's no. Flossie doesn't advertise in the *Blue Book,* a guide to Storyville you may buy at any barber-shop for twenty-five cents a week. And if my friend Clay should hear that secret, wicked voice threatening him on the telephone, it won't be Flossie's voice he hears; it won't be a woman's voice at all."

Then Leo exploded again.

"I just wish the secret voice would try its games on *me!* I'd soon wring the voice's damn neck, if I may so express myself.

"For I have one small talent, Jim, which even you may not have noticed in the old days. If I've talked to any given person more than once or twice, I can always identify that person's voice afterwards, no matter how much he or she may try to disguise it. I can do it blindfolded; I can even do it on the telephone. But, since there's no reason to think I've ever met the owner of the secret voice, that leaves us just where we were before, doesn't it?"

Jim snorted at him.

"If you mean it still leaves us completely in the dark, yes! What's all this about a secret voice? And you might tell me . . ."

"No, Jim."

Leo hoisted himself up, demanded the breakfast bills, and insisted on paying for everybody.

"No, Jim," he repeated, when the waiter had gone. "For the moment, at least, that's all I'm going to tell you: about Flossie Yates, about the secret voice, or about anything else. In the meantime, mind, not a word of it to anybody until I give permission! I know it seems hard lines when you're after a news story. But it's only temporary; unless I'm much mistaken, you'll have a corker of a story (full permission granted) within a very short time.

"Heigh-ho, ladies and gentlemen! It's just on ten o'clock and we're coming into Charlotte, North Carolina. Your Uncle Leo must now sit down for some very hard thinking: this whole accursed situation and how to handle it. Excuse me, will you?"

And there, for the moment, he left them in the air.

Jim's further efforts to question him had no effect. Leo locked himself in his drawing-room, breathing maledictions behind the door. He wouldn't even come out for lunch, which he had sent to him on a tray.

"I've just thought of something else," he said. "Now shut up and go away!"

They had soon crossed the South Carolina border. Jim devoted himself to Jill, whom he found still more fascinating if no less perplexing. For all her good nature, almost her naïveté, there remained that quality of elusiveness which would not allow her to approach the personal, or let him approach it either.

Towards five in the afternoon (the next stop would be Atlanta), they sat together in open air on the platform of the observation car, the last car of the train, watching the tracks unreel and shine by dwindling sunlight. A damp breeze whipped the ends of the scarf Jill had bound over her head; her right arm touched his left.

"Jim, what *is* the matter with Leo?"

"He's worried. He's badly worried. So he's being deliberately mysterious."

"Well, so are you."

"*I* am being mysterious?"

"I asked you about the real people in *The Count of Monte Carlo*. But you wouldn't tell me."

"We were interrupted, that's all. Try again."

"Count Dimitri, the Russian nobleman with the villa, is a real person?"

"He is (or was) very much a real person. Under his own name he *was* a minor nobleman. But he wasn't Russian; he was Austrian. And he wouldn't have had a villa anywhere; he moved about too much. I had to disguise him so completely that nobody could possibly have guessed his identity."

"Why did you have to do that?"

"Because espionage, which seems such a joke to Colonel Harvey and Leo, isn't a joke at all. It's dirty, dangerous work, with long imprisonment or a firing squad if they catch you off base.

"Franz was chronically short of cash, though he had an income from his own estate and got good pay from the Wilhelmstrasse. I met him one night at a hotel in Trouville, when he was half drunk and so fed up with life that he might have put a bullet through his head. Well, I did him a favor. Pledging me to strict secrecy, a pledge I've kept, he told me first a little and then a lot. Afterwards, when I kept running into him all over the continent of Europe . . ."

"That's when started you on the book?"

"Yes. I couldn't use his adventures for the New York *Banner*. I couldn't use 'em in any form if it meant risk to Franz. But with every character and event twisted out of shape or upside down, with suitable additions of glamour and bloodshed, I *could* get away with it as fiction."

"Oh, you succeeded! Those vivid personal details . . ."

"I made the count young and dashing; in fact he was stout, fiftyish, and bald. The fictitious Russian had an English mother, to prepare the ground for revealing him as a British agent. The real Austrian, who hated England, spoke fluent English because he learned it at school; he hadn't even had an English nurse. Count Dimitri never flinched before the most menacing revolver; Franz was one mass of exposed nerves. Having covered my tracks like that . . ."

"And the heroine, Marcia Allison!" Jill said with radiant innocence. "Was *she* one of your women?"

"What do you mean, one of my women?"

"I think you know what I mean."

"And I also know you're dead wrong. Marcia Allison, Jill, was suggested by a girl I once saw for perhaps five minutes in the casino at Monte Carlo. I never learned her name or even her nationality. She was at one of the roulette tables; her elbow knocked some counters off the edge, I picked 'em up and she thanked me. That's all. The next moment her escort, an elderly man who might have been father or uncle or even husband of sixty-odd, drifted up and took her away. She had to be imagined from scraps and patches of other people. When I made Franz fall in love with her . . ."

"Franz. Yes, Franz! What was his full name?"

"I don't think I'd better tell you that, Jill. It's only protecting my source of information, as any reporter should."

"Protecting your source of—!"

Jill's laughter, somewhat overstrained and not altogether convincing, rang out on that platform amid the Georgia hill-country. She whooped and chortled: her head thrown back, her shoulder against his arm.

"Protecting your source of information! Really, it's too funny for words! You think *I'm* hiding some grisly secret . . ."

"Have I said I think you're hiding anything?"

"Not in so many words, maybe. But your looks have said it a hundred times since last night. What did I tell you, Jim? *You're* making a mystery where there oughtn't to be any mystery. Leo won't answer questions, and neither will you!"

"Who says Leo won't answer questions," struck in a familiar voice, "if he thinks they're fit and proper questions to answer?"

And he towered up in dignity, holding open the glass-panelled door. Leo, his tweed cap contrasting with a light-weight suit, swept them a ceremonious bow before he went to lean against the railing of the platform.

"All right, Jim! You're waving your hand like a school-boy who wants to leave the room. We're open to questions now, I say, always provided they're relevant to the issue."

"I'll give you a very relevant one, which I tried to ask this morning. You've referred more than once to what Clay Blake's enemies might do. Just who are these enemies?"

"Offhand, and before this came up, I'd have said Clay had no enemies. Still, who among us is without 'em?"

"That's no answer, Leo. What about young Peter Laird? Didn't they have a row in some bar or other?"

"Yes, but that's all blown over and forgotten. Besides, Pete's not the type. Since you're investigating, though, I'll give you a little tip. Keep your eye on Pete's mother, Mrs. Mathilde de Jarnac Laird."

"The one they call Madam Ironface? Has *she* got it in for my namesake?"

"Judas Priest, no! I say keep your eye on her because I love the old girl, whom *I* call Aunt Mathilde! Cherish Aunt Mathilde. If you've got a problem, take it to Aunt

Mathilde. She's the most sensible and reliable of all the Lairds.''

"Although her son isn't allowed to drive his own car?''

"She won't let such a damn bad driver kill himself, if that's what you mean! Pete Laird oughtn't to be trusted with a wheelbarrow, let alone a new Cadillac. Do *you* drive, Jim? Yes, I see you do. Traffic conditions are easier in New Orleans than in New York. Why not try driving on your errands while you're with us?''

"Where would I get a car?''

"Rent one.''

"Is it possible to *rent* a car?''

"It is if you see my friend Stu Guilfoyle—Guilfoyle's Garage, Chartres Street—and tell him I sent you. Stu may not come up with a Mercer Raceabout like mine, but he'll find you something serviceable. Better buy goggles and a dust-coat, even for a car with a windshield; I always wear 'em. If any errand takes you out to the suburbs, the roads are shocking and you can hardly breathe for dust. Good idea, Jim?''

"Renting a car may be a very good idea, agreed. But I was asking you . . . !''

"Yes, of course!'' The other blinked and snapped his fingers. "Mustn't let a hobby run away with me, as I so often do. You were asking about Clay's enemies, weren't you? Well, now, as regards *potential* enemies . . .''

And yet, despite Leo's professed willingness to help, Jim got little further.

Raymond P. Chadwick, Leo conceded, just *might* cut the throat of the man who had defeated him for nomination to Congress. Leo thought this unlikely, Mr. Chadwick being one with notoriously little fondness for risk. But it remained a possibility. Leo said he could think of nobody else.

Afternoon became evening; evening deepened into night. The three of them dined together on fried chicken and sweet potatoes, a substantial meal if no gourmet's delight. Leo talked freely about motoring; he would talk freely about anything, in fact, except the riddles centering around James Claiborne Blake. Since clearly it was some aspect of this which so haunted or bedevilled him, Jim forbore to hammer at it too long.

Leo's apprehension took no definite shape until the following morning, at which time it struck them like a blow in the face.

Jim himself spent the wakeful night he had feared twenty-four hours earlier, a vision of Jill forever in his mind and forever eluding him. Though he fell into a troubled doze as the train left Mobile, Alabama, at well past three in the morning, he woke again before seven. He was shaved, dressed, and at least outwardly presentable when they rolled into Terminal Station, New Orleans.

The porter had removed his suitcase several minutes before. Jim emerged into the car, a cavern of disarranged green curtains with berth-lights still burning, and descended to the platform outside.

Bedraggled, half-awake passengers were hurrying through the station towards Canal Street. Various articles of luggage from car sixteen had been set in a row on the platform near the foot of the vestibule steps, where the porter bowed above them. Jim found Jill standing beside her own luggage, a valise and a hat-box. Leo, at first seeming unworried, joined them there a moment later.

"Now listen!" he began. "One cab will do for us all. I think you said, Jim, you were going to the St. Charles?"

"First to the St. Charles Hotel, to get a room and have breakfast, and then to the *Sentinel* office to see Mr. Alec Laird. It's an evening paper; he ought to be there by nine-thirty or ten. As for Mr. Clay Blake . . ."

"I live out Jackson Avenue way, as you may or may not remember." Leo waved a hand to indicate. "I'll drop you at the St. Charles, which isn't far from here, and then take Jill wherever she wants to go. Don't worry about finding Clay; don't even bother to telephone; I'll introduce you to him myself. We'll just get a redcap to take our bags, and—" He broke off. "Oh, dear God!"

"What's the matter?"

"In my drawing-room; something I forgot. Now don't move, either of you; stay right where you are. I'll be back in thirty seconds!"

And he sprang up the steps.

It was much more than thirty seconds. Some five or six minutes had passed, and Jim several times waved back hovering redcaps, before Leo descended again. He moved slowly and heavily, turning on them a face of something like collapse.

"Did you find what you wanted, Leo?"

"I found something I didn't want, Jim. Now hearken, brothers and sisters; prepare yourselves for a shock. Though I didn't know it until a few minutes ago, Clay Blake's on that train. He's been on the train since New York, shut up in a drawing-room of car seventeen behind us, having his meals sent in as I did once yesterday. Jesus H. God! I thought this business might be bad, but it's a damn sight worse than anything I ever expected!

"And it necessitates a slight change of plan. I'd better stay here for a little, I think. You get the cab, Jim. I'll phone you later, either at the hotel or at Alec's office. Get the cab, take Jill, and—" Again he broke off. "Just what the hell *is* going on in this place, anyway?"

Jill and her luggage had disappeared.

PART TWO:

QUEST OF PHANTOMS

6

Jim left the hotel at a quarter past ten.

When he had registered there on arrival just over two hours before, he wondered whether anybody would say, "Well, Mr. Blake, and how's the campaign for Congress?" Nobody said it. Colonel Harvey, it appeared, had telegraphed ahead to reserve room and bath, carefully designating him as "my distinguished author, James Buchanan Blake."

They received him with a cordiality near courtliness. He was whisked aloft to comfortable, even sybaritic quarters on the third floor overlooking St. Charles Avenue. Vividly in his mind remained that parting scene at Terminal Station, when Leo hustled him into a cab.

"Where does she live?" Leo had fumed. "How should *I* know where she lives? She's not in the telephone directory, I can tell you. There's more than one Matthews, but no Gillian or Jill, not even a G. or J. You certainly won't find her boss there either."

"What's the boss's name again, Leo?"

"Hollister. Old Ed Hollister, the mystery man of finance. Never mind, Jim; we'll find her somehow, since you're so determined. Now beat it; I must get back to Clay. But I'll be in touch before long."

Once installed at the hotel, despite Leo's warning Jim had leafed through the telephone book in vain. Then he ordered wheat cakes and sausages, to be served in his room. A morning newspaper, its first page devoted almost exclusively to Teddy Roosevelt, arrived with the food. He sat long at breakfast, lingering over coffee and cigarettes. He drew a hot bath and lingered in that, thinking long thoughts.

By the time he took the elevator downstairs, it was almost ten by the clock in the lobby. Buying a map of New Orleans at the cigar counter, he sat down to study it amid marble and red plush. Presently, he folded up the map, put it in his pocket, and went out through the revolving door into St. Charles Avenue.

From what he could recall of one visit here fourteen years ago, his memories were only of pastel-colored houses with courtyards in the Vieux Carré beyond Canal Street, of a luxurious brothel in Storyville, and of one other thing.

At least the telephone book had told him where to find the *Sentinel:* Camp Street. In 1898, as a prospective newspaperman in the best style of Richard Harding Davis, he had already marked that name. Camp Street, roughly parallel with St. Charles Avenue on the side towards the river, contained more than one newspaper office. And he was almost sure he remembered . . .

A changing gray sky held opalescent lights. Leo had been right about traffic, from what he could see now. Though brisk enough along the immensity of Canal Street towards Jim's left, and even here on less spacious St. Charles Avenue, it was not the frustrating tangle of New York. You even noted a few cars amid horse-drawn cabs and wagons, and heard horns honk against streetcar bells.

Jim turned to his right. A short walk west brought him to Lafayette Square, with the white pillars of City Hall looming up on the right and, in the middle, a leafy little park where idlers lounged on benches.

He crossed the street. When he had gone through the park in Lafayette Square—which seemed to contain a statue or bust of almost every picturesque historical figure except Lafayette himself—Jim stopped in realization. Yes, he had remembered! Facing him from Camp Street was the six-story building - of rough-hewn stone which housed the *Sentinel*.

Great tact would be needed now. His approach to the paper's acting owner must be both diplomatic and wary, or he would find Clay Blake's friends leagued against the Intruder to refuse any information at all.

Pondering tactics, he went into a rather gloomy entrance-lobby, with three elevators on the right and, it seemed, the bustle of business offices behind opaque-glass windows towards the left.

Along with three or four others, including a little woman conspicuous for jaw-set, Jim entered the middle elevator and said, "Top floor, please," to the youth in buttons who operated it.

A solitary electric bulb illumined the cage as it rose. The determined-looking little woman got off at the city-room floor, from which Jim could hear typewriters clacking, two telephones ringing in unison, and an insistent shout of *"Boy!"* There was nobody but himself and the operator by the time they reached the top.

He had small reason to hesitate, though. A line of doors with ground-glass panels, no lettering on any of the panels, faced him from the wall opposite the elevators in a broad corridor paved with tile. But well towards Jim's left, at the front of the building, was a single door with the chaste black legend, *Alexander Laird*.

This opened into a reception room with a skylight, heavily decorated after the fashion of the eighteen-eighties: it might have been a reception room at Harper's. *Mr. Laird* and *Private* appeared on the ground-glass panel of another door opposite, clearly leading to an office overlooking Camp Street. At a desk in the middle of the room, behind the glow of the desk's lamp, sat a brisk, poised young lady with a small watch pinned to the bosom of her shirtwaist.

"Yes, sir?"

"I wonder if I may see Mr. Laird? My name is Blake;

here is my card. And you might send in this other card, which is from Colonel Harvey at Harper's in New York."

Neglecting to ask whether he had an appointment, the goddess smiled at him instead.

"We'll not be needing any cards, I'm thinking." She picked up a telephone, spoke briefly to it, and was answered. "Go right on in, Mr. Blake. You're expected."

The office beyond was modern enough. It still held traces of that elder Alec Laird who had occupied the room for so long, including half a wall of framed testimonials and photographs inscribed to him by the great or the near-great. But the past was almost gone.

The younger Alec Laird, a lean, wiry, middle-sized man of forty, with dark hair smoothly brushed and a collar high even for this year of high collars, rose from a massive desk bearing several telephones, and advanced to shake hands. If his saturnine face did in fact suggest some Puritan elder of no very advanced views, it could not have been called an unsympathetic face. His manner, too, was less formal than the visitor had anticipated.

"It's a pleasure to be here, Mr. Laird," Jim said.

"It's a pleasure to welcome you, sir. Colonel Harvey telephoned from New York on Monday afternoon and said you would be in New Orleans today. I've never had the good fortune to meet Colonel Harvey face to face, but we've all heard of him.

"Be seated, I beg," Alec Laird went on, indicating a leather chair beside his desk and himself sitting down. "Only a few years ago, Mr. Blake, these long-distance telephone calls would have been considered a miracle. Today we accept them almost for commonplaces, as we accept motor-cars and flying machines and wireless telegraphy. Which reminds me: you are a much-sought-after man this morning. Leo Shepley has been phoning in search of you."

"Leo's already phoned?"

"Not five minutes before you arrived. When he failed to reach you at the St. Charles—you had gone out, they said—he insisted you must be with me because it had been your intention to call between nine-thirty and ten. I could only assure him I hadn't seen you.''

"Did he leave a message?''

"No message, sir. But he seemed much exercised about something, as Leo so often is, and said he would try again later.''

Alec Laird put his fingertips together and inspected them.

"Now, Mr. Blake. For some time, I believe, you were London correspondent of the *Banner*. And you have written a successful book. I myself, I greatly fear, read nothing published after 1890; let it stand the test of time, and then we shall see. But you have the highest reputation for integrity. I understand from Colonel Harvey you want to do a personality story on our own Mr. Blake, of whom we all think so well hereabouts?''

"That, sir,'' Jim matched his formal style of address, "is my whole purpose in being here. May I count on your cooperation, if I should need it?''

"You may count on it to the fullest extent. And yet there may be difficulties not of my making. For one thing, can you find Clay? You may just have missed him.''

"Just have missed him?''

"Over last weekend, it would appear, there was a conference of various Democratic candidates for office at the Astor Hotel in New York.''

"I remember seeing some item about it in the paper. He attended that conference, did he?''

"So I am informed, at least. Clay may or may not have returned. Of course, I can always ring him and arrange for you to meet him if he *has* returned.''

"Many thanks for the offer, but Leo Shepley's arranging it. Leo probably phoned to tell me.''

"Well, no doubt that's best. Leo is a much closer friend than I am. But there is one other thing, Mr. Blake, which—''

One of Alec Laird's telephones rang. He unhooked the receiver with a certain slight impatience.

"Yes, Miss Donnelly?"

Jim could clearly hear the voice on the wire.

"Will you see Mrs. Laird, sir? And Mr. Peter Laird?"

"What's my wife doing here at this hour of the morning?" Then the acting owner hesitated. "But you said *Peter* Laird, didn't you? Are you referring, Miss Donnelly, to my esteemed aunt and her son?"

"Yes, sir. I told them you were engaged, but Mrs. Laird . . ."

"Yes, the lady does tend to be impatient. Better show them in." Alec Laird looked at Jim as he replaced the receiver. "Not a word of your errand here, please, until—"

Once more he stopped short as Miss Donnelly, the receptionist, held open the door of the outer office.

The woman who swept in, wearing modish clothes and a large hat, did not seem either very old or very overpowering. Forthright and vigorous she undoubtedly was: handsome, well preserved both of face and figure, with coolly appraising brown eyes under ridged gray hair. But the handsome features lacked much play of expression, which may have accounted for so uncharitable a nickname as Madam Ironface.

"Since I was in town for a little shopping," she began, "I thought—"

And it was her turn to stop short, hand raised as though encountering an obstacle.

Alec Laird murmured brief, hasty introductions, presenting Jim merely as "this gentleman from *Harper's Weekly*" both to Mathilde de Jarnac Laird and to the lumpish young man who had followed her in.

Jim had a momentary impression, illusory, that he had met Peter Laird before. Burly, thick-bodied Peter, dark of hair like Cousin Alec, hardly seemed to have shed his puppy-fat even in the late twenties. He combined an apologetic manner with a rather sullen eye.

Miss Donnelly set out chairs for the newcomers before retiring to the outer office. Mrs. Sam Laird and her son disregarded the chairs, Peter perching on the edge of his cousin's desk.

"Yes, Aunt Mathilde?" Alec looked her up and down. "What can I do for you today?"

He very slightly accented "today." The lady raised her eyebrows.

"It's Wednesday, you know," she reminded him. "We just wanted to make sure both you and Sylvia will be with us for dinner tonight. Your father and mother always dined with us on Wednesdays while your mother was alive, and your father would still be there every week if he had the strength to. Don't be so *restless,* Peter!"

"I don't get much chance to be anything else, do I?" the young man complained. "If you'd just let a fellow alone for five minutes of the day—!"

"We know, Peter; we know. Never mind. The high and mighty Mr. Alexander Laird has not seen fit to answer my question. I was asking him . . ."

"At the moment," Alec said, "I see no reason why we *can't* have dinner with you tonight. I'll verify it with my wife, of course. But the high and mighty Mr. Laird, Aunt Mathilde, is a very busy man. He—"

Another telephone on the desk rang shrilly and went on ringing. Alec Laird eyed it.

"That's an outside line; and a private one. The call can't be intercepted by Miss Donnelly out there; it doesn't even go through the switchboard downstairs. But I think I know who's calling."

Standing on the far side of his desk, he caught up the phone.

"So it's you again, is it? . . . No, of course I'm not annoyed; why should I be? . . . Yes, he's here now . . . Yes, by all means speak to him . . . You're not up to any of your games, are you? . . . You'd better not be. . . . For *you,*" he added, handing the instrument across to Jim.

Jim's hello met with almost exactly the greeting he expected.

"Now listen, you old horse-thief!" said Leo Shepley.

"Since I've finally tracked you down at last, give me your best attention. The first part of what I've got to tell you isn't private; at least, it's not *entirely* private. What I'm trying to say, Jim, is that Clay's very much upset and doesn't feel up to meeting people at the moment. Would you mind very much if we postponed the interview until tonight or tomorrow morning?"

"No, of course I don't mind!"

"What we've got to conceal is the reason why he's upset. And the next part of the low-down *is* private. It's so very damn private that . . . Listen, Jim. Is there anybody there with you now? Anybody besides Alec himself, I mean? Just answer yes or no."

"Yes."

"Those phones in the owner's lair have so clear a tone that sometimes you can be overheard speaking from a yard away, unless the person you're speaking to jams the receiver against his ear. But I think I see a way to make this as private as a confessional box. Let me speak to Alec again for a moment, will you?"

A frown had gathered between Alec Laird's brows as he took over.

"In the study, you say? . . . No, there's nobody there now . . . Yes; it can be managed quite easily if you insist it's so very important? . . . In fact, I should prefer it that way. Hold on."

He set down the telephone without hanging up its receiver, and turned to Jim.

"Now, sir: will you come this way, please?"

The office had one other door besides the one to the reception room. This second door, in the wall at right angles to the wall of the reception-room entrance, was of solid oak, with a porcelain knob. Clearly it led to some room at the north-eastern angle of the *Sentinel* Building.

Alec Laird opened the door, ushered his guest in, and stood aside as though exhibiting a museum. And so he was.

Like the office, it had two windows overlooking Camp Street from six floors up. Its decor, though similar to the eighteen-eighties style of the reception room, seemed more stay-at-home and intimate.

Glass-fronted bookcases of dropsical aspect had been ranged against flowered wallpaper. There was an old leather couch between the windows. Against the wall opposite the door, beside what resembled another doorway covered by a folding steel grating, a rolltop desk stood swept and open behind its wooden swivel-chair. There was a telephone on the desk, with a green-shaded drop-lamp hanging above.

Alec Laird indicated everything.

"We call this the study," he explained. "My father furnished it many years ago, and used it as a retreat until he gave up work on the paper. It's kept just as it was when he left; I even have the wallpaper renewed before it turns yellow. Most visitors feel compelled to writhe with aesthetic agony; but, if truth must be told, I'm fond of the old place and won't have it changed."

"What's that door with the grating?"

"That, sir, is the private elevator. There are some, no doubt, who think a private elevator too high and mighty— as we say in the South, too uppity—for this workaday world. That, believe me, is not the reason. My father had it installed when he found his years catching up to him, and had to remodel extensively for the convenience. It goes down to an alley beside the building."

"And the telephone?"

"An extension of the private line in my office. The line is still open. Try it."

Jim sat down in the swivel-chair and addressed himself to carbon.

"As they say in England, are you there?"

Leo's voice boomed back.

"You bet I am, old son; four ways from the ace! Can you talk now?"

"In a moment," said Alec Laird.

Both he and Jim craned round to look through the open

doorway into the office, where Peter sat on the edge of the desk and his mother paced in front of it.

"Peter!" called Cousin Alec.

"Yes, Alec?"

"Be good enough to hang up the receiver of the phone I was using, and don't touch it afterwards under any circumstances."

Peter complied, dropping home the receiver with an audible click.

"Excuse me for existing, Alec, but what were all you people gabbling about? And who's being so gabby at the other end?"

"Nobody who need concern *you*, young man. Now, Mr. Blake, the inner sanctum is yours. Handle things as you think best."

And he went out and closed the door firmly.

"Still with me, Jim?" inquired Leo. "I gather from all that hoo-ha old Stick-in-the-mud played ball?"

"I'm in the study, as you suggested."

"And it's agreed, is it, you don't interview Clay until tonight or tomorrow morning, preferably tomorrow?"

"It's more than agreed. Provided I can file a personality story by late Thursday afternoon, that's all I need."

"All you need? In a pig's eye it's all you need! Jim, I've been having some serious second thoughts about this business."

"I had some second thoughts, too, at the hotel this morning. May I ask one question before I state 'em?"

"We aim to please, brother. Fire away."

"You say my partial namesake is badly upset. Well, what upset him? Is it what you thought it would be?"

"Yes, damn the luck!"

"Then there's proof my second thoughts are right. Leo, it's no go."

"What's no go?"

"The projected big story is no go. It would never do. It must be washed out and forgotten."

"Jim, are you drunk?"

"Far from it."

The changing sky over New Orleans had become darker gray. Little puffs of breeze stirred past the windows. Jim got a grip on the telephone.

"I've been unpardonably dense," he went on. "I let myself be so carried away by the situation that certain obvious implications got lost in the rush. Once we decided they couldn't use Yvonne Brissard against your friend Clay, it had to be something else. I don't know what sort of story Colonel Harvey thinks I'm after, but I do know what he doesn't want. If this were the customary tale of some candidate for office with charges against him—shady financial deals, bribery, corrupt politics in general—it would be easy. But it's not that at all. It's sex, Leo. It's not Yvonne Brissard, but it *is* sex. Sex, the unbreakable taboo!

"I've been commissioned by *Harper's Weekly,* not the *Police Gazette.* In any responsible newspaper I could refer to a sex scandal only obliquely; in a family publication like the *Weekly* I can't refer to it at all. And, if I must keep quiet even about a full-blown scandal with charges already established, how much more silent I must be when no scandal has yet developed and no charges have been made!"

Over the wire came some sound between a grunt and a groan.

"There'll be charges soon enough, Jim, unless you and I take action. Clay wants the whole thing hushed up; I want to nail the bastard who's behind it. You see, that's the private part of what I've got to tell you. Clay's already been threatened anonymously."

"Threatened with what?"

"Unless he withdraws his name from the ballot and resigns as a candidate for Congress within the next twenty-four hours, pleading ill-health or some such excuse, his family and friends will be informed about what he's supposed to have done."

"What's he supposed to have done?"

"Ah, there we come to it!" Leo drew a deep breath. "You know, Jim, you may be right about killing the story for the press. In fact, I think you *are* right; I had doubts as soon as I talked to Clay. And he's not the only load on my mind. I'm beginning to get badly worried about something that involves me, too. I was worried when we were on that train; I'm pretty damnably worried now.''

"Something that involves you, too?''

"Me, your old pal, *moi gui vous parle!* But forget your Uncle Leo, for the moment. Let's agree *any* news story must die the death at once, and get back to our harassed Clay. As I sit here thinking about him . . .''

"Where are you now, Leo?''

"I'm at home, eating a sandwich and drinking, believe it or not, a glass of milk.''

"Where's the harassed candidate for Congress?''

"He's at home, too, or was when I saw him last. He couldn't face the office today. He'll be spending the evening—and the night, too, no doubt—with his fair Yvonne at the Villa de Jarnac near good old Bayou St. John. But there he is now, penned in a corner and thinking the world's come to an end! As I said before, I want to nail the bastard who's behind this. Does that concern you, too? Are you interested in ferreting out the facts, even though you never use 'em?''

"Of course I'm interested, Leo! 'Interested' is too mild a word. In this job, some of the best stories you get are the stories you can't use.''

"All right! You and little Jill,'' momentarily Leo made noises away from the phone, "seemed much exercised about a character named Flossie Yates.''

"Well?''

"Flossie, Jim, offers a certain service to the community. Have you figured out what that service is?''

"No, though I've had one or two ideas about Clay Blake. This alleged 'service,' you said, entails nothing abnormal or unnatural . . ,''

"Nothing abnormal or unnatural, I said, in the way you meant it! Would you like to go out and learn the nature of the service?''

"Why not tell me what it is?"

"Under instructions, and according to my sworn promise, I mustn't tell you that unless Clay tells you. But there's no promise to stop you from investigating. Just how earnest a truth-seeker *are* you, after all? What will you do, where will you go and how far, to get your claws on the facts at last? In short, Jim, have you got the nerve to tackle Flossie for yourself?"

7

ABOVE THE ROLLTOP DESK, in that antiquated room, hung an antiquated framed picture not unskilled of drawing or color. Called *Gentlemen of the Jury* in raised red letters along the lower frame, it showed twelve be-whiskered figures wilting and inattentive under what was presumably a bombardment of evidence.

The murky day threw shadows across it as Jim glanced up. But most vividly he could picture Leo, sitting some distance away over the sandwich and the glass of milk.

"Did you hear what I said?" the other demanded. "Have you got the nerve?"

"I think I can manage, if it's necessary."

" 'Fraid it's necessary, old son. You *could* ask some-body else, maybe; but since you're a stranger here and wouldn't know whom to ask . . ."

"Will there be some risk attached to this, Leo?"

"Only risk to what's humorously called your good name," Leo snorted. "You're in no danger of being clubbed over the head or getting a knife in your back, if that's what you mean. On the contrary! Unless she's paid out some heavy bribe-money, which may be the case, it's Flossie herself who's been running one hell of a risk."

"If these houses in Storyville are operated strictly within the law, how can she run any risk?"

"Because her house isn't in Storyville; it's on the sacred Esplanade."

"On the sacred what?"

Leo snorted again.

"Esplanade Avenue, once sacred to the homes of wealthy Creoles, and still a good neighborhood in anybody's book. I'm looking for her address and phone number at this minute. Yes, here we are! 'Miss Florence Yates, 691 Esplanade Avenue, phone Main 0101.'

"Flossie's a lady of refinement, you'd better hear, or puts up a good show of being one. You'll have to phone first and make an appointment with her, you know. You may not want to use your own name, but you'd better use mine as a reference. Got everything so far?"

"Yes, I think so. 'Miss Florence Yates, 691 Esplanade Avenue, phone Main 0101.' "

"Then here's what you do. Phone today and make an appointment for this afternoon. This afternoon, mind, not tonight; I've got other pursuits in mind for you tonight.

"Treat Flossie as you'd treat a duchess. Begin with some trivial pleasantries; then say you understand her niece is visiting her, or will visit her shortly, and you'd very much like to meet the niece. Let Flossie take it from there, and see what happens."

"Her niece is visiting her. Do I name the niece?"

"No." Leo gave a subdued whoop. "Since you're accepting the challenge and walking into it blindfolded, Jim, more power to you! And more power to me; I may need it. If I weren't so *hellish* worried about Clay and about myself, too, I might almost enjoy what's happening or is going to happen.

"I'd better ring off now; I've got many things to do. But you won't forget about tonight, will you? Be at the hotel after dinner, within easy reach of a phone; you're going to get a message. In the meantime, old son, stay on the alert and don't do anything I wouldn't do. That's all."

The line went dead. Jim also hung up the receiver. He rose to his feet, took a last look around at the antiquated furnishings, and then went back to the adjoining office.

Alec Laird, in high collar and lounge suit so formal it

suggested a cutaway coat without being one, was just closing the door to the reception room.

"Goodbye, Aunt Mathilde. For the last time, you may expect us to dinner unless some crisis arises!"

Departing Aunt Mathilde and her son could hardly have heard the last few words, which were addressed to a closed door. The *Sentinel*'s acting owner turned towards his desk and met Jim.

"It seems most discourteous to turn them out after only fifteen minutes," he said, "and I fear I betrayed impatience from the first. But my esteemed aunt can be something of a handful, Mr. Blake. She means well and she's essentially kind-hearted, but she never lets up; she goes on and on and on. I'm not altogether happy about the boy, either. He won't do a lick of work; we can't interest him in anything except the cars he mustn't drive. Stay, though!—"

Clearly to make sure the visitors had really gone, Alec Laird returned to the glass-panelled door and opened it.

Though the visitors had gone, another presence seemed just to have arrived in their place. The reception-room door to the top-floor corridor was wide open, propped by somebody's left foot. In the aperture stood a big man with an unruly shock of gray-white hair, a yellow copy-pencil in his hand. The corridor lay empty behind him.

"Is it all right, Alec?" he called. "May I exercise a managing editor's privilege of dropping in on the boss without somebody to run interference?"

Alec Laird showed no impatience with this particular visitor.

"By all means join us, Bart! I have something to say; you had better hear it and be in on it."

The newcomer advanced, letting the door swing shut on its air-cushion piston. It would have been hard to determine why he gave the impression of being both shaggy and untidy, since in fact, apart from the shock of hair, he was neither.

"Thanks, Alec," he said. "It's all over the city room, apparently by mental telepathy, that some eminent New

York member of the Fourth Estate has been here with you in the eyrie."

And Jim was introduced to Barton Perkins, managing editor of the *Sentinel.*

Rapidly explaining the errand for *Harper's Weekly,* their host installed them in chairs on either side of his desk, and sat back with his fingertips together.

"Now, Mr. Blake. You have just been on the phone at some length with Leo Shepley. I imagine he *has* arranged for you to meet our candidate for Congress from the Second District?"

"Leo's arranged it, yes. But it's not convenient today. I'm to see him tomorrow, in time to get off a story by phone or wire and meet Thursday's deadline."

Bart Perkins, who seemed to be laboring under strong if suppressed excitement, turned the yellow pencil in his fingers.

"As a matter of fact," the managing editor said, "I'd heard you were supposed to be an old classmate of Leo's. Are you one of the former football heroes, too?"

"No. Baseball was my game; I loved baseball, though I was never better than a tolerable second-string first baseman."

"I wouldn't know about that. I'm a Pennsylvanian myself; got my training in Oil City and Philadelphia; never even strayed south of the Mason-Dixon Line until Alec's father imported me to take over the *Sentinel.* But in my own baseball days . . ."

"If you will forgive me, Bart," interposed Alec Laird, "we have something here that more immediately concerns us than any discussion of football or baseball."

"Of course; I know. Sorry, Alec!"

"No apology is needed. May we continue *our* discussion, Mr. Blake, from the point at which we were interrupted?"

"What exactly were we discussing?"

"You asked whether this newspaper would cooperate with you in presenting to the large public of the *Weekly* some impression—a very favorable impression, let's hope—of our own Mr. Blake from Louisiana. I promised the fullest cooperation, always subject to some small difficulty which might arise.''

"Had you any particular difficulty in mind?"

"Indeed I had, sir. I was approaching it when the invaders entered. I will do so again, though my approach must be somewhat circuitous.''

Alec Laird twisted at a vest-button.

"The whole situation is difficult in itself. With election day not three weeks ahead, we are in a sad muddle about presidential candidates. Mr. Taft, who seems likely to be unseated, has forever maintained the soundest old-fashioned principles, although he does suffer from the horrible stigma of being a Republican. We must support Governor Wilson, I fear. Unfortunately, sir, we have had no responsible Democrat in the White House since the days of Grover Cleveland. If you remind me that since the days of Grover Cleveland we have had *no* Democrat in the White House, I concede the fact but stick to my point.''

"You're saying . . . ?"

"Politically, at least, there are no difficulties about Claiborne Blake. His principles are those of his father or mine; he wants no traffic with sweeping reform.''

"Good for him!"

"I am glad to hear you say so. Clay is an able man, a sound man. Once elected to the House of Representatives, he will have the highest regard for his public duty. If perhaps he seems too popular for his own good, if there is still about him a certain (what shall I say?), a certain flightiness associated with youth, this will soon disappear when he settles down.''

"Alec—!" began Bart Perkins.

But he did not continue. The acting owner continued, up to a point.

"It would be the greatest pity, I maintain, if such momentary flightiness should mar a promising career. While you are with us, sir, you may hear Clay's name linked with the name of . . . the name of . . . !''

"Goddamn it, Alec," Bart Perkins burst out, as the man behind the desk was struck with vocal paralysis, "if you mean the Brissard woman, why don't you say so and be done with it?"

Alec's hand went to his throat.

"Very well. I will be frank and mention her by name, though I had not intended to do so. Many persons, I know, are inclined to treat Clay's association with this common strumpet much more lightly than I do. It is unlikely to do him any irreparable harm. And yet . . . and yet . . . You asked for *my* cooperation, sir. Will *you* cooperate with *me?*''

"In any way I can, believe me."

"You will be discreet, I trust? You won't embarrass *all* his friends unnecessarily? You will let fall no hint, however veiled, of a liaison in the background?"

"Depend on me entirely, Mr. Laird. My namesake seems a very decent sort, from everything I hear; that he's a friend of Leo Shepley would be recommendation enough. If you want me to build him up, I'll build him up to the best of my ability. And forget Yvonne Brissard; I've already forgotten her; she's very small potatoes. If Yvonne Brissard were all I had to worry about . . . !''

"If she were all you had to worry about?" blurted the managing editor, starting to get up with a jump but sitting down again and shifting the yellow pencil to his left hand. "I agree the wench is small potatoes; I've told Alec that. But what about Clay Blake? What else has our gay Lothario been up to?"

Jim spread out his hands.

"Nothing at all that I've heard described," he replied, with strict truth but less than strict candor. "When I spoke of worry, Mr. Perkins, I meant the kind of worry you and I have both known at one time or another: falling down on a story, missing a deadline, arguing with some telegraph operator who sees no need to transmit copy fast. My namesake's behavior is irrelevant. Supposing him to have seduced half the women in Louisiana, that's outside my province. Even if you imagine I would write such muck-raking, do you imagine Colonel Harvey would print it?''

''That *sounds* fair enough, apparently,'' the managing editor admitted, ''so I'd better cease and desist. But I'm a pretty good reader of faces. And there was a look in your eye, Mr. Reporter Turned Novelist, that had nothing to do with the tricks of our trade. What do *you* say, Alec?''

''I say this gentleman is right.'' Alec Laird contemplated Jim with approval. ''I regret having labored the point, and would not have brought it up at all if—''

A light tap at the door preceded the entrance, somewhat flurried, of a dumpy, middle-aged, apple-cheeked woman with a pince-nez, carrying a tray on which cylindrical cardboard container and sugar bowl were flanked by two cups and saucers.

''My secretary, Miss Edgeworth,'' Alec Laird announced to everybody in general.

''It's a little late for morning coffee,'' said Miss Edgeworth, tapping the cardboard container. ''But I met Ruth Donnelly bringing this up from the drug-store. She said you wanted only two cups, sir, though I thought old Mrs. Laird and her son were here. Now I see there are three of you. I can get another cup in half a minute . . .''

''No coffee for me, thank you,'' said Bart Perkins. ''It'll be lunchtime in an hour or so, when something stronger is indicated.''

''Put the tray on my desk, please,'' Alec Laird directed. ''You'll join me, Mr. Blake? Good! Will you be kind enough to serve us, Miss Edgeworth?''

''With p-pleasure, sir, if you'll add your own sugar. The cream's already in. But—but—!''

''Is there something else on your mind, Miss Edgeworth? You seem a little . . .''

''I'm afraid I am, sir. There's been another of those anonymous phone calls!''

"Not *again,* strike me blind?" exclaimed the managing editor. "Who got the call this time, Miss Edgeworth?"

"It was that new girl in your office, Mr. Perkins: Mary Somebody."

"She had the call this morning, did she?"

"No, Mr. Perkins. The actual call came late yesterday afternoon, as she was leaving the office just before dark. She didn't say anything about it at the time. But this morning some p-perfectly innocent man rang up, and by accident began with the same words the phone-fiend had used yesterday. Poor Mary nearly went through the roof. She's in tears and hysterics now, and . . ."

"It's all right, madam!" Bart Perkins assured her. "I'll be along in just one moment to deal with it. Mustn't have my little family upset, now must I?"

The secretary addressed her employer.

"May I add something, sir? That police officer who was here the other day seemed very considerate and understanding for a police officer, if you see what I mean. Don't you think we might . . . ?"

"I most certainly do think so, should police action become necessary. This is really intolerable; trust Mr. Perkins and me! Thank you, Miss Edgeworth; that will be all."

The secretary departed. Jim, having accepted a cup of coffee, opened his mouth to speak but checked himself. It was no time to ask questions about anonymous phone calls, especially since Bart Perkins, though he sat glowering, referred to the matter only in a perfunctory way.

"Who'd have *my* job, for the love of Mike? You were saying, Alec, just before Sara Edgeworth walked in . . . ?"

"We may rely on our guest's discretion, Bart; we know that now. I should never even have questioned it, I was saying, but for a remark Colonel Harvey made about him."

Jim set down his cup on the edge of the desk. "Colonel Harvey took some dig at me?"

"Hardly that, sir. He gave you high praise as a reporter,

but added that you seemed unduly attracted to crime and the sensational.''

"He told me that, too.''

"It seems something of a coincidence that the police officer Miss Edgeworth mentioned, one Lieutenant Trowbridge, should have called here collecting for charity a week ago, since it may be necessary to summon him in his professional capacity. It would seem a really startling coincidence if I told you what Lieutenant Trowbridge insisted on talking about.

"But that's not the point, is it?

"Crime and the sensational!'' Alec Laird seemed to muse. "We have a sufficiency of both in New Orleans, though I firmly instruct Bart and Harry to play them down. My alleged fondness for power, Mr. Blake, is merely the wish that this newspaper may instruct and edify according to its declared purpose. *Are* you so much attracted by crime and the sensational, sir?''

"Not by crime of itself, or by the sensational per se either. To attract the connoisseur of such matters, your criminal case must have a strong element of mystery and some prospect of an unexpected ending. There are few such cases in real life, as Colonel Harvey would be the first to tell you. Offhand, but from fairly wide reading, I can recall only two causes célèbres which occurred in New Orleans within living memory. Each was sensational and sordid enough, but neither had much of the element called mystery.''

"What were the cases, Mr. Blake? Let me see if I remember them.''

"Yes, speak up!'' urged Bart Perkins. "I don't agree with Alec about putting the soft pedal on murder and adultery. You've got to give the customers what they want, or bang goes your advertising and where are you? But at least we've kept out of the red so far, and who am I to argue all day with the boss? What's the first case you're going to cite?''

Jim arranged facts in his mind.

"The first case is the murder of Kate Townsend, a monstrously fat and violent Basin Street brothel-owner, in 1883. Her fancy man, one Treville Sykes, stabbed her to death with a sheath-knife and a pair of pruning-shears after she had attacked him first. The jury acquitted Sykes, who tried to collect her estate and failed."

Tension was gathering in the office above Camp Street and Lafayette Square. Bart Perkins turned the copy-pencil in both hands; Alec Laird had allowed his coffee to grow cold.

"In 1883," said Perkins, "I was fledgling city editor of the Oil City *Derrick*. But I remember that one, because everybody in the country heard about it. Second case?"

"The second case, though less bloody, is no less sordid, its protagonists being Dr. Etienne Deschamps and his Juliette in 1889.

"Dr. Deschamps, a fifty-five-year-old French dentist, settled in New Orleans after political trouble at home. But he never practised dentistry here; he set up as a physician and tried all kinds of quackery, including 'magnetic' cures that entailed the use of chloroform. Being attracted to a laborer's daughter named Juliette Deitsh, he made the girl his mistress and added various trimmings that need not detain us. On one occasion he gave her too much chloroform and killed her, then signally failed to kill himself with stab-wounds. After two trials, as well as several legal delays and stays of execution, they finally hanged him in 1892.

"What made it so sensational is the fact that Juliette Deitsh, though she seems to have entered heartily into the affair and had all the essential attributes of a woman, was only thirteen years old."

Bart Perkins's big hands broke the yellow pencil in two pieces, which he flung into the wastebasket beside the desk as he rose to his feet.

"I don't remember Juliette and the doctor," he said. "By 1892 I'd been shifted to Philadelphia, but I missed the story even if it appeared in any paper there. Now excuse me, will you? I must go along and comfort Mary Rikert before she gets any worse."

And he stamped out, not quite slamming the glass-panelled door.

To Jim Blake had come a great shock of illumination, for the first step that would lead to truth. But Jim tried not to betray this. He also rose, taking his hat from the desk.

"I had better say goodbye, too. It's a pleasure to have met you, Mr. Laird; many thanks for the help you've given."

"To the best of my recollection," said Alec Laird, thawing a little, "I have given you no help at all. But it was only because you asked for nothing specific. If at any time I *can* help you, either now or in the future, pray command me."

"I may take advantage of that offer sooner than you think."

"As regards . . . ?"

"No, not as regards Clay Blake; the prospective interview seems straightforward enough. It's a purely personal matter, which you may consider infernal nerve on my part. I am anxious to find a certain young lady, who has mysterious ways and a mysterious employer, and disappeared from Terminal Station of her own free will. With the resources of the *Sentinel* behind me, my quest should not be too difficult."

"If you will tell me . . . ?"

"Not now, Mr. Laird; not today either, I fear. I shall be fully occupied for the rest of the day, probably during the evening too. I will get in touch with you tomorrow, if I may take the liberty of doing so. Goodbye again, sir; I have received more help in this office than would appear on the surface."

A sense of achievement or near-achievement warmed Jim's heart as he left the office, went down in the elevator, and emerged from the building into the street. But his thoughts did not revolve round Alec Laird or Bart Perkins.

Instead he saw before him a mental image of Leo Shepley, whom he silently addressed.

"Truth remains truth, Leo," he said, "even when we fall slap into the well by accident. Now what sex pursuit is neither abnormal nor unnatural, at least in the way I meant, and yet would wreck a candidate for Congress if too many people heard of it? You don't need to tell me, Leo; I think I know."

8

THE CAR PROVIDED BY Stu Guilfoyle of Guilfoyle's Garage was a fifty-horsepower 1910 Chadwick, dark blue in color, with two well-padded seats in front and one well-padded seat at the back. Though it lacked both windshield and top—there were no doors either—the Chadwick seemed in excellent shape from polished brass headlamps to rear license-plates in the current Louisiana colors of black numbers on a white ground, and exuded an aura of power before you so much as touched steering-wheel or gear-lever on the right-hand side.

Stu Guilfoyle himself, an amiable young man in grease-stained overalls, had stressed such qualities.

"She's my own car, Mr. Blake. I won't be needin' her just right away; I got a Simplex, too. Even so, word of honor, I wouldn't rent this baby to *anybody* 'cept as a favor to Mr. Shepley. When this-yere model first come out, they called her the speediest stock car in the world . . ."

"I'm not much of a speed merchant, you know."

"No harm *havin'* speed, is there, case you need it? Just wait till you hear the exhaust boom through them side-ports in the hood! Now it's a pretty steep price I'm chargin' you, I know . . ."

"That's all right. Will you take a check?"

"Sure I'll take a check; I know it's good."

"While your assistant showed me around, you mean, you got through on the phone to Leo and asked him?"

"No; wasn't any need. I'd 'a' done that, sure, if I'd never heard of you. But he's mentioned you more'n once; I read in the paper you wrote a book everybody's readin'; and you showed me identification, so there's no doubt you're you. All right! Allowin' it *is* a steep price . . ."

"Here's the deposit you wanted. Enough?"

"That'll do fine, sir. Allowin' it *is* a steep price, I'll tell you what I'll do. I'll throw in a dust-coat and a pair o' goggles—*two* pairs o' goggles, case there's a passenger— and stick a couple extra cans o' gas in the back. Which way you headed?"

"Esplanade Avenue."

"Then you're headed right. That's on this side o' Canal Street, in the French quarter. Go straight along Chartres Street and past Jackson Square, which is the one with the statue in the middle and the Cathedral on your left. Six blocks t'other side Jackson Square, turn left or right. You'll be *on* Esplanade: good long street, runs from the river to City Park. Anything else I can tell you?"

"Where do I leave the car at night, if I should happen to be late?"

"Better bring her back here; you're close enough, at the St. Charles. I live upstairs, is all; just punch the bell any hour. There she is, Mr. Blake; if you don't fergit what I told you about handlin' her, you'll be all right."

And so, at shortly past four that afternoon, Jim Blake drove east on Chartres Street towards his rendezvous.

Here were house-fronts of the sort he remembered: dingily pastel-colored gray or blue or orange, some with a gallery of iron lacework across the floor above the street, many so invaded by commerce that their picturesqueness had grown blurred. But, if few traffic problems had seemed to exist on the far or uptown side of Canal Street, the Vieux Carré's chessboard of narrow lanes made smooth or swift progress impossible. Any slowly moving vehicle ahead could hold you to a dawdler's pace until the vehicle turned off somewhere.

Jim had put on the goggles but discarded the dust-coat,

which he threw into the back. The car was not awkward to drive if you remembered its slightly tricky clutch. As he bumped along behind a carriage full of sightseers, just avoiding the stall that would necessitate getting down to crank up again, he reviewed in his mind the few incidents since he left the newspaper office that morning.

It had been well past noon when he reached the hotel. Going at once to his room, he had sat down at the telephone and asked for Main 0101.

The line was busy. Ten or fifteen minutes later the voice which answered, presumably that of a Negro maid, informed him that Miss Florence was at lunch; would he call again after lunch? At his third try, fumingly postponed until one-thirty, he got through without intervention.

"Miss Florence Yates?"

"Speaking."

Perhaps because Jill on the train had not quite called Miss Yates an old bawd, he had expected her to be fat and elderly. Though you couldn't judge by telephone, she hardly sounded either. The voice was cultured, poised, and far from unattractive, a light contralto.

"Miss Yates, my name is Blake. May I explain at once that I am not related to the candidate for Congress? I live in New York, and seldom have the opportunity of visiting here. But I believe we have a mutual friend in Leo Shepley."

"It gratifies me to think so, Mr. Blake. Leo's name is a passport to my door and even to my affections. Did he ask you to ring up?"

"He said your niece was visiting you, or would shortly be visiting you, and described the young lady in such glowing terms that I wondered if I might beg the favor of being presented to her."

"Which niece, please? The dark-haired one or the fair-haired one?"

"Both of them, I understand, are talented and charming."

"I like to think so, Mr. Blake. Indeed, I *do* think so. Are you by any chance free to take tea with me this afternoon, sir?"

"Entirely free, madam. If I were to be invited . . ."

"Consider yourself most cordially invited. The address . . ."

"I have the address, thank you."

"It is rather far up the Esplanade, on the left-hand side as you go north. Shall we say, then, between four and four-thirty? I look forward to making your acquaintance."

"And I look forward to it immensely."

Well, that had been that. Jim had a late lunch in the hotel dining-room downstairs, sat for some time in the lobby studying his map of New Orleans, and went in search of Stu Guilfoyle at Guilfoyle's Garage.

Shortly after four o'clock, then, found him jolting along Chartres Street behind a sightseers' carriage, which he passed at Jackson Square.

There sat bronze General Jackson on his bronze war-horse, raising a fore-and-aft hat. To the north towered the bulk of St. Louis Cathedral, flanked by the Cabildo and the Presbytère. Jim pressed on as well as he could, always impeded by vehicles or pedestrians until he reached the Esplanade and made a broad left-hand turn at its far side.

Though the sky had been threatening rain all day, none had yet fallen. Houses of spaciousness and dignity—some set back from the road and built in what guidebooks called Greek Revival style—lined a spacious avenue bowered with trees. It seemed to Jim that he had driven for some distance, encountering comparatively light traffic in either direction, before he could pick up any number near the one he wanted. Presently, he swung across the road, to pull up before a house which must be as gracious as any in the district.

It was of brick faced with yellow stucco against damp. Though not particularly large, of two rather squat floors, it showed the Greek Revival influence in four slender white pillars as well as the French-Spanish influence in the wrought-iron balustrade of the gallery between the floors. The window-shutters were painted black. Set behind a hedge, its portico shaded by myrtles, it had an aspect grave and melancholy rather than any aspect the initiated visitor might expect.

Jim hesitated for a moment before he mounted the steps to the portico and tugged the brass bell-pull beside the door. A Negro maid in cap and apron, after asking his name, admitted him to a well-proportioned hall, panelled with shiny white wood and floored with squares of black and white marble. Accepting his hat with well-mannered aplomb, she led him to white double doors on the right.

"Mr. Blake, madam."

The woman in the dove-gray tea-gown, who rose from her chair behind a tea-urn near the fireplace, seemed neither old nor quite middle-aged. Fairly tall, with a free stride when she moved, she had an air of sophisticated camaraderie which lacked any suggestion of the knowing or the arch. She would have been very pretty but for a certain haggard look about her eyes. The eyes were dark, like her hair, which glistened with blue-black sheen under the light of small bulbs in a crystal chandelier switched on against that dark day. The setting, a drawing-room of Sheraton furniture and green wall panels picked out at the edges with gilt, formed a suitable background for her personality.

"Do sit down and be comfortable," she said, giving him her hand. "I serve tea in the English way: very strong, and with milk. But of course you may have lemon, if you prefer."

"I've grown so used to strong tea with milk that it would hardly seem the same article with lemon. Just as you serve it, please."

Florence Yates (even in his mind it was hard to call her Flossie) prepared a cup and handed it over when Jim refused sugar.

"*Everything* as I serve it, I wonder? You know, Mr. Blake, you startled me when you phoned. You honestly did startle me, sir. After all, you gave your real name."

Here was a definite challenge. Jim accepted the challenge.

"I gave my real name, madam," he said. "May I ask how you know I did?"

Miss Yates glanced round the room. At the back were double sliding doors, closed. Two heavily curtained windows faced Esplanade Avenue, with a small canvas which resembled a Meissonier duellist, framed but not glass-enclosed, hung on the wall between them. Then Miss Yates looked at her guest.

"Oh, come, Mr. Blake! Surely you don't mind if I . . ."

"If you phoned Leo Shepley and verified my *bona fides?* No, madam, I don't mind in the least. The matter is somewhat more personal and intimate than renting a car."

Miss Yates, who herself had been sipping tea, set down her cup on the table which held the tea-urn. The dark eyes regarded him levelly, if with no less sympathy.

"Shall we stop fencing, sir? You know why you're here; I know why you're here. May I remind you again that I have two nieces, about one of whom you were pleased to speak in the most flattering terms? The elder is Sue, the younger is Billie Jean. Have you any questions concerning them, sir?"

"Yes, madam. I have two questions: one general and one specific. We can make little progress, it's to be feared, until you are good enough to answer both questions."

"Have I not intimated how desirous I am to please? What is any woman's purpose in life, if not that? In this civilized manner, then, let's discuss Sue and Billie Jean. The general question first, Mr. Blake. What is your general question?"

"The question, though general, has some considerable importance. May I ask whether either of the two young ladies is more than thirteen years old?"

A strange expression did flash across the face which seemed so haggard or ravaged despite its beauty. But Miss Yates's tone did not change.

"Yes," she answered. "Sue is fourteen. Billie Jean, though not much past her twelfth birthday, is *exceptionally* mature for her years. Both, as you yourself have said, are charming and talented, with great skill at any polite art which may occur to you. Tonight you may meet one, or you may meet both. What is your specific question, Mr. Blake?''

"I fear, Miss Yates, it will be impossible for me to meet either of them tonight. At risk of seeming unduly to carp, it must be this afternoon or not at all. Now for the specific question. Which of the two young ladies have *you* determined I shall meet here?''

Now the woman's tone did change.

"Here?'' she exclaimed, rising up so suddenly that she jolted the table. "In this house, of all places? Are you mad, sir? Have you completely taken leave of your senses?''

Tall and lithe in the fashionable tea-gown, which had a red rose pinned at the waist, she went at her free stride to the left-hand front window, over a floor of polished hardwood and scatter-rugs. She partly drew back one curtain before letting it fall into place again. Then she turned, vivid against the green-and-gold curtain: head up, shoulders back.

"You call me Miss Yates, which was my maiden name and the one I am compelled to use. Though it has been many years since the most indulgent friend could call me maiden, I am in fact an old married woman, a respectable woman.''

Jim, who had also risen and turned towards the middle of the room, stayed there.

"Just across the street, Mr. Blake, is the home of General Clayton, General Tom Clayton, a noted cavalry commander during the War Between the States. His wife, formerly Margot de Sancerre, was a Creole beauty of ante-bellum days. In their youth, I believe, they were innocently involved in some affair of violence that took place in the Garden District. They are old and frail now, but they are also full of pride. They might represent polite society at its *most* polite. Whatever may be said or done elsewhere, would I jeopardize my own hard-won position by allowing the slightest irregularity on these premises?''

"Miss Yates . . .''

But there was no stopping her.

"If you had really wished to meet Sue or Billie Jean, there is a comfortable apartment in Basin Street where either or both could have given you satisfactory evidence of her skill. And yet you never wanted that, did you? You craved my indulgence under false pretenses. And if, as I now suspect, you are here either to preach or to make trouble for me . . ."

Her voice went shrilling up. And then the whole scene exploded in nightmare.

From the back of the room came a roll and rumble as sliding doors were thrown open. Glancing over his shoulder, Jim could see little more than the outlines of the large, dusky dining-room beyond, and little more than the outline of the squat, dwarfish figure standing there, right arm raised and back. There was a silver streak in the air as the knife flashed past Jim's head and whacked point-foremost into the Meissonier duellist between the windows, pinning it to the wall.

Though Flossie Yates cried out something, this seemed no time to hesitate. Despite the lightness in his chest, despite the hot-and-cold flush that ran over him, Jim plunged into the dining-room after somebody who had instantly turned and bolted.

His assailant, a literal dwarf not much more than four feet high, dashed past a swing door into a modern kitchen that had been built out from the dining-room instead of the detached kitchen usually found behind such houses. He was tugging at a back door both locked and chained when Jim overtook him.

The assailant, though so short, was thick-bodied and wiry, with heavy shoulders. He aimed a groin-kick that missed. He fought and clawed and tried to use his teeth. Jim gave him a hard left under the right ear, then lifted him bodily and banged his head against the wall, keeping the dwarf's right arm locked up behind the back while Jim ran over him for weapons.

The kitchen swam in dusky light. Presently, satisfied, the victor of the contest unfastened the door at leisure, bundled his captive out on a screened back porch, and booted him down some steps into the yard.

"No more knives, Rumpelstiltskin!" he warned. "Don't try anything else either, or you'll get a good deal worse than a kick in the pants. Now mind what I tell you and clear out."

Locking and chaining the back door, Jim returned past a glimmer of silver in the dining-room to join his hostess.

The knife that had pierced the picture was gone. The picture hung straight against the wall, with no mark of disarrangement except a slit across the duellist's throat. Miss Yates, all composure again, sat poised behind the tea-urn.

"Well, madam," Jim reported, "that would seem to be that."

"What did you do to Pepi?"

"Chased him off the premises. There seemed no need to carry it further."

Miss Yates looked at him.

"How can any man on earth," she asked, with an air of refreshed interest, "be one-half so nonchalant as you seem? You're not even out of breath!"

Jim's cup and saucer remained where he had left them, on the floor beside his chair. He picked them up and put them on the table near his hostess's left hand.

"Your own nonchalance, madam, is a thing of sheer beauty. Do you often greet visitors like that? I was told I ran no risk of being clubbed over the head or getting a knife in the back. But I'm always being told or telling myself something which is falsified in the next two minutes. If some other retainer of yours keeps a club conveniently in the umbrella-stand, we may see interesting developments yet."

"You don't think I planned that, do you? God save us, no! It was only Pepi, poor Pepi. So well-intentioned, so devoted to me, and yet so impulsive! He was not trying to hit you, you know: only to frighten you a little. If he had really been trying to hit you, pray credit me, you would be a dead man now. And a dead man in my house, Mr. Blake, would be even more awkward to explain than pubescent girls without their clothes. Speaking of pubescent girls . . ."

"Yes?"

"So often we hear," Miss Yates explained, "that such half-grown nymphs are desired only by the worn-out roué or the man well past his prime. Experience shows it to be not altogether true. Quite frequently my nieces' company has been sought by young men and personable men: as young and personable, sir, as yourself. But you are not here for that purpose, I take it?"

"Frankly, I prefer them more mature."

"Then shall we clear up the question of why you *are* here?"

"Yes, by all means."

"I knew you would call on me today; I knew it even before you communicated with me. I had no cause to doubt your good faith or to refuse my hospitality. That hospitality, I am sorry to say, you abused and violated at the first opportunity. Since you have acted out so elaborate a charade, sir, it can only be to preach sermons or to do me some irreparable harm?"

Jim faced her earnestly.

"Accept my assurance, madam, that it was neither to preach sermons nor to do you the least harm. I wished to prove or disprove a certain theory; it proved itself without much effort on my part. That being so, what happened here today may remain a secret between us. I have seen nothing and heard nothing. Are you satisfied?"

His hostess seemed much in earnest, too.

"Not entirely satisfied, no. According to my lights, Mr. Blake, I am an honest woman. I take no advantage of any man, and seek no advantage either. They may have as many nieces as I can recruit to my family; good luck to them all! Does it surprise you that a woman of admittedly doubtful past should try so hard for a façade of respectability, or even seek to be accepted by polite society?"

"It does not surprise me. But I doubt it can be done."

"It can be done, sir. It *has been* done."

Once more Miss Yates rose and went to the left-hand window, where she turned to contemplate him.

"If you are really a stranger to New Orleans, as you claim to be, can the name Yvonne Brissard possibly mean anything to you?"

"Yes, Miss Yates. I have heard her mentioned more than once."

"Then you know who she is and what she has been. You may perhaps have heard that she is not received by the best circles here. You would not expect her, for instance, to call at the home of General and Mrs. Clayton just across the way, or to be a welcome guest if she did call?

"And yet I must tell you," pursued Miss Yates without waiting for a reply, "that on no less than two occasions last week I myself saw her call there, and be admitted without question or hesitation. On both occasions I was summoned away from the window before I had time to watch her departure. But she called on Wednesday afternoon and again on Friday evening, while her carriage waited in the street.

"I can go even further, as proof that a woman's past is no albatross burden around her neck. The villa Mademoiselle Brissard has been occupying since early spring is rented to her by old Mrs. Sam Laird, Mathilde de Jarnac Laird, a crustier aristocrat than any Clayton or any de Sancerre."

"I *had* heard that, yes. But—!"

"For heaven's sake, my dear sir, whatever can be the matter with you?"

"Nothing. I was pondering another theory, that's all."

"Then don't shift from one foot to the other, I beg, and above everything don't stand there making *faces* at me! If you doubt my word that New Orleans's own Cora Pearl does indeed call on the Claytons, there are other witnesses besides myself. Or if there should be any question you would like to put, please do so."

"One question, if I may. How well do you know Leo Shepley?"

It could not be said that so simple a query disconcerted the poised Florence Yates. But she seemed to look into the past before she answered.

"I know him very well, as he himself must have told you. Poor Leo! Dear Leo!"

" 'Dear' Leo, if you insist. But why 'poor' Leo?"

"It was his mood, Mr. Blake, when I telephoned him to verify your references."

"What was his mood?"

"Shall I find, sir, that the tiger will spring again? Is this some new trap you have set for me?"

"On my solemn word, madam, it is no trap for anybody. When I spoke to Leo on the phone this morning, he was disturbed but no more than that. Has there been any change? Now, you are articulate, Miss Yates; your worst enemy, if you had one, must acknowledge that you are very articulate. Can you describe Leo's mood, perhaps in one word?"

"I think I can, Mr. Blake: he was suicidal. And I don't change or retract a single shade of meaning! The poor man was definitely suicidal."

9

As NINE-THIRTY STRUCK from a clock in some nearby steeple, Jim Blake was still pacing the floor of his hotel room.

He had obtained little more enlightenment from Florence Yates. Either she wouldn't or she couldn't say what had put Leo Shepley in the state of mind she called suicidal; Jim departed soon afterwards. It had been past six o'clock and dark when he returned to the St. Charles. Leaving the car in Common Street near the hotel's side entrance, he went straight to his room. Alarmed, he looked up Leo's number in the phone book and rang through. But he drew a complete blank.

Because both Leo's parents had died since the visit of Leo's classmate fourteen years ago, the former football star had entrusted his well-being to the care of a widowed aunt who kept house for him. A nervous maid, answering the telephone, informed Jim that both Mr. Leo and Mrs. Penderel had gone out that afternoon and that neither had returned, Mr. Leo saying he probably wouldn't be home for dinner.

Jim had to make the best of it. He had promised faithfully he would be on hand for a message that evening. To be within literal reach of a telephone, he ordered dinner sent to his room, ate without much appetite, and glanced through the evening papers.

Still no call from Leo, not even a message left at the desk downstairs: nothing.

The minutes crawled, the hours crawled. Jim paced the floor and smoked, trying to think with reasonable coherence. A rumble of evening traffic rose from St. Charles Avenue. It was almost exactly on the stroke of nine-thirty that the phone did ring.

But it still wasn't Leo.

"Mr. Blake?" began an unfamiliar if pleasant male voice. "This is the other Mr. Blake, Clay Blake. First, with your permission, I'd like to iron out one little problem at the start. We're going to sound like a pair of cross-talk comedians if Mr. Blake solemnly addresses Mr. Blake and vice versa. I've heard so much about you from Leo Shepley I feel I know you already. Suppose you call me Clay, and I'll call you Jim. Fair enough, Jim?"

"More than fair, Clay. Where *is* Leo, by the way?"

"That's one of the things I want to mention. Now look here, Jim! We've arranged for you to interview me tomorrow, if I've got it straight. What if we just hold the interview tonight and get it over with?"

"It won't be necessary, Mist—Clay. Leo said you didn't want to be fired on by strangers today, which is quite understandable. It's very good of you to see me in any case. And it can easily be postponed."

"I'd prefer *not* to postpone it, if it's all the same to you. I wasn't up to much this morning; I'm my own man now. There's very little I can tell you that's not in the record-book. But you sound like the sort of fellow Leo described, and he says you're discretion itself. Could you possibly come out here and see me now?"

"I imagine so. Where are you?"

"Place called the Villa de Jarnac, near Bayou St. John."

(Being consoled, no doubt, by a charmer whose talents had somehow endeared her not only to Clay Blake but to the household of a Civil War cavalry general from the past.)

"Leo says you've heard of the place," the voice continued, "though you may not know how to find it. Leo . . ."

"Is Leo with you, by any chance?"

"No; but he's promised to be here before too long, and stand by as *amicus curiae*. When I saw him last . . ."

"What was his state of mind when you saw him last? Did it strike you as being in any way suicidal?"

"He wasn't in very good shape, if the truth must be told. First he had to pull me together; then I had to pull him together. I think I've managed to do it, though I wouldn't care to bet on anything where Leo's concerned. What about it, Jim? *Can* you come out here now?"

"Of course, if you're sure Leo will be there, too?"

"I'm sure, all right; I'm very damn sure of that much! Finally, about directions. If you just tell the cab-driver . . ."

"A cab won't be needed. I've got a car downstairs, and a map in front of me now. If I go straight out Esplanade Avenue, and start bearing left . . ."

"That's one way of approaching it, yes. But there's a much easier and simpler way, one you can hardly miss. Got a pencil, too?"

"At the ready."

"The Old Basin Canal runs from Rampart Street to Bayou St. John. There's a rumor they're going to fill in the canal and build over the district, which may mean changing street-names and wiping out landmarks. Never mind; let 'em worry about that in the future!

"Take the road beside the canal; follow it straight out. Just before you reach Bayou St. John, past an intersection called Rouquette Avenue, the road forks left and right. Take the right-hand fork and follow that. There are street-lamps: at very long intervals, of course, but there are street-lamps. Count fourteen street-lamps on the right-hand side of the road beyond Rouquette Avenue. The gate of the Villa de Jarnac is just beyond the fourteenth lamp on the right-hand side. There's no name on the gate-posts, but you can't miss it. Is that clear?"

"Very clear."

"It's a fairly short drive, and an easy one bar the not-too-good road. If you start within the next five minutes or so, Leo ought to be here almost as soon as you are, red Mercer and all. Leo . . . You see, Jim, Leo . . . !"

Suddenly the strong voice began to waver and falter.

"What is it, Clay? Is anything wrong?"

"There's nothing wrong, I swear! It's only that . . . that . . ."

"That you're more in need of moral support than you thought you'd be?"

"Yes, I'm afraid so. I don't want to sound like an old woman, Jim . . . !"

"You couldn't sound like an old woman if you tried. And I have a suggestion to make. Leo will be there almost as soon as I am, you say, and there's a street-lamp near the gate? Would it ease everybody's tension if I waited for him there and we arrived at the house together, instead of having me charge in like a leg-man after a four-alarm fire?"

"I didn't like to suggest it, of course. But if you *could* do that . . . ?"

"Oh, I can do it. There's nothing to worry about; keep your chin up; see you soon."

Something of the other's excitement or nervousness had communicated itself to Jim. He took up his hat and the motoring-goggles, hesitating over the dust-coat but deciding he'd better use it. He had just slung the coat over his arm, finding a second pair of goggles in its pocket, when the phone rang again. Again Jim snatched it up.

"Leo . . ."

And again it wasn't Leo.

"This is the desk, Mr. Blake. There's a Miss Jill Matthews here to see you. What shall I tell her, sir?"

"Ask her to wait, please. I'm coming down immediately."

He did not descend on the instant, but stood for a few moments rehearsing words he might say to her. And then, when the elevator had whisked him to the lobby, he spoke none of them.

Jill stood by that part of the reception desk behind which rose the numbered ranks of boxes for keys and mail. With her light, fleecy tan coat over the tailored costume, in a small hat rather than a large one, she herself looked very nervous. But she also looked disturbingly, dangerously seductive.

"I know," she said, and would not meet his gaze; "I deliberately disappeared. I couldn't help it; I had no choice! Are you going to accuse me of being mysterious again?"

"You may not be so very mysterious, Jill, if one wild notion of mine turns out to have any truth in it."

"May I hear what this wild notion is?"

"Not a chance, at the moment. Have you had dinner?"

"Yes, ages ago! I've been arguing with somebody, which is why I'm not as composed as I might be. But I seem to have been arguing all day."

"So have I, in one way or another. Would you care to go for a drive in a rented car?"

"Jim, I'd love to! A drive where?"

"To the Villa de Jarnac. I've just heard from Clay Blake, who insists I meet him there tonight. Yvonne Brissard, that talented *femme du monde,* seems likely to be in evidence. Or do you back away from the elegant Yvonne, too?"

"I'm not frightened of her, and I'm not shocked by her either! But—"

"But what?"

"Nothing; it's only a manner of speaking. Where's the car?"

"Just outside in Common Street. You'd better put on this dust-coat; you'll find a pair of goggles in the pocket. By rights there ought to be a motoring-veil to tie over your hat and under your chin, but . . ."

"I don't need one a bit; I can use my scarf instead." Jill gestured towards the side entrance. "We go out that way, don't we?"

"And there are some fairly elaborate directions. From Rampart Street we follow something called the Old Basin Canal. Past Rouquette Avenue we begin counting street-lamps on the right-hand side of the road. But just where to find the Old Basin Canal . . ."

"It's all right; I can direct you! And there'll be no need

to count street-lamps; I know where the villa is. This coat is miles too big, but it was thoughtful of you to provide one. If you'll help me on with it, Jim . . . ?''

Leaving behind them the shuffle and murmur of the well-filled lobby, they went out into a night breezy but almost warm. And a sense of adventurousness went with them.

Though it took some moments to kindle headlamps and sidelamps, the Chadwick's engine fired up at the first heave of the crank. Common Street, Carondelet Street, then across Canal Street and on, under a pale dazzle of lamps, until Jill told him to turn.

Six blocks along Rampart Street, in the old French Quarter again, they swung left. North Basin Street, the heart of a Storyville stealthily pulsing with night life, also fell away behind.

It would not be true to say that they were soon in open country. But it began presently to feel like open country. Despite joltings from potholes, despite waves of dust sucked in, that sense of loneliness and remoteness seemed to deepen the farther Jim drove northwest through a wind-fretted night.

Almost lost in the voluminous coat, her face behind masking goggles, Jill at first spoke very little. Yet he was intensely conscious of her physical nearness. And she gave certain indications, not covert glances alone but little movements too, that she was conscious of his.

"We're not far from the bayou now," she said, when they had been driving for some time. And later: "That was Rouquette Avenue we just passed; keep to the right. The road begins a wide curve; you'll see (or you'll just barely see, rather) big houses set back at intervals on both sides. There are the street-lamps you heard about, although—"

"Street-lamps on both sides, too," Jim said, "alternately left and right. They seem many hundreds of yards apart, though it can't actually be that far. I'll just try a little speed for a change."

They roared along under that high emptiness. The wind

whipped Jill's scarf and blew darkish cloud-edges across a yellow moon.

"It not only *seems* remote and romantic," she declared; "it would *be* remote and romantic if it didn't give one the creeps at night. What are *you* thinking?"

"This seems the time and place for a quotation. In your presence, my dear, it ought to be a quotation from Swinburne; a quotation from Swinburne is almost imperative. But let's try something else instead.

" 'When the night wind howls in the chimney cowls,
        and the bat in the moonlight flies,
And inky clouds, like funeral shrouds,
        sail over the midnight skies——
When the footpads quail at the night-bird's wail,
        and black dogs bay the moon,
Then is the spectres' holiday—
        then is the ghosts' high noon!' "

Jill sat up straight.

"Jim, what is that? I think I've heard it somewhere, and I'm not at all sure I like it. But spotting the quotation's a different thing. What *is* that verse?"

"You wouldn't vote for Gilbert and Sullivan, would you?"

"It is Gilbert and Sullivan?"

"Yes. In the second act of *Ruddigore* it's sung by the ghost of Sir Roderic Murgatroyd, one of the wicked baronets of Ruddigore Castle. We're not meant to take it too seriously, you know. After warning his listeners that spectral revelry must end at cockcrow, Sir Roderic concludes:

" 'And then each ghost with his ladye-toast
        to their churchyard beds takes flight,
With a kiss, perhaps, on her lantern chaps,
        and a grisly, grim "good night";
Till the welcome knell of the midnight bell
        rings forth its jolliest tune . . .' "

"Stop!" Jill cried. "That may have been written as comic opera, but the pictures it conjures up are *horrible!* W. S. Gilbert has a really *evil* imagination, hasn't he?"

"*Had* a really evil imagination, Jill. He died last year, you may remember, after saving a young lady from drowning in his private lake at Grimsdyke. He's a ghost himself now, and knows all the answers; I wish we did. What are you signalling me about?"

"On the left—we just passed it—is Sunnington Hall, old Mrs. Sam Laird's place. Sunnington Hall and the Villa de Jarnac—on the right—are the only houses for the next quarter-mile. And we shall be at the Villa de Jarnac in two ticks; hadn't you better slow down?"

Jim had already done so. He had been counting street-lamps.

Just beyond the fourteenth lamp-post on the right, as indicated, two stone gate-posts with no gate between them rose up above a low rough-stone wall. At the end of the gravel drive, set well back beyond live-oaks festooned with Spanish moss, stood a massive white house with white columns.

"Why are we stopping here?" asked Jill.

"This is where we wait for Leo Shepley. But we're not stopping here, exactly, and not even stopping for a minute or so. I'm driving a little way in, as you see, and then backing out so we can face the direction we came from. If I can execute the maneuver without stalling this thing . . . reverse gear, now; mind that tricky clutch . . . ah, there we are!

"You see, Jill, Leo should be along at any moment in a Mercer Raceabout. He can't know I'm waiting, to be introduced to my namesake under properly formal circumstances, and I don't want him booming past before I've had a chance to hail him head on."

Jill had not protested, or even asked why they must wait. Though the light of the nearest street-lamp could not have been called bright, it was bright enough to show him her eyes when she removed the goggles and leaned a little towards him.

"We're staying here, are we?"

"For a little while, anyway; I'll keep the engine running. Down there, in the direction we came from, before the road turns, Jill, you can just distinguish the gate-posts of old Mrs. Laird's house by the light of another lamp. What is now our right side, I gather, is the side towards the bayou?"

"Yes, of course!"

"As for the other house, at present on our left: whatever reputation the Villa de Jarnac may have acquired, at least it can't be haunted."

"Why can't it be haunted?"

With his left hand he pointed past her right shoulder.

"There's not a light showing at the front of the house. But you see that thing like an open-ended barn with a peaked roof, built directly against the house's left side with one narrow end towards us? There's an electric bulb burning in there, maybe two or three. You can't see much inside the barn-structure; it's set far back and there are too many trees in between. But there's a good light on the curve of the drive that leads up to it. Ghosts and electric lights are incongruous; they won't mix."

Jill, who had twisted round to look, turned back again.

"What you call the open-ended barn-thing with the peaked roof," she informed him, "was once the way-through to a private racetrack behind the house. A not-so-dignified Creole dignitary named Guy de Jarnac built it years ago. The front's open, yes. At the back he had them build elaborate double doors which could be dramatically opened when he drove through to his own racetrack in a new car. But I don't understand why there should be a light there. The way-through's not used now; those double doors have been locked and barred. The stable's at the other side of the house, and your notorious Yvonne notoriously keeps a carriage, not a car."

"Jill, how do you know so much about the place?"

"First, because nobody can live in New Orleans without hearing everything there is to hear. Second, because—"

She stopped. "Jim, why did you say you're impelled to quote Swinburne when you're with me?"

"Do you really want me to tell you that?"

Jill raised her eyes and spoke softly.

"Please do tell me, if *you* want to! It may seem a little lost and ghostly in this part of the world. But we *are* alone, you know, and free to please ourselves. There can't be any interruptions of the sort that kept happening on the train. —*What's that noise?*"

It was the boom of an engine with its exhaust open. They both saw the car approaching from the direction of the town: at a good clip, though not at top speed. Even at a distance and behind headlamps, there could be no mistaking the red Mercer Raceabout with the brass trimmings. Still less, Jim saw, could there be any mistaking the burly, dust-coated, begoggled figure behind the brass shaft of the steering-wheel. As protection from the wind, the Mercer had only a circular pane of glass, hardly much larger than a man's head, atop a vertical rod on the steering-shaft. But Leo's attention seemed concentrated with a kind of frozen fixity.

And then there was another car.

As the Mercer swept past the home of Mathilde de Jarnac Laird, out from between Sunnington Hall's gate-posts emerged the sleek nose and body of a five-seater Cadillac containing two persons. Its driver, who had no goggles but wore a dust-coat over his uniform, must be Raoul, Peter Laird's chauffeur. Raoul stood up behind the Cadillac's windshield.

"Mr. Shepley, sir!" he bawled, in a voice so loud it carried to Jim and Jill in the Chadwick. "Mr. Shepley!" And then: "Whatever you're gonna do, don't do it! Mr. Peter says . . ."

The Mercer increased its speed. Raoul turned as though for instructions to the occupant in the back seat, who needed both goggles and coat because the car's top had not been raised. What those instructions were became instantly clear; the Cadillac with the self-starter leaped in pursuit.

As the Mercer bore down on the entrance to the Villa de Jarnac, a red Juggernaut with exhaust booming full, Jim slapped dust from his clothes and stood up.

"What's the idea, Leo? This is your old pal speaking! Take it easy, can't you? Take it—!"

A hand was raised at him as though to silence him. Otherwise the Juggernaut paid no more attention to Jim than it had paid to Raoul. It swung between the gate-posts and up the drive towards the house.

"What's the matter with him?" cried Jill. "Has he g-gone mad or something? What's the *matter* with him?"

There was no time to ascertain. The occupants of the gray Cadillac, now clearly as intent as Leo himself must have been, were hard on his track. As the pursuing Cadillac reeled between the gate-posts, Jill spoke again.

"He's not even headed for the front door!" She gasped. "He's making straight for the way-through on the left-hand side! If those big doors are still closed at the back, and he doesn't slow down . . ."

He did not slow down.

Gravel crunched and spurted under his wheels at the turn. The two-seater Raceabout disappeared inside the shed. And then two noises in quick succession exploded against the night.

The first noise, not to be confused with any sound made by the car itself, could only have been the report of a fairly heavy revolver fired indoors. The second, overriding all other noises and blotting them out, was a shattering metallic crash.

Jim looked at his companion, who shrank back in her seat. Fortunately, the Chadwick's engine had not stalled; he put it into gear and took off up the drive, though not at the murderous pace of the other two; a chilling instinct told him he could do little good now. In any case, Peter Laird's car had slowed down before following the Mercer inside.

In a clear space at the pillared portico of the Villa de Jarnac, the driveway divided into two branches. One branch ran closely around the right-hand side of the house, presumably towards a stable. From the corner of his eye, as they approached, Jim noticed another car and chauffeur, the car a Peerless like his own at home, waiting with motor cold and lamps unlighted just beyond that side of the villa, facing outward under the yellow moon.

But he caught this only at the corner of his eye. His attention never wavered from the other branch of the drive and the wicked barnlike structure to which it led, with a light still shining out on gravel.

Stopping the car at a point just before Jill could have got a view of the inside, he switched off the engine, climbed down at one side while Jill climbed down at the other, and circled round the front to meet her.

"Stay where you are!" he said. "Don't try to go in there; don't even look! I mightn't go in myself if it weren't necessary under the circumstances. I'm afraid . . . You won't go in there, will you?"

"Jim, why did you dry?"

"Dry?"

"You said, 'I'm afraid,' and then you stopped as though you'd fallen over something. Why, please?"

"I stopped, Jill, because I'm not sure just what I *am* afraid of. You won't go in? You promise?"

"Of course I won't go in, if you ask me not to!"

But Jim did know what he feared. And he found it.

The barnlike shed was spacious if not particularly high, an oblong some twenty feet wide by a little over thirty feet long. Though there were no windows, its peaked roof had been built almost entirely of heavy glass-squares now dingy and discolored. The inside walls, white stucco like so many outside walls hereabouts, also bore discolorations of time and neglect. The floor was concrete.

Along the left-hand wall Jim saw half a dozen wooden stalls, rather like stalls for horses and about the same size. A heavy workbench, long bereft of tools or equipment, stretched along the middle of the right-hand wall. Against the white-stucco wall at the rear, massive double doors of carved oak, the remnants of a wooden bar still in its sockets, loomed up over a scene of wreckage. Dark beams crossed what would have been the ceiling if the roof-peak had not risen above them. On an electric cord from the central beam a thousand-candlepower Mazda bulb glowed yellow in its wire cage.

The gray Cadillac, empty but for the lap-robe in its tonneau, had been driven well inside, almost to what lay beyond. Jim passed it and stopped.

Leo's Mercer, badly shattered, had run full-tilt into those double doors, splintering the bar across them and partly splintering the right-hand door without carrying either door off its hinges. One smashed head-lamp lay on the floor; what remained of the other had been squashed drunkenly between crumpled front fenders and twisted hood. At least there had been no fire.

Leo himself, in goggles and torn dust-coat, his tweed cap turned the wrong way round, lay on the floor below the right-hand driving-seat. His left cheek was against concrete; above his exposed right cheek, just below cap and elastic that held the goggles, the ugly black stain of powder-burns showed where the bullet had been fired into his head.

Raoul, the chauffeur, a stocky youngish man with a blue jowl, knelt beside Leo. Peter Laird, so shocked and shaken he could barely stand up, had retreated to the work-bench in the middle of the right-hand wall. Hearing Jim's foot-steps, the chauffeur looked up.

"Better not touch him, sir. He's gone."

"Yes, he's gone," said Peter Laird.

Imbued with a kind of restrained hysteria, Peter suddenly whipped off his goggles (he wore no hat) and flung them on the work-bench.

"Aren't many men in the world you can respect, are there? Really respect and look up to; know what I mean? He was one of 'em; he was the real goods; I'd have done *anything* for him." Then Peter burst out: "And now he's gone; he's gone for good; and is that all you've got to say about it, for God's sake?"

"Mr. Peter! Your mother—!"

"She'll have a fit, won't she? She's always having fits. Wait a minute, though!

Jim, himself feeling a little sick, had already removed his own hat and goggles. For the first time Peter seemed to see him and to grope for concentration as well as sanity.

"Look!" he said. "Aren't you the fellow who was in Alec's office this morning? The *Harper's Weekly* fellow?"

"Yes. I—"

"Well, print this! They said he *might* do it: all right! But I didn't believe it, I couldn't believe it; I never for a minute thought he *would!*"

"Would what?"

"What does it look like? It's what they do, anyway; you hear about it all the time! They'll take poison or stab 'emselves just before they jump off a bridge into the water. He drove in here hell-bent; he was always hell-bent. Just before he hit the doors, only a second or two before, he took the gun out of his pocket and . . ."

Now Peter stood paralyzed.

"I can't think straight, can I? We can say that's what he did; we can swear in court that's what he did! But, if that's honest-to-God what he did sho' nuff, where's the gun he did it with?"

"I was just about to ask the same question," Jim put in quickly. "Where *is* the weapon?"

"It's not here, is it? You don't see anything, do you? It's got to be here if he killed himself, hasn't it? And yet . . . !"

Raoul, who had been described as a steadying influence, went over to face the young man.

"If I were you, sir, I wouldn't get too excited. Maybe he threw it away from him, and we'll find it. There's no way out of this place except through the front, where nobody's gone. No place to hide, either, and nobody here but Mr. Shepley when we came in. If you don't mind, gentlemen, we might *all* pipe down a little. Somebody's walking on gravel just outside; I think we're going to have visitors."

They all looked towards the front.

*   *   *

Into the bright light, derby-hatted and wearing a raincoat he didn't need, sauntered a broad-faced man of middle age, the aggressiveness of whose bristling sandy moustache seemed contradicted by an easy-going, ruminating eye. Just behind him came a second newcomer, hatless, very much of Jim's own height and build except that he was fairer of complexion and had fair hair.

When the first newcomer's eye strayed towards that sprawled figure beside the ruined car, perhaps its easy-going expression changed a little.

"My name is Trowbridge, Lieutenant Trowbridge, and I'm a police officer. What's going on here?"

Then the second man spoke.

"My name is Blake, Clay Blake," he said in a voice Jim had never heard before. "And I'd like an answer to the same question."

10

JUST OVER AN HOUR LATER, against that same background of dingy white stucco, the two Blakes, Clay and Jim, had their first opportunity to speak in private.

A telephone call from the Villa de Jarnac had brought the police in force. When measurements were made and flashlight photographs taken from several angles, Leo's body had been removed to the mortuary. Lieutenant Zack Trowbridge, who proved not too difficult and treated Jim in a curious way the latter could not understand, first questioned his witnesses together in the way-through. Then he decided he had better question them separately.

"Seeing it's the cops," Lieutenant Trowbridge had declared, "I don't think the lady of the house'll kick too hard if I sort of commandeer a room for a little while. Wasn't much fuss when I asked to use the phone. Just walk ahead of me, will you?"

A massive and dignified mulatto woman, giving her name as Mrs. Emmeline Peabody and announcing herself as Miss Brissard's housekeeper, met them in the entrance hall of the Villa de Jarnac. The lady of the house, it developed, was not at home. Mrs. Peabody at least partially explained this.

In Mrs. Peabody's terminology her employer was always "Miss Brissard," whereas James Claiborne Blake she called "Mr. Clay." Lieutenant Trowbridge took notes of the account she gave.

On Monday, October 7th, the housekeeper said, Mr. Clay had left New Orleans to deal with some business affairs and attend a political conference in New York over the weekend. On Wednesday Miss Brissard herself had departed to visit friends in Mobile, Alabama. Miss Brissard had been accompanied only by her "social secretary," not even by a maid, leaving her valuable carriage-horses to be "boarded" at a livery stable on Dumaine Street. Though expected back this evening, just a week after she had left for Alabama, Miss Brissard had not yet returned.

Such evidence did not square with certain testimony, true or false, Jim had heard that afternoon. But he made no comment.

Mrs. Peabody then led Lieutenant Trowbridge to a room at the rear of the entrance hall, a room obviously never used or perhaps even entered by Miss Brissard. It was a man's den, no doubt the den of the late Guy de Jarnac, filled with leather chairs, sporting prints, and photographs of early automobiles.

Here Lieutenant Trowbridge had separately questioned first Raoul, then Peter Laird, then Jim, and finally Clay. Jill Matthews, so self-effacing that the headquarters detective all but overlooked her when he met her outside in the drive, he said he would question later, since "our distinguished author from New York" could supply the story.

The interrogation of the four men provoked a kind of minor riot, echoes of which could be heard in the hall outside. At length Lieutenant Trowbridge opened the door of the den and ushered out Clay Blake.

"It won't make sense," he had raved. "The whole damn thing just won't make any sense at all! Now I'd like to talk a little more to young Peter and that chauffeur; where is he? Ah! You two gentlemen," the official gaze rested on the Blakes, "I won't be needing—for the time being, anyway. But stick around, will you? Don't stray too far away."

"And might I," Clay Blake said to Jim, "have a word apart with *you?* The shed out there again, I think. Not the place either of us would choose, but you can hear anybody who comes near, and this is rather important. There's a little something I must attend to here, which shouldn't take more than a minute. Go along to the way-through, if I can persuade you; I'll join you almost as soon as you're there.''

And so, over an hour following Lieutenant Trowbridge's rather mysterious arrival, the two Blakes met for a private talk.

Though Leo's crumpled Mercer was still there, the gray Cadillac had been backed out into the drive. Apart from the damaged car, no trace remained of Leo himself. But Jim still pictured him lying there, in a linen coat torn but clean, when Clay Blake arrived almost within the promised minute. The tall, fair-haired candidate for Congress seemed to have no difficulty in following Jim's thoughts. Evidently they were his own.

"It *is* a horrible business, isn't it? When you remember Leo—so vital, so full of bounce, drinking life like a cocktail and enjoying every sip—it's hard to think of him leaving here as he did leave.''

"I know.''

Imaginative, brooding, in a lounge suit casual but of excellent cut, Clay prowled under the bright light and the glass roof. Then he leaned against the work-bench, left hand in his pocket and right hand raised.

"But can we get one thing straight? I told you when you were telling your own story to Zack Trowbridge here in this shed; I just want to be sure I've made myself clear. Will you accept the fact that *I* didn't phone you tonight and invite you anywhere, though I'm not sorry to have an ally on hand? Will you accept that?''

"Yes. The voice on the phone was strong most of the time, but it wasn't greatly like yours. Yours is heavier, better modulated, the voice of a man who does a good deal of public speaking, as you do.''

"Well, I wasn't the voice on the phone; I can prove I made no phone call from here tonight. And yet . . . and yet . . .''

Again he brooded before straightening up.

"Whoever impersonated me knew a devil of a lot. He knew you and I never met. But he also told you, in part at least, so exactly what I actually was thinking and feeling at the time that he might have *been* me in somebody else's body. For instance . . ."

"Yes?"

"For instance, that part about asking you to call me Clay while I called you Jim. After so much talk with Leo, it had already occurred to me; we might do it. And the part about saying I was my own man again, ready to face anything, but faltering when it came to the pinch. Or saying I thought I could trust your discretion and didn't mind meeting you. Though I'd never have phoned to suggest an interview here, that's just what I felt or believed I felt. Leo *didn't* expect to be on hand tonight; he's never once turned up when he thought I'd be with Yvonne. When was the last time you talked to him?"

"About eleven this morning; he reached me at the newspaper office. He said you'd be spending the evening at the Villa de Jarnac, but didn't tell me Miss Brissard was out of town."

"Leo didn't know. I didn't know myself, until I came out here without even troubling to telephone in advance, and got the note she left for me with Aunt Emmeline."

"May I ask one or two questions about that?"

Clay made a magnanimous gesture.

"My dear fellow," he said, "ask as many questions as you can dream up! This whole affair, which I've tried so hard to keep under wraps, is going to be on display in D.H. Holmes's window. And I don't mind; I've come to a decision. Actually, if it weren't for the brutal, inescapable fact of what happened to poor Leo, I could throw up my hat and cheer. When I think how shabbily I've treated one of God's most stimulating women, expecting her to be at my beck and call practically twenty-four hours a day, I know I ought to be kicked from here to Baton Rouge!

"And I'm going to be absolutely frank, Jim. Except for

one small matter, which you'll presently agree is best kept to myself for the moment, I won't conceal a thing. I'll even tell you what's driven me half crazy with worry. I'll trust your discretion, in short, as Leo did say I could. As regards Yvonne, however, it wouldn't matter a hill of beans if I couldn't trust you at all. Wasn't it the Duke of Wellington who said, 'publish and be damned'?''

"In that Harriette Wilson business, you mean?"

"The notorious Harriette, if memory serves, wrote to him and intimated he might like to make her a substantial payment if she kept his name out of her memoirs. And the conqueror of Napoleon wrote back, 'Dear Harriette: Publish and be damned.' Isn't that true?"

"Yes, I believe so."

Clay Blake took a nervous turn across the shed and then went back to the work-bench, his forefinger still raised for emphasis.

"But the conqueror of Napoleon, I'm willing to bet," he continued, "was never accused of having relations with girls hardly into their teens or not yet at that happy state of womanhood. It's what they're using against your obedient servant, curse 'em; you'll soon hear how they got at me. If THAT were published, even talked about, I could say goodbye to a political career or any other kind of career."

Again Clay crossed to the other side of the enclosure, glancing along the row of stalls against the left-hand wall before he swung round.

"Old Guy de Jarnac, I believe," he added, as though inconsequentially, "used to keep as many as six cars here, lined up for inspection like horses.—But you didn't want to ask questions about my alleged debauchery among the near-nubile, now, did you? What did you want to ask?"

"When was the last time *you* talked to Leo?"

"He phoned me at something past one o'clock, about two hours after he phoned you. He said he'd been in touch."

"At eleven or thereabouts," Jim explained, "he confessed to being very badly worried over something that concerned himself as well as you, though he didn't say what it was. Did he strike you as being suicidal two hours later?''

Clay took out a pack of cigarettes and juggled it for a moment before returning it to his pocket.

''Not suicidal, exactly. More angry and confused than anything else: the word I should choose would be 'simmering.' But it could easily have meant a suicidal mood, I admit. And didn't you hear what Pete Laird was saying in here, just before the arm of the law hauled us indoors for separate interviews?''

Jim studied him.

''Let's leave that in abeyance for the time being,'' he suggested. ''Now Mrs. Peabody, the housekeeper, tells us Miss Brissard has been out of town for a week, and you agree. Are you sure the lady really *has* been out of town since last Wednesday?''

''Of course I'm sure, Jim! What prompts a question like that?''

''I asked it, Clay, because another witness testifies she was very much in town. On two occasions—Wednesday afternoon and Friday evening—Miss Brissard is supposed to have called on General and Mrs. Clayton, of Esplanade Avenue, quote, 'while her carriage waited in the street.' The witness, of course, may not be the most reliable in the world.''

Clay looked him in the eyes.

''Your witness,'' he retorted, ''is either mistaken or lying, and lying wildly, too! Yvonne left on Wednesday morning; she said so here in the note she left for me.'' He ran rapidly through his pockets. ''I don't seem to have it on me now; I must have put it down in the house.

''But to say she's associated with that particular couple, Jim, is not only wrong; it's inherently absurd on the face of it. Yvonne, *my* Yvonne, has no more use for stuffy people than I have. Not that the general and his wife can be called too stuffy, especially Hellcat Tom. But I think you take my meaning. And I shouldn't drop in on him to ask questions. Most of us, nowadays, don't feel about Yankees as he does. Still! Here are two lines of doggerel from the late unpleasantness:

" 'To cannon or bomb or to strong petard
We answer the foe with our Beauregard.'

"And somebody else, possibly in imitation of that, has given us:

" 'When Yankees are struttin' and braggin' and hatin'
Who rides 'em down harder than General Clayton?'

"Since you're a Yankee, Jim, steer clear of Hellcat Tom. He may be well over eighty, but he can't forget that as a cavalryman he was outranked only by Jeb Stuart and Wade Hampton.

"All of which," added the lawyer-candidate for Congress, smiting his right fist into the palm of his left hand, "is relevant neither to our purpose nor to the evidence. I'm not deliberately straying from the point, you know. Have you any more strictly relevant questions to ask *me?*"

"Yes, two more. And the first is very simple. Will you describe Miss Yvonne Brissard, please?"

"Will I—*what?*"

"Just describe what she looks like, as simply as you can."

"I'm not a very detached or objective witness, remember!"

"You're not expected to be. Let's suppose she's got lost in a strange city, and you're trying to find her. How do you describe the lady?"

"Well! 'Is this the face that launched—' No; sorry; no poetic flights! She's rather tall for a woman; comes up to about the lobe of my ear. Hair so dark a brown it looks black. Eyes clear blue, and a smile that would . . . but you don't want that either. Oh, one other thing, for purposes of identification! At the upper outside corner of her left eyebrow she's got a very tiny mole: not a disfigurement at all, more like one of those beauty-spots women had a craze for wearing a few years back. I don't know what else I can tell you . . ."

"There's no need to tell anything else. What you've said will do admirably for the purpose I have in mind."

"If all this is strictly relevant, too, and you seem to be nodding your head at me to swear it is, very well!" Clay drew a deep breath. "What's your second and last question?"

"That's more difficult. It concerns the fact that you yourself were on the train from New York with Leo and Jill and me, only in car seventeen behind us. But it's like a question in court which has to be approached in so round-about a way that it sounds like a whole barrage."

"I'm still entirely at your disposal, Jim. Approach it in any way that seems best."

"Right. Towards midnight on Monday, then, the three of us were in Leo's drawing-room, drawing-room A of car sixteen. We had been discussing the possibility that some enemy of yours might be plotting against you, and how this could be managed if it were tried. All of a sudden Leo had an inspiration. He said he thought he knew; he threw out various references to a wicked game without giving the slightest hint of what it might be. He never betrayed you in any sense, Clay, and never would have."

"Do you think I don't know that?"

To Jim the scene had returned in vivid lights and shadows.

"At the height of the uproar," he went on, "there was a knock at the door by a mysterious somebody who knocked and instantly made off, either towards the car ahead or the car behind. The porter, standing in the aisle at the rear of the car, said the person in question had ducked into the corridor leading to the car ahead. Whereas the conductor, planted at the end of the corridor, categorically denied that anybody had passed that way.

"It was the testimony of the porter, whom Leo called Uncle Mose, which I myself doubted. Leo refused to accept this, saying he'd known the man for years and mentioning, incidentally, that Uncle Mose was also well known to Clay Blake."

Clay stared at him, head a little on one side.

"You don't miss much in the way of evidence, do you? In fact, you haven't missed a thing so far. Well?"

"There's not much more," Jim said, "but it's got to have a meaning. When the train reached Terminal Station this morning, I climbed down to the platform. The porter was there, bowing over the luggage as usual. I tipped him and forgot him; Jill was there, too. Leo joined us in a moment, but suddenly remembered something in his drawing-room, and went back for it."

"It was a nearly full bottle of Bourbon, Jim, which almost got left behind. Well?"

"Leo went back for it. Uncle Mose was no longer in sight either. Leo didn't return for at least five or six minutes. When he did return, startled and upset, it was to tell us you had been on the train all the time, locked up in a drawing-room of the car behind. Everything he said indicated you must be a good deal more upset than he was. And he stayed with you.

"If Leo went back to his drawing-room, he'd have no occasion even to look into car seventeen. There's only one explanation which fits the facts as we know them.

"Leo learned you were there because he'd just been told by Uncle Mose, the mutual friend of you both. Uncle Mose, who at your insistence had kept your presence a secret up to then, felt he had to speak out when you needed help and support at the end of the journey. So Leo went to your drawing-room, where you started to tell him your story.

"All that part of your conduct, Clay, is entirely reasonable and understandable. And yet one move you made badly needs explaining if we're all to stay sane. You yourself were the mysterious midnight presence who knocked at the door and ran. The porter, either devoted to you or bribed by you, would never have told us you ran back along the aisle to car seventeen." Jim looked at him. "But if that's what you did, what inescapably you must have done, just why did you feel you had to do it?''

Clay returned the look.

"Because I was a damn fool!'' he burst out. "It was my indecisiveness again, of course. You'd better hear the whole thing now.''

"If you feel up to telling it.''

"Oh, I'm all right. Somebody has written that the actions we regret in this life are never our sins, but always our stupidities. My mind seems to run on nothing but quotations tonight; sorry; I'll try to curb the habit!''

Taking a key-ring out of his pocket, he twirled it round his forefinger and went on twirling.

"I haven't any sins on my conscience: any major ones, at least, that I've ever been aware of. But stupidities are all over the place, making noises at me like the sound of one vast, concentrated 'Yaah!' ''

Still twirling the key-ring, Clay began to prowl once more. This time it was not the width of the enclosure, between work-bench and stalls. It was the length of that shed, from open front end to ruined car against the double doors, back and forth in both directions, stopping occasionally to glance at his companion. There he paced: hagridden, bedevilled, but immensely likeable. Jim could sympathize with every sentiment he uttered.

"As you've heard,'' he said, "I went to New York on Monday, October 7th, taking the night train that got me there Wednesday morning. Though I did have to see a Wall Street broker about some investments, it was mainly to attend that Democratic conference at the Hotel Astor. But I didn't stay at the Astor. I put up at the Plaza, at 59th Street and the Park, as I always do. And I had no idea Leo himself was in town.

"The Democratic conference didn't achieve much or amount to much. All they did in their speeches was make complimentary remarks about Democrats too long dead to carry any weight at the polls, or tell us what a fine and noble bunch of Americans we were. It's just as well I didn't have to pay close attention and make any decisions. I got it in the neck as early as Thursday afternoon.''

"Got it in the neck?''

"Like this. There was a letter in my mail-box at the hotel. A letter postmarked New Orleans, addressed to me in crude block capitals on the envelope. The message inside had been printed in the same crude block capitals on five-and-ten-cent-store paper.

"I didn't keep *that* message, you can bet; I felt as though I'd been holding a poisonous snake. I tore the thing up and threw away the pieces, but not before I'd read it about fifty times.''

"You remember the gist of it then?''

"Remember the gist of it? I can give it to you *verbatim;* I'm not likely to forget one word. Here it is.''

For a moment Clay stopped pacing.

" 'Dear sir,' it said. 'You are in bad trouble already; you may be in worse before I've finished. What makes you think *you* can serve a term in Congress, when you ought to be serving a term in the penitentiary? We'll see to that, my friend. Unless you instantly obey orders you will get as soon as you return to New Orleans, your family and friends will be regaled with the details of your taste for children below the age of consent. You got great pleasure from at least two such creatures, though the girls themselves got no pleasure at all. Just how young *do* you like them, Mr. Blake? This is only a preliminary warning; you will hear from me again.'

"And it was signed 'The voice.' Nothing else; just 'the voice' in those same crude block capitals.

"My God! Can you imagine how I felt?''

"Yes, I can readily imagine how you felt. But—''

"In honesty as well as in self-defense,'' the other rushed on, "I must insist the charge wasn't true and isn't true. I've heard often enough there are men with a passion for half-formed bodies and the caresses of the immature. I accept it as a fact, as I accept the fact that there are sadists and masochists and the other deviates of the sexologists' books. But my attitude is the same towards each: I simply don't understand how anybody could enjoy it. It's not merely that I'm guiltless; the truth is that I've never even been tempted.

"And yet that's not the point, as you were probably about to say. The charge wasn't true. But what if people believed it to be true? How much of life, Jim, is conditioned by those deadly little words 'what if!' Shall I go on?"

"Yes, by all means continue, again provided you feel up to continuing."

Briefly Clay stopped pacing again.

"Curse it, man, don't you see I've got to get it off my chest now? It's all very well to say, 'Dismiss such things with contempt.' You can't dismiss 'em with contempt; or at least I can't. I also tried to tell myself the note was a crank letter that would have no sequel. Treating it as a crank letter didn't work either. The more I thought the more I brooded and the worse everything seemed to be.

"I spare you my state of mind over the weekend, when I had to drink Governor Wilson's health and agree with the universal sentiment that the Democratic party would have a great renaissance after twenty years. In New Orleans, twenty years ago, they hanged some French doctor for the murder of a thirteen-year-old girl, less because he'd killed her by accident than because he'd seduced her by choice. Did you ever hear of the case?"

"Yes, I've heard of it."

"At Pennsylvania Station, on Monday afternoon, I dived into my drawing-room on that train and said I didn't want to be disturbed except for meals. When Uncle Mose Tompkins told me Leo Shepley was in drawing-room A of the car ahead, I swore him to secrecy.

"And what happened, when I started brooding again?"

"If I could catch Leo alone, I thought to myself, I could tell him my story and ask him how *he* would view the situation. At least I wouldn't have to go round and round in the same old squirrel-cage of imagining the worst that could happen.

"I gave myself enough time, God knows. I waited until nearly twelve, when everybody except a night-owl like Leo was almost sure to have turned in. In my dressing-gown and slippers I went along to drawing-room A, car sixteen. Do you remember?"

Jim remembered.

"I didn't hear any woman's voice," Clay pursued. "But I did hear Leo's voice and what I now know to be yours. If I knocked, it seemed to me, I could always make some excuse to see the old hellion alone. Do you remember what he was talking about?

"Leo uses—sorry; used!—tones of thunder when he believed himself to be speaking in a hushed whisper. In that kind of voice he was sharpening and deepening every fear that had clawed at me since Thursday. He mentioned Flossie Yates, whom I *had* vaguely heard of as a trader in pubescent flesh. He said I was a much less decisive character than I seemed to be. He said being innocent wouldn't matter if somebody were really out to get me. And he added, finally, that a game of that sort was a wicked and foolproof game which never failed.

"I rapped at the door, harder than I'd intended, by a kind of nervous reflex I couldn't control. The moment my knuckles hit that panel, I knew I couldn't face up to it. I couldn't face even Leo; I couldn't face anybody!

"So I turned and bolted. He didn't open the door instantly, you remember. I'm fairly fast on my feet when I need to be, and carpet slippers make very little noise. When I passed Uncle Mose in the aisle, all I had to do was put my finger on my lip; I made it right with him financially later on.

"I'm worse than indecisive; I'm downright weak. I ran like a scared rabbit back to the bolt-hole. And yet, considering all the circumstances and my state of mind, can you blame me?"

"No, of course not," Jim told him sincerely. "Don't call it weak or by any other harsh name; it's what every man among us might have done. If I seemed to find knock-and-run tactics senseless or unreasonable, it was because I didn't know the circumstances, and I apologize."

"Apologize? You did some very shrewd detective work in piecing things together, though it's not likely to help *me* much. Speaking of detective work, what did you do or say that so impressed Zack Trowbridge?"

"Impressed Zack Trowbridge?"

"Don't underestimate Zack. He's pretty shrewd himself; I've had to handle him as a hostile witness in court. You've noticed, haven't you, he treats you with a respect very near deference? But never mind the local police department! Shall we bring my own idiotic saga up to date, and let it go at that?"

Clay now seemed to be making every effort at lightness. He had put away the key-ring, and no longer paced.

"You also called the turn on how Leo found me this morning. Mose Tompkins told him. By that time I'd had six days of stewing myself. Leo gave me a lift home in a cab, and either at the train or on the way home I told him very much what I've told you now.

"I still live with my parents in the house where I was born. Both parents, fortunately, are in the country this week. I kept wondering what other damn haymaker could hit me out of nowhere, and went through the mail without coming across anything except bills. But I soon found out.

"I hadn't more than sat down to breakfast, which was about nine-thirty, when the phone rang. It was a voice, I might say *the* voice. A man's voice, I'm sure, but so soft and whispery that the only possible word for it is 'wicked.' The voice asked whether I hadn't got his letter, and said he was ready to give me orders I'd better obey. I went through the usual business of, 'Who are you? Who's speaking?' But it was no use. Next came the ultimatum. If I don't withdraw my candidacy for Congress within the next twenty-four hours, full revelation will be made about my dealings with one child called Sue and another called Billie Jean. And I can't describe to you how that infernal voice *gloated*."

"What did you say?"

"I told the voice to go to hell and slammed the receiver on him. All the same, I wasn't feeling as big as I liked to pretend. Leo had gone by that time, so I got through on the phone to him immediately. Leo seemed to know all about the wicked voice—in fact, he was the one who called it wicked—and was as soothing and reassuring as possible. But . . ."

Jim held up his hand.

"Wait! Isn't there something wrong here? You said you talked to Leo at a little past one o'clock in the afternoon, which was two hours after he talked to me."

"Don't you be the one to get it scrambled, Jim! You asked me about the 'last' time I talked to Leo. There were two calls: one from me to him between nine-thirty and a quarter to ten, the other from him to me at shortly after one. The second was our last conversation. When I tried to get him again at two o'clock, he'd gone out."

"I've got it straight now, thanks. Anything else?"

"Yes. Just before I slammed the receiver on my old pal the voice, he made one remark that would have scared the pants off a wooden Indian. He said—"

Gravel crunched somewhere outside. Clay checked himself abruptly, trying to look as though he were not there at all. But brisk footsteps approached. Into the shed came the derby hat and aggressive moustache of Lieutenant Trowbridge.

"Excuse me, gentlemen," said Lieutenant Trowbridge, "but maybe we can get some place after all. Whose voice was it, Mr. Blake? And what was it he wanted to tell you?"

PART THREE:

LOVER'S QUEST

11

THIS ATTACK, if it could be called an attack, Clay met with guard raised and little sign of being disconcerted.

"Don't get excited, Zack," he replied. "It was nothing at all."

"Nothing at all, was it? Sure of that?"

"Absolutely sure. I don't know the fellow's name, of course. It was just some lunatic who keeps making crank calls to talk foolishness. You never get rid of him if you encourage him by talking back. The only proper course is to hang up the receiver at once."

Whenever Lieutenant Trowbridge's temper had risen, they were all soon to remember, a kind of strawberry-rash blossomed in his broad face. The strawberry-rash showed plainly now. But his anger did not seem to be directed at Clay Blake.

"I was too far away to catch more than the general drift," he admitted. "So I can't call you a liar—not that I would, anyway—if that's what you say it was. Never mind! Let's see what we've got."

And he answered himself.

"What we've got, gentlemen, is the damnedest situation I ever did hear of! I was hoping we could clear up at least part of it before I landed in the nut-house along with the rest of you. Now a crank's phone call may not help much, one way or the other. But it does give us a jumping-off place.

"All day, it seems, all kinds of people have been making all kinds of phone calls for all kinds of reasons, including Mr. Shepley himself. It might be important, sort of, to find out just what Mr. Shepley was up to during his last hours on earth."

"You never said a truer word, Zack! It's of the utmost importance!"

Lieutenant Trowbridge squared himself.

"Why did he drive out here tonight? When he did drive out, hell-bent for election, no less than four people were waiting for him. Pete Laird and Pete's tame chauffeur, at the gate of Pete's mother's house down the road. The other gentleman called Blake and that fair-haired young lady, at the gate of this house.

"You, sir," he addressed Jim with some deference, "got a phone call from some impostor claiming to be Mr. Clay Blake. That was about nine-thirty tonight, I think you told me?"

"Just nine-thirty," Jim said.

"The impostor invited you out here, seeming pretty urgent about it? He said Mr. Shepley would be coming along, too, and asked you to wait for Mr. Shepley at the gate?"

"Not exactly that, Lieutenant. I was the one who suggested waiting, and he agreed with every evidence of relief."

"Yes, *you* suggested it. We'd better all remember that: *you* suggested it!" Briefly the headquarters detective opened his eyes wide and then narrowed them. "Now young Pete Laird . . . you both heard his testimony, or at least a good part of it, before I hoicked you all into the house. I've got Pete's testimony here, I've got it in my notebook, all clear enough except when he got hysterical once or twice.

"But both you gentlemen, particularly Mr. Clay Blake, are acquainted with all the Lairds, or most of 'em." He appealed to Clay. "While we run through Pete's testimony and try to decide where we're at, will you sort of act as interpreter if I need help? It has to do with more phone calls and Mr. Shepley's movements. Since we're all agreed about the importance . . ."

"No doubt about the importance," Clay assured him. "I was trying to call it to Jim's attention a while ago, but we didn't get very far. Suppose I just repeat what Pete said, or what I think he said, and *you* correct *me* if I go wrong?"

"Can't make a fairer offer than that! O.K., shoot!"

Clay drew back a little.

"A lot of this is hearsay evidence, and would never be allowed in court. But there can't be much doubt it's true; it can easily be corroborated at source.

"Well! At the *Sentinel* office, as at the office of any evening journal, they put the paper to bed between three and three-thirty in the afternoon. But Alec Laird usually stays there until five or even later, being a conscientious sort."

"He's a very fine gentleman, Mr. Laird is! Looks at you like a schoolteacher when you haven't done your homework, but treats you fair and square just the same. I met him myself the other day. Well?"

"At about five this afternoon, when Alec was preparing to leave, Leo Shepley phoned him at the *Sentinel* office."

"That's one of the things I can't get straight. Why did he want to speak to Mr. Laird?"

"He didn't. He was tryng to reach Jim, whom he'd spoken to at the *Sentinel* office that morning. No, Zack, no!" Clay raised his hand. "Though we can't know what was on Leo's mind at that time, since he doesn't seem to have told anybody at any time, he can't really have imagined Jim would stay there from eleven in the morning until five in the afternoon. No doubt it was just on the off-chance. He'd phoned Jim's hotel, found Jim was out, and tried the *Sentinel* just in case. That doesn't matter, but the sequel does matter because it concerns several Lairds.

"Alec went along home. Alec and his wife, Sylvia, were supposed to have dinner tonight with Mrs. Sam Laird and Pete. Whether or not you've heard this, Sylvia enjoys bad health. 'Enjoys' is the word; she's neurotic. When Alec got home, he found Sylvia in one of her fits, swearing she couldn't go out that night or it would kill her. While Alec was trying to persuade her, and Sylvia still wasn't having any, along came another phone call.''

"That was the unknown, wasn't it?''

"Not unknown, Zack; just unnamed.'' Clay looked at him with a hypnotic eye. "Some employee of Alec's at the *Sentinel* had seen Leo Shepley getting partly tanked up in a bar on Bourbon Street. Not really tanked up; Leo hasn't been putting away much booze in recent days. But slightly oiled, very depressed, and muttering wildly if not very intelligibly to anybody who'd listen. He said something about going 'out Bayou St. John way,' and also something about putting a bullet through his head. This was shortly after seven o'clock.

"The *Sentinel* man who heard and saw this thought he'd better phone Alec. He must be a high-ranking employee, whoever he is, if he had the nerve to disturb the boss at home.''

"Right!'' said Lieutenant Trowbridge. "I'll take it from there, if it's all the same to you; I want to make sure how young Pete fits into all this.''

With something of a flourish the lieutenant took a notebook out of his inside breast pocket. But he did not open the notebook; he held it as though he held a weapon.

"So Mrs. Alec Laird, having decided she's not going any place tonight, takes over the telephoning herself. *She* rings old Mrs. Laird's house down the road. Time, seven-thirty. But does she ask to speak to the old lady? No, not by a damnsight!''

"The sad fact is,'' interjected Clay, "that Alec and Sylvia Laird don't get along any too well with the dowager duchess, though Alec tries to conceal it. But they both take an interest in Pete. And Leo Shepley has always been Pete's hero. If Sylvia had to spread a little neurosis even in talking to Pete . . .''

"Which she did, Mr. Blake, and it's not hearsay evidence now. When Pete heard his hero was lapping it up and talking suicide, he says, he'd have gone out to look for Mr. Shepley if he had to search every bar on Bourbon between Canal Street and the Esplanade. Only . . .''

"Only he couldn't," Clay supplied. "Dinner at eight has been a ritual at Sunnington Hall since Sam and Mathilde Laird were married. Pete couldn't have missed it; his mother wouldn't have allowed him to miss it. But dinner's always over punctually at nine-thirty, after which the duchess goes up to her room and (of all things) reads plays until bedtime. To a degree, at least, that released Pete."

"All right, and what does he do then? He's got only one lead, as you might put it. Mr. Shepley'd said something about coming out Bayou St. John way. That might mean Sunnington Hall, or it might mean this house here; it couldn't very well mean anyplace else.

"Maybe the young 'un dithers a little; it'd be only natural if he did. But he got prepared. He had car and chauffeur all ready and alert when Mr. Shepley went sky-hootin' past at . . . what *was* the time? Are you all agreed on it?"

"Nobody took very careful note, Zack. But the consensus seems to be that the shot was fired, and Leo slammed into those doors there, at near enough to ten minutes after ten o'clock. It wasn't late."

"No, it wasn't late. As I say, Pete was all prepared and ready. What he did makes pretty good sense, when you understand everything behind it."

Here Lieutenant Trowbridge inflated his lungs for powerful speech. The strawberry-rash stood out bright red.

"But, beginning at ten minutes past ten o'clock," he roared, "not one damn thing makes any sense at all!"

"It does seem a little confused, doesn't it?"

"Confused? It's crazy! If every witness is telling the truth, and four of 'em at least can be checked on, it can't be one thing and yet it can't be the other. By rights Mr. Shepley ought to have killed himself. But it can't be suicide, because there's no gun."

Lieutenant Trowbridge stood back to look at the workbench, which threw a dense black shadow on the concrete floor.

"I got here myself shortly after it happened. By general agreement, nobody who'd been in this place went out of it for as much as a second. And yet, though the weapon had been held against Mr. Shepley's head—you saw the powder-burns—there wasn't any weapon. I searched for it immediately; I searched with a flashlight; I searched every damnation nook and cranny there is. Well?"

Nobody answered him.

"And yet it can't be murder either," he pointed out, "even if Pete Laird now swears it must have been. Our distinguished journalist, the chauffeur, and Pete himself all have to say there was nobody hiding in this place at the time, and nobody slipped out afterwards. On the other hand, it can't be that somebody among our four witnesses has been telling lies to hide dirty work. Two in one car, Pete and Raoul, and two in the other car, Mr. Jim Blake and the young lady, can all check on each other for every minute of the time. If this was murder, don't you get it, both the gun *and* the murderer have vanished into thin air!"

Still no comment was made.

"Yes," the lieutenant argued, "we've accounted for the four witnesses known to have been at the scene of the crime. We know where they were and what they were doing. In fact, we've accounted for everybody except . . .

"A few minutes ago," he added suddenly, "I came out from the house to do something or other. No, it wasn't to question you people or trap anybody into damaging statements! It was to do something or see about something I had to attend to. And yet I can't seem to . . . Don't mind me, gentlemen; I get like this sometimes; in just a second or two I'll remember what it was. It was . . ."

And then his brow cleared, as though at a great light. Even the strawberry-rash had almost faded. He looked at Clay.

"Excuse me, Mr. Blake, but wasn't it your car and chauffeur in the drive at the other side of the house? They're not there now, are they?"

"Of course they're not there now," Clay said with some asperity. "I sent the chauffeur on an errand; he has instructions to come back. But what's the idea, Zack? You knew that, didn't you? You were within hearing-distance when I told him?"

"I was, Mr. Blake, and that's what reminded me. It's that nigra housekeeper, the one who looks like a lighter-colored Aunt Jemima; she's in a state about something, going on fit to bust! Now you've got a way with servants, Mr. Blake. Would you just step into the house and quiet her down a little, maybe?"

"Yes, certainly. What's the matter with Emmeline?"

"I can't tell you that, Mr. Blake. The more I talk to some of 'em, the less sense I get out of 'em. Oh . . . and before you go, sir, there *is* one other little thing."

"Yes?"

"I said we'd accounted for everybody's whereabouts at the time of the shooting. But we haven't quite accounted for yours. Just for the sake of argument, where were you when it happened?"

"I was in the library at the back on the other side of the house."

"Was anybody with you?"

"Have I got an alibi, you mean?"

Lieutenant Trowbridge hooted broadly at this.

"Alibi?" he scoffed. "That's the best one I've heard tonight, that is! Where would I get off, now, suspecting *you* of funny business? Be a great day, wouldn't it, when *you* had anything against Mr. Shepley? This is strictly to keep the record straight, that's all."

Clay studied him.

"I have no alibi for the very instant of the crime, it's true. But then I haven't got wings or a cloak of invisibility, and I can't walk through walls.

"I heard a car come roaring up towards the house. Though it sounded like Leo's style of driving, I didn't even think it might be Leo; he never came out here at night. The car roared past and, by the sound of it, must have made a very spectacular turn. Then came the gun-shot, or whatever it was, and that appalling crash every-body heard. .

"Another car, which had been tearing after the first, slowed down so much I could hardly hear it. I went out in the hall. Aunt Emmeline, the housekeeper you're con-cerned about, asked me what had happened; I asked her, and neither of us knew. I went outside, where—where I met somebody who moved on. I was still standing there, hearing voices from the way-through, when you yourself walked up the drive."

"Bet it kind of surprised you, didn't it, to see me here tonight?" asked Lieutenant Trowbridge. "There's a story attached to that, too. But it's getting late, you know; reckon it must be close on midnight; we'll have to break up soon. So before you do go, Mr. Blake . . ."

"Forgive my mentioning it, Zack." Clay moved his shoulders. "All the same, I've been under something of a strain this evening. I've lost one of my closest friends, to say nothing of whatever else has been happening. Since you've asked me to soothe Aunt Emmeline, do you mind if I just go on and do it?"

"No, 'course I don't mind! You run along, now, and forget I said anything at all. No tricks or traps, not a bit of it! Don't mind me, as I've told you; just good old blunder-ing Zack putting in his two cents' worth!"

Clay left them. Lieutenant Trowbridge waited until the sound of his footsteps had died away. Then good old blundering Zack addressed Jim:

"There goes as real a gentleman as I ever met! Be a shame, wouldn't it, if he didn't get to Congress after all?" Immense respect had returned to the lieutenant's tone. "Now, sir, there's no point in you and me staying here any longer, is there? Just follow me, will you?"

"Where?"

"Out the front, of course, like this. But we needn't walk on gravel all the way, need we? We'll just cross the drive to the other side, and walk on grass towards the front of the house. This way, please."

It was the drugged, drowsy hour of the ghosts' high noon. A faint white mist rose from dew-wet grass, under spreading oaks with their tracery of autumn. Following his guide, as indicated, Jim passed the dark shapes of the Cadillac and the Chadwick. A few lights burned behind drawn blinds along the façade of the Villa de Jarnac. But Lieutenant Trowbridge was not headed for the portico with the pillars.

Instead he led his companion along beside the left-hand branch of the drive, across the main drive, and around beside its right-hand branch.

The Peerless with the chauffeur, Clay's own car, no longer stood there. Halfway along the right-hand side of the villa, the branch of the drive turned outward at right angles and led to another white structure with a peaked roof, evidently combined stable and coach-house, bowered in more trees.

That drive, in any case, could not have continued to the back. The private racetrack lay there, indistinct under the yellow moon. It had no banked sides, as they were beginning to build such tracks nowadays. But for the fact that its surface was of asphalt, it might have been a dirt track for horses, surrounded by a neat white railing to keep spectators off the course. And it seemed a fairly large one.

Jim had no time for a good look, even if he had been interested. Where the drive turned towards stable and coach-house, a *porte cochère* had been built out over the side door of the villa. At the top of some steps to the side door lurked an indistinct figure.

"Peters!" Lieutenant Trowbridge called softly.

"Yes, Lieutenant?" said the indistinct figure in plain clothes.

"Where are they now?"

"Mr. Blake's got that nigra, the one who was carryin' on, in a room at the front. Where you wanna go, Lieutenant?"

"Library'll do as well as any place. Know where it is?"

"Yessir."

"Then show me. But no more noise than you have to make, mind!"

Less than a minute later they were ushered into a lofty oblong room at the rear. It was the library of one who, like the late Guy de Jarnac, could have done little reading but liked an impressive show. Rows of standard authors in gilded leather or vellum, no doubt bought by the yard like any other merchandise, looked out from shelves amid a profusion of floor lamps and gaunt golden-oak furniture.

Somebody had recently taken down Whyte-Melville's *The Gladiators,* which lay open on a table in the middle of the room. There were several cigarette ends in the adjacent ashtray. Lieutenant Trowbridge struck a big globe-map and set it spinning.

"This is where Mr. Clay Blake was, or says he was," the lieutenant continued. "We're in private now, sir. And when I get a chance to ask the opinion of a famous journalist . . ."

"What gives you the idea I'm that?"

"Well, aren't you?"

"No, not particularly. In this country, Lieutenant, we don't often refer to ourselves as journalists, generally speaking. It's a fair enough description, but it sounds a little fancy to the average newspaperman."

"You're not the average newspaperman, Mr. Jim Blake, or the average anything else! You *are* one of these educated people, aren't you?"

"It could be called that, I suppose. I never thought much about it."

"No, you wouldn't. Now nobody could call *me* educated; didn't even get to finish high school at the Boys' High, the only one we had in those days. But I'm no illiterate, and I know a rip-roaring good story when I run across one. Didn't you write a book called *The Count of Monte Carlo*?"

"Yes, Lieutenant."

"Yes, I know you did. I've read that book three times since it first came out. I may read it again, now I've met you, though I practically know the thing by heart as it is."

Jim offered no comment. The lieutenant was musing.

"I dunno, sir. It's all fiction, I reckon, or mostly fiction. But I dunno. Sometimes I've thought of myself—don't laugh, now!—I've thought of myself as a secret agent like that fellow in the book. Commissioned by somebody's government, with all the kale I need for expenses! Living at swell hotels in Paris and London! Beautiful women all around; some new adventure every time the door opens! 'Course, I never got to France or even to England, though my forebears did come from a little place in Wiltshire, as I've heard my old dad say many's the time. You're not laughing, are you?"

Jim was not laughing, and said so. He thought he could discern, under Zack Trowbridge's bluff exterior, a secret soul essentially as romantic as Clay Blake's or his own.

But the lieutenant's secret soul no longer showed through.

"I don't have to tell *you* what we've got on our hands, do I? It's murder, that's what it is, and what beats me is not so much who did it as how the hell it could possibly have been done! That busted car's a two-seater, isn't it? There couldn't have been somebody hanging on the back, could there, to lean over and stick a gun against the side of the poor devil's head when he drove in?"

"There couldn't have been, and there wasn't. I could see the back of the car, too."

"Even suppose there had been, what happened to him afterwards? Or suppose there'd been somebody waiting there, to jump on the little running-board between the fenders and give it to him? What kind of a murderer was he, a ghost or something, to vanish like a soap-bubble as soon as he pulled the trigger?"

Once more Lieutenant Trowbridge did some mind-searching.

"You see how it is, don't you? We're in the middle of one sweet mess; I'm going to need some help before I've finished. Now you've done some pretty shrewd detective work yourself. I heard Mr. Clay Blake tell you you'd done some pretty shrewd detective work; and, from what he did say, I can well believe it. Why not tag along with me, a man of your experience, and give me help when I need help?''

"Just a moment, Lieutenant!"

"All the time you need; what is it?"

New gulfs were opening; Jim could not shy back from them.

"If you heard Clay tell me that, you must have been hanging around outside that shed a lot longer and a lot closer than you pretended at the time. You may even have overheard everything we said. If that is the case, Lieutenant, just what kind of crafty game are you playing? Twice you told Clay there were no tricks or traps, and yet all the time you seemed to be lurking in ambush. Does this mean you do suspect Clay after all?''

Lieutenant Trowbridge wiped the back of his hand across his forehead, and then looked heavily portentous.

"Whatever I may have heard, sir, whatever I suspect or don't suspect, I'll just keep it under my hat until I know where I am and where I'm going.

"There's going to be a big rumpus about this business. Too many prominent people are involved; I can't go treading on toes or getting out of line too soon, and wouldn't want to even if I could. But I will tell you this much, since I did ask you to work with me and cooperate, and I meant every word of it! What's the first thing that strikes us about the whole case? What was the very first thing you noticed?''

"The first thing I noticed," Jim answered, "was the light."

"The light?"

"A thousand-candlepower bulb was burning, and is still burning, in a way-through which by all accounts is never used now. Who turned on the light? Why?''

"I thought of that, sir, and asked Emmeline What's-her-name about it. You weren't there when I asked her; wasn't anybody there but Emmeline and me. Up above the front door outside, it seems, there's another big bulb. According to Emmeline, it was Mr. Clay Blake himself who turned on the light in the shed, but by accident.''

"By accident?''

"Yes. Our friend came out here tonight expecting to meet his fancy woman, and didn't like it at all when he found she hadn't come back from Alabama. 'This is a fine howdy-do!' says he, or words to that effect. 'Haven't you even put on the light over the front door, so she won't fall all over herself when she does get here?' ''

"Well?''

"In the kitchen there's a board of switches that control several outside lights, including the one in the shed. Our friend pressed what he thought was the switch for the bulb over the front door. Being a casual sort of gentleman, he never looked to make sure and didn't realize until later he'd turned on the wrong light. Emmeline didn't realize it herself, she says, until she heard the car smash and looked out a front window.

"But that's not quite the first thing is it? We've got to start further back. You'll get it at once as soon as I make clear what question I'm asking. Somebody phoned you at the St. Charles Hotel, saying he was Clay Blake, and asked you to come out here. Who did the phoning, and what did he really want?''

"The man who did the phoning," Jim said, "must surely have been the murderer himself. Allowing that this was no slap-dash spur-of-the-moment crime, but was carefully planned in advance . . .''

"It was planned ahead, all right! You can bet your shirt on that!''

"Then the murderer's real purpose, Lieutenant, was to have a witness in the right place at the right time.''

"Got it in one, sir, as I knew you would!'' Lieutenant Trowbridge swelled with excitement. "*You* suggested waiting at the gate, remember? You're a good-natured fellow; you like to oblige people when you can. If you hadn't suggested it, he'd have asked you and made you promise. He knew Mr. Shepley *was* coming out here; he was just getting ready.

"Now I'm not saying our friend Clay Blake is guilty; I'm not fool enough for that just yet. All the same: what do we get from the supposition he *might* be guilty? The first thing he insisted, remember, was that *he* never made that phone call? Also, according to Emmeline, he *claims* he turned on the shed-light by accident."

Jim took a turn away from the table, and came back to it.

"I see. What you're saying, Lieutenant, is that he may have been trying a double bluff? That he did in fact make the phone call, in a voice sufficiently disguised so he could deny it later? That he turned on a light to guide him, and . . ."

"If you've already got some reputation as a detective, Mr. Jim Blake," Lieutenant Trowbridge said admiringly, "you've earned every bit of it! A double bluff for sure, and a pretty good one until it's called. Going on that assumption . . ."

"Easy, Lieutenant! We can't go on that assumption; I don't believe one word of it. To begin with, I like Clay."

"We all like him; that's just the trouble. But you only met him tonight, didn't you? And Leo Shepley, as I understand it, was a very old friend. Don't you want to see us grab Mr. Shepley's murderer?"

"Of course I do! Only . . ."

"Only everything, you were about to say, splits and smashes on the same obstacle, just like the car smashed, too."

"I wasn't going to say that at all. I was going to say . . ."

"If he did do it, how in God's name *could* he have done it? As he said himself, he hasn't got wings or a cloak of invisibility; he can't walk through walls. Nobody can, unless this place is really haunted after all.

"We'd better call it a night, I think. First thing tomorrow morning I'll start tracing Mr. Shepley's movements, beginning with what phone calls he made and received. In the meantime, it'll do no good just to hammer over and over at the four main witnesses. Whoever killed him, it wasn't young Pete or the chauffeur; it certainly wasn't you or the young lady, because . . . Is anything wrong, Mr. Blake?"

"Not necessarily wrong, Lieutenant. I was thinking of Jill, that's all. Where's Jill?"

"The fair-haired young lady, sir? You don't know where she is or where she went?"

"No; how could I? I haven't seen her since Clay invited me out to the shed for a private conference which seems to have been about as private as a political speech in Union Square. She must be with the others, but . . ."

"She's your girl, and yet you don't know where she is or where she went?"

"She's not my girl; I only wish she were! I met her in New York, found her again on the train to New Orleans, and then thought I'd lost her until she turned up at the hotel tonight. Even now I don't know where she lives or how to find her. I ought to have asked her that and insisted on an answer, but . . ."

"Half a minute, now, before you start getting alarmed! Mr. Clay Blake, you'll recall, sent his chauffeur on an errand and told the chauffeur to come back for him?"

"Yes. *Well?*"

"That was it, sir. She left long ago. Our friend sent her home in his car."

12

ON THE FOLLOWING MORNING—Thursday, October 17th—Jim finished breakfast in his room by nine o'clock.

It was no good, he told himself, endlessly to review last night's events, and their conclusion in frustration.

When Lieutenant Trowbridge informed him of Jill's earlier departure, it had seemed to him that Clay Blake at least must know the address to which she had been driven. But it was not only that Jill had left. Charging into the front drawing-room where "they" were said to be, he found the others had left, too: Peter Laird, Raoul, Clay himself. The only person remaining was that massive woman whom Lieutenant Trowbridge had described as resembling a lighter-skinned version of Aunt Jemima on the pancake-flour box. Since it must be plain at this hour that Miss Brissard would not return tonight, she intimated she was ready to lock up when she could get rid of the police.

Nor had Mrs. Peabody been very helpful to Jim. No, *she* didn't know where the little lady had gone. Nobody tole her; it wasn't none of her business, was it?

"Did she leave me any message, Mrs. Peabody?"

"Cain't call it a *message*, no, *suh!* Tole Mist' Clay she right sorry she leavin' 'thout sayin' g'bye, but she got her own troubles, too."

If Jim's theory about her turned out to be correct, Jill could have no troubles of any great weight or complexity.

173

But evidently she thought she had, which may have made all the difference.

After giving Lieutenant Trowbridge a lift home in the Chadwick, Jim had left the car at Guilfoyle's Garage and returned to his hotel. Though he had been impelled to ring Clay at once, the latter would hardly welcome being routed out at far past one A.M.; questions about Jill were better left to the brightness of morning.

Thursday morning did prove reasonably bright, washed in pale sunshine. A man nervous with anticipation finished breakfast by nine o'clock, shaved and bathed in haste, and then attacked by telephone.

Whatever you heard about the leisurely South, they were up and about betimes. Ringing first Clay's home and then his office, according to numbers listed in the book, Jim contrived to miss him twice before nine-thirty.

Some servant at home said Mr. Clay had left for the office long ago. At the office a pleasant-voiced woman, presumably Clay's secretary, replied that he had been there but gone out again.

"You're the other Mr. Blake, sir? Mr. *James* Blake? Mr. Blake's anxious to see you, Mr.—he's *very* anxious to see you, I know. He's got two conferences this morning, and a political meeting this afternoon. But he wonders: could you possibly have lunch with him at Philippe's? . . .

"You can? That's splendid; I'll put it down! Philippe's Restaurant, 83 St. Louis Street, one o'clock? Just ask for Mr. Blake's table—sir."

Lunch would do very well; Jim could file his story afterwards. Meanwhile, it would be better still if he could locate Jill before lunch. And there was a way.

Though the story of tragedy at the Villa de Jarnac could not have broken too late for the morning newspapers, he found no word of it in any paper on sale at the cigar-stand in the lobby. He had thrown aside the papers, and was starting for the *Sentinel* office when he came face to face with Lieutenant Zack Trowbridge entering from the St. Charles side.

The lieutenant, in some strange mood between elation and depression, led him to a couple of chairs in the lobby.

"Well!" he said. "How's it this morning, Mr. Blake? Got some news for you already."

"Anything helpful?"

"May be; may not be; can't tell. Mr. Shepley's parents are both dead, it seems. But there's an Aunt Harriet, Mrs. Penderel, who keeps house for him."

"I know, Lieutenant. It'll be only decent if I get in touch with her and ask whether there's something I can do. She may be glad of help with the funeral arrangements."

"Can't be any funeral just yet; other things to clear up first. And I wouldn't be too quick about tackling the lady. *I've* seen her; she's pretty cut up. Look, now, Mr. Blake! This 'Mr. Blake' business is getting me down; I wish I knew what to call you. I can't call you Jim; you're a gentleman, too. I might call you Dimitri, like the secret agent in the book. But that don't seem right either; it's too foreign; you're about as foreign as a plate of ham and eggs."

"The 'Mr. Blake' business is beginning to get me down, too; it almost threw Clay's secretary a while ago. If you won't call me Jim, as I wish you would, there's a possible if not very satisfactory alternative. Since for some reason you seem to have been so much impressed by *The Count of Monte Carlo*, you might try Franz."

"Franz, eh? It may have to do, though I'm not keen on it. And why Franz? You're no squarehead either, are you?"

"No; my own forebears were Scots. Franz von Graz is just a name that occurred to me, no more. What did you learn from Mrs. Penderel?"

Lieutenant Trowbridge took out his notebook and consulted it briefly.

"Between the time Mr. Shepley got home yesterday morning, and the time he left the house just before two o'clock in the afternoon, he made or received four phone calls. Mrs. Penderel's pretty cut up, as I told you; but she remembers and swears to it. The first call, between half-past nine and a quarter to ten, was from Mr. Clay Blake, just as our friend said it was. At around about eleven, for the second one, Mr. Shepley talked to you at the newspaper office.

"You see, Franz Josef, I'm not counting any attempted calls that didn't get through. He'd tried to reach you at the hotel here, and once at the newspaper office, before he did reach you there. The third call, which seems to have caused all the trouble, came at near enough to twelve-thirty."

"Seems to have caused all the trouble, Lieutenant?"

"Yes, if you can make any sense of it! Mrs. Penderel was just about to go in and tell him lunch was ready, when she heard the phone ring in the living-room. Mr. Shepley answered it himself, as he answered whenever it rang that morning. When his aunt did go in and say lunch was ready, he was just hanging up the receiver. She couldn't tell who'd been speaking to him, and *he* didn't say. But there's no doubt it put him into a very peculiar state of mind."

"Suicidal? Or what?"

"More like angry and confused, his aunt thought. He refused food; he said he'd had a sandwich and a glass of milk, and didn't want lunch anyway. She begged him to eat, as all women do, but it was no go. Then he started tramping through the place from room to room, muttering to himself, like as if he couldn't decide something. Once he stopped and said out loud: 'I haven't any reputation to lose. But, by God, Aunt Harriet, I won't lose my friends!' "

"Was that the only comment he made?"

"The only comment, far as she can remember in her present state of mind. 'Course, she may think of something later. At shortly after one o'clock, when she'd sat down for a bite to eat herself, he phoned Mr. Clay Blake, but didn't say anything important she could overhear. That's four calls; there weren't any more to or from his home. He left the house not long before two. His aunt went out to do some shopping, and didn't see him afterwards."

"Did anything else turn up, Lieutenant?"

"He did own a gun: a .38 revolver, she thinks. But she hasn't any idea where he kept it; seemed pretty certain he was carrying no weapons when he went out. And I could hardly ask her to search the house for it, not at a time like that!"

Returning the notebook to his pocket, Lieutenant Trowbridge stirred restlessly.

"I've got two men tracing Mr. Shepley's movements for the rest of the day. I'm meeting one of 'em at City Hall in about five minutes, so I'd better mosey along. All right! In return for the information I've given you, haven't *you* any mite to contribute? I'd better see the aunt again, much as I hate upsetting her. Any question or questions you think I ought to ask her?"

"Yes, if it can be done tactfully. When did Leo last go abroad, and what place or places did he visit on that occasion?"

Impatience twitched through the lieutenant.

"Look, now! These are *important* questions I'm supposed to be asking, if I've got to start upsetting her again! What's all that got to do with the price of eggs?"

"It may be more important than it sounds. How does the whole affair look to you this morning, Lieutenant? Still so very suspicious of Clay Blake?"

"Now listen, Franz Josef!—"

"If you've decided on Franz Josef, which is even easier to say, we'll leave it at that. But I'd better warn you Clay's story checks out, insofar as I've been able to check it at this juncture. Just before you walked in on us last night, I asked him about Leo's mood when they talked at a little past one o'clock. Though you may well have heard the answer and know it already, I'll remind you just the same. Clay said Leo seemed 'angry' and 'confused,' exactly the words of his aunt. Clay also said 'simmering,' which you are now.

"Some unknown voice, it would seem, phoned Leo at half-past twelve and may have threatened *him* with something.

Threats wouldn't have worked so well with Leo; it may have led to his death. I give you that as a field for speculation at the moment. And now, if you'll excuse me . . . ?''

Both of them rose.

"You leavin', too, Franz Josef? Any particular errand?''

"I've got a little job of tracing to do. If you need me within the next half hour or so, you can find me at the *Sentinel* office.''

They walked west together, Lieutenant Trowbridge turning to the right at City Hall and Jim turning towards the left across Lafayette Square.

Inside the *Sentinel* Building, activity had not yet even begun to work towards that fever-pitch it would attain later in the day, when nerves grew edgy and the man at the city desk started to yell. But there was a sense, which could never have been mistaken by any old newspaperman, of something being up. It pulsed out of the city room as the elevator carried Jim past. It showed in the face of Bart Perkins, the managing editor, whom Jim, at the top floor, met as Mr. Perkins emerged from one of the glass-panelled doors opposite the elevators.

Today the managing editor looked just as indefinably untidy, and his big mop of gray-white hair more ruffled than ever.

"Morning!'' he greeted Jim, jerking a thumb towards the door at the end of the corridor. "Here to see His Nibs, I expect?''

"Yes, that's right. Yesterday Mr. Laird very kindly offered me some assistance; I mean to take advantage of the offer.''

"Well, Alec's there; he's always in early, and it must be at least ten o'clock now. Speaking of yesterday and especially of last night: that was a shocker of a thing, wasn't it, to happen to friends of this newspaper?''

"If you mean Leo Shepley's death, it was a shocker for everybody. I didn't see anything about it in the morning papers, though.''

"My own guess, for what it's worth, is that they're

waiting to see how it's handled by the afternoon papers, particularly this one. We can't kill the story entirely, of course; but Alec will tell you how we're putting on the soft pedal.''

Bart Perkins stared at him.

''And there you were, as I understand it, slap in the middle of everything! Wouldn't care to write us your impressions, would you? No, I guess you wouldn't. When you do do your story for *Harper's Weekly,* what'll you say about crimes of violence?''

''When I do my personality piece on Clay Blake, Mr. Perkins, crimes of violence won't even be referred to. It's outside the scope of any story I was meant to get.''

''Whatever you say, old top, I see what you mean. No muckraking in a clean political campaign, eh? It's got nothing to do with our man for Congress, has it? Unless, of course, the poor devil gets himself arrested for murder.''

''Who said anything about arresting Clay for murder?''

''Nobody, so help me Jinny! Nobody has; nobody will. Just forget *I* mentioned it, won't you? Let's see: didn't you say you were a great baseball player in your college days?''

''I said I was an enthusiastic baseball player of little more than tolerable worth.''

''Well, Clay himself pitched for a championship Princeton team about the turn of the century. You might like to bring that in as a matter of human interest. After all, under the circumstances, you can't have got much useful material out of him last night?''

''I got a very fair amount of useful material, even though the circumstances weren't ideal. And I'm having lunch with him today at a place called Philippe's, where we can round out the details.''

''Before lunch today, Mr. Reporter Turned Novelist''— the managing editor fiddled with his necktie—''*we're* having another conference about the Shepley case, Alec and Harry Furnival and I. There's not much more we can thrash over, but new angles are always coming up. Now run along and beard Alec; I've got an idea he's half expecting you.''

Miss Ruth Donnelly, brightly at her desk in the reception room, made no difficulty about telephoning her employer in the office beyond. Bidden to the presence at once, Jim found Alec Laird, in the customary high collar and very formal lounge suit, rising from his own desk by way of greeting.

"I am compelled to deal so much in clichés, sir," he said as they shook hands, "that I will make only the briefest reference to poor Leo or the deep damnation of his taking-off. Be seated, please."

"Thank you, Mr. Laird."

"Nor will I trouble you with superfluous questions. How properly to deal with this affair has perplexed us all. Charley Emerson, for instance, almost begged to be assigned to it, but . . ."

"Charley Emerson did?"

"You are acquainted with Charley, I believe." Alec had sat down, a frown between his brows. "Yes, Charley's here. He arrived this morning, by the same train you yourself took at an earlier date. Leaving Washington Tuesday night—'in case I should be needed,' he said—put him on my doorstep at an early hour Thursday. When he heard a socially prominent New Orleanian had died under mysterious and tragic circumstances at the home of Clay Blake's dubious inamorata, he was (as the phrase goes) all over me. He volunteered to cover the story without pay and, again to use his own words, 'just for the hell of it.' "

"What did you tell him?"

"That I feared it wouldn't do. Charley was our best police reporter in days gone by. Though sometimes I allowed him more liberty than conscience approved of, more often I had to sit on him when zeal outran discretion. The situation, sir, calls for discretion if it calls for nothing else. And he was too full of cryptic hints nobody could understand."

"How did Charley take it?"

"Not altogether well. When at length I gave him a firm and rounded no, he was out of here in a flash . . ."

"Can anybody go out of here in a flash, Mr. Laird?"

"The phrase was figurative and ill-chosen; forgive me. What should have been said . . ."

"Look here, sir," Jim protested, "I'm not such a verbal purist as all that! I knew very well what you meant; *I'm* the one who shouldn't have butted in. It was just a thought that occurred to me, that's all."

"What should have been said, Mr. Blake, is that he departed in haste, muttering something about taking his wares to the opposition. But you did not come here, of course, to discuss Charley Emerson or his foibles?"

"No, Mr. Laird. It's a very different matter, which I mentioned yesterday just before I took my own leave."

"Ah, yes. You said, if memory serves, you were anxious to find a certain young lady who has mysterious ways and a mysterious employer, and disappeared from Terminal Station of her own free will."

"She turned up again last night. Then she vanished for the second time; she didn't leave a message or even say goodbye. Being a stranger here, Mr. Laird, I can't possibly get on her track unless I have more information to work with!"

Alec Laird fitted his fingertips together, leaned back in the swivel-chair, and for a moment sat lost in thought.

"If I myself ask questions, sir, pray don't think me unduly inquisitive or at all suspicious of your motives. If you would not embarrass us in one respect, assuredly you will not embarrass us in your search for the young lady. What is her name, by the way?"

"Matthews, Gillian Matthews, usually called Jill."

"Matthews, Gillian or Jill Matthews. The name is not familiar to me, but perhaps that's hardly surprising. Does she live in New Orleans?"

"She seems to work here, at all events."

"Have you any information about the employer?"

"Only *his* name. Jill's the secretary of some stock-market manipulator named old Ed Hollister. Or at least I was told so. Leo Shepley, who gave me the information, called him the mystery man of finance and says he moves in such secretive ways nobody can find him. But the resources of a newspaper . . . !''

Now a change had come over Alec Laird, if not a happy one. Though clearly far from unsympathetic, he seemed for the most part dubious and perturbed.

"Are you sure you want to pursue this matter, Mr. Blake? Are you entirely *sure* you want to pursue it?''

"I intend to pursue it," Jim roared, "if it's the only other damn thing I do while I'm here! To find Jill . . .''

"And yet," said the other, "would you be wise in so doing? If you don't want to embarrass others, you surely can't want to embarrass yourself? To inquire after old Ed Hollister's whereabouts, Mr. Blake, would be only a waste of time and an embarrassment, too. May I most earnestly advise you against it?''

"Since it's my time, Mr. Laird, why mayn't I waste it if that's what I feel like doing? But why should it be a waste of time or an embarrassment either?''

Alec Laird leaned forward.

"Because old Ed Hollister does not exist. Leo Shepley invented him for one of Leo's practical jokes, and the name of the mysterious financier has become something of a joke hereabouts. To inquire where he is or how to find him, sir, would be like asking precise directions for the North Pole in order to find Father Christmas.''

After a kind of thunderous silence, which could almost be heard reverberating, Alec Laird spoke in an entirely sympathetic voice.

"This will be a great blow to you, I fear. May I beg, though, that you won't let it distress you too much? May I beg . . . ?''

But Jim, exultant, had leaped to his feet.

"A blow?" he exclaimed. "It's a blow, yes. It's a blow slam-bang in the right direction! It knocks the props out from under *all* the myths; it shows me what I ought to have seen long ago! I'll take my leave again, Mr. Laird, adding only what I added yesterday: that you can't realize how much you've helped me.''

And once more, after a grateful and deeply sincere goodbye, he left that office with head high and heart singing. His theory about Jill had been right after all; in very short order, probably even this morning, he should be able to prove it. He had taken another long step towards truth.

13

COULD SOMEBODY be following him now?

It was not quite eleven o'clock. Having retrieved the car from Guilfoyle's Garage, Jim headed east along Chartres Street. In the dingy, greasy garage Stu Guilfoyle, who obviously knew nothing of last night's events, had been his customary amiable self.

"Didn't have no trouble with her, did you, Mr. Blake? I've given her a goin'-over this morning; she's in tip-top shape. But you ain't got your dust-coat on!"

"No, no trouble at all. I'm not wearing the coat because this morning I intend to stay within well-paved limits; the goggles are here in my pocket. Before I take the car out, though, may I use your telephone?"

"Sure thing. This way."

Stu led him to the cramped cubicle of an office, whose window looked out across an overgrown back yard. A calendar on the wall depicted some fashionable young lady ecstatically holding up a bottle of Coca-Cola with a straw in it. Jim sat down at the phone on the desk underneath and asked for Main 0101. While the ringing-tone sounded distantly, he picked up a pencil and drew squiggles on a pad.

He was answered, as he expected to be, by Miss Florence Yates's maid. A short parley brought Miss Yates herself.

"It's a little early to be disturbing you," Jim told her.

184

"But several important matters have come up since I saw you last . . ."

"So I've been told." The voice betrayed nothing. "Yes, Mr. Blake?"

"And one or two points need to be cleared up. Would it be too much if I asked to come and see you now?"

"You're always welcome here, my dear sir, and I think you know it! Where are you?"

"At a garage in Chartres Street. With luck I could be there in fifteen minutes or less, if that's convenient?"

"Yes, indeed; it's entirely convenient. Do come along as soon as you can!"

Jim hung up the receiver and went to the front of the garage. At the curb outside, facing in the direction of Canal Street, was another almost brand-new five-seater Cadillac, this one bright yellow, with its top up. Beside it, in frock coat and top hat, stood an urbane, silver-haired man with a mobile mouth and a hooded eye. Stu Guilfoyle was addressing him with gusto.

"There's not a thing wrong with her, Mr. Chadwick! Just don't take your foot off the clutch too soon; then she won't stall. That self-starter's a dream, ain't it?"

He turned towards Jim, and became uproariously amused.

"Here, this is good! Mr. Chadwick, meet Mr. Blake from New York. Mr. Blake, Mr. Chadwick. It'd be real funny, wouldn't it, if Mr. Blake in a Chadwick ran smack into Mr. Chadwick in a Cadillac?"

"I sincerely hope he won't," said the silver-haired man. "I'm too old a dog, Stu, to learn the tricks of the young. But you're right about one thing. With a self-starter, you see, my wife and daughter can take over duties that the head of the family shies at. We'll have ladies driving every car in sight before long, don't you think?"

This must be the Raymond P. Chadwick of whom Jim had heard. He made no comment on Jim's name; perhaps he had scarcely heard it. His was the ease of a trained politician, who would have shown the utmost cordiality if he had been introduced to a two-headed dragon.

"So I think I'm safe enough," he added. "However, just in case the gentleman *should* feel impelled to run over Mr. Chadwick in a Chadwick, I'll climb in and be off."

A touch of his foot on a button brought the engine to life. With something of a jerk, but steadily enough after the first few yards, he rolled away towards Canal Street.

After Stu had obligingly cranked up for him, Jim turned in the opposite direction. That was where he began to have the impression that eyes were upon him, and that somebody followed.

It was only an impression, probably illusory. In fact, so far as he could see, nothing followed him except one of the ubiquitous carriages for sightseers, and this soon turned off. He made good time to Esplanade Avenue. A few minutes past eleven found him ringing the bell at the home of Miss Yates.

Admitted by the graceful maid, he was again ushered into the drawing-room on the right. Miss Yates, in a green morning-gown, sat beside one of the front windows with a book in her hand. Though no less *soignée* than yesterday, she seemed even more haggard when she rose and bowed.

"Your servant, Mr. Blake! If you have further questions for me, may we dispense with formalities and get to the point at once?"

"Of course, if you wish it. I believe you said, Miss Yates, that twice last week the notorious Yvonne Brissard called on General and Mrs. Clayton across the street?"

"God save us! Did you come all the way to my humble abode merely to ask *that?*"

"No, madam. There are other matters. You see—"

"How many times must I assure you," cried Miss Yates, "that according to my lights I am a thoroughly honest woman? The suicide of our unfortunate friend Leo . . ."

"Was it suicide or murder, madam? The police seem to think it was murder, and they have good reason."

"It was suicide, I tell you!"

"In either event, Miss Yates, the news has not yet appeared in the press. May I ask how you learned it?"

"A source called the grapevine, Mr. Blake, makes any sensational event common knowledge in a very short time. Can you question that statement?"

"Not as a general statement, though I may question other statements of yours. You have just referred to our 'unfortunate friend Leo.' Were you in fact his fairly close friend?"

"I was. Did he himself not tell you so?"

"He let it be understood. You said yesterday, however, you had telephoned Leo to verify my *bona fides*. I myself could not reach you by phone until one-thirty in the afternoon. At what time did you get in touch with him?"

"To find the poor fellow in so suicidal a mood? As I have good reason for remembering, it was at ten minutes after two."

"No, madam. Leo had left home before two o'clock. The police have a full list of phone calls he made or received before he went out. Unless *you* were the man's voice which seems to have threatened him half an hour after noon, a proposition I take the liberty of doubting, you could not have spoken to him even then; you could not have spoken to him at all."

Miss Yates threw up her hands.

"If we must pursue what now amounts to an inquisition, don't stand there fidgeting and looking tortured! There's a chair just opposite me, by the right-hand window. Sit down, please; let's pursue my sins, or Leo's sins, with some decent appearance of being civilized!"

"*Were* they Leo's sins, madam?"

"I beg your pardon?"

She had sat down. Jim did not immediately follow suit.

"Comparing certain remarks of yours with certain things Leo had said in the course of a lengthy phone call," he continued, "I felt sure yesterday there must be something wrong in the situation as it was presented to me."

"Something wrong?"

"Something false, then. He conveyed the impression, without actually stating it, that he knew so much about you because he himself had employed the service you provide: Sue, Billie Jean, or perhaps some predecessor of theirs. And yet he seemed to think your nieces performed in this house, and added that you must either be running a grave risk or paying heavy bribes to operate on the sacred Esplanade.''

"But I—!"

"Yes, Miss Yates. You made very clear, almost from the start, you would never so jeopardize the position you hope to attain. And yet Leo did not seem to know this. He made no mention of that snug Basin Street apartment, safe beyond touch of the law, as assuredly he must have done if he had ever heard of it.''

"What are you suggesting *now?*"

"I am suggesting, Miss Yates, that Leo never did try the joys of the pubescent, even to satisfy curiosity about what it would be like. In short, madam, he was speaking from hearsay; and he made a mistake.''

Here Jim did sit down to face her. But his tone did not change.

"On the other hand," he pursued, fixing his companion with a mesmeric eye, "you said you knew I would call on you; you said you knew it even before I telephoned. And I don't doubt that: every word and gesture indicated you were expecting me. You didn't communicate with Leo; you couldn't have communicated with Leo. But somebody *did* ring you and tell you to welcome Jim Blake. Have you realized, madam, that this 'somebody' is in all probability the murderer for whom the police are looking?''

The woman was galvanized.

"Murderer?" she echoed. "You're mad! You're stark mad! He would never have—'' She checked herself and stood up. "To demonstrate, sir, that for the most part I have been telling you sober truth, may we revert to the question you asked when you first burst in? It is about Miss Yvonne Brissard.''

"Yes?"

"On the continent of Europe, where they manage these

things better, a *grande amoureuse* will be accepted and even honored by some of the best people. If Miss Brissard has begun to teach us such civilized habits here, more power to her!'' Florence Yates, deeply moved, threw open the lace curtains on the left-hand window. "Look out there, Mr. Blake! Look at the house opposite!"

Jim joined her and peered out.

The house across the avenue, brick faced in pale gray stucco, was of a sort often seen in the Vieux Carré. Its ground or parlor floor had been built up some dozen feet above street-level. The wings of a curving stone stairway with lacework iron balustrade ascended on either side to meet at a white front door between pillars. Sunlight gleamed on its brass knocker.

"General and Mrs. Clayton," Miss Yates reported, "have gone for their customary morning drive; the ogre is absent. Yesterday, Mr. Blake, you seemed to entertain some doubts that Mademoiselle Brissard could be on visiting terms with the Claytons. She has attained more than visiting terms; she makes herself at home. She is there now!"

"I see no carriage waiting."

"She came in a cab, no doubt. Certainly the other woman did; I saw her."

"What other woman?"

"Miss Brissard's social secretary. When they hear that our *grande amoureuse* employs a social secretary, so many obtuse people are inclined to snicker or make ribald jokes. I don't snicker, sir; least of all do I make jokes. More power to her, say I!"

"This social secretary: you're sure that's who it is? And they're both in the house now?"

"I am sure of her identity, though I never heard her name. I saw them both when Miss Brissard was staying at the Grunewald Hotel before she rented her present villa."

The whole emotional temperature of this interview had altered in a matter of seconds. Jim all but seized his companion's arm.

"What's she like, the secretary? Will you describe her, please?"

"Unlike her employer, the secretary is smallish and fair-haired. But she is very pretty, and has a *beautiful* figure. All the men would be after *her*, I am sure, except that she's so self-effacing one scarcely observes her.

"Let it be repeated that the ogre is absent on his morning drive. Mrs. Clayton, who must be years younger than her husband and has a somewhat theatrical presence for so obvious a *grande dame*, is absent, too. Helena, one of the Claytons' maids, is a great friend of Essie, my maid. Not long ago Helena, knowing our interest in these things, ran across the street to tell Essie that Miss Brissard and her secretary have made themselves very comfortable in the back parlor. Should you still entertain any doubt of this . . . ?"

"Yes?"

"Is the matter so important to you, Mr. Blake? Very well. On either side of the house, you will note, there is a wall fronting the banquette, with an open gateway against the house on both sides. If you were to cross the street, enter by one of those gates, and go to the back of the premises, you would find outside stairs leading to a gallery across the parlor floor. You need not disturb anyone or so much as betray your presence. One glance through a window would assure you I speak the simple truth. If the matter *is* so important . . ."

All Jim's earlier excitement had returned in a rush.

"The matter's important, all right, and that's just what I'll do. It's time we cleared up one utterly senseless masquerade."

"Shall I ring for Essie to fetch your hat?"

"No hat will be needed for the errand I have in mind. But I beg, madam, you won't stir from where you are or lock your front door against my return. There are other things of greater weight than my own emotions."

Having said this with as much coolness as he could muster, Jim almost plunged out into the hall. Though he had also said he did not need his hat, he saw it on a table in the hall and took it with him when he descended into the street.

The sun, hitherto so much in evidence, had gone behind a cloud after the fashion of New Orleans weather. A grocer's delivery wagon rattled past, its driver whistling; nothing else seemed astir in Esplanade Avenue.

Jim crossed the street, and at the right-hand side of the house entered the arched gateway in a stucco-faced wall twice the height of a man's head. A brick-flagged walk led him along the south side of a spacious and well-kept garden. A similar brick-flagged path along the north side joined this one where both turned at the back of the house, and became one broader path to coach-house-cum-stable giving on an alley at the extreme rear.

There was the iron gallery along the back of the house, with iron stairs leading up. Slowing his rush, Jim mounted the steps. Beyond the first window through which he looked, which could only have been that of the back parlor Miss Yates had mentioned, he found what he sought.

In a room with two windows, a room richly furnished after the style of post-bellum days before he had been born, two women sat with their backs almost turned. They sat at a table bearing silver coffee-service and Wedgwood china cups.

The woman on the left was Jill, in tailored costume and small straw hat. The woman on the right, slim and lissome, wore a morning-gown of vivid yellow. She might have been in her early or middle thirties. Since she had her profile slightly inclined towards Jill, Jim could see the very tiny mole just above the outer corner of the left eyebrow.

So many emotions boiled up in him that he could not have analyzed them even if he had wanted to. He stood for a moment looking from one woman to the other. Then he quietly descended the steps, and went back by way of the path into the street.

Along Esplanade Avenue, approaching from the south, loomed up a familiar thick-set, derby-hatted figure on a

Ranger bicycle. Lieutenant Trowbridge, his moustache a-bristle, swung in at the curb, dismounted, and propped the machine upright on its metal stand.

"Well, Franz Josef?" he said with broad heartiness. "Discovered anything else this morning?"

"Yes. Have you been following me?"

"Not what you'd call following, no. They said you'd left the newspaper office, but didn't know where you'd gone. I sort of thought you might get the car out, and you had. You used the phone, too, Stu Guilfoyle told me. On a pad beside it somebody'd scribbled 'Main 0101.' "

"I was only making aimless marks, I thought."

"Wasn't so very aimless, Franz Josef. Didn't take long to learn who *that* number belonged to, either!" Lieutenant Trowbridge glanced across the street. "Yes, there's your car outside Flossie Yates's. All right! If you were asking Flossie about her stable of under-age ones, or anything else that's occurred to you, what are you doing over here? This is General Clayton's, isn't it?"

"Yes, but the general's not in. I think Miss Yates could tell us a good deal, though it may not be easy to make her speak. And another point has come up. Listen, Lieutenant! Suppose you learn something which may be revealing or even startling on its own, but which won't help much in solving the problem on both our minds. Could you keep it strictly to yourself?"

"Try me, that's all. Just try me!"

"I'll go even further. *Would* you keep it to yourself, and not make things more awkward than necessary for several persons concerned?"

"Yes, I can promise that. I want to know who killed Leo Shepley and how it was done. Anything else don't matter two hoots in hell!"

"Wait here, will you? I'm going up and hammer at the front door. If they admit me, I'll soon stick my head out and invite you to join the party."

"What's the game, Franz Josef?"

"You'll see."

Now that they had reached at least a minor disclosure which to Jim was a major disclosure, he must keep tight hold on nervous tensions so that his voice would remain coherent. He ran up the steps and plied the brass knocker. A Negro maid in the regulation uniform of cap and apron opened the door on a lofty, tapestry-hung hall at whose rear a partly open door must lead to the back parlor Jim had already seen.

"Yessuh?" the maid began nervously. "If it's for the general . . ."

"It's not for the general." Jim made his voice carry. "May I speak to Miss Jill Matthews, please?"

The maid retreated two steps. From the direction of the back parlor a woman's voice, not Jill's voice but one he had heard before, said, "Surely that's—!" and stopped abruptly.

Inside the parlor there seemed to be a kind of scurry. Then Jill herself, hand shading her eyes, appeared in its doorway. Lovely to look at, infinitely desirable despite a face pink with confusion, she hovered there as though poised for instant flight.

"Better come out, Jill," he called. "You might ask *her* to come out, too. The masquerade's over now, as it ought to be over."

"Yes, it's over," Jill blurted. "And thank God it's over! I've been arguing since Wednesday, though up to this morning I couldn't make her agree to anything at all!" Then Jill's defenses dropped. "But however on earth did you *guess?*"

The maid had vanished. The big front door still stood open behind Jim. He swung towards it and looked down.

"This way, Lieutenant. The thing that must be done had better be done now."

Rather hesitantly Zack Trowbridge mounted the steps, for the first time since Jim had met him removing his hat indoors.

"Yeah, Mr. Blake? What thing?"

"Lieutenant, would you like to meet Yvonne Brissard?"

It was Lieutenant Trowbridge's turn to seem lowering, confused, and dubious.

"Well, now, Mr. Blake, I dunno. My wife . . ."

"It doesn't matter, though. You can't meet her; none of us can meet her."

"Why not?"

The sky had darkened still more, as though for rain. The hall was full of shadows even before Jim closed the front door.

"Because there isn't any Yvonne Brissard," he answered. "At least, there isn't any in New Orleans, wherever the real owner of the name may be."

"Then what's going on here? Why did you ask whether I wanted to meet her?"

"Because there's a lady here you're bound to meet sooner or later. It'll be less of a shock to you both if you meet her, so to speak, under my chaperonage."

Jill had advanced over polished hardwood. Out from the back parlor, eyes dancing and face alight with sheer enjoyment, moved with easy grace the tall, slender woman in the yellow dress.

Jim drew himself up.

"Lieutenant Trowbridge," he said, "may I have the honor of presenting you to the distinguished British actress, Miss Constance Lambert, who as 'Yvonne Brissard' has played her greatest part from the end of March until almost the end of October?" He turned to Jill. "You're her sister, aren't you?"

14

"UNDER ANY OTHER CIRCUMSTANCES, Mr. Blake," Constance Lambert said five minutes later, "I might be annoyed with you; I might be seriously annoyed. But something this morning makes me so happy, so *wonderfully* happy, I couldn't possibly be annoyed with anyone, least of all the man who did that *wonderful*, that so-flattering interview in *Harper's Weekly*! Never mind, for the moment, what makes me so happy. You see . . ."

All four of them—Miss Lambert, her sister, Jim, Lieutenant Trowbridge—sat in General Clayton's back parlor, amid the heavily carved wood, lambrequins, marble-topped tables, antimacassars, and chairs with cushions of overstuffed velvet that marked a post-Civil War splendor from the day before yesterday.

Only Constance Lambert, radiating her famous charm, seemed utterly at ease. The other three were distinctly uncomfortable, Lieutenant Trowbridge twirling his derby hat on his left knee.

"Of course," Miss Lambert continued, "what happened to Leo was absolutely ghastly; I shall never get over *that*, I know. And yet at the same time—let truth be told, though the skies fall!—I *am* happy and I can't help showing it. You see . . ."

"For heaven's sake, Connie," Jill burst out, not for the first time, "do let him speak at least one word, can't you? How *did* you know it was Connie, Jim?"

Jim, seated on the arm of Jill's chair, stared at the coffee-service on the table.

"I was unpardonably dense at first," he said. "But nobody could help noticing when so many little things piled up.

"I think suspicion started with wondering how Yvonne Brissard, a notoriously disreputable character who wasn't received anywhere, could persuade Mathilde de Jarnac Laird to rent a villa Mrs. Laird had meant for a shrine to her brother's memory. Then, if Yvonne could find herself on such familiar terms with General and Mrs. Clayton . . . !

"The only explanation was that she mightn't be disreputable at all, but ultra-reputable: someone these conservative people would have felt honored to receive if they could have done it openly. An imposture of some kind, in short; but what kind of imposture and by whom? You don't want me to go on with this, do you?"

"By gum, Franz Josef," said Lieutenant Trowbridge, snorting like a bull, "but that's just what we do want and no mistake! There'll be trouble if you *don't* go on, I'm warning you! Well?"

Jim pondered.

"In England," he replied, "I knew the world of the theatre pretty well. Not in America, where I don't know it at all. But in London, after seven years, I'd become almost as familiar with stage people as with my own crowd in Fleet Street.

"Take Jill here, whom I first met in New York Monday morning and encountered again Monday night when I boarded the train at Washington. She wasn't an actress; I could be sure of that. She hadn't the theatrical air or manner, which you can't possibly mistake in any actress you ever meet."

"Thanks *so* much," smiled Constance Lambert. "Or— always saving my presence, you mean'?"

"No, Miss Lambert; I needn't apologize. There's nothing wrong with the theatrical manner. It may and usually does mean very good manners, as it does with you. I say only that it exists.

"Well, Jill didn't have it. And yet, from the time that train left Washington, she kept bringing up the subject of the theatre or making gratuitous references to theatrical circles. Last night, at the Villa de Jarnac, she capped it all. When I stopped on the verge of saying something, she told me I 'dried.' That, Lieutenant Trowbridge, is a term they use when an actor or actress forgets the next line. You and I, not stage people, would be inclined to say 'dry up.' But in England, at least, they never do; they say 'dry.'

"It had been Jill, on that train, who asked whether I knew Constance Lambert. There was also an interesting little comparison in the matter of dates, though it failed fully to register at the time. End of February: Constance Lambert leaves London, apparently for Italy. End of March: Yvonne Brissard arrives in New Orleans; the whole dance begins. And Jill has been here for seven months, too.

"*Was* it possible?"

Jim glanced at the actress, who had sat back comfortably with her knees crossed.

"You have a deservedly great name, Miss Lambert," Jim went on. "You have been praised with equal warmth both by critics and by populace in every suitable vehicle from Shakespeare to Shaw. You have appeared several seasons in New York, I know, though I didn't think you had ever appeared in New Orleans."

"Except in my present role, I never have," she told him delightedly. "Else I mightn't have been able to bring it off, might I? New York, yes. That's why Mr. Alden—but never mind. You were saying?"

"If I sought some eminent lady of the stage, admired and respected everywhere, who might be playing a prank of this sort, yours would be among the first names to occur. It did occur. Last night, when I asked somebody for a description of Yvonne Brissard, he gave so striking a description of Constance Lambert that I felt *almost* sure.

"Much other information disclosed itself last night.

Yvonne Brissard, I heard, employed a 'social secretary,' who was said to have accompanied her to Alabama. And Jill, while still professing to be a stranger, knew altogether too much about the Villa de Jarnac: including the fact that those double doors of the way-through to the racetrack had been locked and barred since the new tenant took over.''

"Well, what could I be expected to say?" cried Jill. "But it doesn't matter, does it? Go on!"

Jim put his hand lightly on her shoulder.

"There remained," he said, "only the question of the ease with which 'Yvonne Brissard' had been accepted both by Mrs. Sam Laird and by the Claytons. The difficulties, however, were not really too formidable.

"Puritan prejudice against the stage was already fading when the late Sir Henry Irving received his knighthood in '95. Today, except among the very old-fashioned, it has ceased to exist. Unfamiliar though I may be with New Orleans, parts of the South I know well. If no such prejudice is felt in the best circles of Richmond or Charleston, prejudice seemed still more unlikely here.

"And almost immediately there was confirmation. That inexorable old aristocrat, Mathilde de Jarnac Laird, has an unvarying ritual. Every night, seeing to it that dinner is over by nine-thirty, she retires to her room and *reads plays*. Her fondness for the stage couldn't have been so very secret, could it?''

"*Fondness* for the stage?" echoed Constance Lambert, sitting up straight. "When she was a young girl and a talented amateur (or so she says), she wanted to *go* on the stage professionally, only her brother wouldn't let her. And she's not the only one in her family with aspirations to be an artist. My dear man, if I told you everything . . . !''

"Everything, no doubt, will soon be clear." Jim took up the story. "Mrs. Laird, of course, must have been in on the secret to start with. Regarding the Claytons: I have not yet had the pleasure of meeting the general or his wife. But not long ago, when I had already made up my mind and lacked only a look at the elusive 'Yvonne Brissard,' another witness remarked that Margot de Sancerre Clayton has a notably theatrical manner.

"An elaborate hoax, then, was being perpetrated by Miss Lambert and by Jill, undoubtedly a close friend or a relative. And Leo Shepley must have been behind it. Remembering Leo's passion for practical jokes . . .''

Constance Lambert sprang to her feet and struck a pose.

"Hoax?" she scoffed. "I do protest and asseverate, from the very bottom of my heart, it was no hoax or joke! It was done for the very best possible reason, since—"

"Connie dear," Jill interposed, "can't you let *him* explain? I didn't think I was going to like this at all, and yet . . . no wonder he could write *The Count of Monte Carlo!* Really and truly, Jim, it's the best detective work I ever heard of!"

"*I'd* say it's pretty damn good, too," declared Lieutenant Trowbridge, making a gesture with his hat. "If he can use the same brains on the rest of the business, we oughtn't to have much work left. And Mr. Shepley was behind the joke, was he? Was that why you wanted me to ask his aunt about the last time he went abroad? I haven't had a chance to see Mrs. Penderel again, but was that why?"

"Yes. For whatever reason the three of them planned it, it must have been planned either in England or on the Continent, perhaps in Italy. Unfortunately, Leo had almost thrown me off the track by swearing Jill was the secretary of some nonexistent financier named Hollister. He urged me not to mention it to Jill until she told me, and I didn't."

"He wasn't trying to hoax *you*, Jim!" the girl said with some fervency. "He only did that to shield me, because I begged him on the train to make up some explanation.

"You see, Jim, after meeting you at Harper's on Monday morning, I had started to grow panicky. You hadn't said much, but you had said you were a working newspaperman after a story. So I thought to myself, 'What if it's *our* story, Connie's and mine?' I hadn't any reason to think that; it's the silly, overpowering sort of fear which does jump into one's head, and gets worse and worse as you think about it.

"Afterwards, meeting Leo on the train between New York and Washington, I begged him to think of some explanation that didn't involve me as the 'social secretary' of a notorious prostitute. It was just in case you *did* turn up after all. Leo thought of an explanation; he did make me a secretary. And I was most awfully glad I'd consulted him—anyway, at the moment I was glad—when the train gave that great jump and I landed in your arms *again*. Connie and I hadn't been doing anything against the law, of course. It was just one thing: when you looked at the situation in the cold light of reason, our whole position seemed so infantile and *absurd!* Doesn't that explain whatever may have seemed odd about my conduct, either in New York or on the train?"

"Not entirely, Jill. It doesn't explain why you wouldn't use my drawing-room."

Once more Constance Lambert turned on her charm.

"Doesn't it, Jim?" she asked, dropping "Mr. Blake" for good and all. "That, I'm afraid, is a personal matter my sister had better explain to you in private. No, no, dear!" she added in haste, as Jill made an instinctive movement of protest. "I'm not going to embarrass you or tell tales out of school. However, since *I'm* the one best fitted to explain why I played Yvonne Brissard and had a heavenly time doing it, I had better do the explaining at once."

Having taken the center of the stage, Constance evidently had no intention of relinquishing it. She strolled to the two windows at the back of the room and sauntered past them, for a moment as though studying the bobbles on their curtains. Then she turned back, a dream in her eyes.

"My real name, you know, is Matthews: Constance Matthews. But 'Matthews' wouldn't look so well in lights, as old Benny MacFishbein insisted when I first tried out for rep. I've been Constance Lambert for so many years I can't even *think* of myself by any other name. I've been very lucky, I know. And yet it's meant work, too; God alone knows how hard I've worked!

"I really did go to Italy at the end of February. If *you* ask me nicely, Jim, I can still return and play Marcia in *The Count of Monte Carlo*. It's not a bad part, and I think I might do something big with it. But at that moment I'd just had a row with George Alexander, who can be appallingly exasperating when his conceit shows; the weather in England was awful; and I felt the pressure of things had become just too much!

"Let me see, now," she mused. "At the moment, Jim, you're a gentleman of leisure wth a successful book behind you. But you do represent *Harper's Weekly,* don't you?"

"On this occasion, yes."

"Then you probably know Henry Mills Alden, the editor of *Harper's Magazine*?"

"Yes, very well."

"As I was saying, Jill and I went first to Rome. But there were so many British and Americans they were all over me. 'Do this, Miss Lambert. Do that, Miss Lambert. And you *will* be nice about it, won't you?' It was worse than it is in London sometimes. So Jill and I went south to Naples. We stayed at the hotel; you know—the big one overlooking the bay, where Vesuvius seems so very close, and you see the little lights of the funicular going up the mountain at night. There were scads of visitors there as well, but the only one we took to was Leo Shepley, who seems outwardly crude and isn't."

"Connie—!" began Jill.

"Yes, dear, of course. I *must* keep reminding myself poor Leo's dead, and in some sense it may be my fault he's dead."

"Connie, that's *utterly* silly! you couldn't possibly . . ."

"I know, dear, I know. But I have fancies of the 'what-if' sort, like yours. Just indulge me a little, won't you? I'm coming to the point at once.

"We hadn't been at the hotel more than a week when a letter from Mr. Alden was forwarded by my agent in

London. It was a *charming* letter. He and all his friends, he said, had seen me in New York when I played Candida, and Rosalind, and Marguerite Gautier in *The Lady of the Camellias*. I seemed very young to have accomplished so much and seen so much. Would I be at all interested in writing my memoirs for serialization in his magazine? If so . . . and so on.

"Even in that short time I'd come to be fairly well acquainted with Leo; I'm supposed to make friends easily. And one night, when the do-this, do-that brigade had been at me until I felt I could scream, I burst out a little. I said, 'I've a good mind to *write* my autobiography. And I'll really write it, too,' I said, 'and not get somebody to do the job for me. Oh,' I said . . . what *did* I say, Jill?''

Jill arose from the chair and assumed a tragic air like her sister's.

" 'Oh,' '' Jill breathed in her soft voice, " 'if only I could have peace and quiet to do it! If only I could retire to some place where they wouldn't be at me as soon as I showed my face in the foyer or answered a telephone! But it can't be done in England; it can't be done in Rome; it can't even be done in Naples. Where *might* it be done?' ''

Constance took up that tale.

"Leo, bless him, didn't laugh at me; he was dead serious. 'As long as you remain Constance Lambert,' he said, 'it can't be done anywhere. Furthermore, if you tried to put on some mask of anonymity, they'd find you out in less than a week. But there *is* a way. If you don't mind playing one more disreputable part, in life rather than on the stage, I can tell you where and I can tell you how.'

"Then he gave me a partial history of Yvonne Brissard: who actually, it seems, has gone off to Budapest or Constantinople or somewhere with a Balkan nobleman she used to know in Paris.

" 'If you play Yvonne Brissard in New Orleans,' he said, 'nobody will receive you or even telephone you, or be at you in any way. But are you sure, me dear,' '' and she mimicked Leo's manner to the life, " 'are you sure you want *nobody* to know who you are?' I can still see him looking at me, as though he could see farther through me than I can see through myself, and yet I can't swear I know what he meant.''

"He meant, Connie," Jill informed her with some intensity, "that you've *got* to have somebody to act for in private, even if you can't do it in public on a stage!"

Constance cried out at her.

"This from *you*, an allegedly devoted sister? 'How sharper than a serpent's tooth it is to have a thankless kin!' If that's tampering with *King Lear,* never mind. And I forgive you, Jill, because there may be some truth in it.''

More self-mockery than pettishness gleamed in the expressive eyes.

"The fact is," she confessed, "that none of us likes to be *totally* unknown wherever we go; we need sustenance for self-respect and the ego. Leo explained about the formidable old party, Mathilde Laird, who's just fussy and pernickety, in the main; not very formidable after first acquaintance. He said *she'd* keep my secret if I made her promise, and rent me a beautiful house that was going begging. And the extent of that woman's information! She's seen Duse, she's seen Sarah Bernhardt, she's watched every great artist from Edwin Booth's later years to the present; she knows more stage history than I do!''

Jim intervened. "What about the general and his wife?"

"They've been good friends, too. To meet 'em now, Jim, you'd never imagine that before the Civ—I mustn't say Civil War, must I?—that as dashing youngsters before the Great Unpleasantness that couple were principal figures in a famous murder case solved by Judah P. Benjamin, the lawyer who afterwards went to England and became one of *our* greatest barristers. They've been most sympathetic and helpful, especially the general's wife, and they *are* the best people. It's tragic irony, isn't it, that *I* should blunder into a murder case? And that the victim should be poor Leo himself?''

"It's tragic irony," Jim agreed, "though we'll not dwell

too much on that aspect. Apart from Leo, then, these three elderly aristocrats were the only New Orleanians who knew your real identity?''

''Yes, except for the bank. The manager of the Planters' & Southern *had* to know, or I couldn't have got funds through from London. But the second great virtue of bankers, always putting honesty first, is that they don't talk.''

''One last question, and I will pester you no more. At the beginning of this imposture, I take it, there was no intention of hoaxing Clay Blake?''

Constance recoiled.

''Good heavens, Jim! As I've tried so hard to tell you, there was never an intention of hoaxing *anybody!* It was to give me peace and quiet, which blessedly I've had, so I could get on and finish my book. The only part was being a Creole and speaking French when I had to. They tell me I speak pretty fair French. Anyway, I once played *La Dame aux Caméllias* in Paris; and the notices—I can show you my scrapbook—were positively lyrical. But I haven't been troubled with much French. If anybody ever did fire an incomprehensible sentence I could always draw myself up like this and say''—momentarily a very slight accent tinged her voice—'' 'We are in America, where I was born; please to speak English, if you will.' There was nothing else to it. That I should meet darling Clay, with predictable results, was only what I like to call his destiny and mine. You can't find a hoax there, can you?''

''No, but that's what Leo was afraid of.''

''Afraid of?''

''When the whole truth came out. Even if I hadn't interfered, you couldn't have kept up the imposture much longer, could you?''

''That's what *I've* kept telling her,'' Jill insisted. ''But do you think she'd listen?''

Jim leaned forward, fixing the taller woman with his eye.

''Sooner or later, you know, you'd have had to admit you were Constance Lambert. And then what would have been everybody's verdict? That it had been another practical joke, engineered by Leo Shepley and directed at Clay Blake, one of Leo's close friends.

"It's now much clearer." He glanced at Jill. "What a load of trouble Leo carried when we were on that train. He was worried about a political plot against Clay, yes. He was also worried about what so many people would think was *his* plot, to embarrass and discomfit the very man he was supporting. In the old days, when he did go hog-wild with a practical joke, his conscience wouldn't let him rest until he'd put matters right with the victim. And it explains something he said to his aunt on Wednesday morning. 'I've got no reputation to lose. But, by God, Aunt Harriet, I won't lose my friends!' "

"You're all looking at me," cried Constance, "as though I were the villain of the piece, or at least a wickedly designing woman! Is that what *you're* thinking, Lieutenant Trowbridge?"

"No, ma'am, you're all wrong there," grunted Lieutenant Trowbridge, regarding her with the utmost respect. "All the same, though! If a mere cop *could* butt in and ask you something, too . . ."

"You know, Mr. Trowbridge, you're not a bit like any American detective I ever heard of or read about. Please feel free to ask anything at all!"

"It's a little bit personal, ma'am!"

"I live in public, don't I? *Can* anything be too personal? Ask away!"

"All right, ma'am, if you insist." After staring at the floor for a moment, he looked up suddenly. "Here *you* are, a fine actress and a real lady. What did your swell friends think—old Mrs. Laird, the general and his wife— what did *they* think when you played the high-priced fancy woman and flaunted yourself as one in front of the whole town?"

"When have I ever flaunted myself, Mr. Trowbridge?"

"You haven't, ma'am! It's just what you wanted to avoid, and I can see that as well as anybody. But you started 'em talking; you wanted 'em to talk; you've known what they said. What *did* your swell friends think? If it comes to that, what did *you* think? Haven't you felt just a little bit degraded, sort of?"

"My swell friends, as you call them, have been far less shocked than you credit them with being. In their hearts I know they've enjoyed it. Certainly *I've* enjoyed it."

"Ma'am, are you saying what I think you're saying?"

"I am saying it with all possible clarity. The part I played was that of a *grande amoureuse,* not a common street-walker. If you don't appreciate the difference, ask any woman who'll give you an honest answer. What each of us wants, unco' guid or the reverse, is universal tribute to our powers of fascination. The great courtesan has that; she can walk proudly because she has it, in full conscious- ness of admiration and envy. And my own private reputa- tion, Lieutenant, is not so spotless that I can cry, 'Fie!' or pretend to unco' guidness when I am having an affair with some personable male."

"But Mr. Clay Blake . . ."

"With Clay, of course, it's been a very different matter. Old Mrs. Laird knows, the general's wife knows, I fell deeply and sincerely for Clay as soon as I met him. It's a different thing; it's the real thing. Do you believe *that?*"

"If you say so, ma'am, I believe it."

"And in all this lofty talk about virtue—damn virtue!—we seem to be forgetting why I played the part. Clay's com- pany, after all, was the only company I wanted while I tried to finish that book."

"Ah, now we're on safer ground! Did you finish the book?"

"All but the last chapter, which will bring events up to date. There have been a few difficulties with it, though."

"How, ma'am?"

"As soon as I finish a chapter, Jill types it and tidies up the spelling wherever necessary. But, when I've wanted to write to Mr. Alden in New York, I've had to send the letter to London, where my agent has the envelope retyped and posted there. I'm not supposed to be in this country, you know.''

"We know, Miss Lambert. Well?''

Hands clasped together, body tense in the yellow dress, Constance again seemed to peer out of a dream.

''Towards the end of September, when I'd finished that next-to-the-last chapter, I was *jubilant!* I said to Jill, 'Since it's all finished bar the conclusion, here's what we'll do!' So I wrote to Mr. Alden, saying I was sending my secretary to New York with the manuscript complete except for its final chapter. The letter, I calculated by studying the calendar, would go to London, be reposted, and should reach Mr. Alden early during the week that began Monday, October 7th.

"We studied shipping-lists as well as the calendar. The liner *Olympic* from Southampton was due in New York on Friday, the 11th. Jill would take the train here late Wednesday afternoon and be in New York that same Friday morning. Saying she'd arrived by the *Olympic,* she'd deliver the manuscript to Mr. Alden and camp on his doorstep until she learned what he thought. I felt there were some very good things in it, but I couldn't be sure.

"Well! Having decided that, I said, 'Oh, if only I could go into *complete* seclusion for a week or ten days, not even seeking the man I dote on, while I finished that tricky last chapter!' I thought of going away, but where could I go?

"On the Sunday before Jill was to leave, I was out driving in my carriage. Beyond the Villa de Jarnac there's a long stretch of the road without another house in sight. General Clayton and his wife passed me in *their* carriage, going in the same direction. Mrs. Clayton signalled me to stop, and we both pulled up.

"In rather an emotional way, I'm afraid—I *am* temperamental sometimes; I admit it—I poured out what was on my mind. Mrs. Clayton said, 'Why leave New Orleans at all? Why not come and stay with us? There's a room you'll find very comfortable to write in, and we'd love to have you.' The general said, 'Yes, do that! We can stable your horses and carriage; bring 'em along. You may be working all day, but you'll want a breath of air in the afternoon or the evening.' ''

"The whole *bunch* of you were conspirators, eh?" demanded Lieutenant Trowbridge.

"Yes, I'm afraid that's it. Mrs. Clayton said, 'Tell everybody you're going away, if you like. We have some friends in Mobile, Alabama, who'll back it up if you say you were with them.' I said, 'Yes, but you know the appalling character I'm supposed to be. Somebody thereabouts is bound to catch sight of me; what will the neighbors think?' The general said, 'We are too old, young lady, to give one whistling damn'—yes, he really did say 'one whistling damn' in just those words—'what anybody thinks.' ''

"So you never did leave New Orleans, ma'am?"

"No, I never did. I was glad I'd decided to come here; on Sunday night Clay told me *he* was leaving for New York and a political do. So I couldn't have seen him anyway, that week, and he wouldn't run into Jill when she left on Wednesday.''

"Well, what about it? Have you finished the book?"

"No, not yet. I *couldn't* seem to work for thinking about Clay. But I'd told Jill to phone me here every day and report. And she did. She phoned from New York Friday to say she'd delivered the manuscript to Mr. Alden, and he'd promised to read it over the weekend. There was no occasion for a call until Monday, so that could be cancelled.

"But early Monday afternoon, before she took the train home, she did ring up with the most *glorious* news.''

" 'Glorious' news, ma'am?"

"Mr. Alden *loved* the book! He doesn't even want anything changed: which editors do, usually, I'm told. I'd put in a lot of colorful stories. In my earlier days I did soubrettes for Henry Irving when Irving had lost control of the Lyceum but still played there. Any anecdote about

Irving always goes down well. There was the time Bram Stoker wanted to wipe the floor with Bernard Shaw, and very nearly did. Poor Bram, who died only this year, was once a champion athlete at Trinity College, Dublin. He'd have *slaughtered* that sarcastic devil with the red beard; I wish he had. But I never expected my book to be greeted with a kind of ecstasy.

"All the same, though, Jill seemed worried. She told me how she'd met *her* Mr. Blake—you, Jim—and she had a kind of apprehension the story you were after might be a story about Constance Lambert in disguise."

"Really, Connie," exclaimed Jill, "haven't I explained that already? All Jim wanted, in fact, was a personality piece on your cherished Clay; you know that now; I've told you often enough. Still! If I wanted to claim credit for having premonitions, couldn't I cite that one as accurate?"

"You worry too much, dear." Then Constance addressed the others. "On the phone Monday I told her she worried too much. I told her to take the train and forget it. When she landed back in New Orleans, we couldn't inflict Jill as well as me on the general and his wife. If she ran into some *contretemps* or any situation she couldn't handle, I said, she was to put up at the Grunewald Hotel, where we both stayed when we first arrived. She was to phone me here, and in a day or two we'd both return to the Villa de Jarnac as though we were returning from Alabama. That's where we're going this afternoon.

"There have been some ticklish moments, I know, especially for Jill. But it's worked out just as it should; I flatter myself I planned rather well. This morning I phoned Clay at his office, to tell him I was back in town and invite him to dinner this evening. When he asked me to marry him . . ."

Lieutenant Trowbridge rose up from his chair as though lifted by a sort of slow explosion.

"He asked you to marry him? Still thinking you were Yvonne Brissard?"

"Yes!"

"And *on the telephone?*"

"Yes! Forgive me, Lieutenant; I was too overpower-ingly happy to do anything except *say* yes. Whatever Clay may think, at least he thinks enough of me to give—as the general would put it—not one whistling damn what any-body else thinks. Isn't *that* glorious? Jill's been at me and at me to tell Clay the truth, even if I kept it secret from others. Tonight I can tell him with a clear conscience. And all our troubles will be over."

Jill strode forward and faced her sister.

"You've planned so very well, have you? You've thought of everything? And all our troubles will be over?"

"Yes, dear, I think so."

"Our real troubles, Connie, haven't even begun. You don't see, do you, that we're both standing on the edge of a volcano? And that it's going to blow up underneath us at any minute?"

15

"VOLCANO? Blow up underneath us? Jill what *are* you babbling about?"

"I am not babbling, Connie."

"Then will you kindly explain yourself?"

"I'll try."

The sisters, so very unlike, yet with a certain family resemblance which seemed of the spirit rather than the flesh, made a contrast as they stood outlined in profile against the right-hand window.

Tall Constance, outwardly the more fiery, had charm and attractiveness; but, to one observer at least, she had no more than that. It was Jill, smaller and more rounded, who possessed a sheer allure which unsteadied him: the white-and-pink complexion beneath dark-gold hair, the glance of eyes that could be soft or stubborn, the sense of enormous vitality repressed under that gentle exterior.

Jill looked up at her sister.

"I think you'll agree, Connie, I've rallied round and supported you in everything. Most of it's not been easy. When I've been introduced as your social secretary, or when anybody's bothered to notice me at all, I can almost see the snicker they just manage to hide. I can almost hear what they're thinking. 'Social secretary, eh? Does she make note of an appointment every time the lady of the house goes to bed with her lover?' "

"*Jill!*" cried Constance, genuinely shocked.

"You keep telling *me* to be honest, Connie. Very well; I'll try to prove I can be just as honest as you think you are. *You* may have had a heavenly time playing Yvonne Brissard, and say you don't mind being taken for a harlot so long as the harlot's been successful. *I* minded, thanks very much; I still mind. I begged you to tell Clay the truth. But hasn't it ever occurred to you, as Jim was remarking a while ago, that sooner or later the whole story must come out and be splashed in the press? And the rather awful consequences when that does happen? It *hasn't* occurred to you, has it?"

"Oh, it's occurred to me, dear. And I know how to deal with it when it does."

"Do you really? You're news, Connie; you've always been news. One hint of this, just one hint, and they'll be after you like a pack of jackals!"

"Well, what if they are? Now listen, Jill," pursued Constance, assuming an air of sweet reasonableness, "I've admitted you had a bad time last night. I've admitted that, haven't I? When Jim invited you to the Villa de Jarnac, you went along as though you'd never been near the place before. And you ran all kinds of risks, in the light of what happened. Aunt Emmeline or one of the other servants might have given you away before they realized what was what.

"You had your wits about you, I know. You tipped Emmeline the wink; she kept her mouth shut, and so did the others. When Clay asked you what you were doing there, you said I'd grown impatient with you and sent you back from Mobile to stay at the Grunewald Hotel until I returned. Well, Clay accepted that, according to the story you told me; he packed you off to the Grunewald in his car and thought no more about it.

"But they were all *avoidable* risks, Jill, which you deliberately incurred although you knew what you were risking. You were under no compulsion, I hope? Nobody forced you to go out there in the first place, surely?"

"I . . . I . . . you see, Connie, I . . . !"

"Then do try to face facts, dear; don't make things more difficult for me than you need. Now what's all this fuss and nonsense about being afraid of the press? I've managed 'em before, you know."

"Are you sure you can do it again?" Then Jill flashed out at her. " 'Miss Constance Lambert, last seen as Juliet, has been enacting a very different role for about seven months. What makes you think, Miss Lambert, you have special qualifications for a trade whose true name should begin with the letter *w*?' "

"*Now, really, Jill!*"

"Are you going to tell me my language would make a navvy blush?"

"Not at all, dear, though you might tone it down a little. You're a good soul, sister mine, and very warm-hearted. But you're not practical, as the French would say; you have no eye for business or the box-office. If my next part on the stage is to be Messalina or some other famous nymphomaniac, I shall play it to standing room only for at least a year. *That's* the only effect the press can have. As a matter of sober fact, however . . ."

"Are you off on another flight, Connie?"

"No, my dear. As a matter of sober fact, I was about to say, my next part will be that of Mrs. Clay Blake. A real part, a thrilling part, the part I'm best fitted to play! As for the press, if you're *still* so preoccupied with my technical virtue, here's what we'll do. I'll tell Clay tonight, of course. But nobody else shall get the story unless Jim writes it himself."

"*Jim?*"

"Who else? We can trust *him* to use good taste. Once he's in ahead of the working press," said Constance, beginning excitedly to stride back and forth, "the others will soon stop bothering me and go away. It'll be dead-and-gone news in a day or two. What do you say, Jim? Won't 'Constance-Lambert-as-Yvonne-Brissard' make a neat little feature for *Harper's Weekly*? They call it a scoop, don't they?"

"They call it a scoop in novels and on the stage. Nowhere else."

"Well, Jim, what *do* you say?"

Jim looked her in the eye.

"I don't know, Constance. My editor, Colonel Harvey, did tell me he'd like to beat the wire services with something or other. And there can be no doubt it's news. But the *Weekly* is a family publication which must ignore many of the facts of life. So I don't know. Wait, though! *I've* got an idea, too."

"Yes?"

"I'm having lunch with Clay at one o'clock, after which I'd intended to file my personality story. I can still do that, of course. But, before I do it, I'll phone Colonel Harvey in New York and ask him whether he wants me to go ahead with 'Constance-Lambert-as-Yvonne-Brissard.' If he says yes, then Bob's your uncle. If he says no, I've still got the other story all ready. Will that do?"

"That will be perfectly splendid, I'm sure! And it reminds me. When your American John L. Sullivan was in London some years back, the late King Edward, then Prince of Wales, invited him to one of the Prince's clubs. Your famous prize-fighter—he was knocked out here in New Orleans just twenty years ago, Clay tells me—your famous prize-fighter turned up at the Prince's club accompanied by a young American journalist whom some master of ceremonies refused to admit. Unless they admitted Mr. Brisbane, said the champion, *he* wouldn't go into the damn place himself. So they admitted Mr. Brisbane."

Constance struck an attitude.

"And I'm like the great John L., at least in that respect. Unless the story goes to my own favorite journalist, thanks very much, then nobody gets it at all!"

"But, Connie . . . !"

"Be quiet, Jill! And now, gentlemen, I know you won't mind if I take my little sister upstairs for a private conference that can't interest either the press or the police? It's just occurred to me that—'' She broke off. "Yes, Jim? Something else on your mind?"

Her favorite newspaperman addressed Jill.

"You've been at the Grunewald Hotel since yesterday morning, have you?"

"Yes, Jim. I shall be there until this afternoon, as you heard Connie say. Then we both go back to the villa."

"Where *is* the Grunewald?"

"Baronne Street, quite close to the St. Charles. It's a big white building you can't miss."

"Isn't there a celebrated restaurant, bar, supper-room, something of that sort?"

"You mean the Cave? It's an underground place got up to look exactly like a cave stretching away in the distance. There's a dance floor; they've got entertainers, too, and a small string orchestra. But mainly it's known to connoisseurs for fine food and wines."

"Will you have dinner with me there tonight, Jill?"

"Jim, I'd love to!" Her face lit up, but she hesitated. "That is, if Connie doesn't mind?"

"No, dear, of course I don't mind! Pay your bill at the Grunewald, but don't leave there until after dinner. Then Jim can bring you home in style. And now, gentlemen, you *will* excuse both of us for a few minutes?"

Lieutenant Trowbridge got up heavily.

"Yes, ma'am, we'll excuse you. It's a good thing, Miss Lambert, *you're* not the murderer we're looking for! What with all the voice-changes and tricks you've been showing us for the last half hour *you* could 'a' been the Wicked Voice on the Telephone as sure as shooting!"

"What wicked voice on the telephone? What are you talking about *now?*"

"Just a tricky part of the case, ma'am. Don't matter two hoots; forget it."

"I make one stipulation, though!" Constance said firmly. "If you're having lunch with Clay, Jim, you won't breathe a word of what you know? You won't even hint at it? *I* reserve the privilege of telling him. *Entendu?*"

"Bien entendu. A' voir, chère artiste!"

Taking Jill's arm, Constance led her out and closed the door. Lieutenant Trowbridge wandered for a moment amid the cluttered furniture, then tried to sum up his own state of mind.

"Holy—jumping—gee-whillikers!" he roared, using a thunderous voice for so mild an imprecation. "This thing don't get better; it just gets worse!"

"Having a good time, Lieutenant?"

"No, Franz Josef, I'd NOT call it a good time. I've been sitting here on hot bricks, feeling like an intruder or worse. Any minute, I think, the old general will come charging in to say, 'Cops, eh? What does this cop think he's up to, bringing his big feet into my house?' "

"You're not star-gazing for explanations, are you? You don't seriously think Constance Lambert might be the Voice?"

"No, 'course I don't think so!"

"But it does open up possibilities, doesn't it? We're probably right in postulating the Voice as a man. But it might be a woman. It *could* be Constance Lambert, as you said. In the farthest realm of nightmare it might even be old Mrs. Laird, if she's still actress enough to do a man's voice on the phone."

"Now don't *you* go star-gazin', Franz Josef! I'm confused enough as it is, and that damn voice has got my goat! When I looked for you at the *Sentinel* office a while back, I met the managing editor: big shambling Yankee named Perkins, who kept fiddling with a yellow pencil, but can think straight enough any day in the week.

"It seems there have been some anonymous phone calls to people there. The latest was to a new girl who works in Mr. Perkins's office. The Voice, if it was the same one, accused Mary Rikert of being up to fun and games with her beau in the parish house of the church, and said mother was going to hear all the details. I couldn't get it straight; the girl has hysterics as soon as you ask her anything at all, and I had more important troubles on my mind."

Lieutenant Trowbridge shook his head as though to clear it.

"Also, 'pears to me," he went on, "we no sooner come near a piece of real information than we always get sidetracked. Flossie Yates, now. When I turned up here, didn't you say Flossie knows the answers we want? What did you get out of Flossie, anyway?"

Jim gave him an edited version of that morning's interview with Miss Yates. His companion heard him out in growing excitement.

"That's more smart detective work, Franz Josef! You say you visited her yesterday for a 'purely personal reason.' What was the personal reason? Did you want to know whether Flossie hires out twelve- and thirteen-year-old girls to anybody who's got the dough? *We* could have told you that; we've known at headquarters for some time, though she works out of Storyville and if the girls are proved professionals it's hard to touch anybody. Was that your personal reason?"

"Whatever my reason, Lieutenant, it *was* personal and only to satisfy my own curiosity. She knew I would be going there even before I phoned for an appointment. Somebody had already phoned and tipped her off. Since it wasn't Leo, for whose calls made and received we can account . . ."

"Since it wasn't Mr. Shepley, who else could have known you were going?"

"Exactly. The only reasonable supposition . . . No, that won't work either. We seem to be stymied whichever way we turn."

"Well, we're not going to stay stymied! If you'll just keep your thinking-cap on . . ."

"It's not much use, I'm afraid. I mustn't get a swelled head and believe I'm Sherlock Holmes just because I made a few lucky hits about Constance and Jill."

"They weren't lucky hits, to my way of thinking. You could see what was in front of you; not many people can do that."

"There's a point in front of me now, Lieutenant, except that I can't quite grasp it. When I first met a certain person in this affair, I thought I must have met him somewhere before. I hadn't; it was because he reminded me of someone, but of whom? That doesn't make much sense, does it?"

"It can't make much sense if you don't explain it."

"It won't make much sense even if I do explain it. Meanwhile, I'll go on groping and may touch the meaning. You . . . ?"

"I'm going across the street and have a shot at Flossie myself. Don't worry! I'll use kid gloves; I'll treat her like the lady she thinks she is. But I'll get the truth out of her, so help me!"

All bursting energy, he went to the door with Jim beside him; they strolled along the hall towards the front door.

"I think it'll pay me," said Lieutenant Trowbridge, his hand on the knob, "to keep in pretty close touch with you. Where are you meeting your namesake for lunch?"

"Place called Philippe's. Know it?"

"Everybody knows it. It's quite a joint, strictly for swells. If you're meeting him at one o'clock, don't delay too long 'less you want to be late; it's turned twelve-thirty now."

"One last question, Lieutenant. Are you still as suspicious of my namesake as you were last night?"

"Well . . . now! I guess maybe I must 'a' been in a mood, sort of, like some others I could mention. The mood's not so strong today. I'll still keep an eye on the gentleman, you can bet. But I won't get carried away. Now a last question for *you*, Franz Josef. How the hell," roared Honest Zack, "can a man be shot through the head at the wheel of an automobile when there's nobody there to do it? See you soon, I expect. So long."

The front door opened, and then closed after him.

Jim turned back, to see Jill descending the broad staircase at the rear of the hall. Though she looked rather strained round the eyes, she had regained much of her composure. Impulsively she held out her hand, and Jim took it.

"I've been having quite a time with Connie. I simply can't make her see she needn't go out of her way to *create* scandal. Never mind, though! Am I forgiven for deceiving you?"

"There's nothing to forgive, Jill."

"I really believe you mean that!"

"I mean everything I say to you, my dear; I've meant it since Monday morning. Shall we meet in the lobby of the Grunewald at seven-thirty tonight?"

"Oh, yes, please!"

"Is evening dress obligatory for the Cave, as it is for most such places in London? I brought none with me. If white tie and tails are *de rigueur*, I can always buy something off the peg at one of those shops in Canal Street."

"It's not obligatory, though the older people wear it; dress as you like! —And may I have my hand back, Jim?"

"Not permanently, I hope."

He released her hand. Jill, moving very slightly away from him, stood with her back to a French tapestry whose faded gray-and-green colors evidently depicted the siege of Troy. Again she lifted her eyes.

"You're going to solve this mystery, aren't you, as Count Dimitri did when he exposed Baron von Stubling's treason? You really *are* going to solve the mystery?"

"I hope so, but don't bank on it."

"Is there any way *I* can help you, Jim?"

"I don't know; you might. For instance, leading up to it: does Mathilde de Jarnac Laird know Constance never left New Orleans, but has been staying with the Claytons since Wednesday of last week?"

"No, Jim; there was no occasion to tell her. We've never called at her house, of course; we negotiated things through Leo. And she's never called on us, except once or twice when her son wasn't at home and she could be sure Peter didn't know."

"Young Peter, then, has no idea who Constance really is?"

"Good heavens, of course he hasn't! Do you think his mother would tell him *anything?*"

"Rather a peculiar old girl, in one way or another. To take one aspect of it: should you say Madam Laird is less liberal-minded than the Claytons?"

"In some ways, yes. In other ways, no, distinctly no! The general and his wife, you see, have an absolute obsession about—"

Jill broke off. He had heard no sound of hoofs or wheels in the street. But he did hear the click and rattle of a key in the front door. Alarm flashed into Jill's eyes and seemed to hold her rigid. Jim swung round.

Into the hall, with an effect of shouldering the door rather than merely opening it, strode a craggy, straight-backed old man in frock coat and silk hat, with a gold-headed walking-stick in his hand.

He came to a halt, sweeping off the hat, and drew himself still more upright as he looked at them. Though actually no taller than Jim, he seemed gigantic. And there could be no doubt about the cragginess. He had the white hair and closely cut white beard usually seen in pictures of the late Robert E. Lee. But there seemed none of the kindliness or good nature we associate with a man once known as Marse Robert; quite the reverse.

Jill found her voice.

"Good morning, General Clayton!" she said, with a kind of false brightness. "May I present Mr. James Blake, who represents *Harper's Weekly* in New York? Mr. Blake, General Clayton."

If age had not shrunk Hellcat Tom Clayton, neither had it dimmed his glacial eye or much weakened the pitch of his voice.

"You are from the North, sir?" he asked.

Jim met that level stare.

"I am, sir."

And then Jill rushed in.

"This gentleman was *born* in the North, General Clayton. But he took his degree at William and Mary. A Virginia ancestor of his was one of the college's founders in 1693."

"Indeed?" said General Clayton. "Is it possible, sir, you can recall the name of that particular ancestor?"

"His name, sir, was Septimus Blake."

Some slightly different expression stirred in the glacial face. General Clayton shifted from one foot to the other.

"Septimus Blake?" he repeated. "Squire Blake of Pemberton Hall, Roanoke, whose portrait may now be seen at Richmond?"

"I believe so."

There was a slight, heavy pause.

"My own forebears were Virginians, sir," said Hellcat Tom, suddenly extending his hand. "May I bid you welcome to my house, Mr. Blake, where you will ever find me happy to receive you? But I ask your pardon; I should have known. You have too much the manner and bearing of a gentleman, sir, to be called Yankee in any form or degree."

There seemed no proper reply to this. A frightened maid, who had already come scurrying in with Jim's hat, handed it over in both deference and relief as he made his farewells.

They ushered him to the front door. He went down the steps and across the street to his car, headed for Philippe's, headed for lunch, and headed for another cloudburst of trouble by 2:30 that afternoon.

PART FOUR:

QUEST OF A MURDERER

16

SOME CHURCH CLOCK of the Vieux Carré was striking two as Clay and Jim finished lunch at Philippe's.

They ate under the open sky, where tables had been set out in a patio of gray flagstones and flowering plants. Though there was a fairly large crowd, both for the patio and for the main dining-room indoors, they had been given a favored table somewhat apart from the others. And they had been attended by Philippe himself, great-grandson of the restaurant's founder. Not far away the vast, empty shell of the once great St. Louis Hotel—still fronting Royal Street for a block's length, though now abandoned to rats and ruin—towered up under its balloon-like dome.

Both Clay and Jim ate lightly, consuming only half a bottle of Anjou between them. Not until the coffee had been brought did Clay so much as refer to any matter of relevancy or moment.

Though hardly the haunted, hag-ridden figure of last night, he had much on his mind. Clay's manner seemed almost too easy; he smiled too often. Once he had been called away briefly to the telephone inside, preserving a mask-like face on his return. Then, with coffee poured and cigarettes lighted, he faced his companion earnestly across the table.

"Yvonne's back in town," he began. "She phoned my office this morning, and caught me just coming in again half an hour after you'd phoned and missed me."

225

"You were very glad to hear from her, I imagine. Where was she phoning from?"

"From the villa, I suppose; where else would she be? And 'glad,' Jim, is a very mild word. I asked her to marry me—bang, just like that!—and she said yes. It's not entirely unexpected, is it?"

"Not entirely, no. You said last night you had come to a decision about her, and that seemed a possible decision. Heartiest congratulations, Clay! I know you'll be very happy!"

"I know it, too, and I'm a happy man now. An end of all deception and furtiveness, thank God! Out in the open at last, and doing what I should have done long ago! I'm having dinner with her tonight, so that we can make some plans for the future. Wouldn't care to join us, would you?"

"Thanks, but I'm having dinner with—" Jim had almost said "her sister," but he corrected himself smoothly. "I'm having dinner with Jill in the Cave at the Grunewald. We'll see you afterwards, though. If there should be any champagne available to toast the bride . . ."

"There'll be champagne by the bucket, I promise you! *Gloria in excelsis,* Jim, I'm on top of the world!"

Jim glanced round. At a table on the far side of the patio he thought he had caught sight of a back that looked familiar. But there was nobody near them, nobody within possible earshot.

"Forgive me for introducing the unpleasant, but what about that other matter? The Wicked Voice and its threats if you don't withdraw your candidacy today?"

Tall, fair-haired, mobile of eye and mouth, Clay smote his fist on the table.

"Yesterday morning," he said, "I told the Wicked Voice it could go to hell and slammed the receiver. I'm still of the same mind, only more so. Withdraw my candidacy? In a pig's eye I will! The Wicked Voice may do its damnedest; let it try. Once you knuckle under to threats, once you knuckle under to *anybody*, he's got you on the run and he knows it. I don't amount to much, I know, but I can stand fast and I will! As for the Wicked Voice's latest trick . . ."

"S-ss-t, gently, and not so loud! I think we're going to have visitors!"

Across the patio and among the tables moved Mathilde de Jarnac Laird, closely attended by her bulky son. Though she had a casual air of drifting, she was in fact drifting straight towards their table.

Both Jim and Clay rose up. As soon as Jim encountered Peter Laird for the third time, something clicked like a light-switch in his brain. Clay addressed the poised, fashionable lady with great heartiness.

"Ah, Mrs. Laird! How are you, Pete? Sit down and join us for coffee, won't you?"

"Hello, Clay. And the *other* Mr. Blake. We've just had coffee, thank you, but I *will* sit down for a moment, if I may."

A waiter had darted forward to hold a chair for her. Indicating with her gesture that Peter required no such luxury, she seated herself and contemplated them.

"When you have been as close to any person as I have always been to Leo Shepley (he called me Aunt Mathilde, you know), it seems the height of the unfeeling to take luncheon at a public restaurant the day after his death. But there's always shopping to do, and one must eat *somewhere*. What a dreadful business, Clay! About Leo, I mean. Are the police holding anyone? Do they even suspect anyone?"

"No, they're not holding anyone. And, so far, the only person they seem to suspect is myself."

"*You?* How utterly absurd! Why should they suspect *you?*"

"Mainly, I think, because I was there conveniently on hand before anybody else arrived, and can't supply an alibi for some crucial moments. There's no other possible reason, God knows!"

"Tell *me* something, Clay," interjected Peter, looking up from under his eyebrows. "Why did you go out to

Yvonne's in the first place? Your joy and delight wasn't there, was she?''

"No, Pete, she wasn't there. How do you know she wasn't there?''

"You're forgetting, aren't you? I was there myself, wasn't I, being questioned by that cop along with the rest of you?''

"Yes; sorry; I was forgetting!''

"To tell you the truth''—Peter made a face—"I knew she wasn't there before Raoul and I chased in.''

"How did you learn that?''

"Backstairs gossip. Every maid at our place is as fascinated by Y.B. and her doings as though she had all Y.B.'s talents for her own.''

"Be quiet, Peter!'' his mother said sharply. "Such talk does no credit either to you or to your upbringing. I'll hear no more of it; be quiet!''

Then she looked at Jim, and a smile softened her features.

"When we met you in Alec's office yesterday morning, Mr. Blake, I was not very gracious, I'm afraid. But I had no idea who you were. You're a successful author, among other things, as Alec soon informed us in your absence. May I ask whether you're investigating Leo's death with a view to publication?''

"Certainly not with a view to publication, Mrs. Laird!''

"But you *are* investigating?'' Her eyes would not let go. "What have you learned about us, Mr. Blake? In particular, what have you learned about *me?*''

"Only that you enjoy reading plays, as so many of us do.''

"Only enjoy reading them? Your researches, Mr. Blake, must surely have unearthed the sinister revelation that I was once an amateur actress of no inconsiderable talent? It does seem to run in the family.''

"Yes, madam?''

"Indeed it does. Alec, my severe and formal nephew, has some slight gift along that line, though he has employed it only for charitable entertainments in aid of the

Presbyterian Church. He once gave a capital performance as a comic clergyman whose parishioners are scandalized when someone finds a pack of cards in the tail pocket of their pastor's coat.'' An edge of malice glittered behind her smile. '' 'How well you play a hypocrite!' I said to him, 'the part just suits you.' And he said—well, he made some ingenious retort. He's clever, I give him that, even if he's so fond of power he keeps poor Sylvia completely under his thumb!

"Strangely, Mr. Blake, even Peter is not without talent. I say 'strangely' because of his obvious natural clumsiness and the fact that he lacks the glib tongue of the de Jarnacs or the Lairds. But he did quite well as Tony Lumpkin in *She Stoops to Conquer;* the part suited *him.*''

"Now look, Mother . . . !''

"*Be quiet,* I said. You are sure, Mr. Blake—and you, Clay—you can tell me nothing more about Leo's death?''

"I don't know one other thing, I swear!'' said Clay.

"Then we won't keep you from your coffee. But perhaps, my dear Clay, *I* can help *you* a little.''

"Help me?''

"Oh, not in the matter of poor Leo, which is so completely senseless I sometimes think it can't have happened, and Peter agrees with me. No; this concerns you and your private affairs; it's more personal. One of these days, Clay,'' she looked hard at him, "you are going to get a most staggering surprise. It won't displease you, though it may throw you off balance for a moment. In fact, it should lift you into a higher heaven than any you have yet dreamed of!

"About Leo, however, one thing *does* surprise me. If he had something terrible on his mind, as by general report he must have had, I should have expected him to come to *me* with it, rather than pelt so hard for the home of a woman who must remain nameless. 'Cherish Aunt Mathilde!' he used to say. 'If you have a problem, take it to Aunt Mathilde.' What went wrong with him in the darkest hour?''

She rose up, adjusting the fur-piece round her neck.

"And now, gentlemen, we must bid you goodbye. Remember me, Mr. Blake, if you remember me at all, as an old witch who used white magic in prophesying only for people's good. Come along, Peter. Goodbye, goodbye, *good*bye."

And away they went. Clay stared after them, crushing out his cigarette in the ashtray.

"Now what was that all about? What did she mean, exactly? And, come to think of it, what was *I* saying when Madam Ir—when she interrupted?"

"Something about the Voice's latest trick."

"Yes, of course!" An odd look flashed into Clay's eyes. "Some while ago, you remember, I was called inside to the telephone? Philippe escorted me to it. The phone's in a little booth under the stairs. I picked up the receiver, and . . ."

"The Wicked Voice? Threatening again?"

"Not threatening, exactly. Still gloating, but more challenging than threatening, and even a little conciliatory."

"What did *you* say, Clay?"

"I didn't have a chance to say anything except the noise like 'Ug?' we all make when we pick up a receiver without being sure who's at the other end."

"Well?"

"My unknown friend said: 'Listen to me, and don't interrupt. How's your courage? If you want to prove you've got any, go to number 114-b Conti Street. It's a perfectly respectable place in a perfectly respectable neighborhood, run by a respectable man. Pay a quarter; go inside; try your skill. You've got physical guts, maybe; how's your mental fibre? At least you're in no danger from the baseballs. If you accept this dare, good fool, then I may not do what I ought to do. Don't forget the address: 114-b Conti Street.' And then *he* hung up on *me*."

"Where's 114-b Conti Street? And what's all this about being in no danger from baseballs?"

"The address is just around the corner; we could walk

there in five minutes. I don't understand the part about baseballs, but I used to be a pretty fair pitcher.''

"Are you going?"

"You bet I'm going, old son! Since I was a boy, Jim, I've never been able to pass up a dare. And I want to see what the Voice does when I spit in his eye. Care to come along?"

"With pleasure!" Jim said heartily. "If I can catch somebody's attention, I'll just call for the bill . . . ."

"You'll do nothing of the kind; I invited you. —Philippe!"

A few minutes later, with the bill paid, they went out through the body of the restaurant into the street.

Though the sky remained overcast, still no rain had fallen. With a subdued kind of relish Clay led his companion south to Royal Street and then turned to the right. Another right-hand turn brought them into Conti Street, which ran parallel with St. Louis on the side towards Canal.

More pastel-colored houses, some shop-fronts and some private dwellings, stretched away to the north. Perhaps a little more than five minutes' walk, keeping to the right-hand pavement, brought them abreast of 114-b.

"Is this all right, Clay? Your secretary said you had a political meeting this afternoon."

"Yes, but that's at three o'clock. It's not quite two-thirty now. Look!"

Their destination occupied premises between an old-fashioned drug-store on the far side and, on the near side, a confectioner's conspicuously advertising pralines behind the dummy figure of a colored Mammy with a red bandana round her head.

Housed in a good-sized if temporary-looking structure, rather higher and broader than most buildings thereabouts, appeared what a sign across the façade described as *Test Your Eye: A Trial of Skill* above the representation of crossed baseball bats and a fielder's glove.

In the glass-enclosed pay-box, rather like the pay-box at a theatre, sat a fat elderly man with a goatee beard.

"It's Major Magruder!" exclaimed Clay, striding up to the wicket of the glass cage. "I didn't know . . . hello, Major! What game are you operating these days?"

"Afternoon, Mr. Blake," said Major Magruder, "and hope you're interested. It's just what the sign says: a machine that pitches to you. Self-loading, self-operating, and automatic."

"How does it work?"

"Six pitches for a quarter; you stand and lam at 'em with one of the bats inside. The distance it pitches, mind, ain't *quite* as long as the distance between the mound and home plate, but it's a pretty fair piece. They'd all be strikes if you let 'em go by: a little above waist-high, dead over the plate, and not thrown too fast."

Jim moved past Clay and slid half a dollar through the grill.

"Mr. Blake and I," he said, "would both like a whirl at it. How do we set the machine in motion?"

"*I* set it in motion. As soon as you're both inside, I'll count to twenty and then press this button here. I can calc'late just how long the pitches'll take, and I can hear the bat, too. When the first of you's taken his swats, I'll count another twenty and press the button again. Just imagine the metal arm is Walter Johnson, though you won't be meetin' anything like the Big Train's speed. Thank'ee kindly, gentlemen; go on in."

Clay led the way through a cramped little entry into the blaze of light beyond.

It was a lofty shed which would carry many echoes, illuminated by concealed electric bulbs. At the far end, in what appeared to be a padded rear wall, they could see a dark aperture like an open doorway. In the middle of the aperture loomed some box-like metal contrivance which grotesquely suggested an altar.

On the wooden floor, some thirty-odd feet back from the metal contrivance at the end, a pentagon for home plate had been drawn in white paint. To one side lay several medium-weight bats.

"I don't like this place," Clay said suddenly. "It's got a funny damn *feel* about it, if you ask me. Major Magruder's all right; I know him; but . . ."

"You go first, will you? Pick up one of those bats and face Walter Johnson. The major's almost had time to count twenty, even if he's counting very slowly. I'll stand to the left of you and a little way back."

Clay took a bat at random and squared himself beside the painted plate.

"I can't even hit the thing, probably; haven't touched a bat since I was in college. Never mind; here we go!"

A shiny white baseball appeared up over the back of the altar, where metal glinted faintly. After seeming to hang there for an instant, it flew towards the plate: some few inches above waist-high, not particularly fast, and straight in the groove.

Clay swung hard at it, but there was no clean crack; he swung only into a murderous foul-tip. The ball whacked hard against the wall behind them, which was not padded; it clattered to the floor and bounced amid a fusillade of echoes.

"I still don't like this," Clay declared. "It's too dark in that space behind the machine-thing. But I'll get your money's worth whatever happens. How long between the pitches?"

About twelve seconds, Jim estimated. Another baseball appeared out of nowhere and bore down. This time Clay met it squarely, for what on any field would have been a clean two-base hit to left center. Padded wall or no, the ball smote hard and rebounded in more echoing din.

The third pitch Clay missed completely. But it had to land somewhere; noise never ceased.

"I'll get the next one," he promised. "Trying too hard, that's all. It's only a damn machine, you know. Anyway, the World Series is over."

And then a commonplace play-scene suddenly altered its tempo.

Jim, standing to the batter's left, was keeping alert for

hits that might rebound from the side wall and fly at his head. After the first two pitches he had scarcely glanced at the aperture with the machine.

But he glanced now, and could hardly believe his eyes. There was something besides the machine in that aperture.

A man, face grotesquely daubed to darkness with dirt or soot, stood in semi-darkness a little to the right of the pitching apparatus and behind it. He held a light rifle, which he was raising to his shoulder. And he was turning the rifle not towards Clay Blake, but towards Jim.

Several things ran fast to their end at once. A fourth baseball appeared from nowhere. There was a thud and rattle as Clay dropped his bat. The baseball flew from the machine; Clay caught it with a flat smack against his left palm. As the man with the daubed face fitted rifle to shoulder, drawing his sights on Jim's forehead, Clay sighted, too. Then, with a powerful sidearm delivery, he threw.

The ball, a blinding white streak, took Daubed-face full in the middle of the stomach. Daubed-face pitched backwards, doubled up as though kicked by a mule. His rifle struck the floor before he did, its hair-trigger jarring and exploding the cartridge. At the lash of the shot among all other sounds, stout Major Magruder ran in from the entry, his chin-beard waggling, and stopped, appalled.

"What you doin'?" he shouted. "What you *doin'*, fergossake?"

Almost instantly he jumped aside to avoid a fifth baseball, which flashed out of the machine and whizzed past both Clay and the major before it struck the front wall. As Daubed-face lay inertly beyond the machine, a second and burlier figure with a mud-daubed mask appeared above the recumbent rifleman, and started to drag him out by some back way.

In from the front entrance, enraged, charged none other than Lieutenant Zack Trowbridge, his face all strawberry-rash.

"Stop!" he bellowed to Daubed-face Two, who was still dragging at Daubed-face One. "In the name o' the law, stop!"

He raced for the aperture, dragging an Iver-Johnson .45 out of his hip-pocket holster, and swerving just in time to avoid a sixth baseball, which Clay caught. Daubed-face One, Daubed-face Two, and Lieutenant Trowbridge all disappeared.

"It can't work again," sputtered Major Magruder, almost in tears, " 'less I press the button. But I don't reckon you *want* it pressed again, do you? You can claim a quarter back, if you want it."

"As a matter of fact, Major," Jim assured him, "it won't be necessary either to reactivate the machine or to refund the quarter. Thanks, Clay! That was quick thinking; you quite literally saved my life."

"But *why?*" demanded Clay, dropping the baseball and pressing both hands to the sides of his head. "Couple of cheap hoodlums somebody hired. One of 'em's knocked silly; Zack'll grab *him* even if he misses the other. But why'd the Voice put 'em up to it? Since I was the one they wanted, why go for you?"

"Are you sure you were the one they wanted, Clay? Don't you see what must have happened this time?"

"No, damned if I do!"

Major Magruder had discreetly withdrawn. Jim looked his companion up and down.

"Well, we can easily prove it by questioning Philippe," he went on, "but I should risk a small bet before we do. You were called to the telephone. Though everybody knows you as Clay, which is short for your middle name, your actual first name is James, the same as mine. And that's well known, too. When the Voice asked to speak to Mr. James Blake . . ."

"Are you saying . . . ?"

"Yes. Several persons have told us there can't be any confusion between our names. But there can be. There has been. I didn't have to give my name to Philippe or anybody else. I asked for Mr. Blake's table, as your secretary told me, and was escorted there without further parley. So far as Philippe knew, my name might have been Jones or Brown or Robinson or Woodrow Wilson.''

Clay picked up the fallen bat, lashing it viciously at the air as though to lash at his troubles, before lowering it and facing Jim with the look of a man half out of his wits.

''But this just gets crazier as it goes along! You think the Voice, the one who's been doing all the phoning, is also the murderer?''

''I'm convinced of it. This time, by your own report, you didn't say anything except a sound like 'Ug.' He had no chance to realize he was speaking to the wrong man.''

''But why you? Why should the Voice want to kill you?''

''He must think I know who he is.''

''And do you?''

''That, Clay, is what a friend of yours would call tragic irony. Just after lunch, for instance, I suddenly thought I saw *how* the murder could have been done, the thing that's been driving Zack Trowbridge up the wall. It's simple; it's so damnably and essentially simple it should have occurred to us long ago.''

''It hasn't occurred to *me*. Are you going to enlighten the feebleminded?''

''Not just yet, since at the moment there doesn't seem to be any conceivable way of proving it.''

Jim turned towards the entry, then hesitated and turned back again.

''You asked me whether I know the murderer's identity. Well, I don't. Unless I've missed some fact of glaring importance, which is possible and even probable, the evidence doesn't seem to indicate any particular person; or, rather, the evidence seems to point in three or four directions at once. It might be X, it might be Y, it might be Z; but where's the clear clue to show which?

"The irony, mentioned a moment ago, is that I *can't* be sure who our quarry is. And yet for some mysterious reason he thinks I do know. He's had one go at trying to kill me, and he may try again. Yes, Clay, he may try again."

17

JIM HAD a clear connection. The voice of Colonel Harvey in faraway New York was small but strident, as though the man himself had been shrunk to lead-soldier size by magic and were imprisoned in the telephone.

"You say," he demanded, "Constance Lambert actually authorizes this? She's willing to have me publish?"

"More than willing; she's anxious to have you publish."

"That's a pity, because we can't touch it. The woman's an artist, Jim; she shouldn't be allowed to cut her own throat. Still, I gather, she and Clay Blake *have* been carrying on?"

"If you want to put it like that. But they're going to get married."

"Which doesn't in the least alter the principle of the thing, as John Q. Public will see it. If this story comes out with all details, she'll never be able to play in America again. The League of Women Against Something-or-other will blacklist her at every theatre in Klaw and Erlanger's chain." Colonel Harvey reflected. "We'll work craftily, Jim, and see how the papers play it when the story does break; there may be a follow-up for us. Meanwhile, there's the personality piece. Shall I transfer this call to Ken Lefferts for rewrite?"

"I prefer to write my own copy, thanks. And it's ready."

"What have you done?"

Jim glanced round the room.

"What I always do, and must continue to do until somebody invents a portable typewriter I can take with me. Here at the St. Charles, as at every good hotel, there's a public stenographer and notary public."

"Yes, of course. Well?"

"At two-thirty, an hour ago, there was a dust-up at some place where they've got a baseball-pitching machine . . ."

"You always did have the bull luck to be in the middle of things!"

"It wasn't as much fun as all that, Colonel. I broke away, having work on my mind. I paid the public stenographer for half an hour's use of her typewriter, and turned out twenty-five hundred words demonstrating that Clay Blake's an embryonic statesman who'll be a shining light in the Sixty-third Congress. The story's on the telephone table in front of me."

"Do you want somebody to take it down over the phone? I'm no believer in economy, but . . . !"

"No, not that way either. I couldn't help noticing a Western Union office on the side of the street opposite the hotel only a few doors away. I can send copy by wire at a very small fraction of what it would cost by phone; it'll be in your hands by four-thirty at the latest. And now, if you've got no further instructions, I'll get on with the job."

"No, no further instructions, except: keep your eyes peeled for a follow-up. Good luck, Jim!"

The line went dead. With several typed sheets in his pocket, Jim descended to the lobby and made for the telegraph office across the way. Though still not sure where St. Charles Street became St. Charles Avenue, he pushed through the revolving door on that side and almost ran full tilt into Charley Emerson.

Charley, that wiry little terrier of a man with the gray-black patches of hair on a fire-scarred head, seemed engrossed and enwrapped.

"Hello, Jim. Couldn't keep away after all, you see. Just had to say ha-ha among the trumpets!"

"I didn't really expect to see you, Charley. But I'm not dead with astonishment. What's on your mind now?"

"Can't stop for more than a second or two; I'm after a story."

"I understood you weren't allowed to touch the murder."

"I'm not. But there's been other news in sight all the time. These anonymous phone calls to people at the *Sentinel* . . ."

"You're after that?"

"Very much so. To hear Bart Perkins talk, and Harry Furnival, too—Harry's the city editor—you'd think there had been a reign of terror. Nothing of the kind, Jim! There have been only three calls, including the one to Mary Rikert: never to anybody of importance, and the caller never carries out the threats he makes. Sounds like fright and intimidation just for the hell of it.

"On the other hand, this character they call the phone-fiend has made a high score. One poor old man in the business office was accused of stealing petty cash; he went home and hanged himself. A middle-aged woman who helps with the society news lost her husband some months back. The phone-fiend said she'd poisoned her husband, and that evidence of it was going to the D.A. The lead I've got now . . ."

"Speaking of leads, Charley: when they wouldn't turn you loose on the murder, did you really threaten to go over to the opposition and take the story elsewhere?"

"I made some bluff at it, not being one of God's saints. There's four of 'em: the *Picayune* and the *Times Democrat* in the morning; the *Item* and the *States* in the evening. They'd all be glad to grab old Charley as a free-lance. But I didn't mean one damn word I said, to tell you the truth. Loyalties die hard, Jim, and Alec Laird's been too decent for me to bite the hand that used to feed me.

"You'll excuse me if I chase along now, won't you? The woman who lost her husband is at home this afternoon; I can get a streetcar down there at the corner. And I've got a hot tip. She thinks the phone-fiend *is* a woman!"

"Lord, Charley! Any evidence of that?"

"She thinks there's evidence, at least. It may not be murder, but it's some story if I can trace the phone-fiend and it does happen to be a woman! Making baseless accusations just to terrify is as bad as murder, don't you think? Now all the best, Jim, and cheer-ho!"

Away he went towards the car-stop, weaving in and out among other pedestrians. Jim crossed the road, where twenty more strides took him to the great plate-glass window bearing the name of the Western Union Telegraph Company in white-enamelled letters.

It was a slack time of day. Both the girl behind the counter and the alert young telegraph operator who joined their conversation were deeply fascinated with Jim's proposal to send his story by wire. When he had explained certain terms which would be intelligible to any copy-desk if not to the average telegrapher, and paid the fee required, his typed sheets were borne away. The telegrapher bent absorbedly over a well-lighted desk in a corner behind the counter. The chatter and click of the key began to pulse against a quiet hum of afternoon traffic.

Jim wheeled round from the counter towards the big plate-glass window. Not for the first time that day he had a feeling of being watched and spied on. But once again, it seemed, he must have been mistaken.

Crossing the street towards the telegraph office came nobody more secret or furtive than Lieutenant Trowbridge, attended by the Sergeant Peters who had been on duty the night before. While Sergeant Peters held open the door, his superior officer strode in and greeted Jim affably.

"Well, well, Franz Josef, and how's the Emperor of Austria this afternoon?"

He indicated some chairs at the near end of a two-sided flat-topped desk close to the window. Impelling Jim into one of the chairs, he bent forward and lowered his voice.

"Not very cooperative, are you? You ducked out of Major Magruder's latest business venture 'fore I had a chance to say anything about the two crooks somebody set on you.''

Jim waved his hand towards the chattering telegraph key.

''That's the reason I ducked out,'' he replied in the same low tone. ''Cheap hoodlums, Clay called them, as no doubt they were? The major, I take it, had nothing to do with what they were up to?''

''Not a thing! They got in through the back way, from an alley. They were laying for you.''

''You caught 'em, did you?''

''I caught one of 'em, who's in the hospital. If *you* got a pitcher's fast one square in the belly from not much more'n thirty feet away, you'd be in the hospital, too. The other one dodged me, but I can trace him easy enough.

''You should 'a' stayed, Franz Josef! I had quite a talk with Mr. Clay Blake before *he* had to leave for a political do. He's quite a sane and sensible gentleman, when you get right down to it.''

''Listen, Lieutenant. You were under no pledge of secrecy, of course. When you talked to Clay, though, I hope you didn't betray what you learned at the general's. You didn't tell him 'Yvonne Brissard' is Constance Lambert, or that Jill Matthews is her sister?''

''No, no, I didn't let on! I'm not a gentleman and never claimed to be, but I do have one or two gentlemanly instincts kicking around. That's her private affair; let her handle it. But I've got some news for you!''

''Yes?''

''Since we met the last time, I've seen both the men I had tracing Mr. Shepley's movements yesterday afternoon and evening. Whatever our information's been so far, he *didn't* go on any drinkin' tour of Bourbon Street. He went to his club, where they get drunk in peace and quiet. The club's on Louisiana Avenue in the Garden District.

''But he didn't get drunk either. He had maybe two or three drinks. He sat down by himself without speaking to anybody, or shot some pool all alone, too. About five o'clock he made a phone call, and sat down to think again.

Half or three quarters of an hour later, at five-thirty or a quarter to six, he got up and went out. His car was in the street; he drove away. And that's where we lose him.''

"Lose him completely?"

"Right bang into the blue! So far, at least, we can't find out where he went or what he was doing between, say, a quarter to six, when he left the club, and a few minutes past ten last night, when he went hell-roaring out to Miss Lambert's place in that red Raceabout. We just don't know.''

"If it comes to that, Lieutenant, we don't know your movements either.''

"What have my movements got to do with it?"

"Probably nothing, except that you've chosen to keep them mysterious. *You* turned up not long after the shot was fired and the car went smash. But we've heard no mention of what you were doing there.''

Lieutenant Trowbridge had ceased to bristle.

"Nothing mysterious about it; never was! You know, Franz Josef, people still tend to think of cars as a rich man's plaything. And that's not so.''

"It isn't?"

"Not any longer. Henry Ford's selling *his* car at one hell of a lick. Are you following me?"

"Closely."

"At City Hall," explained the lieutenant, eyeing his companion hypnotically, "there's an Assistant D.A. named Kestevan. It's true he's got a little money of his own; he wouldn't be in the poorhouse even if he hadn't studied law. But he's no Croesus or J. P. Morgan. Well, Mr. Kestevan bought a Ford tourer, four doors and all; goes everywhere in it, not just to the country. He's a friendly sort; he's given me a lift more'n once.

"All right! Last night, a few minutes before nine, there was a phone call to my office. Some anonymous caller wanted to speak to the most experienced detective on the Force.''

"Don't tell me, Lieutenant, *you've* had a message from the Voice?"

Lieutenant Trowbridge was making excited gestures, his strawberry-rash coming up.

"I didn't get it personally, no. But I didn't laugh, later, when I heard about the goddamn Voice.

"At that time, as an ordinary thing, there wouldn't 'a' been anybody at the office. There wasn't anybody, in fact, except the charwoman cleaning up. She answered the phone. If an experienced detective would go out to the Villa de Jarnac as soon as possible after ten o'clock, the caller said, he'd find 'something damnable.' Those were the words: something damnable. And there was something about it that scared the britches off the charwoman. I looked in a little later, just as she finished cleaning, and she told me.

"Well, what was I going to do? Unless you get a lift, there's no way out to that place except by cab. My boss would never pass expense money if I took a cab on the strength of an anonymous tip.

"But it solved itself. I was leaving the office, near enough to half-past nine, when I met Mr. Kestevan, who'd been working late on a case. That was when I remembered he's got a place out near the mouth of Bayou St. John. He said he was going home, and asked if he could drop me some place. There you are; that's the whole story, and I hope it's cleared up."

"Yes, thanks; it's cleared up. Any more news, Lieutenant?"

"A little; not much, but a little. I haven't seen you to talk to, have I, since I put the squeeze on Flossie Yates? I haven't broken her yet, I admit, though she ought to cooperate before long. But what excited me, what really got me going, was a remark Mr. Clay Blake made during our talk."

For the first time the lieutenant seemed to become fully aware of Sergeant Peters.

"Peters," he said, "the maestro and I want to have a little private confab about this thing. Run along to City

Hall, will you? I'll look in on you before I knock off for the day.''

The stolid Peters nodded without comment. He opened the glass door, closed it behind him, and moved off over the pavement to cross the street.

Zack Trowbridge pounced again.

''Though you weren't just sure who's been doing the dirty work, Mr. Blake said, you had a pretty good idea HOW it was done! Oh, Lordy God and everything! Is that true?''

Jim still held the fountain-pen with which he had made a last-moment correction in his copy before handing it over. Though he had put the cap on the pen, he had not returned it to his pocket. He turned towards the counter and the chattering telegraph key beyond.

''Yes, it's true. The coat was clean, Lieutenant! I particularly noted that the coat was clean.''

''What coat was clean? What are you talking about?''

''The problem, you see, may be in finding material proof. There's the bullet-hole, of course, though that's a mere detail.''

''What bullet-hole, Franz Josef? The only bullet-hole I've heard about is the one in Mr. Shepley's head. I've got the autopsy report now; and I've got the bullet, too, after they took it out with a forceps. It's a .38 slug, but what does *that* prove? Will you turn around and look at me, for God's sake?''

Jim, standing at the counter and seeming to study it, did turn. But he did not look directly at Lieutenant Trowbridge; he looked out through the big plate-glass window.

''Sergeant Peters,'' he said in a startled voice, ''Sergeant Peters has only just crossed the street! He's over there and headed west, but he's only just crossed!''

''Sure he's only just crossed! Peters has no wings, any more'n the rest of us. How far away did you expect him to get, in a matter o' ten or twelve seconds?''

''The same distance as—'' Jim stopped suddenly, feeling as though he had been walloped over the head. The fountain-pen dropped from his fingers and clinked on the floor. He stood motionless, rigid, with vivid images rushing back to him.

"What a turnip I've been! What a thundering dunce! The whole business was played out in front of me, yet I never saw the meaning until this minute! Once that key turns and the door opens, every fact is in its proper place as well as easy to interpret. Yes, Lieutenant, I was lucky enough to hit on the 'how.' I now see who, with more than a suggestion of why! And I am going to tell you about it."

The telegraph operator and the girl attendant paid them no attention. The telegrapher was transmitting the last page of Jim's copy; the girl bent above him, reading over his shoulder.

With a great parade of secrecy Jim led Lieutenant Trowbridge to one of the chairs at the desk near the window. The lieutenant sat down; Jim sat opposite.

"Lieutenant," he said in a low voice, "this scene here is all wrong. It oughtn't to be a telegraph office at four o'clock in the afternoon. It ought to be a certain sitting-room in Baker Street. Gaslight instead of electricity. A bright fire burning; fog outside. The acid-stained chemical table, the cigars in the coal-scuttle, the tobacco in the toe of the Persian slipper . . ."

Zack Trowbridge caught the mood with enthusiasm.

"And the hansom down at the door!" he supplied. "The visitor who comes upstairs and keels over in a faint on the hearthrug! And Watson revives him with brandy; he's a heller for brandy, Watson is! You don't have to tell me; I know. Nobody's keener on those stories than I am; almost as keen as I am on *The Count of Monte Carlo*. Well?"

"However, since we can't have that, and must be content with our telegraph office as a background for revelations . . ."

"I'm hopin' for revelations," said the other. "I'm damn well *expectin'* revelations, and I mean to get 'em! But, before you start to reveal, one question. Who knew you were having lunch with Clay Blake today, and when, and where, so that the mixup could occur? I knew it; the two ladies knew it; who else knew?''

"Only one person, so far as I remember, and that fact needs interpretation, too. Now listen, please, and we'll see what we can make of it.''

Jim began to talk.

St. Charles Line streetcars clanged past east and west. Lieutenant Trowbridge's expression, at first thunderstruck, ran a gamut from disbelief through wonder to fascinated interest, and, finally, conviction. The telegraph instrument had long since ceased to click when he sat up straight and snapped his fingers.

"You've hit it, Franz Josef! When you first started, mind, I wondered if you might have lost some of your marbles. But it makes sense, and it's the only thing that does make sense out of all the foolishness! Some very peculiar characters have been known to hang around in that quarter, though nobody thought anything about it in view of the profession involved. But there's a side of it that bothers me. More than one person, eh, has been mixed up in the murder?''

"No, Lieutenant. As I've tried to indicate, there is only one guilty party. The culprit had help, it's true, but was not helped by any person who had the remotest idea it was murder, or that any crime had been committed at all. We've been hoaxed, and beautifully hoaxed, by a smooth-looking, murderous-minded operator who's hoaxed everybody else, too. It's time to end that hoaxing.''

"Yes, that's just it! How do we end it?''

"Only, I'm afraid, by setting the trap I've just finished outlining.''

"But we can't do that!''

"Why can't we do it?''

"Because it's too damn dangerous, that's why! Listen! You're having dinner with the young lady you're so fond of? Right?''

"Right. What if I am?''

"Not thirty minutes ago I bumped into her on Canal Street. She said she was shopping for a new dress to wear tonight. When I told her you'd have got a bullet through your dome at Major Magruder's if Clay Blake hadn't landed a baseball in that crook's solar plexus, I thought she'd have a fit."

"You told her that?"

"It's no secret, is it?"

"Then one more little risk can't do us any harm. Just drop a word in the right quarter, and that will set the trap. You can go even further, Lieutenant." Jim sketched out an addition to the plan. "You want to nab the murderer, don't you?"

"All right! All right! Against my better judgment, and still thinking you're every bit as crazy as *she* thinks you are I'll string along. The inquest on Mr. Shepley is set for tomorrow; it'll be a feather in my cap, I don't mind admitting, if I can nail this killer before they even hold the inquest. So this scheme had *better* work, that's all. It sounds like something dreamed up by Count Dimitri in his villa at Monte Carlo. If it don't work, where are we? We've got the explanation, but we haven't got the Voice."

"Are you sure we've got *all* the explanation?"

"Well, haven't we? We know who, we know how, we can at least make a guess about why. What else is there?"

Conscious of a shadow lurking just beyond the various cards and notices stuck to the inside of the glass-panelled door, Jim rose casually to his feet.

"As in so many cases, Lieutenant, there are one or two extraneous matters to be dealt with before we can write Thirty. Someone, I am now convinced, did follow me in Washington on Monday night. More than once today I have thought (mistakenly, it seemed at the time) I was again under observation. Don't get excited, now! Let it be repeated that these matters are (or seem to be) extraneous to our present investigation. We're lucky we can confront them and get them over with now. Since I seem constantly if unexpectedly to be introducing you to one person or another, let's try it again.''

He flung open the door, and lunged as fast as a striking snake. With his left hand firmly grasping the right arm of somebody standing just outside, he impelled across the threshold a tubby, moonfaced, balding man of just over fifty, whose sartorial elegance was somewhat marred by a bright green Tyrolean hat with a feather.

''Lieutenant Trowbridge, New Orleans Police Department,'' he said, ''meet my friend the Freiherr Franz von Graz, one and only original of Dimitri in *The Count of Monte Carlo*, sometime agent in the service of I won't say whom. He followed me in Washington; he picked up my trail again three days later; and I think we had better learn why.''

18

WEARING WHITE TIE and tails, though he had not troubled with a silk hat, Jim entered the lobby of the Grunewald Hotel at seven-thirty.

The evening clothes he had acquired at the Canal Street shop would have excited no envy either in Brooks Brothers or in Poole of Savile Row. But, for a rush order without alterations, they fitted very well. It was the least he could do, he thought, since Jill had probably gone shopping for formal wear.

And Jill had.

At first glance the lobby of the Grunewald seemed so ornate as to be almost overpowering. Stately pillars of brown-and-white mottled marble, their capitals carved and gilded, soared to a beige-and-brown roof from which hung golden-glowing crystal chandeliers like glass castles. Deep carpeting of a soft pattern muffled the footsteps and muted the voices of slowly moving guests. But you soon got used to the decor; in fact, Jim liked it.

Then he saw Jill. In her silver evening gown, with a touch of blue at the low square-cut bodice, she was descending a broad marble staircase which presumably led to the mezzanine floor. Heavy constraint lay on them both as she greeted him.

"Then you decided to dress, Jim?"

"So did you."

"Yes. It seemed . . . oh, I don't know! . . . more fitting.

Besides, I wanted to. Almost everybody else has, you see."

"Would you like a drink first, or shall we have dinner now? I phoned to reserve a table."

"Let's go straight to the Cave, shall we? There's only one elevator down to it. This way."

As they approached the single cage which would whisk them below street-level, their constraint grew still heavier.

"With the last words I heard you speak this afternoon, Jill, you were putting me in the good graces of old General Clayton. Where did you learn of my family association with William and Mary?"

"I—I read it in the publicity about you. It's true, isn't it?"

"Yes, it's true. Always distrust publicity releases in general, but that one does happen to be accurate. You knew there was such a place as my alma mater, did you?"

"I'm not so ill-informed as you seem to think. There are only two American colleges that date back to the seventeenth century, and that's one of them. Well," she added, as they stepped into the elevator, "what perfectly mad things have *you* been doing for the rest of the day? Apart from almost getting shot, that is?"

"Damn it, woman, you talk as though I *arranged* these things! And as though I enjoyed looking at a rifle-barrel, or having a knife thrown past my head!"

"Somebody threw a knife at you, then?"

"No, that was yesterday."

Jill made a gesture of hopelessness.

"This conversation, Jim, is becoming most frightfully mixed up! Let's drop it, shall we, and stop nagging each other?"

"I was about to suggest it. Your eyes—"

"Well, here we are. It *is* like a cave, isn't it?"

It was. The big cavern, with its circular white-covered tables and spindly gilt chairs, its grottoes and pools, its artificial stalactites and stalagmites, swam in a twilight of concealed illumination.

Jill had recovered both her good humor and her breath-less interest in life.

"The lights," she informed him, "are hidden behind those stalagmites and stalactites. But I can never remember which is which. Are the stalagmites the things like icicles that hang from the roof, and the stalactites that rise up from the floor? Or is it vice versa?"

"It's vice versa. The stalactites hang from the roof, the stalagmites rise up. Often they unite, as some of these give the effect of uniting to form pillars. You see?"

When a Gallic-looking maître d'hotel met them and ushered them to their table, it was not all they saw.

The tables, as yet, had been only sparsely occupied. But there were other occupants for a more intimate atmo-sphere. Lifelike statues of nude nymphs, marble tinted to resemble flesh, lay face-down in shallow pools or perched on rock ledges with their legs in the water. The orchestra, beyond a small dance-floor at one end of the cavern, was playing "Everybody's Doin' It."

At their table, a good one beside a pool whose blonde nymph bore some slight resemblance to Jill herself, Jim ordered mussel soup, lobster Thermidor, and a bottle of Château Yquem.

Jill's gaze flickered round; she seemed to be repressing a giggle.

"There's no dancing yet; that'll be later. The first time I saw this place, you know, I thought those statues were real women. And I wondered how much the city fathers would allow by way of entertainment. It *is* pleasant, though! Whenever I come in here, I feel I've walked straight into the pages of *The Count of Monte Carlo*."

"That's already happened. The count himself turned up this afternoon."

"Really, Jim—!"

"I'm not joking. Franz von Graz, whose real name I so carefully wouldn't give you, camped outside a telegraph office where Lieutenant Trowbridge and I were conferring. So I reached out and hauled him in."

"What did he want?"

"What he's always wanted: money."

"I don't understand!"

"Neither did I, at first. When I told you about the car that seemed to be following me in Washington on Monday night, did I say it had no license-plate?"

"Yes. But I still don't understand!"

"Franz has become very much an Austrian, for the time being; he's got a post at the Austro-Hungarian Embassy. Some of the diplomatic crowd in Washington, it appears, think themselves above such mundane considerations as carrying license-plates, and won't do it. Sooner or later they'll have to conform when they're outside the embassy itself, even if they have a special plate with C.D. for *Corps Diplomatique*. Meanwhile, the law often gets fractured; any policeman who stops 'em can't make an arrest."

"And Franz?"

"Franz picked up my trail by accident. He'd been after somebody at the Senate Office Building, probably dunning *him* for cash, and was on his way back uptown when he saw me go into the Congressional Apartments just before it got too dark to see anything.

"Even Franz didn't have the nerve to follow me in. He was in an embassy car with an embassy driver. He hung around for a good length of time and in a good deal of a dither. Later it seemed easier; I was headed for the station. When I got down to challenge the car, he lost his nerve again and bolted, only to return soon afterwards with a full description of me and find from the redcap who carried my bag I had just left for New Orleans.

"On Tuesday he decided to follow me, and must have arrived this morning by the same train as Charley Emerson, who's here, too. Inquiry at hotels, one after the other, soon located me. Franz still kept his distance, awaiting what he thought was a good opportunity, when I pulled him into the telegraph office.

"Lieutenant Trowbridge scared him badly. But Zack went away, on a little errand we'd planned. It wasn't until

Franz tagged along to the clothing store, where they fitted me out with evening kit, that I learned what was really on his mind.''

"You haven't yet told *me*, you know."

"When I finished that book, early in 1911, I let Franz read the manuscript. He agreed he couldn't be recognized, said I might publish with his blessing if I paid him five hundred dollars quittance. I paid him the five hundred, not thinking much would come of it; most first novels fall dead from the press. But—well, the unexpected happened."

"And now he wants more money? For any particular purpose?"

"Yes. He says he's tired of being a glorified office boy at the embassy. The Wilhelmstrasse will take him back at his old work, he says, if he can get himself to Berlin. He could probably get to Berlin under his own steam, only he won't stir unless he can go in a luxury suite aboard a North German Lloyd liner. That's what he wants."

Vividly, here in the Cave, Jim could remember Franz dodging after him amid the men's clothing, trying to keep the salesman from hearing when he voiced his never-ceasing refrain.

("This book, Jimmee, is *my* book. Wizout me, you agree, there vould be no book and no profit. You vill giff me *some* of the profit, I think?")

Jill was up in arms at once.

"Really! Of all the sheer cheek I ever heard of! You didn't give him any money, I hope?"

"Oh, but I did. I wrote him a check that ought to suffice. First, there was a kind of justice in what he said. Second and more important, your obedient servant could sing a refrain that was a happy refrain: 'My first try at detective work is almost finished; I am seeing Jill tonight, and all is gas and gaiters.' "

"Did it mean so much to you that you were seeing me tonight?"

"You know it did—and does. Here's the soup; it deserves our attention."

Despite such words, despite the excellence of the *potage aux moules* and of the lobster which followed, neither of them ate with much appetite. Each was too acutely conscious of the other's presence. They found themselves darting little glances, beginning to speak at the same time and then pulling up short with more of an explosive laugh than the coincidence warranted.

But they drank the wine, finishing their bottle before coffee. The Cave gradually filled up; the orchestra played a series of selections from various comic operas, including *Naughty Marietta,* Victor Herbert's latest. And, amid nude statues, the intimate atmosphere twined them round.

Who gave the signal for dancing to begin, or if anybody gave a signal at all, Jim never remembered. It was getting on towards ten o'clock when one well-dressed couple took the floor, then another. Jill, who here felt justified in smoking publicly, had just crushed out her second cigarette. Jim did the same.

"Would *you* care to dance, Jill?"

"Yes, please; very much!"

"Over to the left, then. Nowadays," he went on, "there's much talk about a new kind of music that's supposed to have started in New Orleans. But you won't hear it in the Cave."

"No," Jill agreed. "And, except for a constant repetition of 'Everybody's Doin' It,' you won't hear music for the turkey trot, the bunny hug, the grizzly bear, or any of the new dances people write to the newspapers about as being revolting and low. It's still selections from comic operas, mostly. This is the *Merry Widow* waltz, isn't it? You dance very well, Jim."

"I dance very badly. But at least I can keep off your feet."

"I shouldn't mind, really, if you stepped all over 'em. What are you thinking?"

"I was thinking," he said, "that *you* had better stop thinking about Franz von Graz. Franz following me in Washington, and, though you may not have heard this,

Clay Blake innocently giving us all a start when he rapped on the door of Leo's drawing-room at midnight, are both part of the pattern but extraneous to its real meaning. Forget Franz! Forget Clay, even! Let's concentrate on ourselves. What are *you* thinking now?''

"I—I don't think I've got the nerve to tell you."

The music stopped. He released Jill reluctantly, and they both applauded like those about them.

"I *will* tell you something, though! May we go back to our table now?—I wonder," she added a few moments later, "if you'd mind drawing your chair round a little closer to mine? These tables are circular, which makes it easier. There!''

"Will you have a brandy now, Jill? You refused one earlier, but . . .''

"Later, perhaps. Not just for a moment, though.''

They were sitting close together; Jill had turned towards him and looked up.

"I *will* tell you something," she repeated. "You mustn't mind, you mustn't p-pay any attention at all, when I go on about you doing mad things all the time. Provided you keep out of danger, I *want* you to do mad things; I love it! Do you understand?''

"I hope so, because . . .''

"Because why?''

The orchestra had begun again, once more with a Victor Herbert song from *Mademoiselle Modiste*. After a rather long lyric, it approached the chorus. Though nobody sang it, not a listener could have failed to remember the words as the music soared in that gray-green twilight.

> Sweet summer breeze, whispering trees,
>   stars shining softly above;
> Roses in bloom, wafted perfume,
>   sleepy birds whisper of love;
> Safe in your arms, far from alarms,
> Daylight shall die but in vain . . .

"I'll just bet," Jill said in a low voice, "you're thinking of something quite mad at this minute!"

"Yes, I am."

"What is it?"

"I'll show you."

And he took her in his arms.

The kiss was a long one, with ramifications; they were gripping each other so tightly that the world seemed blotted out. It may have been a full minute, even many minutes, before Jim raised his head.

"Yes," he said, "I know it's a public place. And this is an exhibition of bad manners which should never have occurred to me. But at that moment, my dear, I didn't give a damn!"

Jill opened eyes which slowly came into focus.

"I didn't give a damn either," she whispered, "and I still don't! Do you—do you want to know the real reason I wouldn't accept the drawing-room on that train?"

"I want to know anything that concerns you. I love you, you elusive little devil, and—"

"Am I so very elusive now? I never *wanted* to be elusive, not for a minute! You see . . ."

"Well, well," interposed another voice, "and whom have we here? Another of these fellow-newspapermen meetings, eh?"

Exasperated by the interruption, but with much less confusion than he would have expected, Jim looked up to see Bart Perkins, managing editor of the *Sentinel,* in his customary untidy-looking lounge suit. Beside him, resplendent with white tie and tails, stood the silver-haired gentleman to whom Jim had been introduced at Guilfoyle's Garage as Raymond P. Chadwick.

"My friend here," said the managing editor, "has been trying to pump me about Leo Shepley's death. He seems to think we know more than we printed today."

"Well, don't you?" asked Raymond P. Chadwick.

"If you want it straight from the horse's mouth," Bart Perkins told him, "you'd better speak to Mr. Blake here.

Mr. Blake is a former newspaperman who writes popular novels. He was slap on the scene of the crime when it happened."

"I've already made Mr. Blake's acquaintance, Bart, though we had no chance to speak of Leo Shepley or anybody else. I was wondering—"

Jim stood up, and formally presented both of them to Jill. Raymond P. Chadwick was gracious.

"My wife," he said, inclining his head towards the other side of the room, "is waiting for me at a table over there. Why don't all three of you come and join us?"

"*I* can't, as I've explained," Bart Perkins answered. "I promised to meet Charley Emerson at the Absinthe House, and I'm late already."

Jim said that he and Miss Matthews couldn't either. The managing editor did not immediately take his leave, but he did not seem satisfied either.

"What I don't understand, Hap—what I don't understand, Ray—"

"By all means," Mr. Chadwick said amiably, "call me Happy if it makes *you* feel happier. Any lawyer known as Happy is so rare a bird that the public should be encouraged to call him that. What don't you understand, Bart?"

"Frankly, your interest in Leo Shepley. You didn't know him very well, did you?"

"I knew him scarcely at all, though of course I'd met him. No, Bart. It's my eldest son, who is also my law-partner."

"How's Lance concerned in this? Was Leo a great friend of his?"

"No, no! When the firm became Chadwick & Chadwick, some eighteen months ago, Lance married a delightful girl from Asheville, North Carolina. His proud father bought the bride and groom a house in the Bayou St. John area. The next house along is Sunnington Hall, old Madam Laird's property, though that's on the opposite side of the road from Lance's. The next house beyond Sunnington

Hall is the Villa de Jarnac, on the same side as my son's. Sure you won't change your mind and join us, Bart?''

"I can't, thanks just the same. Excuse me: you're not explaining anything.''

"I shall try to be clear,'' said Mr. Chadwick, fastening the fingers of both hands on the lapels of his evening coat. "Last night, in the vicinity of ten o'clock or thereabouts, my son had occasion to look out a front window.

"Around Lance's property there's a rather high wall. Not all the houses have a high wall; some, indeed, have no wall . . .''

"Hell's bells, Happy, you're not giving evidence in court! There's no need to be so *damn* precise. What's this about?''

"In the road just outside Lance's gate, partly visible by the light of a street-lamp, stood a red sports car. He could see only the right front wheel and part of the hood. It was pointed north, the direction it afterwards took.

"Lance had no reason to think it belonged to Leo Shepley, whom *he* knew only slightly. But the late Leo's car is or was a famous one. He thought it must have broken down, as we all know they so often do, and wondered if he ought to offer help. Lance went to find his wife and ask her advice. By the time Shirley returned with him to the window, the car had gone.

"It's hardly important, of course,'' sang Mr. Chadwick, teetering up on his toes as though for a better view of those before him, ''and I told Lance I saw no reason for him to inform the police. Let the police do their own work; that's what they're paid for!

"But it *is* a curious point, isn't it? The car of our late football player either stops or breaks down just outside my son's gate. Shortly afterwards, whatever Leo Shepley may have had in mind, he engages gear and goes bucketing on to the Villa de Jarnac and to death. Yes, it *is* curious.''

Bart Perkins tipped a hand to his forehead.

"Sorry I can't stop for the philosophizing; I must be off.'' And he disappeared beyond a pillar.

"*I* must be off, too." Raymond P. Chadwick made grimaces of impatience. "Miss Matthews! Mr. Blake! My dear young people, if I can't persuade you to accompany me and crack a bottle . . . ! No? Matthews, Matthews! Now where have I heard that name before? Well, at least my intentions were of the best. Sir and madam, goodnight!"

Whereupon *he* went away, not undignified despite a certain pompousness.

Jim, ruffled of mind and shirt-front but in the highest realm of exaltation, swung back to his companion. It was not difficult to recapture the mood of a few moments ago; he had only to look at Jill and see what was reflected in her eyes.

"Shall we have that brandy now?"

"No, please! If we have brandy after all the wine . . . And we don't need it, do we?"

"Agreed, Jill; there's something else a good deal more powerful. Would you yell blue murder if I grabbed you again?"

"Did I yell blue murder when you grabbed me the first time?"

"No, but . . ."

"In London, you know, they'd say it was shocking we didn't choose some dark corner under the stairs, but carried on in public like 'arry and Liz. Even Connie has never carried on in public. And yet I don't care! Nobody *noticed* us; nobody so much as batted an eyelash. Even when those two men interrupted, I wasn't as petrified with embarrassment as I should have been. I provoked it, you know; I deliberately provoked it! After all my good resolutions . . ."

"All your good resolutions?"

"Or what I *thought* were good resolutions! About that drawing-room . . ."

"Yes?"

Jill was leaning closer, though she had become pink in the face and would not look at him.

"I wouldn't accept it, Jim, because—well, because I knew what would happen if I did. Just what happened a few minutes ago. Only more than that, *much* more than that, through the night and into the next day! But my silly, stupid, idiotic conscience was all over me because I *wanted* it to happen and kept wishing for it. Oh, Jim . . . !"

This was irresistible. Public place or no, he caught her for a chaotic, fairly intimate interval during which the orchestra encouraged with a tune neither of them noticed or even heard.

"You know, Jill," he said presently, "there's plenty of time before us to remedy the oversight."

"There is, isn't there? Now release me, please. I *will* sit up straight and be dignified for the time being. Jim, that brandy you've offered so many times. I don't need it and don't really want it, but I'll join you for one if you insist. Yes, as you say, there's plenty of time before us. There's the rest of tonight, for instance."

"Tonight, Jill?"

"Yes, tonight! What's the matter with you? Why are you looking at me like that?"

"I've just remembered—"

"What have you remembered?" Quick intuition kindled suspicion in her eyes. "You're planning something, aren't you?"

"What would I be planning?"

"It's to do with that police officer, isn't it? And it's the wrong kind of insanity that scares me so much?"

"I can't think what you're talking about, Jill."

"You *can* think what I'm talking about! I had hoped, for a little while at least, we could keep away from death and murder. But we can't. Mr. Perkins wanted to talk about it. Mr. Chadwick insisted on talking about it. Look! There's Mr. Trowbridge now, headed straight for this table. And I'll bet you *he* . . ."

She did not finish.

Zack Trowbridge, who had removed his hat but not surrendered it to the cloakroom, sauntered towards them with an air of heavy-footed ease which did not quite mask underlying apprehension. Jill was at him in a moment.

"Just tell me, Mr. Police Officer, if I'm not right in my bet. You *have* come to interrupt us, haven't you?"

Lieutenant Trowbridge became powerfully avuncular.

"Interrupt you, miss? Well . . . now!" He smiled. "I'm sorry, I'm real sorry, but I guess that's about right. I've come to take you along with me."

19

"TAKE ME ALONG with you?" Jill echoed. "Good heavens, are you arresting me for something?"

"Arresting you? No, miss, no; anything but that! Just the reverse, as you might say. I've got authority from the Police Commissioner himself to take you home in a cab; the city'll pay for it. Then I must come back to town on a little business."

"Why can't Jim drive me home, as we'd already arranged?"

"Well, miss, it's kind of a delicate matter. There may be a little trouble, you see; not much, but a *little*. We want you well out of range if brickbats start flyin' or anything. Franz Josef thought . . . Mr. Blake thought . . ."

"Jim planned the whole thing, didn't he?"

Zack rallied valiantly.

"If he did, miss, *I'd* say it was pretty considerate of him. He's got you a good deal on his mind; not that I blame him. Still! There's many a girl I know would feel pleased and flattered to be taken care of, not miffed and put out because a man thought enough of her to keep her out of danger."

Jim stood up and added to this.

"Jill, for God's sake! An old friend of mine was killed, wickedly and quite needlessly, to appease the vanity of a near-lunatic. With anything except the very worst luck, Leo's murderer will be under lock and key inside an hour

265

or so. Are you going to fly into a temper because there's some element of risk attached?''

But he did not know his Jill, who had also risen.

"Oh, no," she said. "Since I've been running from you for the past four days, I mustn't complain if I get a *little* of my own medicine. Whatever you're doing, I don't like it. But then the impetuousness I don't like is all part of the impetuousness I like so very much; it's your character. I must take you as you are, not try to turn you into somebody else.

"And I'm quite content to take you as you are. Do this if you must; do anything you must! I won't nag or interfere; I won't even try. I only pray, my dear, you'll be there to touch me again when it's all over!''

She extended her hand, which Jim carried to his lips. Then he turned to Lieutenant Trowbridge.

"Let's be sure we've got this straight. What's our story, again?''

"It won't be over *quite* as soon as you said, but it ought to be pretty fast when it starts.''

"Our story, Lieutenant?''

"Our story is that Mr. Clay Blake's car has been laid up for repairs. Somebody drove him to the villa for dinner tonight. It's been arranged that you're to drive out there and pick him up for return to town, reaching the villa at round about midnight, more or less.''

"Then it really *is* to be the ghosts' high noon?'' Jill asked. "That wasn't a sneer or a would-be clever remark; it's just what jumped into my head!''

Lieutenant Trowbridge was intent.

"Call it the ghosts' something-or-other; call it anything you want to call it. The point is, Franz Josef, you needn't leave here until near enough to half-past eleven. Let's see: it's now a quarter after ten. That'll give me plenty of time to take this young lady out to her sister's and be back at City Hall easy before you leave the Cave. Ready, miss?''

"Yes, I'm ready," Jill assented. "I won't ask you to be careful, Jim, because I know you can't be careful. And now, as the cooperative criminal says in England, I'll go quietly."

Lieutenant Trowbridge ushered her away towards the elevator, but left her standing by a stalactite-stalagmite pillar while he returned for a final brief word with Jim.

"Sit down, Franz Josef," he said. "I'm going to give you something under the table so's the whole room won't see."

What he handed Jim was a Smith & Wesson .32 revolver, fully loaded.

"Stick that in your hip pocket," the lieutenant advised. "It's a light one, maybe, but the best I could borrow at short notice. Know how to use it?"

"Yes, I know how to use it. But I hope I don't have to use it."

"Sure; we both hope that. All the same! I'm pretty sure our quarry's swallowed the bait, so we'd both better be ready. No horses and carriage in this; it'll be a car or nothing. Just go through with your part of it; leave the rest to me. That's all we can do for now."

This time the detective did depart; Jill waved from beside the pillar, and they both left.

How Jim spent the next hour he would afterwards have found hard to describe. Actually, he did little but sit at his table, smoke, and listen. He considered ordering brandy; but, since he needed a clear head, decided against it. He told himself he was not nervous or jumpy, and knew he told himself a lie.

At eleven o'clock they brought on the first entertainer. A woman in Spanish costume did a Spanish dance with much heel-click and rattle of castanets. Two specialty dancers, both man and woman in evening dress, followed with a number to the strains of *La Paloma*. The floor was being cleared for some pièce de résistance when Jim saw by his watch that it was twenty minutes past eleven. He called for the bill, paid it, and took his departure.

He had left his car in University Place, at the other side of the hotel from Baronne Street. The doorman helped him kindle the lights, and cranked up for him when Jim donned goggles and dust-coat to mount behind the steering-wheel.

He drove the same course as the night before: Canal Street, Rampart Street, then the turn by the Old Basin Canal.

This Old Basin Canal, which he had scarcely observed on Wednesday, was no mere landmark or site of what had once been a canal. You could see dark water gleaming beside the road, under a slight haze and the yellow moon. Oyster luggers and fishing boats still plied there, someone had told him.

The engine boomed sweetly; the clutch was giving no trouble. But three times, before he had passed any place that even remotely could be called suburban, he believed another car must be following.

"Well, here we are," he thought. "In for a penny, in for a pound! Will the attempt be made while I'm still in a built-up area?"

And then, on each occasion, the imaginary pursuer fell back or turned off.

"No," his thoughts ran on, "it must wait for a more remote spot, a lonely spot! Fast or slow, now? Should my pace be fast or slow?"

Something in between, no doubt. He mustn't seem to be running, but he mustn't dawdle either. And what, actually, would be *done* when the time came? That was what he couldn't tell.

He had transferred the revolver to the right-hand pocket of his dust-coat. Carrying a gun, was he? Grotesque! But the enemy had very much been carrying a gun, or Leo Shepley would still be alive.

Something like open country, now, at last!

Unconsciously Jim put on speed; the Chadwick responded to a touch. But the mist had thickened, too; he mustn't go bucketing blindly through it.

Taking the proper turnings, keeping to a steady pace, he suddenly realized he had begun to count lamp-posts on the right.

Yes, he was getting closer. Mist or no, you believed you could scent open water from the bayou. It wouldn't be long now. That house on the right, for instance, set well back behind a stone wall twelve or fifteen feet high . . .

That must be the home of Lance Chadwick, the politician's son, outside whose gate the red Raceabout had stopped for a reason not hard to determine. Jim slowed down to get a look at the place as he passed. That was when he knew, beyond any doubt, that some car *had* begun to follow him, and a big car, too.

All right; and now?

It was what he had expected, what he had come for. Sunnington Hall would be next, on the left; then, soon afterwards, the Villa de Jarnac on the right. If the pursuing car were on his track, he must not turn in at Constance Lambert's. The proper play would be to go booming on past that villa. For his pursuer *must* overtake him; *must* have a chance.

If in fact it were the auto he expected, it should be able to outrun him. Though Stu Guilfoyle might describe his Chadwick as the speediest stock car in the world, that had been two years ago. And a new Cadillac would be bound to pass him in any trial. But at least . . .

Jim glanced over his shoulder. It *was* a big Cadillac, coming up fast. Though he could make out little behind a blaze of electric headlamps, he thought its outline looked familiar. And the top was raised. Yes, the Cadillac could overtake him and must be allowed to overtake him. But he'd give 'em one hell of a race first.

What about that mist?

Oh, damn the mist! Jim touched the accelerator; his three-seater sprang forward, and the Cadillac sprang after it. Sunnington Hall flashed past, the Villa de Jarnac soon afterwards, as they roared north towards completely open country.

And the Cadillac was gaining. After holding his lead for the next quarter mile, Jim let it gain. There were no more street-lamps; they plunged through mist only by the light of their own lamps and the moon's remote eye.

Would the Cadillac try to run him into the ditch? Though this hardly squared with his own analysis, Jim thought someone might have arranged it. And it looked as though the pursuer had such an intent.

Both cars must be doing more than sixty. Despite bouncing, despite jolting, Jim held the wheel rock-steady. Up crept the pursuing car, closer and still more close.

But the Cadillac did not run him into the ditch; it did not even try. Something else happened which all but climaxed that wild ride.

As the Cadillac drew abreast on Jim's left, he could see the chauffeur at the wheel behind the tall windshield. Then the tonneau of the Cadillac moved level with the Chadwick's driving-seat. There were two figures in the tonneau. One of them, face masked by goggles, leaned out with some object in his hand.

That Jim's car had a right-hand drive probably saved his life. He saw the flash and heard the concussion as somebody fired a bullet point-blank at the left side of his head.

Somebody else in the Cadillac yelled, "You're crazy! You're completely—!" But the boom of both engines drowned out other words.

On went the Cadillac, though at somewhat reduced speed. Jim did not go on at all. Since it had finally happened, he pulled up and stopped. For that moment, when he jumped down and peered back, the road behind him seemed empty. Then other headlamps appeared and took on clarity. A Ford tourer drew level, its driver a man of youngish middle age with a woman on the seat beside him. The woman was Miss Florence Yates.

Down from the tonneau, as the Ford stopped, jumped Lieutenant Zack Trowbridge. He had a wild look on his face and an Iver-Johnson .45 in his hand.

"You didn't tell me you were gonna race him!" he said in no mild voice. "If you wanted to race him, or make him race you, how'd you expect Mr. Kestevan's Ford to keep up? This is Mr. Horace Kestevan, our Assistant D.A. The other 'un you know.'' Lieutenant Trowbridge stabbed a finger in the direction taken by the Cadillac, now out of sight. "He took a shot at you, didn't he?"

"And missed by a wide margin, I'm glad to say."

"Was it . . . ?"

"I couldn't be sure. He was wearing goggles."

"If the Ford couldn't catch either of you, it damn sure can't catch him now. And yet we've *got* to catch him! Do you think *you* could catch him?"

"I don't know; I can try. Jump in, before I feel too much reaction from being shot at.''

"Are you all right, Franz Josef? You're lookin' a little bit white."

"Yes, that's what I meant. Jump in!''

"I think, Lieutenant," said Horace Kestevan, "you had better do as the gentleman suggests. I am in no hurry to get home tonight, especially under the present circumstances. And this lady and I are finding much to talk about. Meanwhile . . .''

Jim gave Lieutenant Trowbridge the spare pair of goggles from the dust-coat's left-hand pocket. The engine was already so warm that one flip of the crank set it thudding. Saying no word, Jim concentrated on driving until they picked up the Cadillac's tail-light well ahead. But Honest Zack remained vocal enough.

"I didn't *see* how it could come unstuck," he raved. "It *wouldn't* 'a' come unstuck, either, if this hadn't turned into a race. Step on it, Franz Josef; you've gained on 'em! But if they want to race AGAIN . . .''

They could not seem to make up their minds. The Cadillac suddenly spurted ahead, then hesitated as though uncertain. The mist was clearing; the countryside, like a dead world except for its lush vegetation, stretched emptily ahead; Bayou St. John lay to their left. Jim opened the throttle wide, lessening the distance between himself and the other car as it had previously done to him.

Over the road arched great live-oaks festooned gray with

Spanish moss. A moment or two later, as Jim seemed inexorably to overtake that red tail-light, the car ahead was inspired with new, Satanic life and leaped away.

"What's goin' on up there?" demanded Honest Zack. "He's off his nut now; he's as mad as a hatter! Is he using that gun to threaten the driver, maybe? The driver slows down; up comes the gun. You do the same thing, Franz Josef! Give this bus every ounce of speed she's got; keep your foot on the floor. If his little game's to threaten 'em, I'll soon put a stop to *that* foolishness, you see if I don't! Step on it, now!"

Jim's car met the challenge, its exhaust thundering through the side-ports in the hood. In that seesaw race, advantage first with one and then with the other, the Chadwick began to close in again. Though you could see nothing through the rear window in the Cadillac's raised top, you sensed activity inside. Lieutenant Trowbridge stood up beside Jim, balancing precariously with the Iver-Johnson in his right hand.

"Cadillac, stop!" he bellowed. "In the name o' the law, stop!" He lifted the .45 and fired in the air, with stunning report. "Stop, you hear, or the next one goes through a tire! If you don't stop . . ."

The Cadillac swayed towards the other side of the road, but slowed down. Jim could now hear a voice, as though in response to some threat or protest.

"Oh, I'll stop!" the voice yelled. "You want to get us *all* arrested and wreck the car, too?"

Once more the Cadillac swayed, but did not go out of control; it came to a halt. The engine was switched off. After a bursting kind of pause, during which you might have counted ten, there was another concussion of a revolver shot.

Jim stopped the Chadwick ten feet behind the other car. Lieutenant Trowbridge, his face terrifying in goggles, jumped down and strode forward. He looked into the back seat of the Cadillac, then into the front, then into the back again.

Returning his own gun to his hip pocket, he faced back towards Jim.

"There's two innocent men here," he said heavily. "One in front, one in back. The other one in back, the one who's not innocent . . ."

"Yes?"

"He held out just so long. When the time came, he couldn't bear it. He put the gun to his own head, and he . . . 'Tain't pretty, this ain't, but then it never is. And, anyway, it saves us the rumpus of a trial."

"Well, Lieutenant, were we right?"

Lieutenant Trowbridge reached into the tonneau of the Cadillac, as though to haul something forward on display. But he changed his mind in the same instant. Though he walked slowly back to meet Jim's eye, he spoke in a voice far louder than was necessary.

"Oh, we were right," he answered. "The murderer is the man you said it was—Alec Laird. And Flossie Yates is his one and only legal wife."

20

IN THE LIBRARY at the Villa de Jarnac, under tiers of books which glowed with rich bindings even though they had been bought by the yard, five persons sat over coffee on the night of Sunday, October 20th.

Jim Blake and Clay Blake had finished dinner with Constance Lambert and Jill. Lieutenant Trowbridge, though invited, had been unable to join them until a few minutes ago. Now Honest Zack, beaming and triumphant, swallowed coffee with a shark-like air of meaning to swallow the small cup as well.

But Clay Blake showed no triumph. Seated close beside a radiant Constance, he remained moody and abstracted as he glanced across at Jim.

"Alec Laird!" Clay pronounced the name as though summing up. "He *was* a consummate hypocrite, then? I can hardly believe it even now!"

Jim nodded.

"When the possibility of his guilt first occurred to me," Jim said, "I could hardly believe it either. I liked the man; for all his seemingly austere ways, I found him sympathetic. I wasn't alone; he's been fooling most people for years. But, once you began to think, the weight of evidence was too much.

"The only one who saw through him was Mathilde de Jarnac Laird. I didn't like the Duchess of Sunnington Hall; I still don't like her, having no fondness for fussy and demanding women who tell everybody what to do. But she had him pegged from the start. Remember our lunch at Philippe's, Clay? When she was telling us about her nephew as a first-class amateur actor, she as good as said straight out he was a posturing hypocrite, and did say straight out he was so fond of power he kept his wife completely under his thumb.

"Alec Laird's fondness for power has been commented on by more than one person, including Alec himself. As acting owner of the *Sentinel,* of course, he had a great deal of open power and authority. His real taste was for secret power, power behind the scenes, power of life or death over those who never saw him but only felt the lash. That's the key to his character. And don't forget he completely dominated a neurotic wife, which is an important part of the story.''

Constance Lambert smoothed her skirt.

"I can't (or at least I shouldn't) enter this discussion at all,'' she declared. "I never even met Alec Laird. And yet I've heard so much about him, from one person or another, I think I might make an intelligent guess. Speaking of wives, isn't there some question about who *is* his wife? What I can't understand . . .''

Lieutenant Trowbridge called for order by rapping on the center of the table.

"The one *I* can't understand . . .''

"Yes, Lieutenant?'' prompted Jim.

"It's *you,* Franz Josef!'' the other boomed with great heartiness. "You call yourself a newspaperman. And you're a good one; you pieced the whole thing together less'n twenty-four hours after Mr. Shepley was shot.

"But you haven't been behaving like any news-hound I ever heard of. Practically all the papers in town, to say nothin' of some New York papers and one wire service, have offered you all kinds of fancy prices if you'll write your story of how you did this and how you got on to the truth. And you back away from 'em. You hand me the credit, which is fine for yours truly but not fair dealin'.

You won't write; you won't even talk. It's as if you just wanted to sweep the pieces under the rug and forget 'em!''

"My conduct as a newspaperman, admittedly," Jim confessed, "should make the ghosts of Horace Greeley and both Gordon Bennetts gibber at me every night. But you're right, Lieutenant. It's an ugly business and I do want to forget it, so that—well, so that I can go on to more important things."

And he looked at Jill, who said nothing but made a face of happiness.

"All right, Franz Josef! Now that we've got full statements from the two innocent parties, Pete Laird and his chauffeur, we know practically everything that happened and can supply any bits they didn't see. What others want to learn is how you put it together. If you won't tell the world, at least tell these good people here. Tell it as you told it to me in the telegraph office Thursday afternoon. Fair enough?"

"Yes, fair enough."

"While we're on this subject," interposed Clay, looking at Constance, "I'll make a confession, too. I've already explained to Yv—sorry; I can't quite get used to calling her something else—I've explained to my Dulcinea what the Voice (and Alec Laird was the Voice), what the Voice accused me of."

"Really, Clay!" Constance murmured. "It's not necessary to . . ."

"It *is* necessary, Dulcinea. Though Jim has been trying hard to conceal this, too, I was accused of spending my nights in orgies with girls of twelve or thirteen years old. Don't look so shocked, any of you," he added, though in fact nobody did look shocked; the women merely looked thoughtful, "but there's the truth. It can be faced now, faced and stared down. So, Jim, you might tell us what made you so sure that damned deacon was the Voice and the murderer, too."

Jim spread out his hands.

"It wasn't much, but you may as well hear. I first met

Alec Laird in his office on Wednesday morning. While we were talking, Peter Laird and Madam Ironface walked in. I knew he was anxious to get rid of 'em, but at that time I couldn't dream just how anxious he was.

"In their presence, Leo Shepley telephoned on a private line. Leo, obviously still with no suspicion of Alec Laird, asked for the call to be transferred to another room, the so-called museum adjoining Alec's office, where he could speak to me in complete privacy. That room has not only a private telephone; it has a private elevator.

"It was a long conversation, and an important one. Leo told me to get in touch with Florence Yates, and how to approach her. He told me you, Clay, would be coming out to this villa on Wednesday night, and he told me how the Voice had threatened you on the phone. He told me everything, in short, which could have been of use to somebody who afterwards decided to kill Leo.

"I spoke of these matters to Leo; I spoke about them to nobody else until much later. If anyone could have overheard that conversation . . . !

"But, apparently, not a soul could have overheard it. Alec Laird had ordered the receiver hung up in his office, though the line remained open because I was using it in the adjoining room. All the time I spoke to Leo, it seemed, Alec Laird was engaged with his aunt and his cousin. And a heavy door had been closed between the two rooms.

"When I left the phone and rejoined him, to all intents and purposes he was just saying goodbye to his visitors at the door to the reception room. He even addressed some remark to 'Aunt Mathilde' as the door closed. And I accepted all this, at the moment; I was very dense!"

"For the love of Pete, Franz Josef," Lieutenant Trowbridge burst out, "will you stop saying how dense you were and just tell 'em what happened?"

"Realization," said Jim, "didn't dawn until the following afternoon, when I was in the telegraph office with our watchdog here. His assistant, Sergeant Peters, left us to cross the street. I looked out of the window, and for some reason was surprised to see Peters had only just crossed the street. It was about the same distance Madam Laird and her son, after leaving Alec's office, would have had to cover before they reached one of the three elevators out in the corridor.

"Then I woke up. I remembered what *had* happened on the top floor of the *Sentinel* Building Wednesday morning. After (presumably) speeding his parting guests at the door of the private office, Alec Laird spoke only a few words to me before he turned back to that same door and opened it.

"The door from the reception room to the corridor was open, too. Bart Perkins, the managing editor, stood in the doorway. And the corridor lay completely empty behind him. There was no sign of two guests who were supposed to have left Alec Laird a very few moments before.

"That wasn't all. A girl named Ruth Donnelly, as a rule, guards that reception room like a good-natured Cerberus. But Ruth Donnelly hadn't even been there.

"Bart Perkins entered the sanctum to confer with his boss and with me. Soon afterwards Alec's secretary, Miss Edgeworth, appeared with a container of coffee and two cups on a tray. She had taken the coffee from Ruth Donnelly, who had gone downstairs to the drug-store for it. Since the receptionist wouldn't have left her post unless Alec Laird had sent her, we can see very clearly what must have happened.

"Madam Laird and Peter couldn't possibly have left the office when Alec pretended they did. He must have shooed 'em out almost as soon as he planted me at the telephone in his father's museum. He sent Miss Donnelly for coffee to get her out of the way. He picked up the receiver of the private phone on his desk. He, and he alone, could have heard every word except the beginning of my conversation with Leo. When he heard us both ring off, and knew I would be joining him very shortly, he ingeniously improvised those 'parting words' to an Aunt Mathilde who wasn't there, since there was no receptionist to testify he'd been talking to an empty room. He was very clever, as the same Aunt Mathilde also said.

"Once we see the truth of that particular incident, everything else falls into place. And it's almost time to recapitulate."

Lieutenant Trowbridge looked from one to the other of the listeners.

"Got it?" he demanded. "Alec Laird knew my friend Franz Josef would be getting in touch with Flossie Yates, who can find some attractive small girls for men who like 'em at that age. So Alec phoned her first. 'There'll be a gent after you soon,' he probably said. 'If *he* wants some of your wares, Flossie, be nice to him!' Thinking to himself, I'll bet a nickel, he might just add Franz Josef to his private list of victims."

"List of victims?" echoed Jill. "That wasn't *really* why you went to see the Flossie woman, was it, Jim? *You* didn't want . . . ?"

"No, of course I didn't! From further revealing indications in Alec's office, I believed I knew the nature of the threat being used against Clay. But I had to make sure by questioning the woman herself. I couldn't know at the time, of course, that Alec Laird was doing a good deal of telephoning the same day."

Clay, who had been brooding in a cloud of cigarette-smoke, now raised his head.

"Alec was the Voice, but was he the only voice? It's now common knowledge that various persons holding minor positions at the *Sentinel* were frightened, as I was frightened, by threats never carried out. Are you saying the boss himself sat like a spider and took pleasure in terrorizing the meanest of his employees?"

"As we've been told, Clay, he went to the office early and stayed late. Nobody, not even the managing editor, dared intrude on him without being announced. And he had his father's retreat, the study adjoining the office."

"Granted a poisonously sadistic mind," Clay admitted,

"it's quite on the cards. But why did it have to end in murder? Why kill Leo?"

"Because Leo had tumbled to him; he had no choice. Also, since a great part of the game was to destroy you . . ."

"To destroy *me?*"

"Yes; hadn't you sensed it?" Jim met his look. "From statements made by Peter Laird and the chauffeur, as Lieutenant Trowbridge has remarked, the police have learned virtually everything. First, however, let's glance at the evidence, as presented to us both on Wednesday and on Thursday; let's see if there aren't indications in it."

"Well?"

"At nine-thirty on Wednesday morning, Clay, the Voice phoned you and said your family should hear all about those under-age playmates if you didn't retire as a candidate for Congress.

"At eleven or a little later, when I talked to Leo, he was upset and disturbed. But clearly, as already indicated, he had no suspicion of Alec Laird or of any particular person.

"Then what? At twelve-thirty, before Alec must have left the *Sentinel* office for lunch, Leo gets the mysterious call, undoubtedly from the Voice, which sends him straight up in the air.

"When he'd talked to me, an hour and a half earlier, Leo conveyed the impression that he himself, L. Shepley, had been enjoying the favors of pubescent girls. That's what I understood; and the Voice, listening in, must have understood it, too.

"The Voice, so to speak, started to lose its head. The latest victim was on the run—you, Clay, seemed to be on the run—and Leo could be put on the run, too. So, with what appeared to be heavy ammunition, the Voice phoned Leo and uttered dire threats about disclosing *Leo's* improprieties.

"But it was the wrong weapon, the Voice's big mistake.

"We have now been able to determine what had really been worrying Leo when he talked to me. The whole business of Constance Lambert's masquerade must soon become public. When it did, the world might think—you, Clay, particularly might think—it had been nothing but a rather cruel practical joke designed to make a fool of you.''

''But it wasn't anything of the kind!'' cried Constance.

''Agreed; we now know it wasn't. Still, that's what had been on Leo's mind: up to half-past twelve on Wednesday. After twelve-thirty, when the Voice phoned with threats, the worry had been wiped out. He was in a state of sheer rage.

''I must now cite a clue (or, rather, two clues) which none of you except Jill will remember. Only Jill and I were present when Leo made either remark.

''On the train from New York Leo had said, with excessive modesty, that he had one small talent. If ever he heard a person's voice more than a few times, he insisted, he would never afterwards fail to recognize that voice, no matter how much the speaker tried to disguise himself. Leo said he could do it blindfolded; he said he could do it on the phone.''

''And so he could!'' exclaimed Clay, sitting up straight. ''I've heard him do it! Then Alec phoned Leo as the gloating Voice? And, for all Alec's acting ability, Leo knew who he was? That was the way of it?''

''That, undoubtedly, was the way of it. It fits in with something else Leo had said on the train, even before he mentioned his talent for identifying voices. He was discussing your character, Clay. He said he thought a threat or a crisis would find you indecisive . . .''

''Well, I am. Only luck and the grace of God kept me steady when those threats had me in a corner!''

''Leo told us he could be sure of that because, deep down inside him, he tended to be indecisive, too.

''And we find this well instanced by his behavior after that midday phone call. He had been praying the Voice would get after him, who had no reputation to lose. And the accursed Voice had. And Leo knew it was Alec Laird. He would have to act.

"Did he act-at once? No, not by any manner of means! He paced the floor, muttering to himself. In your own description, he simmered. At just before two o'clock, he left home—for his club.

"Leo had true iron in his soul. Sooner or later, of course, he *would* act. But not just yet. Hence that long afternoon, and even part of the evening, while he made up his mind how to handle this.

"He had recognized Alec Laird. While speaking to his would-be tormentor during that crucial phone call, had he given any betraying sign of recognition? Leo was no actor, you know, and Alec's cleverness needn't be stressed again. I think Leo *had* given some sign to the Voice; that, as early as twelve-thirty on Wednesday, Alec feared the game was up and Leo would have to be disposed of.

"Very well. While this was occurring in one part of town, what occurred elsewhere? I went to see Miss Florence Yates. And Miss Yates swore to me, among other things, that Leo Shepley was in a dangerously suicidal mood."

"For heaven's sake," Jill burst out, "how *does* the Flossie woman fit into all this? *Was* she Mr. Laird's real wife, now his widow?"

"Patience, Jill. Lieutenant Trowbridge will tell you in good time. As for the information she relayed to me: she hadn't spoken to Leo, as she said she had. The murderer had phoned her with instructions, preparing the ground for a crime that must now be inevitable. Perhaps, as the lieutenant suggests, Alec did tell her to treat me kindly. But he did much more. *He* told *her* not to be surprised if Leo Shepley killed himself; and she, believing this as she usually believed what he told her, passed it on to me. The spider was already preparing his first plan: if he had to kill Leo, it must be thought a suicide.

"Should you doubt this, recall ensuing events.

"Afternoon became night. At nine-thirty the Voice, pretending to be Clay, phoned me at my hotel and spun a yarn designed to lure me out here as a witness for what would happen.

"I swallowed the bait, Jill, and I brought you along. There we were, waiting at the gate of this villa. A red Mercer Raceabout, with a begoggled and dust-coated figure at the wheel, came roaring up. It was pursued by a gray Cadillac containing two persons. The Mercer swept past us, up the drive and into the way-through. A shot was fired; the car smashed. We gathered round a scene of wreckage, to hear what Peter Laird *said* had been happening that night.

"At five o'clock that afternoon, according to Peter, Leo had phoned Alec Laird at the *Sentinel* office; Leo was supposed to be searching for me. As a matter of fact, Leo did phone Alec at five, but it wasn't in search of me.

"Let's return to Peter's story. Alec went home, Peter said, where Alec received the most mysterious message of all. Somebody from the *Sentinel,* never identified or even inquired after, is supposed to have telephoned Alec at Alec's home, telling him Leo Shepley was touring Bourbon Street bars and threatening suicide.

"Leo had been doing nothing of the kind, as the police soon proved; he never left his club that afternoon. The 'mysterious informant' was an invention who never existed.

"At seven-thirty Sylvia Laird, whom the world knows as Alec's wife, did actually phone Sunnington Hall and speak to Peter. She said she and her husband would not come to dinner at Madam Laird's that night, and repeated the tale of Leo's mythical doings in Bourbon Street.

"All this information, both the true and the false, we heard through the mouth of young Peter Laird. But who was the source of everything? Who stood behind it, and from whom did it stem?"

"You mean Alec Laird, don't you?" demanded Clay. "Yes! He didn't go home when he was believed to have gone home; he stayed at the *Sentinel* office. Since he badly needed and would need an alibi for the whole evening, he would establish one. And it wasn't difficult. Sylvia Laird may be neurotic and a nagger, but she obeys him implicitly. So he phoned Sylvia and ordered her to ring Sunnington Hall with the story he wanted told. There was his alibi if anybody questioned it. Am I right?''

"Entirely right," Jim agreed. "The true parts and the false parts in that story are as easy to separate as the true parts and the false parts in the story of the murder. We were hypnotized from the start into taking a wrong view of the murder, which ought to be corrected now. This crime, apparently, was committed at ten minutes past ten. Leo Shepley, apparently at the wheel of the Mercer . . .''

Constance Lambert put up her hand.

"Just a moment, please!" she cried. " 'Apparently' at ten minutes past ten? 'Apparently' at the wheel of the Mercer? Are you telling us it wasn't Leo who drove that car?''

"It couldn't have been, I'm afraid. Leo had been dead since about nine o'clock. Shall I deal with that part of it?''

"If you don't, *I'm* afraid both Jill and I will have a fit!''

Jim assembled facts in his mind.

"The first time I saw Peter Laird, I thought I must have met him before. I hadn't, of course; it was because he reminded me of somebody. The light didn't switch on until I saw him for the third time at Philippe's restaurant on Thursday.

"He reminded me of Leo Shepley. He's got the same wide and heavy, almost top-heavy, shoulders, as well as the same bulky body, though Leo was principally muscle and Leo's admirer is mostly puppy-fat. They don't look alike, of course; Peter is dark and Leo had light-brown hair. But the build is exactly the same. Let Peter wear goggles to mask his face and a dust-coat like Leo's, let him be seen only by the uncertain light of a street-lamp as he sweeps past . . .

"From the first moment I saw the real Leo's dead body beside the ruin of his car, there were some troublesome features in believing what we were meant to believe. Leo's dust-coat was quite clean, which it couldn't have been if he'd driven out from town; my own clothes were soaked with dust. As I walked past the Cadillac drawn up behind the wrecked Mercer, I did notice a big lap-robe in the tonneau.

"I walked towards Leo's body, starting to bend down. The chauffeur, who was already kneeling there, said, 'Don't touch him!' If I had tried to touch him, either the chauffeur or Peter, or both, would have got in my way and prevented it. They had only to keep *anybody* from touching him until the autopsy people took over afterwards, and the real time of his death could never be determined. The question wouldn't even be asked, because we all thought we knew."

"You say 'they' had only to do this or that,'' cried a not-quite-stammering Jill. "When the truth dawned on you, didn't it make you suspicious of Peter and the chauffeur?"

"Not when I realized, at the Western Union place on Thursday, that Alec Laird must be the murderer, and that any accomplices after the crime were only unwitting accomplices. Leo was shot in Alec Laird's office, his body conveyed downstairs by private elevator, and transported under a lap-robe in the tonneau of the Cadillac to the place where the others set the scene outside Lance Chadwick's house.

"I will mention only one more point, and let Lieutenant Trowbridge fill in the few remaining details from statements made by Peter Laird and Raoul Dupont.

"Leo phoned Alec Laird at five in the afternoon; Alec Laird admitted that much, since he had no idea where Leo might have been phoning from, and some outsider might be able to enlighten the police. Leo wasn't looking for me. He told Alec that Alec had damned well better stay at the office; Leo would be coming to see him.

"If Alec hadn't already guessed Leo knew the Voice's identity, he could be sure by that time. And he waited; he waited a long time. Leo didn't leave his club, well out in the Garden District, until about a quarter to six. Even then he didn't drive straight to the *Sentinel*. He cruised and cruised, still making up his mind. It was well past seven o'clock, and Alec Laird had already prepared an alibi in case he *had* to commit murder, when Leo left his Mercer in the alley beside the building and took the private elevator to the top floor.

"What happened when those two first confronted each other? We shall never learn; both of them are dead. But, since there's such a great deal we do know about later events, Lieutenant Trowbridge had better cross the *t*'s from the statements made by Alec Laird's unwitting accomplices."

"How *could* they have been 'unwitting' accomplices?" asked Constance.

"You'll see. Lieutenant?"

With a great flourish Honest Zack whipped out his notebook; but, as usual, he refrained from consulting it.

"This part," he explained, "even Franz Josef couldn't have reasoned out from the evidence; we didn't have it as evidence. Young Pete and that chauffeur never did tell me the truth until after Alec was dead, and they had to speak up to save their own necks.

"All right! At seven-thirty Wednesday night, as we've heard, Sylvia Laird phoned Pete and told him that string of whoppers her husband told her, 'specially about Mr. Shepley touring bars and talking suicide. She made it convincing, because she believed it; most people believed Alec. Pete believed it, too; his great hero, it seemed, might do something desperate.

"So he hung around close to the phone afterwards, in case there should be news. There was news. Shortly before eight—Pete's mother hadn't yet called him to dinner—Alec Laird himself phoned from the *Sentinel*.

" 'Have you heard anything about Leo?' asks Pete. 'You bet I've heard something about Leo,' says Alec, or fancier words to that effect. 'He's here now; he's in my office, and I'm calling from the extension in the next room. He's in a pretty bad state; seems intent on doing himself in.' See what Alec was leading up to?

" 'I've been trying to argue him out of it,' Alec continues. 'But he's a big man, and strong; I don't know what to do if he gets violent. Look!' says Alec. 'I know *you* can't come here; your mother won't let you skip dinner. But that chauffeur of yours is a pretty husky lad, too. Why not send him in with the car? Tell him to wait in the alley beside the building; he can lend a hand if I need help.'

"So Pete sent Raoul in the Cadillac with those instructions. Until nine-thirty Pete stayed chained to his mother's dinner-table. Shortly after that, when the old lady had gone upstairs and was out of the way, Pete phoned Alec.

" 'Leo?' says he. 'He's done it!' says Alec. 'About nine o'clock, before I could call for help or make a move of any kind, he pulled a gun out of his own pocket and shot himself.'

"A while ago Franz Josef asked what happened when Mr. Shepley and Alec Laird first confronted each other. To judge by evidence we found after Alec's death—aside from what Pete and Raoul told us, I mean—you can see what happened during the whole interval.

"Mr. Shepley was going to have this out with the Voice. His aunt didn't *think* he took his own .38 revolver with him, which only means she didn't see it. He took the gun, all right! He didn't mean to use it, naturally. He'd just show it to the damn Voice to prove he meant business. That was *his* mistake.

"At first, I reckon, Alec denied everything. When Mr. Shepley wasn't having any, he tried to justify himself with all kinds of fancy words. That didn't work either. Alec owned a .38 of his own; kept it in a drawer of that desk in the museum, along with a box of cartridges. He could always use that. And he had to use something.

"Things got stormier and stormier. If Mr. Shepley had taken a long time about making up his mind, Alec *seemed* to take a long time about doing a killing he knew he had to do sooner or later. But it wasn't that way, not really. Alec couldn't take chances; he had to be sure there was nobody left on the top floor, who might walk in on him by accident.

"Then he got his opportunity. When Mr. Shepley thought of violence, he never associated it with *guns*. Like most of these big athletes, he'd think of using his fists. And he got careless.

"After showing the gun to Alec, he put it down on a table or a desk and more or less forgot it. While he paced the floor, as they say he always did, he wouldn't pay too much attention; he didn't see Alec slide up against the table and hide that gun behind Alec's back. The man who was soon to be a victim sat down again. When the lid blew off, it was because . . . didn't you make a suggestion, Franz Josef?"

Jim nodded.

"Leo, who never thought this hypocrite was dangerous except in making malicious phone calls, must have said something like, 'I've had enough of this! I'm driving straight out to Sunnington Hall; Aunt Mathilde's going to hear the whole thing.' "

"And the murderer, who had no choice now," supplied Honest Zack, "yanked up the victim's own gun and let him have it through the side of the head.

"It didn't take him long to work out a new plan. He needed help with the new scheme, but he knew very well he could get help. At nine-thirty he phoned Franz Josef and arranged to have a witness waiting at the gate out here. That was done in short order; he had the rest of the hocus-pocus ready when Pete's call came through soon afterwards.

" 'Yes, Pete, Leo shot himself,' says Alec. 'But we don't want scandal, do we? *You* don't want it known your hero went crazy and took his own life? All right! If you'll help out a little, and take a very small risk, too, we'll turn this into a murder. Nobody'll be arrested for the murder; nobody'll even be blamed for it; your hero had no enemies, and there isn't any murder.'

"Would that reckless young fellow help out? You bet he would! Raoul was waiting downstairs in the Cadillac, with instructions to obey Alec in everything. And Alec told

Pete just what to do. Pete was to leave Sunnington Hall and jog along the road to the gate at Mr. Lance Chadwick's house, where Alec and Raoul would join him, and Pete would hear the rest of the scheme.

"Alec *can* drive a car, I've since learned, though he don't own one and seldom does drive. He keeps a carriage and horses; he'd sent 'em home that night, ordering the coachman to keep his mouth shut or see trouble.

"There were two cars down in the alley, the Cadillac and Mr. Shepley's Raceabout. With a box of .38 cartridges in his desk, Alec slipped a new bullet into the murder gun as replacement for the one he'd fired.

"Alec and Raoul, who's an old-fashioned loyal retainer and cooperated all the way, got Mr. Shepley's body downstairs. They put it in the back of the Cadillac, covered with a lap-robe. Alec drove the Cadillac, an easier job, while Raoul, the professional, drove the trickier Raceabout. Alec, Raoul, and Pete met outside Lance Chadwick's house, where Alec explained.

"If Pete wore goggles and a dust-coat, at the wheel of the Mercer he'd be taken for Mr. Shepley as sure as you're born. They did one other thing, which no watcher in the house overlooked. While Alec gave 'em the details of his plan, they backed both cars into the drive so they wouldn't be seen when Franz Josef drove past.

" 'Here's the gun, fully loaded again; no shot seems to have been fired,' says Alec. 'You, Pete, are to imitate Leo's drivin' style; you're known as a crazy driver anyway. Go tearing down the road, up the drive, and into the way-through. Just before you slam the car into the locked double doors, lean out and fire a shot at some place where they won't soon notice the bullet-hole. Then drop the gun on the floor, with one bullet gone. It'll seem like murder, but nobody'll be blamed. Have you got the nerve to do all that?'

"Yes, you can bet Pete had the nerve! He'd lean down, he said, and fire the bullet into the wall under the work-bench on the right, where there's always deep shadow night or day. But Pete had one little improvement he didn't mention.

"After Franz Josef and this young lady had driven past, they were ready. Raoul drove the Cadillac to the gate of Sunnington Hall, where it waited the right moment to chase the other car. Pete, disguised at the wheel of the Mercer—"

"Wait!" cried Jill. "When the Mercer went past Jim and me, it was Peter Laird we saw? If Raoul drove the Cadillac, who was the other person in it?"

"You didn't see another 'person' at all, miss. What you saw was Mr. Shepley's dead body. The other person didn't move, did he, except as the car moved?

"After the smash, remember, Franz Josef didn't exactly rush into that way-through. They had time to put the body on the floor beside the wrecked car. Then came the 'improvement' Pete was thinking about. He didn't get a bump or a scratch when he slammed into the doors; he'd had smashes before. But he didn't drop the gun on the floor, either; he deliberately stuck it in his own pocket.

"This was going to *be* murder, no doubt at all! So first Pete pretended he thought it was suicide, all the time believing it *was* suicide. Then he could 'discover' there was no gun, so it had to be murder. None of 'em realized they'd created an impossible situation. And Pete put on a pretty good show."

"Well," volunteered Clay, "his mother said Pete could be quite a competent actor when he had to be. What happened to Alec, while this was going on?"

"There was no car for the master-mind. He just walked back towards town, where he picked up the cab that took him home. Get it all now?"

"Not entirely. Jim's suggested that this second plan of Alec's was somehow intended to implicate *me* . . ."

"He couldn't be sure it would, Mr. Blake; he thought it might. He knew you were here on Wednesday night. Pete Laird knew 'Yvonne Brissard' was away from home, so

Alec probably knew it, too. And he envied you, Mr. Clay Blake. The men like you, the women fall for you . . .''

"With both Sylvia Laird and Flossie Yates backing him to the hilt, surely *he* had no reason to complain?"

"Maybe not, sir; but the natural-born criminals of this world don't see it that way. Anything else you want to know?"

"Well, yes. I've sometimes felt Alec sounded a little too unctuous when he praised me. But that's not the point. Never mind how he felt about me; why did he go crazy and try to kill Jim?"

Using all the suavity he could command, Honest Zack turned to the gentleman mentioned.

"If you'll play this one, Franz Josef, that should wind it up."

"Having visited the newspaper office on Wednesday morning," Jim said, "I also visited it on Thursday morning. I still had no suspicion of Alec Laird, who was all cooperation. He began by talking about Charley Emerson. When he had refused to let Charley handle the story of the murder, he said, Charley was out of his office 'in a flash.' In all innocence I asked, 'Can anybody go out of here in a flash?'

"It wasn't until later that afternoon, when I recalled how Mathilde Laird and her son seemed to have gone in a flash on Wednesday, that I understood something besides the identity of the murderer. The murderer thought I had been referring to that miraculous exit; he thought I was on to him, and very briefly he showed it. So he first sent two shady characters to take care of me . . .''

"Some very shady characters," interjected Lieutenant Trowbridge, "have been known to hang around Alec Laird, as I mentioned to Franz Josef Thursday afternoon. But, being as he owned a newspaper and would have a lot of panhandlers after him, nobody thought anything of it. Franz Josef only told one person where he was having lunch: he told the managing editor . . .''

". . . who also told me," Jim supplied, "that he and

Alec and the city editor were having a conference before lunch. As we now know, Bart Perkins told Alec Laird, who tried to set me up for his rifleman. When that failed . . .

"When that failed," Jim continued, "I knew he'd try again. He couldn't have realized how little actual evidence there was against him. Even finding the bullet-hole under the work-bench in the way-through wouldn't have implicated the master-mind. He thought only that I must have discovered his game; as, by that time, I actually had. He would try again, and do it himself.

"The trap was set. Lieutenant Trowbridge dropped in at his office very late Thursday afternoon. Alec learned I should be driving out here alone that night, and at what time. I had something on my mind, said Honest Zack, which I wanted to tell the police first thing Friday morning. And that did it.

"Once more, of course, his dupes were Peter and Raoul. They hadn't the least idea what he meant to do. He said he doubted that even a new Cadillac could overtake a 1910 Chadwick in first-class condition; he made it a challenge. They realized some hinge had slipped in his brain only when he pulled out his own .38 revolver and fired at me point-blank. There's good stuff in both Peter and Raoul; it was a relief to hear from the lieutenant that no charge of any kind will be made against either. But that *is* the end."

"No, it is *not* the end!" protested Jill. "What about Flossie Yates and *her* part in it? We were promised that, weren't we?"

Lieutenant Trowbridge uttered a reminiscent chuckle.

"I tried my damnedest to break Flossie. She wavered once or twice. But no attack *quite* worked until I challenged her claim to be a respectable married woman. She went up in the air like the Wright brothers, and out came her marriage lines."

"The real thing?"

Honest Zack looked wise.

"Alec Laird and Florence Yates," he said, "were secretly married by a justice of the peace in Shreveport fifteen years ago, when Alec was twenty-five and Flossie several years younger. That's a decade before he married Miss Sylvia de Vere of Charleston. You don't need to guess who bought Flossie that fine house on the Esplanade. It's going to cause all kinds of a hullabaloo when the lawyers try to settle up Alec's estate, but that's no business of mine, thank God. In stories, you know, any holier-than-thou character always turns out to be a hypocrite leading a double life. Alec Laird's been leading a double life for fifteen years or better; I'm glad to see it can turn out that way in things that really happen.''

After a long silence, when much might have been said but wasn't, Jill rose to her feet.

"Jim," she suggested, "would you care to take me for a little stroll in the grounds? It's not late, you know.''

By way of the *porte cochère* on the south side, by way of the gravel drive leading east, they emerged into a warm, fragrant night with no mist under the moon. Jill, face rapt, walked a little way before she put her hand on his left arm.

"You know, Jim . . .''

"Yes, my dear?''

"You saw through the whole thing and solved it before anybody else had an inkling! Really, Jim, I'm so proud of you I can almost forgive you for risking your life *every* time you get the chance!''

"And I'm so proud of you for being you," he assured her, "I've been singing loud hosannahs all day long. But, although everybody's happy, there's a practical point to settle. Constance and Clay are to be married as soon as possible. When do you and I go to the altar?''

"Oh, Jim, need we? I'd love to be your wife; you know that. But isn't it too hasty? Shouldn't there be a sort of trial run while we discover whether we're suited to each other?''

"If we don't know now how completely suited we are, when in God's name arc we ever going to learn it? Thursday night, after the kafuffle was over, both you and Constance asked me to stay here until morning. What you and

I discovered about each other, in the course of a *nuit enchantée . . . !*"

"Though I've already proved I'm absolutely shameless and indecent where you're concerned," Jill cried out, "couldn't you at least *pretend* otherwise? Can't you leave me one shred of modesty at all? Still! You might stay here tonight, if you wouldn't hate it. Towards morning, when other matters are off our minds, we could always discuss marriage again."

"Every generation, Jill, has a grouse against the preceding generation. At the moment we're young and full of beans. But one day, before too many rolling years have whitened our heads, we're going to be oldsters ourselves. What will they say of *us?*"

"They'll say," she replied happily, "we were prudish and (what's the new word?) inhibited. That's it! They'll say we were so prudish and inhibited we couldn't have enjoyed ourselves at all! That's what they always say, isn't it?"

NOTES FOR THE CURIOUS

1

NEW YORK

Since the House of Harper has published my own books for forty years—I handed the manuscript of a first novel to the late Eugene F. Saxton in summer, 1929—the reader may be assured that background details of the old building in Franklin Square are as accurate as they can be made from study of two books called *The House of Harper*, one by Eugene Exman (1967) and one by J. Henry Harper (1912), as well as from the personal reminiscences of a lady, Mrs. Frances Zajic, who worked there and remembers it well.

In the library at the present Harper office, 49 East 33rd Street, I was able to read through a bound volume of the *Weekly* for the entire year 1912. Most of the political remarks attributed to Colonel Harvey in Chapter 1 will be found in his editorial comment during that three-cornered presidential campaign. Though he does not say editorially that he considered Governor Wilson guilty of the blackest ingratitude, his subsequent conduct, when he became as strong a Republican as he had previously been a Democrat, shows this to have been the case. And the new Cadillac with the self-starter gets considerable advertising from January onwards.

This story does not linger in Manhattan. But the various volumes of *Valentine's Manual of Old New York* (new series, edited by Henry Collins Brown, 1916-1926) supply facts and dates about the Pennsylvania Station, the Public Library, and the Woolworth Building, which last-named did not officially open until 1913.

And the New York-Atlanta-New Orleans Limited, number 37, was a real train; its schedule may be looked up in the *Railway Guide* for October, 1912.

2

WASHINGTON

Nor does the story linger here. Background and atmosphere come in part from my own very vivid childhood memories, verified wherever possible by research; my father was elected to Congress in that same year 1912.

The Congressional Apartments did very much exist, as described and on the site assigned. Among the tenants were Representative W. N. Carr of Pennsylvania, his wife, and their small but noisy son. Visiting Washington many years afterwards, I was not surprised to discover that the apartment house had long disappeared. But with something of a shock I found the present Supreme Court very close to the same site.

The toy streetcars of that date were a reality, too. They had no overhead trolley even then; all wires ran underground. Whenever the car rounded a curve, after dark, its lights would go out and then flash on again.

Union Station and the Library of Congress remain pretty much unchanged.

3

NEW ORLEANS

To enumerate the multitudinous books on the Crescent City would be merely to repeat a list set down at the end of my previous novel, *Pupa La-bas*. But again I am happy to acknowledge the invaluable assistance so generously given by Miss Margaret Ruckert, of New Orleans, who shares my fondness both for antiquarian research and for detective stories.

Miss Ruckert chose the route, beside the Old Basin Canal, by which Jim Blake and others are made to drive from Rampart Street to Bayou St. John; the canal no longer exists. Miss Ruckert also provided the name of the actual high school Lieutenant Trowbridge would have attended, as well as the name of the real (and unopposed) candidate for Congress from the second Congressional District of Louisiana. The latter was Mr. Henry Garland Dupré, who remained so long in office that one lady, then very young, thought he must have been elected for life.

All motorcars which appear in these pages will be found in the text and the color photographs of a work both fascinating and exhaustive, Ralph Stein's *The Treasury of the Automobile* (New York: Golden Press, 1966). And, though I can point to no baseball-pitching machine in New Orleans, then or later, I once faced such a contraption in my own home town.

4

THE GRUNEWALD HOTEL

This hostelry, now the Roosevelt, has undergone such changes that a visitor from 1912 would be unlikely to recognize his surroundings. But elderly connoisseurs still recall it with affectionate nostalgia.

The lobby and the Cave are described from picture postcard views preserved at the New Orleans Public Library. Thanks must go to my daughter Bonita, of Appleton-Century-Crofts, who found these views and photographed them for me in their original color. *Vive le soleil d'antan!* As with the St. Charles, still happily functioning as the Sheraton Charles, the Grunewald's spirit has never died.

5

THE PEOPLE

Apart from Colonel George Harvey, and a few others mentioned only in the background, no character in this book ever existed; let me hope it will not be suggested that none ever could exist. A lunatic in Milwaukee really did wound Theodore Roosevelt on October 14, 1912. All the rest is moonshine.

But, though these people are imaginary, every writer's characters must be put together from scraps and patches of persons he has actually known. Both Jim Blake and Clay Blake may be found among your friends as well as mine. During a quarter century's residence in England I have met actresses who suggested Constance Lambert, together with one or two young ladies not unreminiscent of Jill. Neither you nor I may ever have come face to face with a murderer, but on the fringe of our lives may well lurk some potential Alec Laird.

The two criminal cases cited by Jim in Chapter 7—Kate Townsend hacked to pieces in her brothel, and the death by chloroform of little Juliette Deitsh—were genuine cases célèbres of their time. One or the other is mentioned in almost every book on New Orleans, and both will be found admirably detailed in Robert Tallant's *Ready to Hang*.

6

THE COUNT OF MONTE CARLO

Should any reader feel surprised to find Jim Blake writing a novel of espionage in 1911, I had better point out that both William Le Queux (1864-1927) and E. Phillips Oppenheim (1866-1946) preceded him. Already Conan Doyle, with short stories of Sherlock Holmes's adventures in espionage and counterespionage, had been at the same game at a still earlier date.

FINE MYSTERY AND SUSPENSE
TITLES FROM CARROLL & GRAF

☐ Allingham, Margery/MR. CAMPION'S FARTHING $3.95
☐ Allingham, Margery/THE WHITE COTTAGE
    MYSTERY $3.50
☐ Ambler, Eric/BACKGROUND TO DANGER $3.95
☐ Ambler, Eric/CAUSE FOR ALARM $3.95
☐ Ambler, Eric/A COFFIN FOR DIMITRIOS $3.95
☐ Ambler, Eric/JOURNEY INTO FEAR $3.95
☐ Ball, John/THE KIWI TARGET $3.95
☐ Bentley, E.C./TRENT'S OWN CASE $3.95
☐ Blake, Nicholas/A TANGLED WEB $3.50
☐ Boucher, Anthony (ed.)/FOUR AND TWENTY
    BLOODHOUNDS $3.95
☐ Brand, Christianna/DEATH IN HIGH HEELS $3.95
☐ Brand, Christianna/FOG OF DOUBT $3.50
☐ Brand, Christianna/GREEN FOR DANGER $3.95
☐ Brand, Christianna/TOUR DE FORCE $3.95
☐ Brown, Fredric/THE LENIENT BEAST $3.50
☐ Brown, Fredric/MURDER CAN BE FUN $3.95
☐ Brown, Fredric/THE SCREAMING MIMI $3.50
☐ Buchan, John/JOHN MACNAB $3.95
☐ Buchan, John/WITCH WOOD $3.95
☐ Burnett, W.R./LITTLE CAESAR $3.50
☐ Butler, Gerald/KISS THE BLOOD OFF MY HANDS $3.95
☐ Carr, John Dickson/CAPTAIN CUT-THROAT $3.95
☐ Carr, John Dickson/DARK OF THE MOON $3.50
☐ Carr, John Dickson/THE DEMONIACS $3.95
☐ Carr, John Dickson/DEMONIACS $3.95
☐ Carr, John Dickson/THE GHOSTS' HIGH NOON $3.95
☐ Carr, John Dickson/MOST SECRET $3.95
☐ Carr, John Dickson/NINE WRONG ANSWERS $3.50
☐ Carr, John Dickson/PAPA LA-BAS $3.95
☐ Carr, John Dickson/THE WITCH OF THE
    LOW TIDE $3.95
☐ Chesterton, G. K./THE MAN WHO KNEW
    TOO MUCH $3.95
☐ Chesteron, G. K./THE MAN WHO WAS THURSDAY $3.50
☐ Crofts, Freeman Wills/THE CASK $3.95
☐ Coles, Manning/NO ENTRY $3.50
☐ Collins, Michael/WALK A BLACK WIND $3.95
☐ Dickson, Carter/THE CURSE OF THE BRONZE LAMP $3.50
☐ Disch, Thomas M & Sladek, John/BLACK ALICE $3.95
☐ Eberhart, Mignon/MESSAGE FROM HONG KONG $3.50

☐ Eastlake, William/CASTLE KEEP	$3.50
☐ Fennelly, Tony/THE CLOSET HANGING	$3.50
☐ Freeling, Nicolas/LOVE IN AMSTERDAM	$3.95
☐ Gilbert, Michael/THE DOORS OPEN	$3.95
☐ Gilbert, Michael/THE 92nd TIGER	$3.95
☐ Gilbert, Michael/OVERDRIVE	$3.95
☐ Graham, Winston/MARNIE	$3.95
☐ Greeley, Andrew/DEATH IN APRIL	$3.95
☐ Hughes, Dorothy B./THE FALLEN SPARROW	$3.50
☐ Hughes, Dorothy B./IN A LONELY PLACE	$3.50
☐ Hughes, Dorothy B./RIDE THE PINK HORSE	$3.95
☐ Hornung, E. W./THE AMATEUR CRACKSMAN	$3.95
☐ Kitchin, C. H. B./DEATH OF HIS UNCLE	$3.95
☐ Kitchin, C. H. B./DEATH OF MY AUNT	$3.50
☐ MacDonald, John D./TWO	$2.50
☐ Mason, A.E.W./AT THE VILLA ROSE	$3.50
☐ Mason, A.E.W./THE HOUSE OF THE ARROW	$3.50
☐ McShane, Mark/SEANCE ON A WET AFTERNOON	$3.95
☐ Pentecost, Hugh/THE CANNIBAL WHO OVERATE	$3.95
☐ Priestley, J.B./SALT IS LEAVING	$3.95
☐ Queen, Ellery/THE FINISHING STROKE	$3.95
☐ Rogers, Joel T./THE RED RIGHT HAND	$3.50
☐ 'Sapper'/BULLDOG DRUMMOND	$3.50
☐ Stevens, Shane/BY REASON OF INSANITY	$5.95
☐ Symons, Julian/BOGUE'S FORTUNE	$3.95
☐ Symons, Julian/THE BROKEN PENNY	$3.95
☐ Wainwright, John/ALL ON A SUMMER'S DAY	$3.50
☐ Wallace, Edgar/THE FOUR JUST MEN	$2.95
☐ Waugh, Hillary/A DEATH IN A TOWN	$3.95
☐ Waugh, Hillary/LAST SEEN WEARING	$3.95
☐ Waugh, Hillary/SLEEP LONG, MY LOVE	$3.95
☐ Westlake, Donald E./THE MERCENARIES	$3.95
☐ Willeford, Charles/THE WOMAN CHASER	$3.95

Available from fine bookstores everywhere or use this coupon for ordering.

Carroll & Graf Publishers, Inc., 260 Fifth Avenue, N.Y., N.Y. 10001

Please send me the books I have checked above. I am enclosing
$_____ (please add $1.00 per title to cover postage and
handling.) Send check or money order—no cash or C.O.D.'s
please. N.Y. residents please add 8¼% sales tax.

Mr/Mrs/Ms _____

Address _____

City _____ State/Zip _____

Please allow four to six weeks for delivery.